About the Author

This is the debut novel from Roger Colston, who is a sixty-three-year-old retired engineer and lives alone in Dorset with his two dogs.

The Adventures of an Aspiring Maniac

R.A. Colston

The Adventures of an Aspiring Maniac

Olympia Publishers
London

www.olympiapublishers.com
OLYMPIA PAPERBACK EDITION

A CIP catalogue record for this title is
available from the British Library.

ISBN: 978-1-80439-146-4

First Published in 2024

Olympia Publishers
Tallis House
2 Tallis Street
London
EC4Y 0AB

Printed in Great Britain

Dedication

To the weird, wonderful, and downright ludicrous that has inspired this book.

Acknowledgements

Thanks to Mum for listening when she would probably rather not, and to James, a wonderful nephew, for his support, advice, and constant enthusiasm. Also, to Harvey Starte of R&C, for clear, invaluable advice.

Education

Jonathan Piper had a normal, almost happy childhood – at least, up until the age of nine, when on an overcast, drizzly day in 1974, his parents, two older sisters and himself moved north to start a new life in Sheffield. To him, it seemed a charmless place compared with the semi-rural tranquillity of Sussex they were leaving behind.

For a quiet, introverted boy, school was a place of terror – something that had nothing to do with education. Well, it was education of a different kind. It was all about the pressure of daily social intercourse with other human beings of the same age. Something, if given the choice, he would avoid like the plague. He didn't fit in Sheffield, but yearned to, if just to make life more bearable. He both despised his surroundings and yet yearned to be a part of it. He wanted to disappear, to be invisible, and blending in with a crowd seemed the only way of achieving it. He detested drawing attention to himself, but soon attracted the attention of bullies as someone who didn't quite belong, didn't talk with an accent befitting a boy at a Sheffield comprehensive. An Anti-Jonathan Piper Club was soon established.

His parents had high hopes for him as an academic over-achiever. Why? he wondered. They had no idea what school was all about for their son. To them, it was about education, qualifications, and the importance of gaining a successful career in later life. But to Jonathan, that was nothing to do with anything.

The taunting and general abuse increased to various incidents where Jonathan learned all about humiliation. He often had his clothes stolen in the changing rooms after showering, which the P.E teacher also found amusing. Jonathan had talent but it was suppressed, partly by his own personality and other people's perception of him. In football, he always played in defence and spent most of his time being shouted at by the goalkeeper. Only the loudest of the loud mouths got to play centre forward, regardless of talent. He decided he hated football until a few occasions when, just because of the absence of the loud mouths for a few

11

weeks, he accidentally got to play centre forward, enjoyed the freedom of it, and scored goals. But sadly, this rare enjoyment of school was short lived.

He sometimes got attention from girls, not unwanted, but attention he didn't know what to do with. And, he thought, they were bound to ask what for many would seem like the obvious questions: 'Why do you put up with it?' 'Why don't you stand up to them?' Which on several occasions he was asked. Fear was the main obstacle of course. But Jonathan was a very private fourteen-year-old who hated being the centre of attention, and whose main objective in life was to avoid other fourteen-year-olds. School was not the best place to achieve this. And the last thing he wanted to do was to become the playground entertainment for the rest of the school on a regular basis, which 'standing up to them' would have required.

Jonathan's friendless existence continued, during which he often dreamt of being back home in Sussex, only for his alarm clock to bring him back to the grim reality of his new life. One of the club's most enthusiastic members, Kevin Porter, one day discovered an old disused well, after tripping over its protruding concrete slab cover on a patch of waste ground near his terraced home. With considerable effort and a few items taken from his father's shed, he got the cover off and found a ten-foot drop with dirty water at the bottom. He knew he wanted to use this well to do harm to something or somebody but wasn't quite sure how yet. For the moment, he just enjoyed his secret hiding place's potential – potential for something destructive and sadistic.

One afternoon, Jonathan accepted an invitation from an associate of the main members of the club to meet them after school. Mainly because there wasn't the slightest hint of ridicule in the manner of the boy that invited him, which was so rare, it caught its unsuspecting victim off-guard. Such was the magnetism of Porter in getting others to participate in a cause that only he himself knew. Jonathan didn't know what he was accepting, but he met with them nevertheless, clinging to some faint hope that somehow his days of being their victim were coming to an end. But ridicule was, without doubt, the only reason for the invitation.

Jonathan almost felt a sense of belonging for the first time ever in his new environment as he and three other boys got off a bus and started to cross the waste ground, with the promise of having their tea at the home of Kevin Porter. The boys were cordial with Jonathan, as people usually are when luring somebody to something. As they walked, Kevin did a lot of smiling and winking at his two mates, who were not sure why, but just assumed their leader had a plan that was sufficiently detrimental to Jonathan to be exciting.

As they approached the well, without warning, Kevin suddenly wrestled Jonathan to the ground.

'In there! In there!' he shouts his instructions, as the other two assist with dragging the victim along the ground and the sliding of the concrete cover he had left half-open in preparation.

A few seconds later, a helpless Jonathan is dropped about ten feet down into the well. As he hits the filthy water below, it rises up completely smothering him but the swimming lessons of his former childhood in Sussex at least give him the ability to tread water for immediate survival, due to the lack of solid ground beneath his feet. The shock of the last few seconds was almost too great for him to follow another natural instinct. To cry. But as he gazes upwards in disbelief at his smiling teenage torturers, the tears begin to engulf his eyes.

'I always said he belongs in a sewer!' one of the boys shouts with excitement.

And with that in mind, Kevin Porter, the main instigator of hatred to Jonathan, unzips his fly and urinates in the well onto his victim's head. The other two gleefully follow suit.

Completely at the mercy of them and whatever they decide to drop onto his head, Jonathan's terror alone is almost enough to cause suffocation as he gasps for air while treading the freezing water.

As the fun and excitement begins to wane, a decision is made to just leave him there, as their tea awaited them and they wouldn't know how to get him out even if they wished to. But as their victim's screams were in danger of attracting the attention of passers-by, the only solution was to replace the concrete slab before leaving. Having done so, they proceed with their euphoria to Kevin's house for tea, with shouts of 'Leave him there to die!' – each of them keen to declare their solidarity to the cause.

Alone, freezing, and in pitch darkness, with nothing to hold on to and only his continued ability to tread water stopping him from drowning, Jonathan cries hysterically with vague thoughts of his family and never seeing them again. He screams for help before realizing its futility as his voice echoes around him. His brain is induced with all manner of mental disturbance for the future – if he has one.

The euphoria continued at Kevin's house between the baked beans on toast and trifle, and stern, worried looks from Kevin's mother who could sense the unusual amount of excitement and sniggering between the three boys. It died down a little later that evening when, together in Kevin's bedroom, they pondered on what they had done and its possible consequences but none of them dared to be the first to show any real signs of regret.

Having kept himself afloat and alive for the last three hours, the only relief was that of occasionally managing to wedge himself between the two walls surrounding him – head pressed against one, feet against the other, for the maximum of a few minutes' rest before inevitably slipping back again into the bottomless pit of water. Foremost in his mind was the increasing, terrifying awareness of everything being futile: shouting for help, treading water, breathing, living. Only the fear of drowning energised him, but that energy was fading fast.

In what was a slow, gradual descent back to reality and the flicker of common sense they usually possessed, just before it was time for them to part company for the evening, the now slightly subdued trio decide to tell Kevin's mother, triggering a panic in the adult world, the immediate intervention of the emergency services and concrete cover being removed, to find a traumatised, freezing, exhausted boy. But still alive, having miraculously kept his head above water for the last five hours. And as the first bit of light appears in his tomb, he cries with relief as he listens to the comforting adult voices telling him not to worry. His day ends in hospital under heavy sedation, but still shivering uncontrollably despite the layers of thick, dry clothing. He is visited by his bewildered parents, disturbed at the complete transformation of the son who had left for school that morning in the usual unenthusiastic fashion and by his inability to speak of his experience, or about anything else.

Kevin and his second-in-command Alan Marsden were very close and from similar backgrounds, and seemed destined to stay in contact for the rest of their uneventful lives of mainstream normality. At times, harmless on the rare occasions they were alone, but together seemed to feed each other with an energy for the destruction of others. The other member of the trio, Phillip Reynolds, had started at the school in the second year when his biggest fear was being bullied himself. But, upon discovering there was already a regular victim, figured that by eagerly participating he was somehow deflecting the unwanted attention away from himself.

The near-death experience of their classmate resulted in them having to endure a boring lecture the following day in the headmaster's office on the subject of 'maintaining the school's reputation and high standards' – standards that the deluded headmaster actually believed existed. There followed a brief, relatively quiet period of adjustment of their youthful minds to what they had done, during which they were almost frightened by the force of their own collective hatred. But the displays of bravado soon resumed as the leniency they had received began to sink in, confirming they had 'got away with it', and that it wasn't such a serious matter after all. The incident was dismissed by the adult world as nothing more than adolescent malarkey; or, as one teacher described it, 'high spirits that got a little out of hand'. The fact that the 'high spirits' by-passed Jonathan completely was seemingly of no importance to anyone. For his torturers, that was the end of the matter and life returned to normal quite quickly. But a vacancy now existed for another victim, as this one was never to return to the school, his 'education' about to follow a very different path.

Life continued at the school in Jonathan Piper's absence, and the name soon became a distant memory.

The Reluctant Clown

Currently buried somewhere in the mind of the sedated, shivering, hospitalized mess of a schoolboy, was the personality of a likeable and amusing young man trying to evolve. Someone who often made people laugh without trying and was often bewildered as to why they were. But only in the right company could this ever be an asset, and Jonathan was never in it. It was more of a hindrance when needed to be taken seriously. To the adolescent minds of his classmates, to throw somebody down a well and urinate on them seemed the appropriate way of dealing with what was likeable and amusing. For him, making people laugh was not something he tried to do as an only means of defence against bullying – as so often stated by famous comedians as being their first inspiration -- but more something he was cursed with that exacerbated it. Going to school was like being the medieval jester in the royal court, simply there to be laughed at, never to be taken seriously. Only by force, could the smiles and laughs of the audience he was reluctantly entertaining ever be removed.

Further Education

Jonathan fitted in as a full-time resident at the adolescent unit of St Mary's Psychiatric Hospital like a hand in a glove. He had always assumed he would never fit in anywhere in Sheffield, but this was a completely different side of it. And although now affected by chronic claustrophobia and regular nightmares of being buried alive, such was his sense of belonging in his strange new world that the torture of school and his previous life in the outside world was largely forgotten. The relief of no longer having to endure full-time education, the slim chance of ever returning to it, and being sedated by psychiatric medicine of one sort or another, all combined to give him a strange feeling that perhaps he was one of the lucky ones who had managed to escape.

His experience of school had set a precedence for the future, in that he avoided the mainstream of society, and found himself drawn to those struggling on its margins. Although surrounded by other patients around his own age, they were struggling on the margins as he was. He experienced something like friendship with a fellow patient for a while, only for the boy to be transformed into a kind of human statue by a change of, or increase of, medication. He would just sit there with mouth permanently half open and a steady stream of saliva coming from it. But Jonathan still had a feeling that the statue was his friend, even when, for psychological or medicinal reasons, it was incapable of doing anything other than dribble. And he would still talk to it, without needing a reply.

Another girl, suffering from manic depression[1], was living the high life. She danced around in her nightie, shouting, laughing and waving to anyone who walked past her cage. This was a locked bedroom on the main corridor next to the office, with lots of windows, where patients stayed while being closely observed by the staff, or anybody else for that matter. She was clearly seen with her nightie almost covering her, but not always. Then, a short time later, this same girl could be found sitting on her own in the day room, fully clothed and quietly reading a book.

---

[1] now more commonly known as bipolar disorder.

But unlike most of his fellow inmates, he was not mentally ill. More the victim of catastrophic circumstances, and society and its shortcomings. But some of the medication he was being given *was* for the mentally ill, and he was fast becoming dependant on it. There was a thin line between what he was suffering from and mental illness – sometimes so thin it wasn't actually there when it was needed.

Initially, Jonathan had been reluctant to go directly from his brief stay in a physical hospital to a long stay in a mental one. More grief, he predicted. But any such feelings were soon dismissed, and his new abode became more of a dependency; knowing as he did, that school had to be avoided, and that, as soon as he was discharged from the hospital, he would find himself back in the horrors of full-time education in the mainstream world outside. Somewhere, that the longer he was away from, the more terrified he was of returning to. And if the taking of whatever medicine they wanted to give him meant he was labelled as mentally ill, thus maintaining the current blissful status quo, so be it.

There was the occasional reminder that the hostile mainstream world was still out there when the staff and patients went out on day trips on a coach. Some of the patients, who were visibly more disturbed and /or had the wrong colour skin, attracted attention and abuse from passing youngsters, and the occasional raised eyebrow of adults. But life in the 'funny farm', as Kevin Porter and his gang would call it, became more and more comfortable. Thus, a sanctuary from all that needed avoiding. And he developed an unlikely social life with his psychiatrist Dr Heinbecker and a few of his colleagues. They told him he was articulate, as though it were an asset, as if to infer that he should do something to put it to good use, without suggesting what. A Dutch national, his long hair blew around in the wind when he drove his open-topped Volkswagen Beetle. Jonathan soon had long hair also, that blew around with the doctor's, as he was driven to the leisure centre to play squash. The border between psychiatrist and friend became a little blurred, as was everything else in his life.

Jonathan was always much more able to make a friend of someone a lot older than himself, more able to fit in to the adult world than that of the child. He could be articulate and witty, often in a sardonic kind of way, and the psycho-medics genuinely liked his company and didn't laugh at him, which was a rare thing. And this brief interlude of socializing and exercise was considered by the experts to be therapeutic. It was, but it couldn't last forever, and it's ending wasn't a happy one for the patient.

Not long before Jonathan's sixteenth birthday, his friend left St Mary's with his Volkswagen Beetle and his promotion from registrar to consultant. He had a leaving do, to which only staff were invited. Sixteen was the age at which your time was up at the adolescent unit. If you were still in a bad way, you would then proceed to the much larger adult unit, most likely with a 'section' of the mental health act to restrict your movements.

Dr Heinbecker left recommendations for the future treatment of his patient: that he should be allowed to stay at the unit for a while longer while he attended a local college of further education starting in September, and for him to continue with the taking of several different psychiatric medicines that the doctor, in his wisdom, had prescribed. One of which, as stated in its accompanying literature, was 'for the treatment of schizophrenia for short periods only'.

Jonathan was not a schizophrenic, but fast becoming an addict to medicine for schizophrenia amongst other things. He missed his only friend, dreaded September, and felt abandoned and betrayed. Somehow he knew the doctor's recommendations were the wrong direction for him to go in, but, with no idea of the right one, reluctantly conformed. Because he had proved to be 'articulate', his faring in an I.Q test, and being a member of a family of academic overachievers, he was cursed with continuing education despite leaving school with no qualifications. But what were the alternatives? Long term unemployment? Another piece of debris on society's scrapheap? The doctor wasn't about to recommend that.

So, on a wet Monday morning in early September after being wished good luck by a few of the staff, he walked with dread and fear to the college. On arrival, he was welcomed by a smiling lady member of staff of some kind, who, after asking for his name, informed him that the principal of the college wanted to speak to him before he went to his classes; but added that this was 'nothing to worry about at all'. Jonathan worried, as he and the staff walked towards the principal's office. Outside the door, the lady smiled again and wished him luck before leaving him, as if exciting things were about to happen, and told him to knock on the door.

'Hi there! You must be Jonathan Piper no less. Come in and sit down,' said the cheery principal, as if presenting a TV game show. If the casualness of his manner was meant to calm the new student, it was failing.

'I'm Mr Thomas. Well, Geoff, I prefer to be called. Anyway, I'm the principal of the college. We've heard a lot about you.'

This was worrying. Jonathan didn't know whether to feel flattered, insulted, or if he should just make a run for it. The phone rings.

'Excuse me.'

There's a lengthy pause while the principal discusses more urgent matters with the caller. He then turns back to Jonathan, as if waiting to be reminded of what they were talking about.

'Yes, Jonathan! We've spoken to your doctor...'

'Heinbecker?' Jonathan assists, with an unsettling feeling that this was going to take some time and that maybe he should be somewhere else.

'Yes, of course, Heinbecker. So, myself and my staff here are well aware of the problems you've had, and I want you to know now that it will make no difference whatsoever to the way you will be treated, or to the quality of the education that we feel we provide for our students.' The conversation now felt more like a well-scripted advertisement for the college. 'You are no different to any other student and will not be treated as such!' Geoff continued sternly, pointing his finger in Jonathan's direction, making the new student half expect to hear an *'Is that clear!'* at any moment.

There's a knock at the door.

'Excuse me a minute, Jonathan.' The principal gets to his feet and answers it.

'Geoff, good weekend?'

Jonathan hears a cordial chat from outside the door. The phone rings again while Geoff is outside chatting. Jonathan's feelings of unease and doubt about his, or rather Dr Heinbecker's, reasons for him being there are exacerbated. Eventually, Geoff returns.

'Sorry about that, ah... Jonathan. As I was saying... Now, also, as a college we usually don't accept students without the sufficient O-Levels. But, after meeting with the team, your good Dr Heinbecker and his colleagues, we feel that it's appropriate for us to break our own rules!' Geoff smiles broadly at Jonathan, as his sentence reaches its unruly climax.

Jonathan doesn't feel like he's expected to say anything, so just sits, with the occasional cross between a half-smile and a grimace.

'And we fully understand your reasons for not having any O-levels through no fault of your own.' Another big smile, leaning forward on his swivel chair.

The phone rings.

'Apologies again, Jonathan. It's a bit like that here. You'll get used to it,' he jokes, as he answers it.

A longer conversation ensues, Geoff obviously feeling that there is no great urgency to end their meeting. A bewildered Jonathan doesn't really know what he should be doing, saying, or thinking.

Eventually, Geoff turns his attention back to him.

'Well Jonathan, just to say that it's great to have you here, and if there's anything you need to see me about, if you're concerned about anything at all, do come and see me. I'm always here to help.' As he speaks, he gets up from his chair. Jonathan follows suit, and they make their way to the door.

He leaves the principal with the sound of his phone ringing once more. His new student is now about an hour and a half late for whatever he's supposed to be doing, at wherever he's supposed to be doing it. After a few minutes of aimless wandering, he goes back to the principal's office to get some guidance as to where he should go now. The door is ajar, and Geoff is nowhere to be seen.

'Hello,' he calls out. Nothing.

Now, there's a more prolonged period of aimless wandering – often getting in the way of other students happily going this way and that, looking like they had the luxury of knowing where they were supposed to be and at what time they were supposed to be there. Never could anyone be more accurately described as being the victim of do-gooders as Jonathan was at this moment. Purely by following the smell of food and the noise of chairs being moved about, he found where lunch was going on, but didn't get any, as there was some kind of system to do with paying for it that he wasn't told about. He felt embarrassed and *'different'*, as he held up the queue when he got to the front of it. He was told by an impatient dinner lady that there was now another room that he needed to find, where in future, he had to order a dinner and pay for it, and then be given a token or whatever. Feelings of hunger and anger towards all the con artists who made this horrific day possible ensued.

In the afternoon he wandered around some more, occasionally trying to get the attention of somebody to help him, mostly without success. He followed a man who was trying in vain to find the right room for him, disturbing numerous classes that were already in session as they did. Having already decided that whatever was left of his life will definitely not include anything more to do with organised, or disorganised, education, he left the building, earlier than the scheduled time. The relief was overwhelming. At last, alone, outside in the fresh air, and free to get much needed crisps and chocolate from a shop and wander back to the hospital, or *home*, as he had very much come to think of it as.

Why was he back early? was the question from one of his least favourite members of staff as he entered the hospital. He didn't know where to begin with an intelligible answer to it. The only speech he could muster was 'I'm not going back there' to which he was reminded of the enormous efforts of Dr Heinbecker and his team to get him in there. Feelings like – *well you wouldn't be grateful for the efforts of the SS to get you into Auschwitz would you* – were going on his head. He was now unpopular with the staff, some of whom he had almost come to regard as makeshift parents. And that hurt. He missed Heinbecker like never before. He would surely have had the opportunity and ability to explain to the doctor about what had happened that day, and would surely have been understood. But now, in his friend's absence, he felt surrounded by those who now regarded him as a waste of space who had no intention of 'bettering himself'. And so, by what felt like an extraordinary act of heroism, he went back the next day, if only to ease his new-found unpopularity with the usually sympathetic staff.

Whatever improvements were made the next day, they were small; no lunch again as by the time he found the lunch-ordering-and-buying room it was closed for lunch, but a class he was supposed to be attending was finally located. He was escorted to it by an irritated college secretary, who assumed that Jonathan had arrived late the previous day and therefore missed the induction period, and treated him accordingly. It was halfway through a science lesson and he struggled to find a chair to sit on, and when he did, the chair didn't have a desk to go with it, much to the amusement of other students. It was just like old times, being laughed at in a place of education; where once again, it was not possible to think about the academic work that had to be performed there. There were too many distractions. At school it was bullying, and here, it was being a displaced misfit with neither map nor compass to help him find his way around. He felt an overwhelming, frightening confusion about who he was and what he was doing. As if suffering from a complete lack of identity.

Earlier that day when he asked for the help of what looked like a tutor, with handbag over her shoulder and a mass of books under her arm, she had asked him, 'are you a student?' She had laughed at his hesitancy in answering such a simple question. He nodded, without being really sure what he was. Not exactly a student, but someone who was 'no different to any other student', but obviously very different indeed? One thing was becoming clear through all the obscurity: while he was receiving his sympathetic, supportive chat from the principal (with its numerous interruptions), all the other new students had received the vital information that was their timetable and guided tour of the college. He managed to find his way back to where the fiasco started, the principal's office, to vent his frustration. He opened the door to find the phone ringing and a once again absent principal, who was 'always here to help'.

Jonathan left early again, with the same relief at getting out of there as yesterday, but this time, with complete surrender. No matter what the consequences would be, or the opinions of people who had no idea of the predicament he was in, he was not going back. He enjoyed the stillness of walking home, not caring about what the rest of his life would bring. The kind of peace seemingly only attainable after complete surrender.

As it was against the rules for any patient of sixteen-years-old to remain at the adolescent unit unless they are being 'supported' in some kind of work, training or education, Jonathan was evicted back to his family's home. It now felt much less like his home. But in the first bit of luck he had had for some time, there was now about three million unemployed, and him joining their throngs wasn't exactly going to make the front pages.

The experience had taught him that education was about as desirable as dysentery. Something to be avoided at all costs. And the Unemployment Benefit he would now claim, would be inadequate compensation for the enormous debt that society owed him. And so, a very long period of unashamed 'scrounging off the state' was about to commence.

Homeward Bound

There wasn't much of a farewell for Jonathan on the morning of his departure from St Mary's as the staff had run out of sympathy and other young inmates were too wrapped up in their own worlds to care who was coming or going. He had been there for two years, and two out of sixteen was a long time. He had become institutionalised, and now returning to the relatively normal surroundings of house and family would take some adjusting to. He would surely miss the place and its mayhem that had become almost run of the mill now. How would he cope back in the real world where anything out of the ordinary was immediately noticed and mocked? Where he had been so thoroughly mocked, despite being nothing particularly out of the ordinary. But it now felt like he was, and as he walked out of the place laden with his belongings, he wondered what on earth the future had in store for a boy with no qualifications and no obvious talents in any direction. A complete mystery.

At home, his sisters, who had each other and their own busy private lives, were largely indifferent to their brother's departure and now return to the family home. The main feeling they had regarding him was embarrassment, as rumours had circulated at school as to the reason for his sudden exit. But it was never spoken about in the house, and whether they knew the full extent of his humiliation, would remain a mystery. There was always an undercurrent of disapproval from his father, but he experienced something like unconditional love from the type of mother who was mainly concerned with the safety and well-being of her children, rather than if they'll turn out to be serial killers or prime ministers. Or serial killing prime ministers, which was rare.

Often his evenings in the house after dinner would be spent in the dining room playing scrabble or cards with Mum. The sisters would be upstairs with their much-valued privacy and sometimes friends. Dad would be in the lounge slumped in front of the telly, often asleep. His mum liked board games, but the rest of the family were not so keen. Her son was lost and needed company, and him playing games with her almost made him feel like his presence in the house was serving a useful purpose. Any other time when his dad was absent and the lounge was his, he'd play loud rock music on the Hi-Fi music centre. And again late at night, but as the rest of the family had things they had to get up for the next morning, they had gone to bed. Then, he would listen through headphones, and often fall asleep, only to have a near heart attack when his dad would come in and tap him on the shoulder and tell him to go to bed. He was jealous of his sisters, and resented them entering the lounge as they did, with their friends and their smirks, as he enjoyed the likes of Black Sabbath and Jimi Hendrix at anti-social volume levels. They were more fans of the 'proper music' of Bob Dylan. They both attended the same college and would soon be leaving home for university. Their brother looked forward to it. His parents, who had created a Catholic household, were more fans of the Pope, and the clergy in general, who were regular visitors to the house, along with headmasters, doctors, lawyers, and other assorted dignitaries that could be enticed. Although it was never spoken, their son was fast becoming a disappointment, but he didn't care. In his opinion, any aspirations they may have had for him (pre-mental hospital) were misguided.

In his mind was the most enormous but fragile of egos, in which he alternated between being far superior to the rest of the human race, and hopelessly inferior to it, almost on a daily basis. He began to write poetry, clinging desperately to the belief that each completed work was a literary masterpiece. Thus, making him some kind of misunderstood genius, which justified his failures in the conventional world in which he didn't belong. A Van Gogh of literature. What genius didn't have psychological problems? It was a bubble that when burst would leave him in complete despair.

Jonathan had to go back to the main adult section of St Mary's once a month to see a doctor and get his supply of pills, which were being continuously prescribed with little discussion Although considered by a succession of doctors to be an 'essential part of his treatment', they were slowing him down, and he was one of the few sixteen-year-olds who needed an afternoon nap. By now, he had made several attempts to come off them, often inspired by comments from well-meaning acquaintances who couldn't understand why he was on them in the first place, which resulted in severe panic attacks and insomnia, often lasting for days.

But because the medication was not considered addictive by the medical establishment, he was told that he was not addicted to it. But, as his behaviour proved when he was without it, he must need it, and was only capable of leading something like a normal life with it. At least, that was the official line, a glowing advertisement of the product that needed to be shifted, in bulk, just like toilet roll or super glue. With this reasoning, it was almost possible to eliminate the whole concept of addiction, at least to the more gullible of patient, which Jonathan certainly was. And after several days and nights of panic and sleeplessness without it, he was inclined to believe this confusing and dubious of hypotheses and return to the stuff, giving him almost instant tranquillity and a good night's sleep. Thus, making it yet another failed attempt at ridding himself of it and adding to the overall confusion about himself that was rapidly increasing. This became a vicious circle that would go on for years, keeping it continuously flowing in his bloodstream.

He quite happily attended these monthly appointments, as it was familiar territory; he still had an emotional attachment to the hospital, and it gave him somewhere to go. His only other excursion to the great outdoors being to 'sign on' at the dole office for his benefit, once a fortnight. And as unemployment was a mass phenomenon, bullshit as to what one had done to look for work was not required, so it was a fairly painless experience. But the feeling that he was unemployable and wouldn't be able to cope with a job if he was given one, wasn't.

Just as victims of rape often feel dirty and somehow stained after the event, a victim of extreme humiliation can't help feeling that they are simply not worth it, and that, if other people knew what had been done to them, they would keep well away. There was a fair amount of this line of thought, often subconscious, that would forever obstruct any hopes of a social life. Especially with the opposite sex. It was his understanding, like most of the male teenage population, that girls had to be sufficiently impressed and tended not to be by the writing of poetry, being a misunderstood genius, and the taking of tranquillizers and anti-depressants. The impressing of girls would have to involve deception of such magnitude to be truly exhausting to the drugged-up teenager.

At home, the hostility increased between him and his dad, who he blamed for moving him to his troublesome new life in Sheffield, just as all had seemed to be ticking along merrily in his previous one. Sometimes only thought, but often erupting to the surface. His mum, like many others, was often spoken to disrespectfully when a tired, agitated husband returned from work, making Jonathan feel that he should stick up for what was essentially the closest thing to a friend that he had. But when he did, his interventions didn't go down well with either parent. And now, as he was getting closer to the age when he was no longer their responsibility, he really was completely and utterly dependent on the goodwill of his father, who had the power to turn his life upside down at any moment by chucking him out, into the shark-infested waters of bedsit land. The dependency didn't sit comfortably with the boy.

To Jonathan's further distress, Mum and Dad, although uninvited, insisted on accompanying him to the hospital for his next appointment with the doctor, where the family's domestic strife was voiced loud and clear. This resulted in him being allocated a social worker, whose main objective was to get Jonathan out of the family home. And ultimately, she did; coming up with what was regarded by many as the excellent idea of shipping him to the 'caring environment' of a home for teenagers with 'mental health problems' in London. Although Siberia would have been a better location, in his dad's opinion, all concerned were satisfied with the new arrangement. Except Jonathan. But off he went, with seemingly little choice in the matter.

An Impoverished Alien in Wonderland

Jonathan's agreement to this move wasn't exactly given or required. At seventeen, he was not quite old enough to legally make his own decisions. His feelings about it were mixed. Its only attraction was that he was returning to the South of England, somewhere he had pined for after the relatively happy pre-adolescent childhood he had had there. But this would surely be a very different environment. And although obliterating his Sheffield past appealed to him immensely, starting a new life in London was a tall order. A place where new lives could wander off in all sorts of destructive directions for the young and vulnerable.

He was now a disturbed character; but being trapped in a hole in the ground, where your only means of escape was the faint possibility that the people who put you there would have the good sense to report what they had done, tended to create a disturbance. His anger towards the culprits had not yet fully fermented. He was too busy grappling with the present day. But he was slowly becoming aware that their actions then, were somehow controlling his life now, in their absence. He imagined them fitting themselves neatly into apprenticeships or further education, while he moved himself awkwardly between one establishment for the problematic, to another.

The social worker commented on the 'great reputation' of their destination, as she drove him down the M1 to it, without specifying what that reputation was for. But as he had heard similar things said about the college where he spent two days of aimless wandering, her comments were stored in a part of his brain marked 'cods wallop'. As the world whizzed by, he enjoyed the peace of being nowhere. Between one place and another. Having left one place of trauma and having not yet arrived at the next one. He dreaded arriving, and that peace being disturbed, and predicted what would happen when they did. He would be introduced to smiling, welcoming members of staff, who would in turn introduce him to non-smiling, non-welcoming teenage inmates. And that was exactly what happened.

The place was a shock to the system, even for Jonathan and his past experiences. The type of old Victorian house in which bells were rung and servants appeared, but after decades of gradual decline, its residents were now very different. At first viewing, most of the inmates could be more accurately described as juvenile delinquents than 'teenagers with mental health problems'. People he was more likely to be a victim of, than having any kind of affinity with. And to his horror, his bed was one of five in a dormitory room. There would surely be problems when his still frequent nightmares of being buried alive, and other confinement in small spaces, became loud and vocal.

Although he wasn't quite there yet, his assumption about adulthood was that it was freedom of choice about all sorts of things, including where you lived and the company you kept. No more being put here and put there at the convenience of adults. And he couldn't wait for it to begin. Once again, he was being shackled with others his own age, which past experience had taught him was the exact opposite of what he wanted and needed.

Each resident was given what was called a 'key worker', a member of staff to sort of guide and befriend them. Jonathan's key worker Clive was one of the few positive things about the place. They had an understanding and seemed to enjoy similar things, including rock music.

Clive would often invite Jonathan to tag along when he went out to see a film or some live music. They had some good trips out, and the big plus of London for Jonathan was that now going out anywhere was an adventure, seeing so many places for the first time. Clive's company provided much needed respite from the constant, unavoidable presence of other teenagers, with its hostility and competition.

As well as Clive, he formed an unlikely attachment (friendship being too strong a word) with a skinhead girl. It was a busy time for youth culture. A rehash of mods, rude boys, post-punks, new romantics, skinheads and skinhead girls (like skinheads but female, with a little tussle of fringe at the front of their otherwise shaved heads) and Doc-Martin boots were mandatory for both sexes. She was one of those. Any attachments to girls were rare and unromantic. With his rarely washed long hair, and acne that he never considered putting cream on, he gave off clear signals that he was unavailable for such things. But for a while they frequented the local pubs where they didn't get hassle about their age and the showing of ID. And on occasions she was something of a bodyguard when he had drunk too much and become annoyingly sociable with strangers. She had a softer side to her, underneath the brash, aggressive exterior, often reserved for her contact with the staff. Their outings didn't last long but were precious to Jonathan. To get anything other than abuse from fellow inmates, was almost flattering.

He had been an Arsenal fan in his first decade in Sussex, which seemed like a good idea after they won the double in 1971. He took them with him to Sheffield for a while, before his enthusiasm for football waned a little, when the traumas of school and the preoccupation of daily survival took over. The few happy memories of being alone with his dad, were their rare trips to the grounds of Wednesday and United when Arsenal were the visitors. So he now made a few solitary trips to see Arsenal at home, and then got lost trying to get to an away game at Spurs. But at least he was out and about and travelling on the tube, which excited him greatly.

He loved wandering around in a big city where nobody knew him, with the kind of sight-seeing that almost felt too good to be true for someone of his lowly predicament. Never had that been so apparent than on one occasion while drinking tea in the café at Hyde Park when the place was invaded by a group of Harrods-carrier-bag-carrying Yuppie types, asking for Darjeeling, and shouting to each other with such cries of 'Crispin! Crispin! How many sugars, darling?' Just to be within spitting distance of someone called Crispin, was a novelty only London could provide. A bizarre moment when people who should never be in the same room as each other, were. No chance of bumping into old acquaintances and people he had the misfortune of going to school with here, he thought.

The staff at the house tried to keep some kind of order and would hold 'emergency meetings' when breaches of the house rules occurred, where the alleged culprits were interrogated by the rest of the house. Theft, glue-sniffing, failure to do household chores, and not getting out of bed in the morning at the set time, were among the usual offences that warranted such a meeting. These would sometimes turn violent, especially when inmates accused each other of theft of their belongings. But when Jonathan first arrived at the house, he had an acoustic guitar with which he was making very slow progress at learning to play. When that went missing in his second week there, he reported it; there was no meeting, and he never saw it again. Only the fact that he knew he was never going to be the next Segovia, or Jimi Hendrix, made it bearable. But it felt like abuse nonetheless, and he had his suspicions as to who was responsible. Suspicions he had so far kept to himself.

One such meeting took place around a bed in his dormitory that was still occupied at eleven o'clock. The rule was that the accused had to attend the meeting, so if their crime was the fact of still being in the bed, the meeting would come to them. Chairs were set up around it and much talk ensued about how such indiscipline was detrimental to their well-being, and so forth. This bizarre spectacle was one of the house's 'progressive techniques' Jonathan's social worker had so enthusiastically remarked upon on their journey down here – talking to him as if he were a fellow social worker, when he hadn't got a clue what she was talking about.

It was hoped that such an extreme response would embarrass the culprit into submission, prompting them to get out of the bed, but it rarely worked, prompting only feigned unconsciousness and loud snoring as an act of defiance. All residents had to attend, including Jonathan. Never one to join in a collective tirade against an individual, himself having been so often a victim of such, he sat there silently, with dread at ever being the subject of such a meeting, with his sensitivity and loathing of drawing attention to himself.

He had recently discovered alcohol, and realised that when he drank, a chemical reaction occurred in his brain and body. But not the same chemical reaction that one might expect to occur between the booze and the pills (marked 'avoid alcohol') he was still taking and much dependant on. But the type of reaction where a Walter Mitty-style transformation occurred with his personality. And with the thought that all he had to do was drink the stuff in order to escape from his prison of being an introverted young man with no self-confidence or worth, there was no stopping him. But it was almost suicidal in the wrong company, in which he usually found himself. Also, the fact that if there was still drink to be drunk and they hadn't as yet rung the bell for last orders, he would have to continue to the bitter end. On one such evening, the end was more bitter than usual.

31

All the inmates were invited to a party in the local area where they helped themselves to the free booze. When there was none left and it seemed to most normal guests like a good time to leave, a drunk Jonathan decided he was not quite as close to oblivion as he would have liked. And so made the suicidal gesture of threatening the largest male inmate of the house who he suspected of stealing his guitar and anything else of anybody's that had gone missing. It was really meant as a joke, but at the end of the night he could hardly stand up and his jokes weren't funny. So he was promptly punched and kicked about the place by the 'thief', and later by his friends who joined in.

Whether Jonathan was an alcoholic was debatable, but lager and bottles of barley wine were doing for him what cocaine was doing for a lot of other wealthier folk, and the idea of stopping abruptly when his drinking had been gathering momentum all evening, was like trying to stop a train. Any thought of doing something as rational as going home after you've heard a bell ring for last orders was downright impossible. The same rational thinking that millions of other heavy drinkers didn't have a problem with. To them it was an enjoyable pastime. To him it was something far deeper; more like psychotic drinking than alcoholism, if there's a difference.

As he ran from the scene, he must have looked something like the naked child that ran towards the camera screaming and crying with bombs going off behind her, in that famous photograph that depicts the Vietnam war like no other. Having lost both his shoes, clothes torn and blood coming from various bits of him. This was a well-heeled neighbourhood where you had to be a millionaire to buy any property in it, where there were regular sightings of celebrities off the telly, but the locals were hardened to the general mayhem from the teenage luni-bin nearby. So the only reaction would have been the odd raised eyebrow or the twitching of curtains, as he ran down the road screaming.

But someone must have called an ambulance as there was now one following him. Luckily, one of its occupants got out and bundled him in. So now, getting much needed respite from what felt like the youth club from hell, he found himself in the more peaceful surroundings of the local hospital. Its physical department was on the lower floors where he spent a few days being treated for his wounds and generally observed, as his head had taken a pounding from a lot of feet and a brick wall. The mental department was on the upper floors, with suitable restraints so inmates couldn't throw themselves out of it. This was to be his next stop, for a week of heavy sedation. But not enough to stop the fear and contemplation of his immediate future, and the possibility of more violence should he return to the house. It was considered justifiable by staff at the hospital if he refused to go back there, who suggested he be transferred back to the adult section at St Mary's. Although this was immediately attractive purely as a means of escape from his current dilemma, did he really want to be back in the bosom of the mental health system, and in Sheffield? He had begun to enjoy some things about his new life in London, just not the accommodation. Something there was no choice about. Leaving there for a penthouse suite in Mayfair overlooking Hyde Park, was never going to be an option.

Jonathan's stay at the hospital was uneventful, except for a bizarre encounter with a psychiatrist who entered his solo bedroom, wearing a suit and glasses and wielding a clipboard. He asked the patient two staggeringly irrelevant questions.

'How many units of alcohol do you drink per week?'

The doctor wished he hadn't asked as the answer was a long one, and didn't come until after Jonathan had asked the doctor what exactly was a 'unit of alcohol'.

'Well, it depends on whether I go to the pub or not,' he rambled, 'and if not, I sometimes go to the off license and buy four cans and usually drink them all that day but sometimes I don't.' The doctor, who was expecting an answer involving one or two numbers to put neatly on his clipboard, was getting more and more frustrated. But this was a seventeen-year-old boy who was heavily drugged and recovering from being used as a football only a week ago.

The doctor's second question went quite differently, in that the one-word answer the boy was trying to give, which should have been sufficient, apparently wasn't.

Doctor: Are you a homosexual?

Jonathan: No.

Doctor: Why not?

Jonathan: I don't know.

Doctor: You don't know if you're a homosexual?

Jonathan: Ah, I don't know why I'm not.

Doctor: What's wrong with being homosexual?

Jonathan: Nothing.

Doctor: Maybe you would feel better if you just admitted it. It's nothing to be ashamed of.

Jonathan opened his mouth to speak, but nothing came out. It was trickery of some kind, like being cross-examined in a witness box, but his heavily sedated brain couldn't quite manage the hostile response such (interrogation?) required. Lost for words, he was reduced to staring at the doctor with vacant eyes and a sagging lower lip, not unlike a very tired Labrador. He wondered if his visitor was actually a salesman promoting homosexuality and would get commission for every new recruit he managed to convert. And, whether the new recruit would get some kind of discount, a 'Crackerjack' pencil[2] or something more sinister. With a less sedated mind he may have thought of asking the doctor the obvious counterattack, 'Are you a homosexual?', but really, the conversation was much too much like hard work. He'd struggle to get a clear head round it, let alone the one he'd got now, with its mixture of the usual pills plus a few extra 'temporary' ones.

At last, the doctor, thankfully returning to something like normal behaviour, looks at his watch and says, 'Good heavens! Is that the time? I must be off.'

He smiles at Jonathan as if everything was satisfactory and he had passed a test of some kind, and after scribbling a few notes on his clipboard, promptly gets up and leaves the room without another word. He then enters the room next door and starts another conversation. Jonathan puts his ear to the wall trying to listen to the chat, in case it was the same as what he himself had just endured.

With almost disbelief, he pondered. Could he really be giving out to one and all the impression of being gay, and all his problems stemming from his refusal to accept it? Or maybe his reactions were being tested like a rat in a maze in a laboratory. If so, what on earth could have been deduced from his reactions to being (accused?) of being gay? Or had the conversation just been some kind of rehearsal for a forthcoming Monty Python sketch?

---

[2] the usual modest prize given away on the 1970s children's TV programme of the same name.

After a welcome visit from Clive, and some assurances that there would be no repeat of the violence on his return, he made the decision to go back there. Lucy, his skinhead friend, had come to the hospital to meet him, having volunteered to accompany him on the walk back. Although too embarrassed to show his true feelings to the shaven-headed, Doc-Martined girl, her presence was a big comfort to him at a time when he needed it. He dreaded his next sighting of the six-foot plus, fifteen-stone monster that had beaten him up, who he was sure would be revelling in his destructive achievement. And would be difficult to avoid, as sadly, they shared the same dormitory. Jonathan would have to suppress a lot of anger and hatred, and sleep with one eye open, in order for life at the house to continue with any degree of peace. In these cramped conditions, the potential for clashes of personality with catastrophic results was vast.

Life stumbled along awkwardly at the house. A sober Jonathan couldn't bear drawing attention to himself, and so was content for the matter of his beating to be swept under the carpet and left there. Merciless revenge being forever something not to be indulged in, unless one wants to be confined to an even more claustrophobic community than this. And one where the going out for some light relief wasn't an option. But the 'progressive' staff had other ideas, and to his horror, he learnt that the matter was to be the subject of an emergency meeting. During which, the monster was pressured into apologising for his actions, with extreme resistance. Jonathan still hated the bastard but was touched by the pressure applied by the rest of the house, inmates included. And was pleased he made the decision to return, but in his fragile existence, being pleased was a state of mind that was usually short lived.

Mainly due to homesickness, although there was no clear definition of where home was, Jonathan felt an urge to go to the Sussex town of Horsham and revisit some old haunts of his childhood. This was difficult financially as the train fare alone took up a large chunk of his meagre benefit money. But off he went, looking like something of a lost cause, with his long, dark, unbrushed hair, cagoule with a hood, dirty, and now unfashionable, flared jeans. His appearance was a guarantee of being ignored in London, where the sheer mass of people prevented anyone paying too much attention to anyone else, but of definitely being noticed in Horsham. On arrival, he had a brief look at the timetable for the last train home but as a large part of his brain didn't want to return 'home' (at least not until the need for shelter was truly overwhelming), none of the information really sank in.

He stood outside the primary school he had attended, gazing at the carefree looking children running around and laughing in the playground. He felt comforted, as he reminisced for the days before education became such a problem. But there was also a feeling of having been normal in this place, and now wasn't, and a bewilderment at how that change had occurred.

Just to confirm those feelings of abnormality, his presence attracted the attention of dinner ladies supervising the children's playtime. And as one of them walked towards him with a stern look of disapproval, he walked on.

In the afternoon, he wandered down a long peaceful road with houses on both sides, where neither sight nor sound of human activity interrupted the bird song. On this road was an old detached house which was his home from birth to nine-years-old. Happy times here, he remembered, as he stood outside the place and listened to the occasional train passing on the railway line behind it. A non-threatening, almost comforting sound. He felt a long way from London, where there were too many sounds going on to be able to appreciate any particular one. His mind wandered over memories of watching his dad light fireworks while he and his sisters stood on the path keeping a safe distance, wrapped up warm on a freezing bonfire night, and splashing about in the paddling pool in the summer.

He knocked at the house next door which used to belong to the Taylors, former close friends of the Pipers. And sure enough still did, as the door was opened by a now older looking Jean Taylor. She looked slightly disturbed at the sight of the stranger in front of her, who looked nothing like a Jehovah's Witness or a door-to-door salesman. He introduced himself to a few gasps and smiles from Jean, who let him in and promptly put the kettle on.

'What happened to you? We've heard all sorts of things about your goings on,' she said, with more than a hint of disapproval in her voice.

Jonathan shuddered at the thought of what she might have heard and didn't answer. It was not a question that could be answered in one or two sentences. She got some photos out of a drawer and passed them to him. There were some old black and white ones showing Jonathan and her son as toddlers. The two boys would play together while their mums chatted over tea and biscuits.

'You remember Peter, don't you,' referring to her son, now doing 'so well' in the RAF.

She was quite blatant in her comparisons between the downtrodden boy sitting in front of her, and Peter, of whom, she showed him what seemed like endless photos. Mostly in uniform, at various official military gatherings. She had always been proud of her son, and now to see his former playmate in his current dishevelled state, had somehow increased that pride.

Jean, with fond memories of her friendship with Jonathan's mother, felt duty bound to take care of the wayward son while he was here, and so insisted on cooking a meal for him.

'Where are you going now?' she asked, looking out the window at the dusk and rain.

His response was vague about getting the train back to London, the times of which he wasn't quite sure. She said that she thought the last train left quite early, and as he was a fair distance from the station, he may not make it in time; without it sounding like an invitation of shelter for the night. Remembering his family's strong connection with the Catholic church not far away, she suggested he make his way there. The priest, who she thought was the same one who had been there since his childhood days, 'May remember you and be able to help'. He doubted that, but took it as his cue to leave. Which he did, thanking her for her kindness.

He took her advice, as now there was no other option, and knocked on the door of the priest's house. Sure enough, he was confronted by the same but now older and more miserable priest that had baptized and confirmed him, and was promptly told to 'piss off'. After explaining his situation and previous connections with the church, he was then offered the shelter of the man's garden shed. In which, he shook the night away in the freezing cold of the January night – a stone's throw from where he used to play football on the green after mass on Sunday, in those far off, naïve, carefree days when it felt like church and school were somehow his saviour.

In the morning, he made his way back to the station with the welcome warmth of the sun to defrost him. He returned to the house in the middle of the afternoon where he collapsed on the bed, in the rare bliss of an empty dormitory. But a few minutes later, his sleep was disturbed by a member of staff, telling him he was to be the subject of an emergency meeting caused by his failure to do the household chores he had completely forgotten that he was supposed to be doing that morning. He was informed that the meeting that he must attend will take place in the dining room in five minutes. Still lying on the bed after a brief period of indecision about whether he should or could attend the meeting, he fell into a deep sleep. He was soon woken again by the movement of chairs being placed around the bed, as if some kind of ritualistic exorcism was about to take place. He was told by the now seated congregation that, because of his failure to attend the meeting, it would take place here. All highly officious, with what was painfully obvious being pointed out. Household chores were a much-needed therapy, encouraging the resident to take responsibilities and stick to them, he was told, and that this would benefit them in their later lives. There was always a therapeutic aspect to such occasions. Never before had he been so desperate to sleep and to be left alone to do so. He didn't have the energy to explain his sleepless night with his body shaking uncontrollably with the cold, like being pushed down an endless flight of stairs while you're attached to a trolley.

With his return to full consciousness came a feeling of increasing paranoia. Intensified by the discovery that the monster was in the audience, glaring at him with a slimy grin, while the straight-faced spokesman went on to describe Jonathan's laziness, amongst other alleged shortcomings. This seemed well out of character for this particular staff, who seemed to have turned into a dictator now he was in the role of spokesperson, supposedly speaking on behalf of 'the house'. As if a sudden surge of electricity had passed through his tired body, Jonathan suddenly rose up off the bed staring straight at the spokesman and headed straight for him. He barely had a chance to do any damage before being paralysed by male members of the audience, including the monster, gripping each of his limbs and head. They were suitably prepared for what was a fairly regular conclusion to such meetings. It was a pointless attempt at violence with no chance of getting anywhere, but in some ways an appropriate response to a cowardly verbal attack on him by someone who was heavily backed up by his cohorts. It was this reminder of school and his abusers that triggered Jonathan's rage, so strong and powerful when there was three of them, united in their fight for one common cause: his destruction.

The consequence of his outburst was expulsion from the house, leaving him undecided as to whether to be angry, relieved or depressed. The struggle was over, before the next one commences. And hopefully, the pause between the two would be long enough to be enjoyed. Where was he supposed to go now, being as The Ritz and The Dorchester were fully booked? After words with Mum, fortunately it was an option to go home to them in Sheffield but he would have to be on his best behaviour when he did.

Ironically, it was the monster who offered to help him carry the remainder of his belongings (that he hadn't already nicked), and walk with him to the tube station. Either he had a newfound respect for his victim or was sympathetic at the harsh treatment he was receiving. Whereas *he* went unpunished for putting a fellow inmate in hospital; Jonathan's punishment for trying to do the same to a member of staff who was administering 'therapy' was severe. A big difference, so it seemed.

'You take care, all right,' said the monster in a stern voice, as they waited on the platform. Jonathan nodded, with a little reluctance to accept the last-minute friendship of what had been a major source of his struggle in living there. He promised to keep in touch with Clive who had been such a comfort, but sadly absent on the day of the fateful 'emergency meeting', and who had tried in vain to get justice for his beleaguered charge. Although it had been a daily struggle to maintain what sanity he had, he was sad to be leaving London.

He boarded the train for Sheffield, full of regret and sensing his parents' reluctance to have him back. His dad's mainly, but if Dad was reluctant, Mum would join in. She was that kind of wife, loyal to a fault, and had surely had enough of trying to keep the peace in her home. But what were the alternatives to inflicting more of his company upon them? Where else could he go, with only a weekly giro[3] consisting of barely enough for a round of drinks in the great metropolis, let alone putting a roof over one's head?

---

[3] very often how benefit money was paid, in the form of a *giro* cheque, usually sent in the post, before direct transfer to bank accounts was introduced.

Homeward Bound Again

Mum put on a convincing display of being pleased to see him, and Dad felt obliged to join in. Although mentally disturbed, Jonathan was alive and well and thankfully didn't have to become a 'rent boy' hanging around Piccadilly Circus, at a time when AIDS was just about to kick off. Not a career option he would ever consider,(so long as other options were available) but, he had heard, was the fate of a few ex-residents of the house, whose fondness for glue had escalated towards other substances. Self-destruction, of one sort or another, did seem to be the price that would have to be paid for remaining in London, the great city of dreams that had never been kind to its paupers. So, count his blessings he did, on his return home.

His sisters had dispersed to university. He enjoyed their absence and settled down to an altogether cosier existence of being alone most days while Mum and Dad were at work, and the playing of board games with Mum in the evening. He could watch all manner of nonsense on telly during the day and play loud rock music to his heart's content. It could be said that music and solitude were his two favourite things. He yearned to play raucous guitar solos that would tear stadiums apart in front of screaming fans, but it would have to remain a dream as his fingers were never going to do what they should. He liked solitude because so much of being with other people was problematic, it seemed.

He resumed his outpatient appointments at St Mary's to get his medicinal fix. God knows why, but it was the status quo which had to be maintained, or else decisions would have to be made. They made him tired and sluggish, but this could be used as justification for not seeking employment should he get pressure of that sort, and it got him out of the house every few weeks. And, as he was now back in the bosom of the family, this was no time for the disruption of another attempt to come off them, and its subsequent madness. After a brief chat, which always started with the doctor's attempt at a comforting smile and the question, 'So, how are you getting on?', he got his supplies and went home.

His drinking was pretty much stagnant at this time, as he had no social life and there were no pubs nearby. To him, alcohol and pubs definitely went together, because he lost the inhibitions that so controlled his life when he drank, and he could chat-up girls, whether they liked it or not. Mostly, they didn't, and it often led to problems when their boyfriends arrived or came back from the loo. But sometimes they did, as if they liked a man with self-confidence, and on a few rare occasions he miraculously managed to pass for one. But the timing had to be precise; he had to have drunk enough to be witty and charming, but only when there wasn't enough time for him to continue to the bitter end and *really* start making a fool of himself, did he have any success. But he managed to make a date with one or two girls, while in this semi-drunk state. However, when the time came, despite a yearning for female company, he wouldn't turn up. The daunting task of trying to imitate a normal person for an entire evening, was just too much effort. During which, he would surely be asked questions about himself, and for every one of them, a bogus, acceptable answer would have to be found. The charade didn't interest him, as it would mean an element of controlled drinking and trying not to go over the top. Sex definitely interested him, but the delicate social stepping stones that hopefully led to it were far beyond his capabilities.

On a rare occasion when he did find the courage to turn up for one such 'date' (and could remember having made it), he found himself walking along the pavement with the girl in question. Having told her all kinds of stuff about his job, car, and flat, he realised he was bullshitting himself into a corner. So much so, that when a bus approached its stop in the opposite direction, with him still in mid-sentence, he quickly made his escape, jumping on it with impeccable timing just before it closed its doors to pull away again, with the intention of finding a pub a safe distance away and getting as much down him as possible in the short time left before last orders. Drowning his sorrows at being a sad enough person who would do such a thing. Still, the social aspect of drinking was very important, even if it did sometimes result in him being arrested or hospitalized.

Despite his efforts to conform to whatever would keep the peace at home, after a few episodes of late-night drunkenness, the old feelings of dependency on his dad re-emerged. And now more dependent, as he was definitely old enough to be turfed out into no man's land. And so, he made a few attempts at moving out, which sadly, involved trying to fit in at various places where solitude was hard to come by due to the shared facilities. Not an easy task for someone who had felt that they fitted in perfectly in the often psychotic surroundings of the adolescent unit at St Mary's. One place, where the other tenants were much older than him, appealed to him initially for that reason alone. Youngsters his own age needing to be avoided. But he got a lot of disapproval, mainly because of his appearance and unemployment, offending their somewhat conservative values with his remarks about avoiding work, rather than looking for it. So, he left there and moved to a bedsit, where the other tenants were young and unemployed which appealed to him initially for that reason alone – a break now needed from the more geriatric, conservative types. But, upon realising that a vulnerable tenant had just moved in, they proceeded to nick his stuff and hassle him regularly to buy drugs from them. So he left there, and his long-suffering father waited outside in the car for him to emerge with his belongings. Full of enthusiasm, *of course,* at his son's imminent return to the house.

But one day, the wind must have blown him in the right direction, as he ended up moving into the YMCA, which looked like an office block, right in the centre of town. A big place, not unlike an institution, and with its mass of residents, provided the sort of anonymity he craved. Life soon became bearable here, and he had at last, it seemed, successfully left home for good, too much rejoicing in the Piper household.

There was a pub down the road which was frequented by a few of his sister's former friends who he had met before, and who treated him much like an annoying little brother. Something he was used to. But it was company of sorts, for someone who had very little else. But his drinking took off here once again. He was barred several times by usually the most tolerant of landlords. And on another occasion when he wasn't quite as close to oblivion as he would have liked at closing time, he accepted an invitation to go back to a bloke's flat with the promise of more booze to be had there. But on his arrival, realised they were alone, despite the man's words of, 'A few of the lads are coming back to my place'. When they were alone, drinking Lager from cans, the bearded, thick-set, tattooed man, who looked like he dug roads (with a pneumatic drill – not his actual fondness for them), made suggestions of a homosexual nature. But then, fortunately, paused to get more cans from the kitchen, giving a plastered Jonathan the opportunity to chuck himself out the window. Which he then did, frantically, as if his life depended on it, oblivious to what floor he was on.

Luckily, it was only the second, and he survived the ordeal with the only pricks up his bum coming from the holly bush in the flower bed that he landed in. Luckily also, the man, who was a regular at the pub, kept himself to himself from then on, seemingly desperate for the other regulars not to know of his preferences. It was never mentioned again, and sort of assumed and hoped that Jonathan was so drunk that he didn't remember any of it. Especially as the man was a coach for a local youth football team in his spare time, whose players consisted of some of the other pub regular's male offspring. But Jonathan did remember and joked to himself that one day he'll write a book about his near misses with homosexuality: from a doctor insisting he was, to chucking himself out the window to avoid it, to staying at the YMCA, which with its solely male clientele, had a reputation for it, which was perhaps a fair one, although he hadn't mingled sufficiently in the place to find out. Not that he was at all homophobic; there being plenty of far more appropriate directions for his hatred. Just a quirky feature of his youth that he seemed to be irresistible; but sadly, only to the same sex.

One morning, Jonathan waited at the bus stop for his usual journey to the hospital for his appointment and collection of pills when along came another resident of the YMCA who he had seen there once or twice. They both waited for the bus. Jonathan half-smiled, with caution, not wanting to encourage any more sexual advances, and then continued examining the pavement beneath him. The middle-aged man could have almost passed for a doctor himself, had he not been chewing gum, smoking, and waiting for a bus. His dress was formal, brown lace-up shoes, proper trousers – not jeans – and an open-necked shirt. He had an overcoat draped over one arm and carried a briefcase.

'Going anywhere nice?' the man asked.

Jonathan was hesitant in his reply, as there was a real stigma attached to his destination to many locals in the narrow-minded community. And as this was a fellow resident who looked like he was on official business, further caution was needed. But, as Jonathan nervously gave a truthful answer, while unable to think of a plausible, non-truthful one, he discovered that the fellow resident was also a fellow patient, and also bound for St Mary's to receive his monthly injection. After which, he would go round the hospital, and wherever there was a piano and an audience, entertain the troops. That was what was in the briefcase. Music. And this was music to Jonathan's ears. Mental hospitals were more like home than anywhere else, and he loved live music in whatever form. Even Bob Dylan, if there was nothing else.

As they continued chatting on the bus, it became obvious that he didn't need to ask for permission to accompany 'Dennis' on his piano-playing trip round the hospital. Up until now, Jonathan's visits to St Mary's had been purely functional, and brief. But this was all about to change.

A Mad Hatter's Tea Party

Jonathan enjoyed his visit to St Mary's like never before, and it seemed to open up a whole new world for the directionless young man. Dennis was truly a master of the keyboard, churning out the old-time classics at a relentless pace, and often with a touch of vaudeville thrown in. Getting up off his piano stool during the last few bars of a song, ready for the finale: a glissando[4], followed by a thump on the keys, before much exaggerated bowing to the audience at the end, as though impersonating a classical pianist, soaking up the thunderous applause at the Albert Hall. Often, a humorous attempt at drawing attention to the lack of it when being ignored by a drug-induced audience, or, to raise a titter in an elderly audience who needed cheering up. Although the maestro explained his 'paranoid schizophrenia' and injections at the hospital for the treatment of it, he seemed like a calm, laid back sort of bloke – something Jonathan was not, or had become not, since his Sheffield schooldays. It was difficult to tell how much all that had affected his personality.

This was an asylum originating from the Victorian era. A huge place, presumably to cope with the overcrowding at a time when a young girl having a child out of wedlock and the breaching of other social norms was presumed to be insanity. There were some quite disturbing (to the uninitiated) and amusing sights here. It is a widely held opinion that the best comedy is often achieved by the straight-faced comedian putting on an act of being totally unaware of being funny. A lot of the inmates here fitted that description exactly, only it wasn't an act. After lobotomies and electric shock treatment had been used to cure their ills, they were unaware of a lot of things. Dennis, with his other talent for doing impressions, would sometimes imitate them, in a mocking, yet affectionate way.

Requests were often made at inappropriate times. An old man enters

---

[4] a quick running of the fingers or thumb across the keys of a piano – often followed by an abrupt thump on the keys, as performed in this case.

45

the room with a face lacking any expression and shouts his request in order to be heard above the rendition of *The Girl from Ipanema* currently being played.

'I'm in the mood for love!'

'I'm sure you are,' Dennis replies, grinning, as he looks at Jonathan sitting next to the piano.

This was followed by a choir of seated inmates pausing with their puffs on cigarettes for a moment, in order to sing the next few lines of the requested song in a loud, shambolic fashion; as the pianist continued his way through the Brazilian bossa nova classic, oblivious to the disorderly vocals around him. Dennis later explained that the same request by the same man would be called out every time he entered the room, regular as clockwork. And, that there was some doubt as to whether it actually was a request, or the man was shouting it purely because he was in the habit of doing so every time he heard music. Like one of the various catchphrases that could often be heard being blurted out for no apparent reason. Once again, Jonathan had entered a bizarre, psychiatric world, and one where he increasingly felt he belonged. A refuge from the real one. Out there. Where he didn't.

The more appreciative audience was usually found in what was known to the patients as 'The Tea Bar', or the more sedate, 'Patient's Lounge', to the staff. A lounge where the upholstery was ravaged by cigarette burns. A sort of canteen where volunteer ladies would serve tea, cake, crisps, biscuits and individual cigarettes. Patients would gather in it, making the journey from their various wards in the hospital during its opening hours. The patients had all the essentials supplied on their wards, but cigarettes and money were strictly rationed. Everybody smoked, so there was a constant preoccupation with trying to get one's next fag, like seagulls in a never-ending search for food. The pitiful sight of people trying to light dog-ends they had just picked up off the floor was a common one. Individual cigarettes were often traded like currency and promises of settling petty debts were made with them. During which, the occasional argument would break out, before the volunteer ladies would restore order with threats of contacting the relevant wards for the removal of the disorderly. There was a Dickensian style of poverty and persuasion among the desperate; for a smoke, or a few pence for a cup of tea after all money had been spent on fags. But some of the 'desperate' could often be seen wearing smart, expensive, if ill-fitting clothes, and jewellery. As if what money they had was concealed from them, and being spent on non-essential, non-tobacco-related items.

Respectable civilians from outside who had come to visit their loved ones and take them to the Tea Bar, were always a target for scroungers. A dishevelled man with tobacco-stained fingers and teeth approaches a table with the smile that he uses for business purposes, where two ladies are chatting and drinking tea. One of the ladies, a patient who knows him, proudly introduces her sister, and the old chap comments on her beauty which he says the other sister has 'definitely inherited'. The sisters smile sweetly and blush just before he ruins the moment with an open hand outstretched and the fatal words, 'Any chance you could spare…?'

When Dennis entered the place, it lit up, as if Liberace[5] was gracing it with his presence. As he was the bringer of music and the fond memories of youth it restored, he was important.

Looking smart with his brief case full of sheet music, he would mingle with the audience, asking about their ailments, if there had been any improvements, and if they had a special request for him to play. Jonathan sometimes felt he was cramping the great man's style with his scruffy attire and reticent demeanour, but his company always seemed to be appreciated on the now frequent occasions he accompanied his musician friend. It was common knowledge that Dennis smoked and left particularly generous dog-ends, so his ashtray would get immediate attention at the end of each performance. And sometimes during.

But Elsie didn't smoke, and to anyone that would listen, would declare her disgust at the general rabble surrounding her that did; except Dennis of course. 'Cadgers, the lot of 'em'!' was her particular, much-repeated catchphrase on the subject. Together with her aged friend, they would make the long journey from their geriatric ward at the other end of the hospital to the Tea Bar. Beads round their necks and handbags round their arms that swayed chaotically as they staggered down the long corridors gripping the hand rails for dear life. Swollen ankles, and feet looking squashed inside small brown lace-up shoes, squawking at each other almost unintelligibly as they walked. Both barmy, but very proud

---

[5] flamboyant American pianist of the period.

snobs. Elsie however, the severest of the two in that department; disapproving of much that went on in the Tea Bar but determined to get there. She would dish out the insults and scornful looks when she and her friend were eventually seated at a table, their teas brought to them by the volunteer ladies. Her insults were never returned by the 'cadgers' and ashtray-sifters they were aimed at, who looked up to her like she was the Queen Mother. She repeated herself constantly, and in her more light-hearted moments freely admitted that she was 'as bald as a coot', because all her hair fell out on the day her husband died in 1948, and never returned, due to the shock.

'Only a young man he was.'

She wore different wigs that would sit on her head slightly tilted, as if at any moment would fall off her head and onto the table. She often moved suddenly, jerkily, especially when her chat was interrupted by a 'cadger' swooping in on the ashtray on the table for a choice dog-end; or when she banged her fist on it to help get her point across, but the wig only ever wobbled precariously. She would proudly tell all, and did every time you saw her, that she was once a 'chamber maid waitress' in 'all' the hotels in an area of Sheffield that was posh in her day, but had since become notorious for its prostitution and drug-dealing. Testimony to the many decades she had spent away from the real world. But in her day, probably the naughtiest thing that ever happened there, was the scandalous act of young ladies doing the Charleston with the occasional ankle on display.

'Not much call for chamber maid waitresses there now, Elsie,' Dennis interjected, with his usual mocking yet affectionate grin during one of Jonathan and Elsie's frequent chats. But she wasn't listening, clinging to her memories of the place, where iron railings and blue plaques (declaring that the great and the good once lived there) could still be seen outside the few listed buildings that remain, now cowering below the tower blocks.

Jonathan took to this place like a duck to water. People either out of society altogether, or very much on the margins of it like he was. Strange, he thought, that the wind had never blown him in the direction of the Tea Bar during one of his many previous visits. If he had ever fancied a cup of tea while there collecting his medication, he would surely have stumbled upon it. But this being the adult section, had given him expectations of shouting, violence, strait jackets, and dangerous people, so better keep one's visits brief and unsociable he had thought. But the atmosphere in the Tea Bar couldn't have been further from it. Bearing in mind that most of the patients were now old and when they were first admitted, stuff like infidelity and illegitimacy seemed good enough reasons to lock people up, they may not have been too dangerous in the first place. Despite the 'paranoid schizophrenia' (including Dennis) and 'severe personality disorder' (including Jonathan?) that was contained here, it was mainly a peaceful, charming place, lacking any real malice. Testimony perhaps, that the psychiatric establishment often did get it right with its medicine, if not so much in Jonathan's case.

He would often jokingly refer to Dennis as 'a menace to society', spouting the cliched words of judges before the sentencing of paranoid schizophrenics, or 'serial killers', as they are often otherwise known as, which they both found quite amusing. As well as Dennis, there was other such diagnosed people in the Tea Bar, quietly sipping their tea and putting tobacco in their pipes, who had never harmed anybody. But alas, this didn't sell newspapers.

To Jonathan, what was so infectious was that, despite the humour and comical characters, nobody seemed to laugh at anybody else. A refuge, it seemed, from the outside world where they did, with malice. And so, becoming rapidly absorbed by the place, he began to make more frequent visits, alone, without an appointment, and without Dennis. At times, when not on the official business of getting his medication, or being Dennis's chief applauder and tea-bringer, he was self-conscious of his presence, wondering if he may be asked what he was doing there, and if the volunteer ladies might not serve him. Which, to the directionless young man with no sense of identity or belonging to anything, would hit him like an arrow through the heart. But this never happened. And, as he was essentially a caring person, would often converse with patients of the more downtrodden and less devious kind, and so made a few friends; despite the conversations at times wandering in and out of the absurd. But whenever Dennis was going there, Jonathan followed, for the added bonus of the piano playing which always brought a lively atmosphere to the place.

Dennis was twenty years his senior, and also originated from the South of England but had moved from one place to another on his own many times.

A genuine rolling stone, something Jonathan truly admired. But this was how Dennis's periodic psychosis had helped him on his way, when he explained that his moves had coincided with him being 'high'. Deluded into believing that the local people of wherever it was he was planning to move to knew he was coming, and would therefore be shouting, cheering and waving upon his arrival. But the disappointment when they weren't, and the shock of being a stranger in a strange town would throw him off balance, often landing him in the local mental hospital where pianos were played and new friends quickly found. He freely admitted to being gay and only really attracted to non-gay males younger than himself, of which Jonathan was a good example. So it was never going to be easy looking for a partner who would reciprocate his feelings. Perhaps there was a homosexual interest in Jonathan, the possibility of which the young man didn't want to get close enough to find out. If so, it wasn't the first time, and surely wouldn't be the last. But sexual matters aside, his friendship with Dennis was a guiding light when he desperately needed some kind of direction, and it was a rare thing that he wasn't required to give anything back – apart from being expected to accompany his friend to the windswept terraces of Bramall Lane whenever his beloved Norwich City played Sheffield United. This was always followed by a visit to the nearby Railway Tavern in search of paid piano-playing work which the stingy landlord always declined despite the obvious appreciation from the music-starved regulars, singing away as Dennis charitably gave them a few tunes for free before leaving.

Another much-neglected piano was the Bechstein upright that sat in a large, semi-abandoned church hall opposite the YMCA. Dennis was given permission to practice on it and would do so for hours. Often oblivious to Jonathan standing in the doorway, savouring the wonderful acoustics of the place as his friend attempted the mastering of Gershwin's *Rhapsody in Blue* and other challenging pieces. Usually followed by enthusiastic applause from the one-man audience that would pleasantly startle the musician who thought he was alone. Special moments that cemented their friendship.

Lured by the prospect of having his own flat, and being closer to the hospital, Jonathan accepted an offer of accommodation. Staying at, and 'keeping an eye on', the council flat of Eric, who was always away on business. That of being an almost permanent inmate of the hospital. A

50

manic depressive, his brief stays at the flat in the outside world would send him sky high, attracting the attention of the less than understanding neighbours. Religion was a major part of his madness, as could be said for the world in general.

'Whoever shuts their ears to the cry of the poor...!' he shouts, unable to finish his quote from the bible due to the crush of neighbours, who had heard that the crazed 'bible-basher' would sometimes give his money away to worthy causes. Them. After one such incident of charitable donation, he had laid down in the middle of a busy road refusing to move until he was given a cigarette. Behaviour that prompted a swift return to the hospital, 'sectioned' under the mental health act, where he was unable even to go to the Tea Bar unsupervised. And on the few occasions he did, there were heated exchanges between deranged landlord and tenant, during which, rent in advance was demanded, to compensate for the twisted generosity to the locals that had left him charmless and tobaccoless.

Eric was like a clockwork clown that the neighbours would wind up when they wanted some entertainment. After which, he would have to return to the hospital to wind down. A viscous circle that went on and on being repeated. But a situation that meant that the increased chaos of landlord and tenant living together was avoided. Although intelligent and well-spoken, he had extremely childlike ways and charisma that should be packing them in at the London Palladium. Like a crazed Groucho Marx minus the cigar, he bobbed up and down on the spot with excitement when he told a joke that usually started with a 'knock, knock', and then fell about laughing at it. With this behaviour, combined with a height not being much above the average ten-year-old, he had a way with children. However, there was much debate locally as to what that way consisted of. Of course, he was suspected of being a paedophile; a suspicion not uncommon of any man living alone on such an estate. But one thing was sure, the local children couldn't get enough of him, his sweets, his smiles and his jokes. And Jonathan, alone in the flat of the great absent one, was a poor substitute. There was a knock at the door.

'Can Eric come out to play?' he was asked by a group of straight-faced small children.

'Well, I don't know. It's way past his bedtime,' Jonathan jokingly replied to the miniature audience of disappointed faces.

As if from nowhere, a committee of adult locals appeared behind the children, with revulsion at the sight of him. Mostly the parents, but some having just come along for the potential aggro.

'Another paedo!'

Jonathan, despite his inner terror with fears of being lynched and hung up from the nearest lamp post, managed to find some sensible words. 'Well, don't let them come round here then.'

It was a rare moment when words seemed to save the day, when he somehow managed to find the obvious counterattack at the right moment. Rather than the usual thinking of it later and wishing he had said it earlier. And in this case, there may not have been a later if he missed the first opportunity. The crowd just stood there wondering what had happened; were they being given some sound parental advice from a nutter associate of Eric the paedo? Momentarily stunned into silence, they didn't have an immediate answer, and to his relief he then managed to shut the door, before a few more shouts of 'weirdo'! 'nutter'! 'pervert'! came through the letterbox.

It was obvious that no housework had been done here for so long that special equipment not sold in ordinary shops was essential for the doing of any now. Eric's social worker, who sometimes came round to check up on the place and declined any refreshments when he did, strongly disapproved of him being there. Giving Jonathan the feeling that his days there were numbered, even if the neighbours hadn't already seen to it. At first, he was seduced by the big plus of having his own flat, with the imagined inviting of girls he may meet in local pubs back to it. But right now, found himself grappling with what felt like an avalanche of minuses.

The Tea Bar had never been more of a safe haven than what it was now. He was now part of the furniture, and the only hostility he ever experienced was forgivable, being caused by the sudden changes of behaviour of those suffering from a sudden change of medication, who would just as quickly revert back to being their usual charming selves. As the outside world became more horrific (Eric's neighbourhood in particular), his dependency on the tranquillity of the hospital increased.

Jonathan got in the habit of drifting down to the local pub with a few outpatients that happened to be in the Tea Bar after it had closed, quite early in the evening. The 'outpatients' were men in a similar situation to himself, but a decade or few older. Living close by, they had to see a doctor and collect their medication or receive their jab every few weeks or so, but used the Tea Bar as a social club much more often than that, as did Jonathan. But when they went down the pub, the outpatients had soft drinks. Thus, sensibly avoiding the collision of booze with tablets or injection, and by about nine o'clock would have usually dispersed in different directions to go home. Here, the differences began, as Jonathan was neither capable of avoiding alcohol, (as suggested on his pill bottles), or leaving the pub early. So, arriving at the pub early and not leaving until it was compulsory was a potentially fatal combination. He resented being alone and listening to the laughter of groups of young happy drinkers around him, and the more he drank, the more likely it was that that resentment would overflow.

On one such occasion when forced to leave a pub at closing time, and once again, not quite as close to oblivion as he would have liked, he grabbed hold of a large bottom, belonging to a woman getting on a bus. It wasn't done with any aggression, malice or humour, it just looked nice and difficult to resist, even more so after alcohol had done its job of enhancing anything nice and diminishing anything negative (like consequences) from his brain. But such mitigating circumstances are never usually taken into consideration, and the next thing he knew, a car pulled up next to him as he staggered along on the pavement. Several young men got out of the car with the worst of intentions. On seeing a glass bottle in a rubbish bin close by, and with a mixture of seething hatred and determination not to be victimised, he smashed it and waved it about in the general direction of their faces with shouts of 'Come and get it'! By some kind of miracle this had the desired effect, and they promptly got back in their car and sped off, making do with shouts of abuse out the window as they did, leaving a half-comatose Jonathan free to stagger home to bed. It would take some years to accumulate enough wisdom to grasp the enormity of good fortune in this, and other similar incidents where he had escaped unharmed.

On one less fortunate drunken return to Eric's flat, it became obvious that the vile neighbours had stepped up their campaign of terror. A window smashed, and his more treasured belongings missing or broken. His records ruined, and now no means of playing them, and the word 'PAEDO' scrawled on the wall with a permanent marker pen. There was no doubt about it, living in the flat of a suspected paedophile also made you one in the eyes of the Great British public; that same mass of people that believed everything it read in newspapers. Resistance was futile. But lacking the wisdom to grasp that, he went out in the street and shouted insults at whoever was listening. That was his last memory of the evening, after which, he presumed, he must have been beaten up, due to the pain, swelling, and slightly deformed facial appearance in the mirror the next morning. Without fully realizing it, there was an internal rage going on at the now absent school bullies which was manifesting itself in other ways, towards other people who looked like, sounded like, or whose behaviour closely resembled that, of the vermin who put him in that well.

Thankfully, there was no shortage of outpatients who would welcome some extra cash and were willing to have Jonathan stay with them. One, who was more than willing, due to his heavy drinking and chain smoking that had to be financed, spieled off the virtues of his one bedroomed council flat as keenly as an estate agent trying to sell a mansion.

'What about the neighbours?' Jonathan enquired with scepticism.

'Never see them! Never hear them!' were the assurances quickly fired back.

'Neighbours', now on a par with gangrene in terms of undesirability, who, when gathered in small groups (as was usual at the last place) became something of an infestation.

So, he began to drift from one chaotic situation to another, often just having a settee to sleep on when there was no spare bedroom. Sober, he was good company for the patients he had genuine affection for, and could make them laugh without trying, and this paid dividends. But because of the drinking, he didn't last too long in each place before one catastrophic incident or another put an end to it.

He yearned to have his own place, and as he had been on the council housing list for some time, eventually, his wish came true. A small self-contained flat, it had a balcony with a panoramic view across the city from which the Arts Tower and cathedral spire could be seen on a clear day. And, as this was a work of architectural genius – a block of flats built like steps going up a hill – he was high up but still close to the ground. Potentially useful to eliminate the risk of another drink-related catastrophe. It was bliss. A momentous occasion, marking the end of chronic dependency on others for shelter.

One day in the Tea Bar, which he now had to get the bus to, but which didn't make his visits any less frequent, he got into a conversation with the most charming of female inmate. Bridget was short and stout, about fifteen years his senior, with a lovely smile and deep brown eyes that seemed to light up when she spoke. A loud cheery voice, and a rare occasion when the broadest of Sheffield accent was a joy to listen to and not at all threatening. He had noticed her before, but she was usually unavailable to talk to due to the amount of visitors she got, friends or relatives that she would sit with in the Tea Bar. And he wouldn't have known what to say anyway should he have got the opportunity. So up until now, she hadn't taken up too much space in Jonathan's brain. But now, in this rare moment when her entourage of hangers-on were absent, she sat opposite Elsie who, in her almost regal status in the Tea Bar, gave the young lady the usual, much-repeated stories of her past, in between disparaging remarks about those around her. Which, in a bizarrely ironic way, was all part of the old lady's charm to which nobody took offence.

'Don't you bother with girls, Jonathan?' Bridget asked, as he walked past their table.

'I don't know any,' he replied, concealing his excitement at being spoken to for the first time by a lady he had so admired from a distance.

'Well, you know me,' she said, disagreeing with him, in a very matter of fact way.

The rarity of common sense being present in such a conversation was a joy to behold. Such straightforward practicalities that were usually stifled by the fear of rejection. The main reason there has always been a huge market for alcohol ever since it was discovered that if you left fruit lying around for long enough and drank it, it would set you free. And Jonathan relied heavily on it for anything remotely amorous to ever take place. But a sober Bridget, with her almost childlike, no-nonsense approach, obviously didn't. Jonathan fancied her, enormously. He 'ummed' and 'arred' for a bit, while trying to get his brain into some kind of order before he actually spoke.

'Well, maybe we could go for a drink sometime,' he mumbled, without having a clue as to how that could be achieved with her being an inpatient on a ward and so on.

'Yes, that would be nice,' she replied.

He felt excited, flattered, and close to collapsing or exploding all at the same time. But go for a drink they did, and for once he was in a pub without any concern for the drink itself, what it was or how much of it he was going to consume before last orders. He was on something resembling a 'date', the connotations of which were usually terrifying. But on this one, where the attraction was obvious to both parties and the smiles and looks were far more important than words, he felt almost relaxed in her company. She neither knew nor cared that he drank excessively, and strangely enough, he didn't feel the need to do so while he was with her or to try to impress her. This priceless association had to be treasured.

From then on, his visits to the hospital were even more delightful, when she would come out of her ward alone, and meet him in an often deserted Tea Bar. No possibility of refreshments as it was closed, but it provided an opportunity to be alone with her. Something he craved. The thrill of hearing her approaching footsteps and subsequent smile as she entered the room, was giving him all he needed right now.

Everything in the garden was lovely while she was a patient in the hospital, and they could enjoy each other's company in its tranquil surroundings. Although their attempts at having sex within the confines of a cubicle in the ladies toilet were uncomfortable, they were certainly memorable. But when she was discharged a short time later, complications of the outside world began to emerge, and her absence was endured, painfully. In his naivety, he had never wondered about her marital status, and it became obvious that she was not single. Her arrival for an outpatient appointment with another man, after he had craved her company for so long, filled Jonathan with a chaos of negative feeling he had to suppress. But, as it turned out, the man was not her spouse but a friend of the family who had been appointed her minder for her visits to the hospital. She was under suspicion of something by her absent spouse, and, by what Jonathan perceived as, her overbearing family and friends.

On one such occasion, he invited Bridget (and her minder!) round to see his new flat, after he saw them in the Tea Bar. The minder seemed all right, if a bit dopey, but even if he was 'The Dalai Lama' with bells on, he was never going to be anything other than a nuisance, stopping the couple being alone together. But it was preferable to not seeing her at all.

This was followed a few days later by a threatening visit from a bloke, who definitely was her spouse, and as charmless and ugly as the rest of her followers. Maybe he should have expected this, having unwittingly revealed the location of his new flat, but he didn't, and it shook him up. Where would he go when he's shook up, happy, sad, or all points in between? The Tea Bar. On the bus up there the following day, he was full of the same familiar feelings he'd had since his time spent alone in the well, treading the freezing water to stay alive. That of suppressing more anger and hatred than the human body could contain.

Everybody was bigger and tougher than he was. Or there was just more of them.

For once, he didn't want to see Bridget up there. He just felt like consoling himself in the company of the outpatients. But she was there, with the usual entourage, and the outpatients weren't. She had been threatened by her bloke into revealing Jonathan's address, who now joins the queue for tea with torturous feelings of having been betrayed.

He sat as far away from her as possible, the rain preventing him from taking his tea outside to be alone with the flowers. She didn't look in his direction, but her entourage did, treating him to the occasional snarl. A charmless bunch, he considered, as if hoping that some of her charm and good looks would rub off on them if they hung around long enough.

Months went by and life stumbled on without her, with him having no idea when she would next grace the Tea Bar with her presence and listening to reports of sightings of her from well-meaning friends, to which he shrugged his shoulders with feigned indifference. But one morning as he gazed out the Tea Bar window with Dennis in full swing on the piano, she walked in, and calmly and silently standing next to him, waited for him to notice her presence. And when he did, her smile was glorious to behold as they embraced. He looked all around for any sign of the disapproving committee that usually surrounds her. To his joy, and for whatever reason, they were absent, and remained so on the blissful future occasions of her outpatient appointments at the hospital. This gave them ample opportunity to indulge their passion for each other in the privacy of his flat, and a stroll in the nearby botanical gardens holding hands before putting her on her bus home. The threatening visit from her loud-mouthed bloke had not deterred him, and after these happy afternoons spent with her, was stirred into thoughts of fighting back should the festering vermin reappear.

Although pining for more of her company, with Bridget and his new flat had begun an upward trend, a period of comparative stability in which thoughts of the future and what he intended to do with it were now possible. With this in mind, and a lull in his drinking habits, he managed to scrape enough money together for driving lessons and a test, which went well, and the instructor was confident he would pass. To Jonathan, it felt as if he had almost joined the human race, doing something 'normal' people did. However, in what felt an almighty kick in the teeth of the kind he was more familiar with, he failed test after test after test; and when he could afford no more had to commandeer the services of his dad for the use of his car, and money, to finance his stubborn determination to continue. Just at a point when he had begun to feel more independent from the family! Ho-Hum! And so, now in his dad's car, he failed test after test after test before his dad pleaded with him to see sense and give up, as he was obviously 'not cut out for driving'. But Jonathan knew that he was, and with precious little else he was 'cut out for', it became a somewhat deranged battle of wills with his dad. But after a few more failures, increasing the already negative image he had of himself and the need for serial killing of the bastards with clipboards that sat unimpressed in the passenger seat, was forced to surrender. And did, with gritted teeth, empty promises to pay back the debt he had now incurred with his dad, and a possible entry into the Guinness Book of Records for driving tests failed. He had so wanted to achieve something without having to rely on anybody else, especially not his dad, and had failed miserably on both counts. The perceived injustice was stored in his brain with a load of others, somehow stirring an internal rage that festered within him.

As has often been said, life is full of ironies, and Jonathan's was no exception. In that, what he had so craved in recent years was to get his own place, after the traumas of living in other people's. Now he had it, and in the relative peace and comfort it provided, nagging feelings at the back of his mind that he must leave Sheffield for good, wouldn't go away. The days of sheltering anonymously under the then three million unemployed were over. He would have to get a job of some kind, and in his current habitat, there was no incentive to do so. But a job would be a drastic change, and somehow it felt like a drastic geographical change would have to accompany it. Since stumbling upon Dennis, he had made a lot of other dear friends, but they were all as far away from the idea of employment as it was possible to get. (Unfortunately?) he was not a 'paranoid schizophrenic' who was going to be left undisturbed to claim benefit for the rest of his life, and that life, if spent in Sheffield, would forever remain in the shadow of what happened to him at school.

Life trundled on with him surviving more alcohol-induced mayhem while nursing the now enlarged chip on his shoulder brought on by his recent attempt to learn to drive. He craved more excitement than this, without quite knowing what. Bridget had somehow managed to convince her overbearing family that Jonathan was history, and so their blissful meetings continued but were confined to whenever she had an outpatient appointment at the hospital, which she was now miraculously allowed to attend unsupervised. All was lovely, but stagnant. And that stagnancy increasingly bothered him. So much so, that in what must have been a gale force wind pushing him in the terrifying direction of employment, he applied for a job as a live-in washer upper/kitchen assistant at a restaurant in Hounslow, near London. He had heard of it, somewhere in the direction of Heathrow Airport, which for some reason was advertised in the Sheffield Mercury. Perhaps to entice applicants with the promise of free accommodation in the promised land that was London, which Jonathan certainly was. But the money was pitiful, as expected, because of it. With almost reluctance to move in the direction his mind seemed to be taking him, he dreaded any success with it, but the ball started rolling when he got a letter telling him where and when to turn up for an interview.

Jonathan took an immediate dislike to his interrogator at his first ever job interview. Somewhat creepy, middle-aged, and with a foreign accent, the man proudly introduced himself as the owner of the restaurant. There was a hint of menace about him and a face that seemed incapable of smiling. He sat very close to a thin, sleek, Italian-looking, super model-type, brunette female companion of at least half his age, who said little and whose presence seemed to be purely for decoration. Their matching expensive jewellery told Jonathan they were a couple, and, due to the lack of Ferraris in the area, the owners of the bright red one that was parked outside the place when he arrived. The rather out of place, crucifix-shaped ring attached to the man's left ear that wobbled with the movement of his head as he spoke, suggested an insecurity with the glaring age gap that existed between him and his far more youthful spouse. That, and the neatly trimmed, greying, goatee beard, that looked like it never left the house without a thorough preening, told Jonathan they were unlikely to hit it off should they be unfortunate enough to ever meet again.

Despite the aversions, he bluffed his way through it, purely focused on the accommodation side of the job and the drastic change of life and scenery it would provide. The charade of trying to promote himself was truly gut-wrenching, something that went against the very core of his being and which included a mention of his previous stay in London, which sounded reasonable as long as he didn't go into any detail (which he didn't). But what they didn't want was someone too impressive and career-focused, who might use the job as a trampoline to better things. Jonathan was definitely not in that category and may have unwittingly increased his chances (of success?) by not dressing up, and not looking like the sort of person who would wish to aspire beyond the dizzy heights of washer upper/kitchen assistant.

The only time these two got anywhere near a smile was when they spoke about the 'annual turnover' of their beloved restaurant, and how they had 'built it up from nothing'. As they did so, they looked at each other adoringly and he placed a hand on top of hers, as if they were alone. But the nauseating self-congratulation continued on the pretence of being essential background information for the benefit of the interviewee. Like he was supposed to give a toss at how much money they were making. To Jonathan, their affection was a revolting spectacle, and his mind wandered into quiet character assassination of the pair. Was it his money and Ferrari she found so irresistible? He suspected it was, as the man had all the *charisma* of a Nazi doctor in a concentration camp. How exactly was he going to leave behind the charms of Bridget, the gaiety of the Tea Bar, and the music and humour of dear friend Dennis, and replace them with people like this?

The inner conflict continued, with him alternating between wanting and not wanting the job with equal certainty on a daily basis. But deep down, he knew he was in the grip of a comfortable trap in Sheffield, one that he had to break free of completely for any progress ever to be made in his life. So having made sufficient effort to hide all the negative emotions that had engulfed him at the interview, he soon got a letter telling him he had got the job, and where and when he would be met in London to take him to his new home and place of work. The news was both distressing and pleasurable, in equal measure. Distressed at parting with his flat and people he would undoubtedly miss but pleased that he was at last leaving the past behind – largely, the humiliation of his schooldays and being stuck in the well. Although the past could not be erased, moving to a new place where there would surely be no time to think about it, seemed like the next best thing.

At the Tea Bar, there wasn't much in the way of sadness among the outpatients at his imminent departure. More concern about the enormity of the challenge he was taking on, to which Jonathan nodded his understanding, as if confirming his own insanity. But the next and last time he saw Bridget, they spent the whole afternoon fully clothed and without her usual smiles. What did she want him to do? In a last-ditch attempt at reversing what felt like the madness of his departure, he asked her if she would leave her bloke and hangers-on and come and live with him at the flat. She didn't reply. He took it as a no. He wasn't too sure either as to whether that would cure his long term need to wander, despite his feelings for her. Their parting was inevitable. And painful. They kissed and waved and blew more kisses as they walked in opposite directions in a busy Sheffield street.

What was he doing? He wasn't really sure.

Moving on and Seeing What's Out There

He boards the train with as much of his stuff that he and Dennis can carry to it.

'Sometimes you've got to move on and see what's out there,' Dennis encouraged his troubled friend with a comforting smile as they said goodbye.

The train moves off and Jonathan waves a sad farewell to a good friend and much-needed stabilizing influence amongst the chaos of his young life. But also a source of inspiration, with his many moves here, there and everywhere, of which, somewhere amongst the reluctance and confusion of Jonathan's mind, was a keenness to emulate. They didn't make any definite plans to meet again, as they both knew the score. Such was life. Leaving a lot of friends in one place for strangers in the new one was never going to be easy.

His instructions were to wait at a certain place at St Pancras station, and 'somebody' will be there to meet him. Who knows, this 'somebody' might be the girl of his dreams who he's going to spend the rest of his life with, he thought, trying to be positive. But sadly, no chance of that, as already standing there on the platform when he arrives is the creep he had endured at the interview. 'Graham', despite the foreign accent. Something didn't seem right, and Jonathan wondered about his new employer. An ex-Nazi perhaps, still on the run after the liberation of his concentration camp after World War 2, adopting the most English of names as a cover? But he would have had to have been in short trousers and sucking lollipops at the time of the atrocities. Or some kind of gangster, which would explain the car. Well, Nazi or gangster or not, at least for the moment he had someone to help carry what was really too much for one person. They shook hands in an awkward, reluctant sort of way, as if merely conforming to what was expected of them.

The Ferrari is now open-topped, and Graham's beloved who was at the interview, gives Jonathan the faintest of half smiles from the passenger seat. But he was pleased to see her, if only for the fact that she seemed fairly honest, and he didn't quite trust the mysterious Graham in the driving seat. A possible witness if he tried anything dodgy. They both tried to smile to put him at ease, but it was as if their faces couldn't quite manage it. In wonderment, Jonathan gets into the exquisite machine and it roars off suddenly, causing him to give an anxious look at his luggage that is piled high on the seat next to him. They explain about the 'slight change of plan'. The 'somebody' couldn't make it, and they thought they would 'come into town for some shopping' and therefore would be able to come and pick him up themselves. Was he supposed to feel honoured? At least he was getting his one and only ride in an open-topped Ferrari, as he gazed in wonder at the hustle and bustle of surrounding streets as they flew by. But it wasn't long before he started feeling car sick. It was either the sight of them holding hands and trying to smile at each other, or the fact that he was doing about seventy-five mph on the elevated bit of the A40 with one hand on the steering wheel, or the mixture of both, that had brought on the nausea. If somebody was being driven to their place of execution in an open-topped Ferrari, the feeling they would have would be not far from the one Jonathan had right now. But he reminded himself of Dennis's parting words that summed up the spirit of exploration: 'see what's out there'.

Fortunately, he had his own room, but unfortunately, it was directly above the nightclub/restaurant. Not much sleep to be had here, he thought. He was introduced to the chef who he 'would be working closely with', who was young, French, and seemed OK. But was the chef aware that all his new assistant was capable of in the kitchen was washing-up, and he wasn't great at that? Not yet.

Not required to work until the Thursday evening, he tried to settle in a bit. He was still completely dependent on the pills for sleep and something resembling sanity, but not organised enough to consider the inevitability of running out of the stuff soon after his arrival.

After a few days without them and no sleep whatsoever, he found himself running through the town in a panic attack trying to find a doctor's surgery, which would have been closed anyway had he found one. Passers-by made what they thought was humorous comment upon seeing his obvious distress. He noticed a branch of the Samaritans and knocked at the door frantically, and a kind lady sat him down and encouraged him to take deep breaths. She made him a cup of tea after he had calmed down sufficiently to drink one, and then began to write a list of doctor's surgeries near to where he was staying. Eventually, he got his prescription fix, after having a difficult time convincing a suspicious GP that he wasn't a 'junkie'. A young person desperate for drugs tended to create that assumption, even when the drugs in question were not the sort that provided a 'buzz' no matter what you did with them. But as usual, they did the trick, and enough serenity was restored for him to start his first ever shift of work at the agreed time, grabbing a strong coffee where he could to cope with the sleep starvation.

At the interview, Graham the creep neglected to ask him about his skills in the kitchen, as if it wasn't important. But now it was, so it seemed, and things had to be done fast. As there was a never-ending supply of dirty dishes, pots and pans, there was no time for helping the chef with the chopping up of vegetables and things of that nature that he was now told was part of his 'job description'. Maybe the previous kitchen assistant was some kind of octopus on speed, he wondered. While Jonathan did his best to imitate the multi-limbed sea creature on performance-enhancing drugs, a casual, jewellery-laden Graham came into the already overcrowded kitchen as fast-moving waiting staff awkwardly weaved their way around the human obstacle without a word of insubordinate complaint. He just stood there, arms folded, shaking his head.

'Jonathan, Jonathan. Oh dear!' came the loud verdict on his first-night performance from the loathsome boss at whose mercy Jonathan now found himself, as the provider of the current roof over his head amongst other things.

This felt horribly familiar territory from incidence of his past, and Jonathan's way of dealing with it was to just continue working as if nothing had happened, feigning obliviousness to present company. But inside he felt sick at his decision to give up everything to be here.

At the end of the night, he found himself scrubbing and mopping the kitchen for the continuation of its 'maximum hygiene rating' or some such nonsense, which he was told was very important. After that, he assumed he was going to be spoken to about whatever was deemed unsatisfactory with him, but to his relief the place was now empty, and in a state of exhaustion he made his way to bed. At least it was close by. All the other staff were foreign it seemed and didn't exactly warm to him, as though it were a club for foreigners who had reluctantly had to accept a British member. He lay in bed pondering the new trap he had found himself in, and an escape plan was beginning to emerge. But he would have to stick it for at least a month until he gets his month's wages. Then what?

At weekends, the place turned into the most nauseating of rowdy millionaires' club, when the odd Lamborghini or Maserati could be seen parked outside alongside the usual Ferrari. After closing time, a drunken Graham would entertain his similarly drunken cronies. Jonathan did his best to avoid them or any other human contact after he'd finished work, feeling sure he would be the butt of any jokes if he took a wrong turning on his way to bed. He found himself in the most unlikely situation of being surrounded by booze, but where the drinking of it was not an option and all he could think about was getting away from it and the atmosphere it created. Not to mention trying to sleep directly above such an atmosphere, of which karaoke was a regular excruciating feature. To sum up his feelings about his new home: it was like walking into a pub where it's impossible to get served despite the lack of customers, because the barman is too busy with his cronies at the other end of the bar, cracking loud, unfunny jokes. And being imprisoned in it for life.

His Mondays, Tuesdays, and Wednesdays, when he didn't work, were what made life bearable, when he was free to wander around the centre of London, which now felt more like home than anywhere else. But he was chronically lonely and missed Bridget, and as he walked along The Mall towards Buckingham Palace, he looked up at all the official, white stoned, stately buildings, and imagined her smiling and waving to him from one of the many windows. Just as Marilyn Monroe had done to her friends in the street below in the film *The Prince and the Showgirl.* How much he yearned for that fantasy to become reality, but had to concede to the unlikelihood of ever seeing her again.

This drastic change to his life and new merciless surroundings were keeping him sober for the time being. He didn't have the urge to drink in semi-deserted pubs on his days off, and certainly didn't have the urge or opportunity to drink at his place of work. But in the back of his mind nested a feeling, that maybe when life was less fragile and he had really cracked it with this move, he would treat himself to an almighty piss-up.

So maybe it was a good thing that he was nowhere near cracking it, as it wouldn't take too many nights of being drunk and disorderly here to end up homeless, with nothing. And as there was now a chronic shortage of obliging friends with spare rooms or settees, homelessness would mean just that.

His ability to cope with the non-stop work at the restaurant improved. As the main incentive was to get out of there as soon as possible, he didn't stop for anything. Doing his best to ignore negative remarks about his work from the chef, which would invariably find their way to Graham – of whom, his loathing was so intense, it was almost impossible to suppress. He went to bed each night wondering how much longer he could stick it.

He began to notice one middle-aged cockney lady barmaid, who was strangely not at all foreign and seemed to be as lost and uncomfortable in the place as he was. They had only ever exchanged a few pleasantries, but one afternoon shortly after the sound of raised voices, she came into the kitchen looking flushed. She told Jonathan that she had just had a big bust up with the boss over her wages being short 'again!' and, as he had just laughed at her, she had told him 'where to stick it!' She then gave Jonathan her phone number and told him that, if he ever got the same kind of grief, to ring her, and she will get him a job at another place where she works on and off and is a friend of the boss there. His good fortune at having what appeared to be a freshly dug tunnel out of the place, made the remainder of the month far more bearable. And on at last receiving his month's wages, he rang her, she kept to her word, and he ended up with a job as promised, at 'Rockerfellaz', a huge nightclub and restaurant a few miles away.

'You'll like it there,' she assured him. Feeling gratified that she was doing somebody a good turn and depriving her slimy ex-boss of his washer-upper.

To Jonathan, the relief was intense. No way could he stand another month of slave labour and disapproval at this hellhole, where he had sensed the approach of an unhappy ending. He piled himself and his belongings into a taxi, with caution, trying his best to conceal his departure. Still unsure of 'Graham', his obviously false name, and equally slippery looking mates. His destination was a bedsit he had previously looked at and thankfully was now able to pay for, as promised. Sadly, it took up a large chunk of his new-found wealth, as the new job was not 'live-in', but it seemed quiet and overlooked a garden and something resembling countryside beyond it.

The work and hours were much the same as the last place as expected. Fast and furious, and early hours of the morning finish. Washing-up, not being any kind of vocation, just something he had stumbled upon that was currently keeping him afloat in his new life. And now, due to the size of the place and vast numbers of customers, would be done on a more industrial scale.

Jonathan, being the sort of person who was far more likely to be thrown out of a nightclub than ever being comfortable in one, looked around the place with unease. Mainly at the assorted personnel, wondering from where his next problems were going to emerge. There were some lovely looking waitresses and barmaids and mean looking bouncers. The former being the property of the latter, he assumed, and strictly off limits for someone struggling to survive by washing dishes. But the manager of the restaurant and Jonathan's immediate boss, 'Mr Ramaj', probably looked the meanest of all. He had had no say in the recruiting of the new washer upper. That was decided by the senior lady manager of the whole place, who was friend of the barmaid, who was enemy of Graham at the previous place. Mr Ramaj, a well-built man in his forties, was from one of those countries in the middle east that was constantly at war and was a veteran of the army of his homeland. In which, presumably, one was exposed to hostile fire almost immediately after conscription and forever thereafter. Jonathan feared the worst, but the sense of humour of the man soon became abundantly clear, often to be found chasing his waitresses about the place after making obscene suggestions to them. Much laughter from all concerned.

'I'm gonna put out the new serviettes, Rammy, like you said, OK?'

'OK, but give me blowjob before you start. Don't forget now.'

'Not again!'

'You promised.'

This was the kind of semi-deranged banter partially caused by severe overwork that could often be heard when 'Rammy' was on duty. All too comical and silly to be regarded as sexual harassment with no such sexual acts being performed, and with similarities to Eric in the far-off crazy world of St Mary's, his enthusiastic laughter at his own jokes enhanced them.

The phone rings.

'It's Mrs Ramaj. Says you're due back at the monastery,' was the ironic wit as the boss made his way to the phone.

Everybody smiling, except a now straight-faced Mr Ramaj. Two things that were guaranteed to put an immediate end to the frivolity, were an impromptu visit from either his wife, or the owner of Rockerfellaz. But mainly, this was a happy family of staff of whom Mr Ramaj was very much the father, turning the place into a daily pantomime — despite looking like Stalin's most dedicated henchman.

The man's way of restoring order amongst the chaos was to stand there with a look of despair, arms outstretched, and a shout of, 'For faarrrk's sake!', followed by the name of the individual who was not up to speed. Often 'Jonathan', when he dared pause for breath in between the scrubbing of giant saucepans one could almost have a bath in. But Mr Ramaj became more of a much-needed friend than a boss, and someone Jonathan would arrive early for work to have a chat with, and often confide his troubles to. Another large establishment with more than a hint of insanity, Jonathan's dependency on it became firmly established.

Again, there were many foreigners among the staff, but unlike the last place, this was a source of comfort. Mainly a large happy community from Ghana, West Africa, who all seemed to know each other very well as if they had all come to Britain on the same boat specially to work at Rockerfellaz. Big laughs with them in between the constant dirty plates, pots and pans, his words not always understood by the Africans but it not seeming to matter. Once again, Jonathan's ability to make people laugh, which seemed to alternate between being a curse and an asset depending on the circumstances, here, was definitely an asset.

He also got to know Jan, an attractive, down to earth, English waitress in her thirties, who, when they were chatting and he explained a bit about his circumstances, offered him a spare room in her house. To which he gulped with excitement and anticipation only for it to be quickly followed by the news that her husband and five children also lived there, and the latter all under ten-years-old! Surely, she may need her husband's agreement to make such an offer, he wondered, but didn't say, while not wanting to disturb what was potentially wonderful news both socially and economically, as his rent would be considerably reduced. The house was small and terraced and he asked himself, did they really have room for anybody else? But he moved in, to what was his third address in as many months, and had to be very careful not to tread on or trip over any small bodies that were crawling about. Now, he was not so dependent on Rockerfellaz for company. Jan was always keen to chat with him, despite the frequent wailing of small children in the background. He began to be quite fond of her, but once again, feelings of any kind had to be suppressed, especially when you are never more than a few inches from homelessness. And for this same reason, he dared not have an alcoholic drink. For the same reason one should not pour petrol on a fire.

At Rockerfellaz, the work was fast, furious and relentless, and Jonathan wasn't the only one whose sanity wavered a little from time to time. Having resumed the driving lessons and arranged his next bash at the driving test for the following morning, he arrived for work tense that afternoon. How much more disappointment with it could he stand? How much more hatred for the Ministry of Transport, or whatever corrupt organisation had benefited so much from his numerous failures, could he contain? Also, with it occurring in an unfamiliar area where he had often got lost as a pedestrian, didn't increase his optimism. As usual, he commenced his shift by chopping up lemons in the kitchen for the bar staff. The chef, who liked to talk to anyone considered beneath him, as though they were a kind of sub-human species, complained about something he either had or hadn't done. The usual trivial reminder of the pecking order that existed in the kitchen – only this one badly timed. Jonathan, with knife still in hand, and chef a safe distance behind him in the doorway of the kitchen, does a ninety-degree turn. 'Piss off!' was Jonathan's blatant, impassive response to the criticism, with a mind far away on more important matters; before continuing the slow, unprofessional manner with which he chopped up lemons.

With your ninth driving test the following morning, you don't mince words. Chef goes to the big, big boss, the one above Jonathan's middle eastern friend, and the one above the lady above him who'd given him the job and, to add a bit of weight to his story, says that he has been 'threatened with a knife' in the kitchen. The kind of manipulation of a rather dull truth, that those employed in the news media so excel at.

Mr Ramaj is then ordered to sack Jonathan immediately; orders he tries his best to ignore. At least for tonight, as the usual mid-evening chaos

69

was now in full swing, and he didn't want to have to do the washing-up himself. Jonathan carries on as normal, ignorant of his imminent dismissal. He then goes home to bed, gets up the next morning and passes his driving test—to much rejoicing in Jan's household. Small children were thrown in the air, and thankfully, caught. He then came to work as planned, early as usual, this time to report his success to Mr Ramaj who he knew would be delighted, who tells him he is fired with immediate effect and is 'very sorry'. It took a while for Jonathan to close his mouth and regain the ability to blink.

'I never threatened him with nothing!' he pleaded for the defence. 'I had a knife in my hand 'cos I was chopping up lemons!'

'I know, I know,' an equally distraught Mr Ramaj consoled with head bowed, finding himself awkwardly positioned between two warring factions, and still without a plan of how tonight's washing up would be done.

In a normal place of employment, when your boss tells you, you are fired, it is assumed that this is a permanent arrangement. You do not assume that you will be reinstated in a week's time, after your replacement has just walked out, and the piles of dirty plates, pots and pans are now something of a safety hazard. Especially to the fast-moving waiting staff, in and out of the kitchen like whippets. But after a dismal week in which Jonathan (assuming the arrangement was permanent) went around frantically looking for other work, that was exactly what happened; during a phone call one chaotic Saturday night as Jonathan sat idly at Jan's house.

'You gotta help me out, Jonny! You wouldn't believe what's going on here!'

'Oh, I'm sure I would,' Jonathan jested casually, while hearing raised voices in the background as the music thumped. But it was good to feel wanted again, even though it seemed appropriate at this moment to keep that feeling to himself. 'Give me half an hour,' he continued, with a sigh.

It was obvious his friend had had little choice but to blindly follow orders from above to sack him. During that lost week of being, as far as he knew, unemployed, and having spent what should have been rent on his recent driving success, he'd been touched by Jan and husband Steve's support for him. Steve also 'helped out' at Rockerfellaz when they were desperate, and neither of them liked the conniving chef with an exaggerated sense of his own importance.

As Jonathan returned to the place, with suspicious looks from menacing-looking bouncers on the door, it soon became obvious that he was being smuggled back in secretly without the consent of the esteemed hierarchy that had ordered his sacking. They wouldn't know what this 'knife-wielding' washer-upper looked like: a factor that Mr Ramaj had quietly suspected and intended to take full advantage of. As they walked through the dimly lit 'shop floor' with its thumping music and loud drunken conversations towards swinging double doors that led to the bowels of the place, the big, big, boss that had so absorbed the chef's exaggerated tales of terror in the kitchen and ordered the 'immediate' sacking of the culprit (whoever he was), was coming the other way. In the split second the two bosses clocked each other, a cautious Mr Ramaj swapped places with Jonathan, concealing him with his bulky, sixteen-stone frame, and smiled at his boss with the usual cheery 'Good evening, sir'. With that obstacle safely passed, Jonathan was then led to the kitchen which looked like news footage of Beirut in the 1970s.

'Right. OK?' said Mr Ramaj, with a loud clap of his hands and a look of satisfaction, while trying to avoid standing in one of the many greasy puddles of water with bits in that now littered the tiled floor.

Jonathan, never a slouch when there was hard work to be done—at least, not since having entered the fast, furious, and somewhat alien world of employment with its suggestion of 'survival of the fittest'—began the clear-up operation. He was welcomed back by the Ghanaians who collected and washed the mass of empty glasses in their room opposite the kitchen, with the usual cheeriness. The big question that remained was what would be the seemingly highly influential chef's reaction to the washer-upper's reinstatement? But, as the forever stern-faced, withdrawn young man seemed even more distant and silent, it was assumed that a deal of some kind securing that silence had been achieved by the much accommodating, but resourceful, Mr Ramaj.

One Thursday night, after Jonathan left work in the early hours and there wasn't much activity in the streets outside, a car pulled up alongside him as he walked on the pavement. A man in the back seat wound down the window and asked him for directions. Just as he was getting into his stride with the *turn left heres* and *right theres*, the man, and another one in the passenger seat, suddenly got out and bundled him into the car.

'What the hell!' was all he had time to say.

But then, upon catching a glimpse of the familiar, crucifix-shaped ring dangling from the left ear of its driver, realised it was none other than Graham the creep, boss/owner of the previous place, whose mouth on this rare occasion had managed a disturbing full-smile. In a state of terror, he tried to make a plausible explanation for his sudden departure from the man's restaurant, while grappling for the door handle at the same time. But it was hopeless.

'I don't like being made a fool of,' Graham said calmly, as he drove into a patch of waste ground where Jonathan was dragged out of the car, and punched and kicked repeatedly by the three men.

It was unimaginable terror. To be a victim of this sort of thing again, but now without the usual anaesthetic of alcohol was more than he could bear, feeling the full, terrifying force of each thump. Fortunately, the unconsciousness that followed, prevented the full-scale panic attack that otherwise would have done, as he was left bleeding in a heap on the ground.

The furore must have attracted somebody's attention, as he woke up in hospital the next day with several broken ribs, one side of his face swollen up like a balloon and an almighty headache. His primary concern, after that of needing strong painkillers, urgently, was for his precious psychiatric pills, which he hadn't got with him. Who knows what would happen if he didn't get them! Such was his dependency.

'Don't worry about that, we'll give you something else for the time being,' the nurse assured him, smiling.

But her words were no assurance at all. When he asked her what was to him the all-important question, if, what they were going to give him was addictive, she gave a firm 'No', as if it were a stupid question.

'Because I'm already addicted to stuff that isn't, you see,' he explained impassively, without a trace of sarcasm, while just trying to verbalise his anxiety about adding to his current list of medicinal addictions.

His words prompted a concerned look from the nurse, convinced she was dealing with either a patient suffering from severe concussion, or an undesirable drug misuser, who, judging by the gobbledegook being spoken, was quite possibly still under the influence of something he shouldn't. It was moments like this when the lunacy of his chemical situation was glaringly obvious. But, with an overwhelming need to avoid any further agonizing movement of the face, he quietly surrendered to his powerlessness of resisting anything they wanted to do with him.

His activities were restricted to drinking through a straw and pestering the staff for a bedpan, in between long periods of thought and worry. Questions needed answering. Like, was it a coincidence, or did Graham the creep and his cronies know where he was working and about what time he would be leaving? He suspected the chef's involvement, who had had to put up with his reinstatement after he had fought so *valiantly* to get him sacked. But then, how would the chef at Rockerfellaz know that he had worked at, and absconded without word from, Graham's place? What could he do even if he had answers to any of these questions? Not a lot, he conceded.

The new psychiatric pills (whatever they were) and pain killers took effect, and he dozed off, despite the constant noise around him. Beds being moved, patients trying to get the attention of nurses, and some sort of building work going on outside his window. He slept right through to the late morning of the next day. The thinking continued, and when he thought of those he'd left behind in Sheffield who were dear to him, who he had known a lot better than the comparative strangers he had here, was close to tears. Then thought of Dennis's parting words: 'Sometimes you've got to move on and see what's out there'. But 'what's out there' couldn't be relied upon for being a palm tree-ed, golden-sanded isle of peace and tranquillity, as Dennis would know only too well.

73

A Quietly Desperate Yearning

He had feelings of course for Jan, his new landlady. But time after time, any women that Jonathan gravitated towards or who gravitated towards him turned out to be married or otherwise shackled in some way. These were always unfortunate coincidences, not matters of choice; as he had no idea of the marital status of the women before he decided to gravitate towards them, or vice-versa. But on this occasion, having had the luxury of knowing Jan's unfortunate marital status from the outset, such gravitation had to be resisted. With her being his landlady, he had the added luxury of being able to predict what the punishment might be for transgression. Eviction, at the least. Possibly a few more broken ribs, at the worst. And so endeth the luxury.

However, the charming and beautiful Ghanaian waitress at Rockerfellaz (also married!) assured him that if he went to Ghana he would be guaranteed at least one beautiful wife. After his initial excitement, enhanced by the long-held belief that he was and always had been in the wrong country, he decided that knowing his luck this probably wasn't the case, and she just had shares in the Ghanaian tourist board.

The Road to Recovery, with Potholes

In between the bedpans and long sleeps, there was plenty of time for reflection.

Revenge would surely be sweet if he ever managed it, he considered. And about the many times people had done things to him that had left him broken, demoralised, sedated, or having his meals through a straw. Those people had then been able to continue their comfortable lives as if nothing had happened. Every time, he would have to swallow his pride, suppress his rage, and do nothing, for the sake of the continuation of life and liberty. The only revenge he could think of that was a possibility right now was via the police. It was after all, illegal, wasn't it, to attack people in this way? He knew exactly who had done it and where they could be found. But then the creep knew where *he* could be found if he returned to Rockerfellaz, he assumed, and the man obviously knew people who were happy to help him carry out his dirty work. Such assistance was a common thing, it seemed, but Jonathan had never experienced such luxury. It was always him, alone, against the world. So if he just let it be and did nothing, perhaps that might be the end of it. On the few occasions in the past when he had sought the retribution of the law, what was the result? Sweet FA! The thought process that eventually led to a decision to do nothing was an exhausting one.

Just at that moment when his thoughts could not have been more troublesome, the perfect tonic for his ills walked in: Jan, her husband Steve and the five kids. How lovely. How touched he was that they would bother to come and see him. He hardly knew them, despite living in their home for nearly a month. He felt guilty about any feelings for Jan that he may have indulged in now her husband was here, and all showing much concern for his well-being. They assured him that his room and all his stuff was safe, and how much they wanted him to come back. Jan was very much the spokesperson, who it seemed 'wore the trousers' in their marriage, but Steve wasn't showing any visible objections to her words. Jonathan couldn't do much except nod enthusiastically, which he did.

75

They were very casual about what had happened. All smiles, as if he had merely fallen off a step ladder or something. No enquires about who could have done it, if Jonathan knew who had done it, or why they had done it.

'Oh, remember that time when those blokes set on you and Trevor, and we had to get an ambulance and everything,' Jan said.

'It happens,' Steve said, nodding his agreement: a man of few words and seemingly fewer thoughts. One of the lucky ones, Jonathan conceded.

They were the most accepting of people who somehow managed to lighten his brain about the whole incident, as they constantly tried to stop the smaller children climbing all over him. The older ones just stood in the background, silently, looking confused about what was going on, who this bloke was that had recently moved into their house, and why he was now in hospital looking like something out of a horror film. Jonathan waved to them in an attempt to lessen their trauma as they got ready to leave. He squeezed Jan's hand and shook Steve's to try and show his genuine appreciation, as his face wasn't capable of much expression and speech wasn't getting any less painful. They were enroute to the park for the swings and roundabouts, Jan explained, and she gave him one last smile just before her head disappeared round the door. He momentarily entertained thoughts that she might be quite fond of him, only to remind himself that such indulgence needed to be avoided. Similar thoughts in the past of this nature had proved to be delusions of grandeur: feelings that were almost as common as those of inferiority in his confused mind that tended to fluctuate between one extreme to the other. Especially on matters of self-image regarding the opposite sex.

'You need to rest,' said a nurse, who came in with his pills a short time after Jan and the family had left.

Yes, he thought, it's funny how a few visitors and the thoughts and feelings it creates, can be so exhausting when you're at your weakest. But their visit had certainly hastened his psychological recovery.

In time, his ability to speak slowly returned. Smiling, which had been impossible, was now possible but painful, and he avoided it. But almost had no choice about doing so, when one particular cheerful and attractive nurse came in to change the bandage that was tightly wrapped around his torso. As she did this, the pain slightly interfered with his enjoyment of the close contact. But she was very talkative and he enjoyed listening to her, up until the point when she said, 'You remind me so much of my husband.' To which, he groaned.

Nice visit one afternoon from just Jan and the few of her kids that had not yet been exposed to the trauma of school.

'I can't wait,' she said, referring to the glorious day when they all went to school, giving her some much needed peace. 'Freedom at last! A few hours anyway.'

'Oh god, school. Things could be worse, I suppose,' Jonathan mumbled to himself, recalling the horror while feeling a sudden surge of gratitude that that particular avenue of pain had ended.

'Oh no, they love it,' she said.

Jonathan couldn't quite get his head round that last statement. Perhaps school had improved. Perhaps bullying was now punishable by death and a public execution in the playground, he mused, managing a faint but painful smile as he did.

Apparently, one of his efforts to find work during the week after his dismissal from Rockerfellaz had born fruit. She had had a phone call from an agency who asked if Jonathan could go to a shoe factory not far away. He apologised to Jan for this and explained that he'd had little choice but to give out her phone number so they can ring him when they've got work. He dreaded these moments of cautious explanation, as sentences of more than a few words were still a painful challenge. Him, having no experience of employment agencies, and not much more of employment itself, thought that you just go in their office and you come out with work. But no, they want a phone number, so *IF* they've got work for you, they can contact you.

'Oh, don't worry,' she said. 'You've gotta do what you've gotta do. I told them though, that you've had a bit of an accident and were in hospital.'

He thanked her sincerely, becoming acutely aware that he was unintentionally, but increasingly, falling into her debt. The meagre amount of rent he had been able to give her so far, was by no means adequate enough reward for her friendship and kindness. As she got up to leave, he felt the overwhelming urge to squeeze her hand once more. But he knew he would enjoy it, and the mere fact that it would involve enjoyment made it something like adultery, in Steve's absence. Oh, the perils of having a conscience!

When alone again he reflected on the chaotic work situation. Being sacked, then making desperate efforts to find work, then being reinstated, and now daywork in a shoe factory? And he had forgotten to ask Jan who was doing the washing up in his absence. Would he be going back to Rockerfellaz? What was he meant to do in a shoe factory? Make shoes? When your entire work history consists of a few months of washing-up and occasional chopping up, any other type of work sounds daunting. And if he doesn't get out of this hotel for the downtrodden soon, the laziness will set in like rigor mortis and he'll be paralysed with it, he thought, just as his favourite nurse entered the room with a smile, a cup of tepid Ovaltine and a straw. Ho-Hum! His brain, scrambled with nervous anticipation of his release, soon packed up for the day, and he dozed off.

A week passed by much the same, only now he was having to do some walking and gentle exercises in preparation for his discharge. Once again, he found himself in even more debt to Jan, as the staff explained that they did not have any ambulances available to take him home the following day. Did he have any family who could come and pick him up?

'Ah… well, no, not exactly,' he dithered. 'I have a sort of landlady.'

The lady administrator of some kind became impatient. She had hoped for a more straightforward answer, and usually got it, as most normal patients did have close relatives to pick them up. But they obviously needed the bed he was occupying, so when she asked him for the telephone number of his 'landlady', he reluctantly gave it. As he had so recently apologised to Jan for giving out her phone number, his head sunk in despair at having done so again. How was he ever going to get out of her debt?

The following morning, Jan, on her own, stands outside of her car, leaning against it with arms folded, looking gorgeous as ever in denim jacket and jeans, her long blonde hair blowing in the wind. She smiles as she watches him struggling along attached to the arm of a nurse. On arrival at the house, he stumbled as he got out of the car, almost falling to the ground, causing Jan to grab hold of him with both arms wrapped tightly around him, and they hobbled along like this to the front door. Jonathan stopped breathing temporarily as the pleasure overwhelmed him, far outweighing the pain. To surrender to his feelings for her was potentially fatal and he was terrifyingly close to doing so now. And the post-surrender homelessness would seriously complicate the already complicated.

'Hello, you old cripple!' Steve laughed, as the shambolic procession continued through the door and up the stairs. The most casual of men, he didn't move an inch from his armchair to assist with the manoeuvring of downtrodden lodger, or to control the children currently throwing toys at each other and screaming.

This was too much. Get rid of any feelings for Jan now, he told himself, as she laid him on the bed. His body, almost frozen with fear of further enjoyment, as he desperately tried to conceal the unwanted erection in his trousers. His dependency on the couple now reaching a peak, with thoughts of being anywhere other than the comfort of their house at such a vulnerable time, being unimaginable.

He really shouldn't have been discharged so soon, but there was a flu epidemic going around and they needed the beds, so it was a case of continuing his recovery 'at home', whatever that was. Unable to manage the stairs unassisted, he spent most of the time in his room reading books – the only remotely purposeful thing he could do to get his mind off the lust for Jan, anger and hatred for his most recent abusers, and general fragility of his existence that he could do nothing to strengthen. Jan was here, there and everywhere, dropping off kids, picking up kids and so on, in between the hoovering and dusting of the immaculately maintained house. Steve worked Monday to Friday but sometimes popped back home for lunch.

The uneasy feeling of dependency on the couple continued. He had paid hardly any of the previously agreed rent in the short time he had been there. Firstly, because of his dismissal from Rockerfellaz and subsequent week of unemployment. Then, he was back at work for barely a week before being hospitalised for the next two. But for the moment, Jan wasn't exactly breathing down his neck for it.

'Don't worry,' she said. 'Just get yourself well so you can get back to work.'

A statement that was somewhere near the current state of play, only simplified several thousand times. Where exactly would the 'work' come from, that he so needed to do when well enough to do it? Especially as, according to Jan, all was ticking along merrily at Rockerfellaz in his absence. And, a phone call back to the agency that had asked if he could go to a shoe factory had achieved nothing more than him leaving a message that wasn't returned. The insecurity of it all was acutely felt from behind the closed door of his bedroom. A fact-finding visit to Rockerfellaz was top of his list of priorities, just as soon as he was well enough to venture out into the big, wide world again.

As he came through the door of the blissfully peaceful restaurant/nightclub; as it usually was in the middle of the afternoon, the way in which Mr Ramaj usually restored order was now a form of greeting, as he stood there with arms outstretched.

'For faarrk's sake, Jonny! We've been worried sick! Good to see you.'

They both laughed, which occurred so easily in each other's company. All these people Jonathan currently knew were priceless in terms of lightening the usual darkness of his mind.

To Jonathan's relief, it was agreed that he would resume his duties as it had been 'barmy' in the kitchen. It usually was, but had now plunged to new depths, so it seemed, despite Jan's unsettling reports of the opposite. And, that if Jonathan could wait for a bit after his shift for him to lock up the place, Mr Ramaj would then give him a lift home, just in case of any repeat of the violence. Five-star treatment, for which Jonathan thanked his friend, genuinely touched by all the kindness he was receiving. At least now, he could give Jan some rent and feel a bit less of a non-paying guest.

So, he did what had been his usual Wednesday to Saturday nights that week. And with trepidation, rang the agency again that had rung while he was in hospital, which resulted in a day's work at a 'Johnson's shoe factory' the following day.

'Doing what?' he asked.

'No idea,' was the tired, dismissive answer, plus a name of somebody to report to.

'Nothing sexual, is it?' he asked the agency lady, feeling the need to lighten the atmosphere. It didn't get a laugh but it wasn't his finest material.

So off he went to the great unknown with no idea what he was going to find, just like so many other explorers in history that had gone before him. The person he had to report to was the manager of the packing department, and his search for it took him across a busy shop floor with the constant rattling and grinding of machinery. The work force were about ninety per cent Pakistani, Indian or Bangladeshi. Some were standing next to their machines chatting, despite the constant din. This felt like a strange new world, and an interesting one.

On arrival at the packing department, it was like the old days of the Raj. A long line of South Asian men, mostly of pensionable age, but working tirelessly packing shoes into large boxes, with a young Englishman giving out the orders in an arrogant, impatient way. Jonathan proceeded to take the finished large boxes into an old industrial lift which sent them down to the loading bays to be put on lorries. Most of the workers spoke English. If you spoke to the ones that didn't, the others would translate, always in a cheery fashion. Jonathan immediately warmed to them, and to his relief wasn't surrounded by others of his own age and nationality. It was as if they had something in common, despite the obvious difference of him being young and one hundred per cent British. With him never quite belonging in his own country.

It wasn't long before he settled into a routine of working here Monday to Friday, plus the usual Wednesday to Saturday nights at Rockerfellaz. Sundays were spent in a state of horizontal exhaustion but both places needed his services, and he took advantage of an opportunity to strengthen his fragile existence, after a period of chronic dependency on the goodwill of others. To increase the need for the workaholism, he bought a car from an Asian colleague, a Ford Cortina Mark 3 well into the autumn of its years. But to Jonathan, a dream come true. A nostalgic object of wonder, having seen them in car chases in episodes of *The Sweeney*[6], and regularly been taken out in the one belonging to the father of a boyhood playmate in Horsham. And a source of amusement when he went home with it. Steve pointing out the little pile of rust that appeared on the ground when the doors were closed with a bit too much force.

In the following months, it was as if work had replaced booze as his chosen method of self-destruction. But the money he saved gave him a much-needed feeling of security. Jan, although pleased with the rent she was now getting, was less keen on his company. Without realizing it, his determination for progress had had a dire effect on his personality. The closer it got to Christmas, the workload at Rockerfellaz increased to the usual festive chaos. His passion for the car and the independence it provided, when coupled with the gradual onset of nervous exhaustion, was like a bomb waiting to go off.

Arriving for work, he usually parked in one of the side streets

---

[6] British TV cop show of the 1970s. A must for old car enthusiasts.

opposite Rockerfellaz, that all looked pretty much the same. After work one night in the early hours, he discovers the car is gone; and in a panic attack filled with paranoid delusion, storms back into the kitchen where he promptly pins the chef to the wall by his throat, demanding to know what he has done with his beloved Cortina. Already suspecting the chef of supplying information that resulted in his beating at the hands of Graham and his cronies, it all just boiled over. But his judgement was severely impaired by the mania that possessed him.

'What would I want with an old clapped out thing like that!' exclaimed the chef, after the pressure on his wind pipe was released, by bouncers, more used to ejecting customers for such behaviour. But ejected and humiliated he then was.

'You knew about this, didn't you!' he shouted at the few other members of staff dotted around that he didn't like, as he was dragged outside, only rescued from another beating by Mr Ramaj's intervention.

'Go home Jonny, for faarrk's sake!'

The next morning the phone rings at Jan's. It was the husband of one of her waitress friends who lives in one of the side streets opposite Rockerfellaz.

'Has anyone lost a Cortina?' he asked with a knowing laugh. 'Well, there's one parked outside just a few doors down from us.'

Jonathan walked down there quickly with a sense of impending shame and embarrassment. His relief when he unlocked the door and started the engine, was quickly followed by a feeling of terror that he was going mad. And not in the shelter of a luni-bin where such things were expected, but in the real, non-psychiatric world!

It gradually sunk in that he had been in the wrong side street the night before, going barmy at the sudden lack of car. Later, he took it to work at Rockerfellaz, early as always for the chinwag, which this time would have included a sincere apology to Mr Ramaj. But before he had the chance to speak, his now unusually serious boss told him he was fired and 'this time it's for good'. He bowed his head and mumbled the prepared apology, now selfless in its intent, and walked out.

To see his boss being just that and no longer a friend was truly disturbing. And perhaps equally so for his boss, at having to say such things. But Jonathan had a habit of dragging harsh words out of people that were dear to him, that they would rather not have to say. Not that he could empathize with them. He couldn't begin to realise the effect he had on others. It was always the other way round. He wasn't important enough to affect other people; of that he was sure, if only in his sub-conscious mind. And almost looking down on people who valued him, with feelings like: why would I want to be a member of a club that would have somebody like me as a member?

Rejected and bewildered, he drove home, trying to make sense of it all. In an act of what was largely self-discipline, he had taken advantage of an opportunity to recover his losses. A lot of the money gained was rightfully paid back to Jan. All positives. But the thin line between self-discipline and self-destruction had been crossed. Not that he was aware such a line existed. It was all so confusing.

There was a subdued silence at Jan's place; even amongst the children, who could perhaps sense a stillness in the air. Words were deemed unnecessary. She had witnessed his psychotic display and now, it seemed, was already aware that he wouldn't be working tonight.

'I've left you some dinner in the oven,' she said, confirming it.

He pined for the Tea Bar, and the company of Dennis, Eric, and the outpatients. The kind of society where such outbursts were almost acceptable, run of the mill, and never threatened to distract from the ongoing search for cigarettes. St Mary's. He belonged there and now had an overwhelming feeling of regret at parting with it. But he was lost in a very different world now, which suddenly was all too apparent.

Rockerfellaz and Mr Ramaj were gone, and things weren't quite the same at Jan's any more, but he still had the shoe factory as a means of socializing and income, and now, with just the one job, was less overworked. Although it was casual agency work, he was needed there constantly and getting more used to it. He would often go down in the lift with the boxes to the loading area and watch the spectacle of the reversing of articulated lorries onto the closely set bays, where the boots and shoes would be loaded onto. He enjoyed the hectic atmosphere down there with vans and lorries coming in and out most of the time. It was welcome relief from the long hours of tedium and clock- watching upstairs in the packing department.

At times, without the surge of adrenalin needed to power him, Jonathan's chemically induced fatigue seriously impeded his ability to do a week's work, and he pondered the ridiculousness of his situation. Here he was, a young man trying to hold down full-time work, still firmly attached to the anti-psychotic and anti-depressant pills, like a ball and chain around his ankle. He felt strongly that the time had come to rid himself of it for good. And the mayhem of his previous failed attempts to do so brought him to the inescapable conclusion that he would have to be confined to the local mental hospital for the duration. Or in other words, try and persuade the powers that be, that that was what needed to happen. There would surely be more derangement, and he would rather it took place amongst the deranged, than out here in the real world where he would be misunderstood and more vital friends would be lost.

There was never going to be a good time to do this, but now was as good as any, he considered. After his outburst, the subsequent shock of being sacked for real by his friend Mr Ramaj, and a big change in Jan's attitude towards him, making it painful to live there, he needed a change of scenery. As he had no idea what life would be like without the pills that had been swimming around his bloodstream for the last nine years, he decided not to go back to Jan's after his discharge from the hospital. Wherever that was. If he was going there at all. And where he would go instead of Jan's was another mystery. He would cross that bridge when he came to it. Working for the agency, he was free to come and go as he pleased, telling them when he would work or not, rather than the vice versa of normal employment. A freedom that needed to be taken advantage of while it existed, he further considered. He would just have to hope that they would have the wisdom and means to send him back to Johnson's shoe factory, in a month's time, or however long it takes, as this had been the only thing in his life that had been going well in recent months. And as such, something that really ought to be gripped as though life depended on it.

His next step in the plan was to try and see his usual GP down at the surgery to explain his case. Easier said than done. Seeing a different doctor, who didn't bother to read his notes and acted purely on his or her assumptions of the patient, would surely be a spanner in the works. Dr Thackeray was by far the more likely medic in the building to understand his motives. For a patient fast becoming one of the most misunderstood in medical history, his favourite doctor had to be seen. Luckily, he made it over the wall of stern, disapproving female receptionists, and got an appointment with the familiar and affable Dr Thackeray. The man had an air of cynical humour about him, as if he had seen it all, and was content

84

just to plod along until the glorious day of his retirement. And no manner of lunacy could shock him and remove the tired half smile that seemed to permanently adorn his face. Doctor and patient had a fair amount in common, despite the completely different worlds they inhabited. But they were on opposing sides of an enormous barrier. Dr Thackeray was in his profession, the supplier of drugs, of which Jonathan was the recipient, and, to a large extent, 'guinea pig'.

Although he was a broad-minded chap as far as his position would allow, it was inevitable that the doctor would spout what felt like the bible of his profession, by saying, 'Well, you know these tablets are not addictive, don't you?' Which he then did.

What his words actually meant were: *at the moment as far as we know, there have been no reports of patients becoming addicted to this medicine.* But, for the sake of keeping up the pretence of the medical profession knowing exactly what they are doing, instead his words came out as, 'these tablets are not addictive'. This was the wall that had to be scaled.

Having heard it all before, the doctor's cliched words just increased his determination to get off the stuff, thus, never having to listen to them again. It was the patient's cue to then try and explain what had happened in his numerous attempts to come off the so-called 'non-addictive tablets', while trying not to sound like he possibly knew more about it than the doctor, as he had actually taken the stuff and the doctor hadn't. He also explained that having no family in the area for support, only fragile friendships; and as he was currently living in a house with, and owned by, some of these said friends and their small children, his accommodation was also fragile, and he was therefore very vulnerable indeed.

It was a quite brilliant act of persuasion by Jonathan, that any salesman or barrister would have been proud of, but it was the truth, the whole truth, and nothing but the truth. Perhaps a rare thing in these professions. The doctor seemed to agree with what he had just heard, merely from the fact that he had temporarily lost his usual, cynical, half smile. His pupils dilated and his mouth remained slightly open throughout. And was speechless, while the barrage of information sunk in. After which, he agreed that it 'might be an idea' if the patient were removed from normal society while he did this. He then made a phone call while scribbling things down on a piece of paper as he mumbled into the phone. His words were as unintelligible as his handwriting, and all Jonathan could really make out of the conversation, was his diagnosis of 'dependant personality'. Not exactly flattering, he conceded, laying the blame squarely with the patient rather than the medicine itself, of course. But at least it sounded like the medic was managing to get the cooperation of whoever he was speaking to. He ended the call and informed his patient that he was now expected to arrive there of his own accord next Monday by lunchtime, and to bring the drugs he was currently taking with him. Mission accomplished. Common sense had prevailed but only after Jonathan had bombarded the most educated of professional with it.

Had anyone ever left a doctor's surgery feeling so pleased and proud of their achievement in getting themselves into a mental hospital? An unusual ambition, that would have surely been treated as a prime example of insanity if anyone ever had. The complexities of his arrival at such an ambition shouldn't be examined too closely, it felt, in order to avoid a severe headache while trying to make sense of it. So he didn't. Just enjoying the contentment that he was somehow moving in the right direction. But it had been mentally exhausting, as if trying to come up with a plan to take the Crown Jewels out of the Tower of London, just for the afternoon. And then put them back again without being noticed.

A Strange Farewell

Sticking to the plan rigidly meant removing the option of returning to Jan's after his hospitalization. For better or worse. And that meant explaining his intentions to her and her husband, who had been so good to him, on the morning of his departure for the hospital. Their association had always been a fragile one. Either being ended in the way it was now, or by him giving in to, and making public, his true feelings for Jan. Something he had been very close to, and whether reciprocated or not would surely have led to more disruption and a far more hostile exit from their home than this one. And so, he proceeded to empty his room of all his stuff and load up the car, with Steve's help. They would soon need the spare room anyway, they explained, for their eldest daughter now yearning for her own room. But there was a sombre atmosphere in the house that morning. They had become a lot more distant since the incident at Rockerfellaz, not quite sure what their lodger was doing, or whether he was sure what he was doing. All this talk of mental hospitals and medication was well out of their range of life experience and not something they felt able to comment on. Except for a last minute reminder from Jan that he was supposed to be taking his medication with him to the hospital. He had forgotten.

'Ah!' he exclaimed, with a smile and a shake of the head, prompting a smile from Jan. Lightening the atmosphere somewhat.

What on earth was he going to do without her? He had lost count of the favours she had done him and given up hope of ever repaying them.

Jonathan turned and walked to the kitchen to get his pills from a cupboard before leaving. But as he did, the doorbell rang, and he eavesdropped on the conversation at the front door.

'We're looking for a Jonathan Piper,' were the words that followed the introductions of two police officers. 'It's about an incident that took place at Rockerfellaz on Friday the...'

Jonathan stopped breathing. He followed his first instinct and exited the kitchen into the back garden, and with pockets stuffed with medication attempted to climb over the fence into next door's garden. Nothing must be allowed to disturb the plan which had now rendered him homeless. But on realizing that he was about to demolish the couple's fence and had been spotted by the neighbour looking out of her window, he surrendered, gave up his escape, and made his way to the lounge. As he did, it slowly dawned on him that the pinning of obnoxious chefs against walls by their throat was, although commendable by some, actually illegal. Chef had obviously alerted the police, who would have been assisted in their enquiries by ex-friend and boss Mr Ramaj, who knew where he lived. As Jonathan opened the lounge door, a panic attack had set in. Was this ruin? Was it worth pleading guilty but insane, and explaining that he was just on his way to the appropriate place for those of his calling, if they would kindly leave him to it?

'Ah, thanks for calling in, Dave,' Jan said to him cheerily as he entered the room, with Steve and the two coppers standing by the window.

She winked at him repeatedly, and he quickly got the gist of what was happening.

'OK, no problem,' he responded, nervously. But, gaining a bit more confidence, as by some kind of miracle it looked as though visiting plod were almost indifferent to his presence, while being engaged in conversation with Steve.

'No, we haven't seen anything of him. He just left without a word,' Steve told the officers as Jonathan and Jan walked past them, with the chaos of small children assisting the obscurity.

'Well, if you have any more trouble with it just give me a bell,' Jonathan said to Jan by the front door, doing his best to imitate a passing handyman, despite the obvious lack of tools. Doing his best to join in the façade while trying to conceal his disbelief at what was occurring.

Now safely outside in the street, every bone in his body wanted to run to the car, and freedom, but having spotted a few curtains being twitched at the sight of a police car, decided a brisk walk was a bit less suspicious. Nobody had ever been so keen to get to a luni-bin, with the possible exception of a prisoner serving life for murder, having successfully convinced the psychiatric 'experts' he was mad. Thanks to the dear friends he was trying to distance himself from (although right now wasn't quite sure why), the plan appeared to be still on, as he continued towards the car with frequent anxious looks behind him. And not just any car, but a dishevelled Cortina: now a rare species, the police would doubtless have been told about as being the focal point of the offending incident. Safely in it, he roared off; all his possessions in the boot and piled up on the back seats, and medicines next to him on the passenger seat. Which, he would have surely forgotten had his beloved ex-landlady neglected to remind him. There wasn't time to dwell on the sudden, disturbing increase in the debt that was now owed to the couple. Firstly, giving him shelter in their already overcrowded house and rent-free during his frequent mishaps; now they had moved on to 'perverting the course of justice' to protect him.

'Well, if he does turn up again, be sure to contact us. This is a very serious matter,' the more senior of the police duo gives as his parting words to Jan and Steve on their doorstep as a shell-shocked Jonathan picks up speed on the dual-carriageway towards his rural retreat.

The couple nod, with feigned sincerity.

Jonathan arrives at what now felt more like a hideout. He had brief chats and games of table tennis with other inmates that were capable of such normalities. Very familiar surroundings. The doctor he saw in a brief exchange of words in the lounge made the same comment that Jonathan had heard and ignored many times, that the tablets were not addictive but that they would 'cut it down gradually in case of any ill effects', which sounded much like a contradiction, albeit a caring one. But his thoughts were elsewhere, and he felt an urgency to make contact with what had been home until today. Jan and Steve had to be thanked sincerely for their almighty gesture, allowing him to make his escape. But it was the kind of extreme favour that so often had to be returned. It was unsettling. He had somehow descended from being seriously in their debt, to being at their mercy. No way could he cope with his complicated life being complicated further by an intrusion from the police. He asked for directions to a payphone and made his way to it armed with as much coinage as he could accumulate.

'Listen, Jan, that was so good of you. I don't know what to say. But thanks, thanks so much, really. I don't know how I'm gonna…'

Jan interrupted to explain the finer details of the near-catastrophic misunderstanding.

'It was Steve! He thought you'd already gone, the dozy sod. He's standing there giving them the bullshit of how you've disappeared and that, and you're in the kitchen! I couldn't believe it! I had to do something! But anyway, we got there didn't we?' She ended with the kind of chuckle that so typified why he adored her.

Luckily for Jonathan, it sounded like Steve was (suffering?) from a disorder whereby the telling of the truth to the police was not only immoral but physically impossible. He apologised profusely for all the hassle he had caused them.

'Oh, don't worry about that. Just you do what you've gotta do and get off these tablets. They won't know where you are. After you'd gone, I showed them your room and luckily there was nothing in it. And as you won't be coming back anyway.'

Jonathan detected more than a hint of disappointment and feigned indifference in her last sentence. And it was devastating to listen to. Then, as if with no choice in the matter, unable to stop his words spilling out, he explained his real reasons for not coming back. That he was 'too fond' of her, that having to listen to her and Steve having sex through the wafer-thin wall was excruciating. He spoke of his affection for her as though it were more like a severe bout of constipation than anything to do with romance. It certainly hadn't served any useful purpose and had been more of a threat to his already precarious survival.

'It's OK, love. I knew already,' she responded, in her usual down to earth way, but sounded as if she was struggling to breathe as she spoke.

Somehow, he knew she knew, and that his feelings were reciprocated. But it was best for all if she didn't verbalize them.

'For god's sake, don't tell Steve,' he begged. Fearing that the man may suddenly break with his principles and assist the police with their investigation, possibly leading to him doing his planned cold turkey in a police cell. 'But thank him for me, won't you, please.'

'Of course.'

'So, it's best I don't come back, Jan. You know,' he continued.

'Yeah, I know,' she agreed, with a sombre tone in her voice.

With what was probably impeccable timing before the conversation had a chance to get any more intimate, the pips[7] sounded, he had no more change, and they were cut off. But much to his relief, the truth had at last been spoken, hopefully without causing too much damage, as it had a habit of so often doing. In his fragile existence, it seemed, feelings of love had to be suppressed in just the same way as those of anger and hatred.

---

[7] A repeated bleeping noise, heard when the call is about to be terminated unless the payphone is fed with more money; often endured by the masses before the invention of the mobile phone, and with it, a new era of telephonical perils.

Madness in the Countryside

The positive, rational thoughts about what he was doing, that he had arrived with, gradually began to diminish after a few days. On arrival, he had handed over his supply of pills that he'd been taking since Dr Heinbecker first prescribed them nine years ago, and that was the last he ever saw of them. They were now replaced by pills of a different shape and colour, and the attitude of the staff giving them out was that it was none of the patient's business what they were. They had their orders from above and it was not open to discussion. This was obviously not going to be the clear-cut operation that he had planned. He began to feel disorientated and unsettled, and ultra-sensitive to what he perceived as any negative attitudes or the faintest of criticism towards himself. Even more than usual. And there was plenty of it for him to perceive; him being the kind of patient who was a little too concerned with his own well-being for the staff's liking. Definitely not what they were used to.

At times, his feelings could only be described as weird, and there was no way of knowing whether caused by the medicinal changes, or if it was just him. The fact that he didn't know if the planned reduction of his pills had actually started, didn't help to clear the fog that was rapidly taking over his brain. He desperately needed to see the doctor again: that semi-sensible one he bumped into when he arrived, for confirmation of something. At least, he had seemed to have an idea who Jonathan was and what he was doing there. Something that Jonathan himself was now having serious doubts about.

In his wanderings in the hospital grounds, he stumbled upon what appeared to be a bungalow out on its own. Too small for a ward, his curiosity led him in, and there was seated a group of patients, some of whom were obviously identifiable as such due to their sudden nervous twitches or pointless, loud, repeating of certain words; with none of the serenity of Buddhist chanting. The others were doing basket weaving under the supervision of a young man and woman who spoke to their patients in a loud, slow, caring sort of way, as though they were a substitute for children. Jonathan had an overwhelming sense of not belonging here, despite in the past having had an overwhelming sense of belonging in similar environments. But life had changed a lot since then, and having recently suffered the comparatively normal problems of overwork and car ownership, the scene that confronted him seemed to add to the general confusion of identity, and a disturbing feeling that quite possibly, he didn't belong anywhere.

Jonathan was asked by the young man staff if he wanted to do some basket weaving but the man's words seemed tinged with hostility, as though he were speaking to an intruder, exacerbating Jonathan's feelings of being one. He declined the offer with an equally cold and straight faced, 'No thanks.'

'What are you doing here?' the young woman staff asked him, in a very similar way to that of her colleague.

Jonathan, feeling immediately intimidated by the question, wondered if perhaps there was some hidden meaning to it; a slur of some kind. What are you doing in this room right now? Or what are you doing in this hospital? Now, amongst all the other fog in his head, was a feeling of having no legitimate reason for being here: in this room or this hospital, as what felt like was being insinuated. He had somehow lost all trace of the original, positive, rational thinking, that had brought him here. And being constantly reminded that the tablets were 'not addictive' exacerbated the psychological chaos. Usually, he had the common sense to dismiss these words, but now strangely, he didn't.

But one thing that *was* clear, was the verbal attack being aimed straight at him, and he shouted his reply, in what felt like an honest, necessary act of self-defence, with wide, menacing eyes.

'What's it gotta do with you why I'm here?'

Young man staff gets up off his chair and calls (security?)

'There is a man here who has just wandered in and is being disruptive. Can you please come and take him away?' was the request of the young man staff, who then took his seat and resumed helping the basket weavers. Jonathan just stood there in a trance, incapable of making a decision to move in any direction.

He had observed since his arrival, that there was some male (nurses?) whose role it seemed, apart from chatting up female nurses, was that of bouncers. Moving patients to where they didn't want to go, with a lot

92

more force than was necessary. He had witnessed one such incident on the ward earlier that day. This is precisely what happened next, when the same 'bouncer' burst in through the door and immediately put Jonathan's arm behind his back in a lock. Before he had time to fully grasp what was going on, he was being frogmarched back to the ward where he was told he was being 'sectioned' to the order that he is not allowed to leave the ward under any circumstances. And this frogmarch having occurred just a few metres from where his car was parked, somehow added to the overall sense of unreality. The car that he had voluntarily driven here with such a sense of purpose, in what now felt like a previous life. His 'sectioning' prompted a whole mass of questions that needed answering, as his mind and body entered panic attack mode once more.

If he wasn't allowed off the ward, was he therefore not allowed to leave the hospital as that would involve leaving the ward? And with him being a 'voluntary patient', as quoted by Dr Thackeray in his attempts to get him in here, should he just leave voluntarily? But would he then be chased by a frenzied nurse/bouncer if he did? Was he physically able to drive his car out of here, despite the fog now taking over his mind? Should he at least try, while still in possession of the keys? If he was and he did, where would he go? Would they get the police after him? And if they did, would a prosecution for assaulting a chef be added to the chaos? What exactly were the pills they were now giving him? Was he in the process of becoming addicted to something else? What should he do? Why had he come here in the first place? Would he ever get out?

His questions led him back to the nothingness from which he had started, as though trapped in a psychological maze with no exits.

The nurse/bouncer that had escorted him back in an armlock had briefed the night shift when they arrived, as to his 'disruptive behaviour' at the occupational therapy class. Thus, spreading his unpopularity further and increasing the usual tension at the giving out of medication. 'What are they?' he asked.

'Pills! Take them!' was the stern reply, as if implying that force may be applied if he didn't. After some hesitancy, he took them, but his ignorance of what they were was terrifying. Had he now started going backwards in his effort to free himself of medication and put his mental patient days behind him? Was his former life outside the hospital in the process of being dismantled, never to be returned to?

Confusion doesn't often get described as 'horrific', but that's exactly what this was. As if by coming to the hospital of his own free will, he had somehow entered an abyss from which there was no way out, and in which, he was descending rapidly.

Thankfully, there was some light relief at the end of an arduous day of psychological torture, as he entered the lounge full of empty chairs and a TV, from which *Top of the Pops* was blaring out. An inmate in another world and dressing gown and pyjamas was the only other person in there. The man looked deadly serious as he attempted some kind of belly-dance to the latest release from *The Pet Shop Boys*. Jonathan sat down quietly, for fear of disturbing the spectacle of the large stomach going in and out with hands positioned behind his head, prompting a rare smile from a member of staff on the face of a passing West Indian nurse. 'Lesley, you silly boy. What do you think you're doing?' she said to the dancer, who continued, oblivious to anything going on around him. She shook her head in disbelief as she then smiled at Jonathan, who was still a long way from being able to return the gesture, but the music, and the abandonment it created, somehow eased his turmoil. Which, on this day, had been so severe, he even managed to get some comfort from what was currently in the pop charts: something avoided in normal circumstances.

The following morning, after another sleepless night with his body engulfed in a spasm of tension, he caught sight of the doctor he had spoken to briefly on arrival, while his head was full of more judicial matters. He remembered the man's words of 'cutting down gradually in case of any ill effects', which had put him at ease, if only for the recognition of his reasons for being there. But now, just getting a glimpse of the man was a relief, as if a possible lifeline back to reality, after the constant unreality of the last few days. Although there was plenty of private consulting rooms on the ward, it was as if Jonathan's situation didn't warrant the using of one, or it seemed, him being assigned and introduced to any particular doctor. And so, this second-class patient was reduced to hovering around, desperately trying to get the attention of the doctor whose name he still didn't know and didn't bother to ask. Waiting, patiently, but determinedly, for him to finish a conversation with a colleague in a corridor. But, having taken his eyes off his prey for a few seconds, it was now on its way to the car park with car keys in hand. Jonathan gave chase, looking anxiously behind him for anyone chasing him.

'Excuse me, Doctor. Excuse me! Can you *please* tell me what these pills are that they are giving me? I've been in a right state. I haven't slept, I'm just... well... I don't know. I don't how to explain.'

The doctor looked at him vacantly, as if he had no idea who the obviously disturbed, pyjamaed man was that was addressing him. And as a result, Jonathan's spirit sunk to new depths of despair, as if his 'treatment' was about to reach a whole new level of weirdness. *Please, don't insist I'm homosexual. Not now! I'm not in the mood!* he thought to himself, as he gazed at the still confused doctor, waiting in anticipation for a desperately needed, intelligent reply. But anything was possible in such places, past experience had taught him.

'Ah . Jonathan Piper. We met briefly the other day,' he reminded, trying to maintain a level of politeness and civility, despite an overwhelming urge to scream. 'I'm coming off of tablets.'

'Oh yes, yes, of course!' The doctor's return to consciousness was like a flicker of light at the end of a long dark tunnel. 'Well, it's exactly what you've been taking, but a much milder dose.'

'So you've cut it down then?' Jonathan asked, as if not quite believing the sensibleness of what he thought he just heard, and quietly clamouring for it to be repeated.

The best answer he could get was a nod of agreement, as the busy doctor looked at his watch. Jonathan felt close to doing something embarrassing like crying or kissing the doctor's hand, with the relief of getting this vital information and being spoken to like a human being and not a monkey that's had its brain removed. But he settled for an apology for his 'disruptive behaviour' at the basket weaving place, in case it had somehow affected his treatment.

'It was a misunderstanding,' he explained. 'I've had so much confusion.'

But the doctor showed no sign of awareness of the incident. Jonathan looked him straight in the eye for any sign that his described symptoms made any sense to the man, as if trying to determine if this was perhaps what he was supposed to be feeling right now, after the reduction. But the doctor just nodded and smiled, and it was obvious that the brief bit of information he had managed to get, was all he was going to get. But those few words appeared to be delivered with sincerity, and as such, had given the patient a renewed sense of direction, reducing the confusion and making life more bearable. At least one person in the place, knew and cared what he was doing there. Maybe he should have at least got the doctor's name, he then considered, as he watched the man get in his car; as he was invaluable to him right now. As if the only source of democracy in an otherwise dictatorship.

Later, he wandered in the grounds again. All this bland place had going for it was the countryside surrounding it, he thought, as if assessing the merits of a holiday cottage. He was hoping to stumble upon something like the Tea Bar, which would have been like an oasis in the desert. But there was nothing like that here. St Mary's had been a wonderland of magic and excitement compared with this. But the stark contrast between the two could be a blessing, as he vowed that if he got out of here safely, he would never again set foot in another mental hospital. Probably a healthier attitude than being addicted to the one in Sheffield.

Suddenly, he remembered that he was 'sectioned' and therefore banned from leaving the ward. He turned and looked back at it, half expecting to see somebody coming after him. But there was no one. He was sure he'd been seen leaving the ward by at least three female members of staff who were chatting and made no attempt to stop him. He carried on walking, and his thoughts turned to the nurse/bouncer who had 'restrained' and 'sectioned' him. Obviously an unstable man, a frustrated wannabe dictator who dished out his punishment without any authority or cooperation from fellow staff to enforce it. The three nurses who were sitting comfortably, engrossed in conversation as he exited the ward, looked like they would not have moved had he been the Grim Reaper with scythe.

Later on that day, the nurse/bouncer had just started his shift, and the sight of him made Jonathan feel sick with rage, recalling how the arm-locked escort had made him feel when at his most vulnerable. The need for revenge was becoming like something living inside him, desperate to get out. He approached the table where the man sat alone.

'What is it you do here?' Jonathan asked, while among the safety of potential witnesses milling about in the dining room. Some of these were visiting social workers from outside, unaffected by the sickness inside.

'What?'

'Why don't you get yourself a proper job?' Jonathan asked, in a rare moment when he managed to shed a few layers of inhibitions and say exactly what he thought, while completely sober. And it was glorious.

Doing the same while drunk came naturally to him, and he had the scars to prove it. Looking into his eyes, he guessed the nurse/bouncer would be seething and desperately wanting to kill him but couldn't do a thing to satisfy his cravings. The grimace on the face of the man told him he was right. Jonathan's words hushed the rest of the dining room, and a now attentive audience observed the proceedings with almost expectation of violence. The nurse/bouncer specialised in restraint when there was no need of it, and was aware of the thin line between that and assault, and he liked assault. But now, there were witnesses that no restraint was required, as Jonathan just stood there calmly, no danger to anyone, giving his words. While at the same time, administering maximum unease.

'Go and sit in there!' the man ordered, pointing at chairs in the lounge.

'Or what?' Jonathan replied, feeling a rush of excitement as he did so.

This caused the man to instinctively get up off his chair, then noticing the assembled company watching, got back in it and lit a cigarette. This was about as heroic as a sober Jonathan ever got. But would there be consequences? No way did he want to jeopardise his 'treatment'. He had been reassured that if the doctor could be trusted, he *was* in the process of coming off his pills and therefore moving in the right direction; and at times, didn't want to breathe in case the air produced blew him in a different one. The man was now seated and silent, nervously fiddling with a cigarette lighter while puffing on a fag, but Jonathan dare not feel victorious. Life was never that easy. But somewhere inside him was a growing feeling that vermin like this had to be stopped.

One morning, Jonathan lay in bed while other patients in his dormitory were washing in the bathroom. Suddenly, he felt a pillow over his face that was then pressed hard over his mouth and nose, with incredible force. In a state of terror at being starved of oxygen, this was surely it, his life done. But just at the point when he felt himself about to be transformed into another state of being, the pillow was removed. He raised himself upright gasping for air, to see nurse/bouncer laughing at him as he walked towards the door and left. In a severe state of shock, his immediate concern was to regain normal breath. And after doing so, followed his instincts to raise the alarm. He entered the office where two female nurses were playing cards.

'He just tried to suffocate me! That nurse. The blonde-haired one!'

They completely ignored him, except for one who raised her eyes above her hand of cards and looked up at him for no more than a second.

'Put a pillow over my face!' he continued, looking directly at her, expecting, hoping, to see a flicker of concern on her face. There was none. Did she not believe him? Did she believe him, but it was a regular occurrence and therefore didn't warrant any concern? Who knows. It was like being on the set of a disturbing, psychological thriller of the late 1960s. Only for real. Actually living it.

Subdued by the incident and lack of reaction to it, he wandered in the grounds just to get away. He kept going over again and again in his mind, the terror of being unable to breathe, the relief that he now could, and the ease with which somebody else could stop it and start it again at will. All very similar feelings to what he experienced after being forced into a well, the lid being closed, and the relief at being pulled out of it. On his return to the ward, he avoided looking at and listening to the perpetrator who was still 'on duty', as a survival instinct, as if unable to contain the hatred that such exposure would cause. Hatred that couldn't be acted upon if he was ever to get out of this nuthouse[8] unscathed. He demanded to see the doctor, whose name he still didn't know, to tell him of the incident.

'The one with glasses and bit of a beard. You know.'

The staff were silent, just giving him the usual, puzzled, vacant look, as if they were visitors from another galaxy who had only just arrived on earth. Relishing being unhelpful, as if they knew and disapproved of him, and his reasons for being here.

As usual, all Jonathan could do was think his revenge. The man was obviously a psychopath trying to get out, he considered; who had chosen this kind of (work?) for the domination side of it. The arm lock, the pillow

---

[8] one of many derogatory terms for a mental hospital and its inhabitants, but in this case, reserved purely for its staff.

over the face. He assumed he had an unfortunate spouse who was regularly chained, gagged and strapped for his own personal amusement.

Jonathan could only suppress the compulsion to tell the absent doctor of the incident, and his personal diagnosis of the culprit; if only to satisfy a need for revenge that couldn't be obtained any other way. But, before he had the chance to do this, the presumed-absent psychiatrist suddenly appeared in front of him, and gave him the 'good news' that he was now off of any medication, as last night's pills were the last he was going to be given. This really was music to the ears of an otherwise traumatized Jonathan. But the next bit of 'good news' the doctor seemed more excited about giving, he wasn't so sure about.

'Dr Palmer will be assessing you herself, *personally*, on her next visit to the ward,' as though this were a great honour for any patient to be considered worthy of her attention; whoever she was. 'And, strictly off the record of course, (big smile) I can't see any reason why she would want to keep you here for say, any more than a week.'

Jonathan could understand how this could be perceived as good news to a patient who had a loving home to go to after their discharge. And it was good news to him also even though he didn't; mainly due to the antagonism inflicted upon him by the staff, that had made his stay such a precarious ordeal. But he was grateful for the update from the doctor, that at last it seemed, he was gradually moving in the general direction of accomplishing his mission.

He had never heard of Dr Palmer, but assumed she must be someone of great importance, as the mere mention of her name seemed to get the adrenalin flowing and pupils dilating in the *ordinary* doctor stood before him. After all his mental preparation, Jonathan forgot to mention the pillow incident. Semi-deliberately. Just in case the bizarreness of his accusations was deemed delusional, bringing an abrupt end to the progress: him being treated (or punished?) by his discharge being postponed, and new medication being prescribed. In which case, he too could end up belly-dancing in front of *Top of the Pops* as his only source of amusement.

His first impressions of life completely without the pills were that he was OK, if everything was OK. And right now, it was, it seemed. His worries, that the complete withdrawal from the tablets he'd taken for so long may turn him into a non-dischargeable monster, had proved

99

unfounded. He was off them, he had just about hung on to his sanity, and his discharge was imminent according to the doctor. But he was soon to return to the outside world homeless, and that definitely had the potential of not being OK. But the break from the comfort and shelter of Jan's place had to happen at some time and was never going to be easy. As he enjoyed the relative peace and tranquillity of the hospital grounds for the last time, it was surely the calm before the storm that he could almost sense gathering.

It was as if the ward was being visited by royalty when Consultant Dr Palmer graced it with her presence one morning. The white-haired lady in late middle-age was escorted around it by a female nurse, and they stopped for a brief word with several different inmates in turn, in which she looked at them with the most gracious of smiles. But if an inmate took up too much of her valuable time or raised their voice, the smile would waver somewhat, and the procession would move on. There was a queue of mortals waiting to be 'assessed' by the good lady, and Jonathan, he presumed, was in it somewhere.

'Dr Palmer will assess you herself, *personally*', were the ordinary doctor's words. But this seemed anything but personal, as he was led into a large room with the Consultant on her throne in the middle of a semi-circle of seats, flanked by more junior members of staff occupying the other ones. Some of these were the few nurses with whom he had managed to get on fairly well up until now, having the occasional game of table tennis with, in his less confused moments. But it appeared that the now sadly absent, ordinary doctor, was not the only one in awe of the great Dr Palmer.

There were similarities to James Bond films here, as 007 received the most courteous and formal of introductions to his seated arch enemy before the hostilities commenced.

'You are wasting our time,' she began. 'These tablets you have been taking are *NOT* addictive, and therefore there is no reason for you being here. You are simply trying to draw attention to yourself.' Her words were followed by the most authoritative of self-satisfied grin.

And so, having been misunderstood by the so-called experts yet again, it was official: he was a time-wasting, attention-seeking junkie. And, increasing the insult further, her words were accompanied by nods of agreement from various minions, who never had the guts to show their true feelings to his face when the opportunity was there. Temporarily lost for words, he opened his mouth to speak but nothing came out. But it then dawned on him, that once again, his rage had to be suppressed so as not to jeopardize his imminent, drug-free release from this hellhole. Especially, as the great lady, who seemed to be missing either a tiara or a black cap on her head, was about to pass sentence. Immediate discharge. Now sentence had been passed, he rose to his feet and walked slowly and calmly towards the woman with a menacing stare, prompting her vast collection of bodyguards to raise to theirs.

'Drop dead, you fucking ugly, old cow!'

His words were clear and precise, and prompted scornful looks from her more loyal servants, but awkward smiles from others who secretly understood the motivation for them. One such awkward smiler, a young female administrative type, then found herself forced to apologize for the embarrassingly audible, uncontrollable sniggering her initial smile had now descended into.

'Please, excuse me,' the red-faced, visibly distressed young lady pleaded, in between almost barks of laughter, as her eyes welled with tears and shoulders quivered. A display that momentarily caused all eyes to focus upon her and not him, as those around her began to wonder if first-aid might be necessary.

It was, what he hoped would be, the last word on the slime that was the psychiatric establishment, as he then calmly retreated out of the room with a smile at the embarrassment he had caused, as the unfortunate woman sniggered on. Allowing himself a rare moment of victorious gloating as he did. A job well done. Thus, completing his 'assessment'.

Jonathan started packing the car with his things. He said goodbye to the few inmates that had been a source of comfort, but was ignored when he did the same to the few staff he had previously got on well with. Such was the influence of the much-revered iron maiden. He was sad that the ordinary doctor was absent, and therefore couldn't be thanked for being the one thing that had held him together. Maybe the man was now locked in a dungeon somewhere underneath the hospital, wishing he hadn't spoken to a patient like a human being, Jonathan considered. Also, the irony of him being so publicly insulted by the esteemed lady, about whom, he had received such hype from her biggest fan: the ordinary doctor, who would doubtless have strongly disapproved of his counter-abuse of the goddess of psychiatry. So, maybe just as well he *was* absent and therefore spared the trauma of witnessing his beloved being so crudely insulted.

With faces at the window, as if checking to see if he was actually going to leave so the celebrations could commence, the car was now packed, and he got in it. But going he was not. The battery was flat. Deep sigh! Luckily, Steve had given him jump leads which were in the boot. Although he had also given his lodger a rough demonstration of what to do with them, so much had happened between then and now, and that valuable lesson was now ancient history. And after the turmoil of the last few hours, all he could do was sit there, head rested on his arms that were rested on the steering wheel and try to clear his head, before filling it again with the practicalities of getting the car moving.

Eventually, he unpacks some of the baggage that was now crushing the jump leads. He then puts the bonnet up with leads in other hand before the dreadful realisation that another car has to be involved in the proceedings. This wasn't happening, surely! Was it? And so, he decides to walk to the car park of the nearest other ward where nobody knew him. But dare not enter the other ward uninvited for risk of spreading his unpopularity further and stirring nurse/bouncer into action once more, as per his previous uninvited visit to the basket weavers. So, he just waits outside in the full-up car park for one of the many car owners to emerge. Maybe they were having a similar inquisition here, he wondered; with the same unnecessary hangers-on, nodding in agreement to whatever was being said. That might explain all the cars. If he'd gone back to what was his own ward carrying the jump leads seeking assistance, he would doubtless have heard something like: '*you've been told to leave the hospital!*' It was that kind of place.

After an hour of waiting and being stared at suspiciously by the foot traffic coming in and out, he then asked a smartly dressed lady motorist in the politest way possible, if she could oblige. Although the man looked a bit odd in her opinion, and unsettlingly more like patient than staff, the jump leads hanging over his shoulder suggested his intentions were harmless, and she drove him to his car. After a bit of fumbling about under the bonnets of both cars, the beloved Cortina was purring again. He thanked her, and off she went, and off he went. But then stopped abruptly upon seeing what looked like the blonde hair of nurse/bouncer coming the other way; approaching the main car park behind the wheel of a distinctively immaculate, standard-issue boy racer, Ford Escort XR3i with huge spoiler. Jonathan, still in the driver's seat with engine running, concealed himself with a hand against his head as the man walked past and entered the hospital. He then got a flat-head screwdriver from the glove box. Should he or shouldn't he? he wondered, while repeatedly tapping the tool against the palm of his other hand, deep in thought. He couldn't quite get his head around the full list of possible consequences of trashing the XR3i, now its driver was absent; but it somehow felt immoral that someone should be able to inflict such terror with that mock suffocation, and suffer no repercussions whatsoever. It was a golden opportunity for revenge, feeling almost like a god-given blessing from above that had to be taken advantage of. And so, in what felt like god's work, after a quick look around for onlookers, he violently stabbed all four tyres in a few seconds, followed by a deep scratch along both sides for good measure. Luckily, he remembered to keep the engine running while he got out of his car to do this. Thus, enabling a quick getaway from the scene of the crime without having to seek further assistance with jump leads before doing so. An easy mistake to make after a traumatic afternoon, that would have surely led to an even more traumatic evening. But, after administering the most satisfying of justice, he roars off.

'YES!'

Followed by a concentrated stare in the rear-view mirror. The joy of revenge was sweet. And up until now, very rare.

Eventually, when his driving ceased resembling that of a getaway driver after a bank robbery, he pondered on the very real problem of having nowhere to live. And surely now, too late in the day to find one. He habitually drove in the direction of Hounslow, but then asked himself why. He could go anywhere. He didn't belong anywhere. He had nowhere to go. Just as these thoughts were pounding his head, he felt his breath become laboured, as though descending from indecision into confusion, and from there into the paralysis of a panic attack. But, in an attempt to fight it, he comforted himself when he remembered the shoe factory, and the possibility of going back there. And to Jan's for a visit; if they could put the honesty of their most recent phone call behind them and resume the dishonesty of their friendship. It was better than nothing. She and the children would surely be pleased to see him, if he could revert back to the old Jonathan. The one with a sense of humour, that wasn't striving so hard for progress and independence.

So Hounslow it was. At least a fairly painless decision had been made about that. He drove on, oblivious to the very little petrol he now had.

Back to ('Normal'?)

Not an ideal situation, approaching dusk with only a car for shelter. And not an option to get even the cheapest of Bed and Breakfasts. To splash out on the luxury of a bed and four walls for tonight, could make the difference between taking up permanent residence in the car, or finding a proper place to live, from which he could pick up his life where he left off. Every penny was needed, for petrol, and hopefully, tomorrow's pay out on a room or bedsit of some kind, somewhere. And he needed to start looking early. So, on finding a secluded lay-by, still as much in the countryside to feel safe, he turned off the engine and lights, and tried to arrange himself in a position on the back seat for sleep to be possible. It started raining outside, and he counted his blessings, thinking of the unfortunates who didn't even have the luxury of a rusted old Cortina to keep the rain off, as he listened to its patter on the roof. Bit of regret now at removing the option of returning to the comfort of Jan's place but he knew he had to stick to the plan rigidly, and this was never going to be an easy bit of the plan to stick to. Despite the discomfort, a feeling of contentment came over him as he reflected on his 'assessment'; getting the last, loud and abusive word, and the general disturbance it created. And imagining nurse/bouncer finishing his shift to the sight of his car with four flat tyres was the equivalent of the most tranquil of bedtime stories being read to a five-year-old, and at last, he drifted off into blissful sleep. Only to wake up again at one o'clock when the temperature had plummeted, and spent the rest of the night wide awake, shivering, with a pain in his back.

Proper *'begging for change while sitting on the pavement'* type homelessness was like quicksand, and he was tiptoeing on little bits of rock around its edges, only just avoiding the drop.

The next day was a long one of scouring newspapers and ads in shop windows and fumbling about with small change in phone boxes; in many of which, the phone had been cut off permanently and only bare wires remained. Towards the end of it, with time running out and the prospect of another night in the car looming, he got himself installed in a room in a small shared flat with three other young people. A bad decision for someone with almost an aversion to people his own age, but one made out of desperation and fatigue. The latter increased by the sight of the naked mattress on the bed, prompting him to put common sense aside and pay the necessary in order to collapse on it, immediately. The room was OK, and it was the prospect of the peace and solitude in it that was more appealing right now than the girl who showed it to him, after introducing herself as the 'partner' of the absent male owner. After initial obligatory introductions with the others, he proceeded to avoid them like the plague. He had no interest in trying to make polite conversation in the shared lounge, while the TV blared out the screams and explosions of an action movie. And with nothing at all odd about them, something that had become an essential ingredient in a friend, they seemed destined not to get on. But it was a base for the time being.

The next day, the next phase of the plan was put into place: a visit to the agency in the centre of town to see if he can resume work at the shoe factory. To Jonathan, it was vital that he did, both financially and psychologically. The stability of the familiar being paramount to ease himself back into life without the pills, with unnecessary complications being avoided. But he was greeted by a stranger, with doubts.

'Mmm. Well. Johnson's, eh? We've got quite a few people down there already right now, as it happens. But we've got a milk processing plant, if you fancy going there?'

Jonathan squirmed uneasily in a swivel chair, trying to give off an air of nonchalance while feeling that his fragile existence was hanging in the balance. He had a funny feeling there was some kind of future for him at the shoe factory. And, with his complex personality, considered that there must be hundreds if not thousands of places of work, at which, he would feel like a square peg in a round hole. So this rare one with a square hole, must be treasured and preserved at all costs.

At that moment, a familiar face entered the office who, from memory, made an immediate connection between Jonathan and the shoe factory.

'Yeah, let's see if we can get you back in there,' the man muttered optimistically as he picked up the phone. Jonathan, now much more at ease, apologises for his absence in the last few weeks without delving into the complicated reasons behind it. This was a delicate situation governed by fate: the right person at the right time, talking to the right person at Johnson's. The agency man ends his call, swivels round in his chair and points at Jonathan.

'Tomorrow?'

'Yeah.'

'Then assume it's every day unless the manager in the packing department says different.'

Mission accomplished.

So, to his relief, the mundane routine in the packing department resumed, only now without the chronic, drug-induced fatigue that had so hindered his previous life there. He was pleased to see the line of South Asian workers once again. It was the nearest thing to home that he had.

At every opportunity when his absence wouldn't be noticed, he squeezed himself into the lift with the large boxes packed with shoes to the loading area on the ground floor. Fortunately, the ten-second journey in the darkness of the aged metal box, wasn't quite long enough to stir any feelings of deja vu from being stuck in the well. The claustrophobia of which, he had been plagued with ever since.

'Been on holiday, have we?'

'Yeah, something like that.'

'It's all right for some, innit, eh.'

The predictable chat made him feel accepted and normal. Although the truth was far from it and could never be spoken. He was suddenly aware that the whole notion of 'holiday' had become a far off, unattainable thing, that normal people indulged in. A distant memory from a bygone age, the nearest he would get to now, being a mental hospital in the countryside.

He watched the articulated lorries being reversed with such precision. The drivers then getting out and 'dropping their trailers': lowering the legs on which it sat and driving out from under it with just the front cab bit, then hooking up to the trailer next to it with a loud click as it connected. This was exciting to him, and from somewhere, an ambition was emerging; and like a small boy, he longed for the day when he could do the same.

One day, after chatting with some of the loaders, he learnt that a vacancy existed for a driver of one of the company's smaller lorries. He dismissed with a laugh the suggestion that he should apply, pointing out the *slight* obstacle of him not having an HGV license.

'You don't need one,' he was told.

An ordinary car license was sufficient to drive it and apply he did. So, after a bit of manoeuvring and reversing observed by the boss and admitting that he had no experience of driving anything bigger than a car, to his amazement, he got the job. Maybe, it was a way of avoiding the hassle of advertising it and interviewing strangers from outside, he later considered; and therefore, had nothing whatsoever to do with his qualities as a human being, or driver. So, he now had the security of a permanent job at Johnson's, and the sudden change of fortune for the forever-struggling young man was almost beyond belief.

After what felt like a perfect day, he drove back to the shared flat. But once there, it became obvious that his popularity was decreasing rapidly. It seemed that tenants were expected to socialize in the lounge, and failure to do so was treated with derision and suspicion. And, what exacerbated the already tense situation, was his decision to celebrate his new found security with a pint of bitter in the local pub. One, that after a period of abstinence, never tasted so good. This, he had planned long ago, just as soon as he had 'cracked it' with the move down south. He hadn't, but right now, it felt very much like he had, and the first one led to the second and so on, until he had lost count, and his marbles, and once again, there was no chance of him leaving voluntarily. And certainly not in this case, to the solitude of a room in a flat where he was increasingly unwelcome. Strangers in the pub, including a small group of females, seemed a far more attractive proposition for socializing, when he'd drunk enough to do so.

He staggered his way to the flat. The others came out of the lounge to see what all the crashing and banging was about as he walked into the closed doors of other people's rooms, eventually finding his and collapsing on the bed. He woke up four hours later to the silence of the middle of the night, fully clothed and having wet himself and the bed several times, and his bedroom door still wide open. For the first time in his drinking career, he shook uncontrollably, but not with the cold. His instincts told him, that his precarious existence could not withstand such mayhem. Years ago, in the luxury of his own flat in Sheffield, maybe, but this was a different world.

His room looked and smelt bad, and the last thing he felt capable of doing right now was cleaning it. And he assumed it would be on display for all to see while he was out, as there was no lock on it. When he first arrived with his stuff, he had asked about it, only to be treated to a lecture about 'trust', and how it 'eliminates the need for locks'. In an ideal world perhaps, where fairies sing you a lullaby every night before you go to sleep after another hard day of picking money off trees, but in this one, he would much rather have one; and the lack of security made him wonder where his belongings might be when he got home from work tonight. Outside the front door perhaps?

Was today supposed to be the first day of him driving the lorry? He wasn't sure, but the thought of it was now terrifying. He had to be at work at eight o'clock. Now five o'clock, and his bedroom feeling more like a prison cell, he changes into his work clothes and tip toes out the front door to his car. A relief to be moving. Escaping from one catastrophe before arriving at the next, and the shaking stopped. But the optimism he felt yesterday for the driving job had been replaced by dread and fear. As if the driving of a larger vehicle somehow represented destruction on a larger scale.

The area around the shoe factory was as much like home as anywhere else, and he felt safe in its familiar surroundings. A dual carriageway, but usually slow moving with numerous traffic lights and entrances to retail parks either side. Allied Carpets and Safeway Supermarket were the main attractions, and the area couldn't be more impersonal, which right now suited him.

Thank God for the staff canteen, he thought, as he tucked into a bacon and sausage sandwich and a *proper* cup of tea, not the peculiar liquid that comes out of a machine pretending to be it. No matter how much technology moves forward, machines will never get the hang of making tea, he thought to himself with a faint smile. Even when robots are driving lorries! Which moved his thoughts swiftly back to the present and the day in hand with its mass of uncertainties and the smile disappears. What will he be doing today? The euphoria of yesterday's brief driving lesson and chat with the boss of the despatch and goods-in area, Mr Montague, had overshadowed the making of concrete plans as to where and when he would actually start. Or maybe plans *were* made, but after being told he'd got the job, was too excited to listen, and already planning the celebratory drink.

After he managed to track down Mr Montague, it transpired that he had spoken to the manager of the packing department who had agreed that Jonathan could be 'borrowed' for the day to be briefed about what he was to be doing in his new job.

The managers of different departments were mostly white and English, despite the mainly South Asian work force. Which implied there wasn't much opportunity to work your way up for those of a different race. But there was no obvious unrest in the place about the way things were. British and Pakistani blended together with apparent ease. Mr Montague was no exception to this, but unlike the other managers was very much the down to earth cockney.

The enjoyment and subsequent horror of last night was largely forgotten, as he found his way around this new and challenging world giving it his full concentration. To his excitement, he was given the keys to what was to him, the monster of all juggernauts, and he drove the 7.5 tonne vehicle along the dual carriageway, with Mr Montague directing him. It was a fifteen-minute journey to a large warehouse where Johnson's stored much of its shoes that were ready for despatch, soon to be loaded on to lorries. He was shown the tricky procedure of unlocking the warehouse, involving an alarm that he would have twenty seconds to turn off 'before all hell breaks loose'. And had some tuition on a forklift truck, essential for the loading of lorries that would come here, Mr Montague explained.

Without knowing it, the man really was the world's greatest at putting people at ease, and putting this most recent of mental hospital resident at ease right now was among his finest achievements. With absolute calmness and humour, he explained all to his inexperienced twenty-four-year-old driver. For someone with so many failed driving tests to his discredit, Jonathan took to the driving of lorry and forklift truck well, and managed to surprise even himself with his abilities. He was to be assisted by Sadiq, 'a young chap from Pakistan', who also drove the lorry and forklift truck. Jonathan had mixed feelings about this. Not the greatest of socializers with the young, as his current accommodation had proved, but at the same time unsure whether he could cope with all this alone; despite Mr Montague's frequent assurances that it was a 'doddle'. The day's work was near its end, and Mr Montague locked up the warehouse. As he did, Jonathan paid close attention to what felt like a big responsibility that would soon be his, and then drove them back to the main factory.

'Oh, there he is now,' Mr Montague observed, as they came round the back of the large, somewhat antiquated building to see a slightly-built young man, dwarfed by the huge, metal, sliding doors of its loading area he was standing in front of.

'You must be Sadiq,' Jonathan greeted tentatively.

The young Asian nodded and smiled. Although of similar age to himself, he seemed a man of few words and similar temperament to his much older fellow countrymen in the packing department. A bonus, as who exactly was meant to be assisting who in this future partnership wasn't made too clear, and therefore, petty, child-like squabbles about who was going to do this or that, including the driving of the potential vehicle of mass destruction, needed avoiding. The young Jonathan was becoming acutely aware of the need to concentrate on what he was doing and not how he was feeling. A relatively new idea, that in this environment especially, needed adjusting to.

Mr Montague, who insisted he was to be called Vic in future, told Jonathan to come and see him first thing tomorrow and they would take things from there. Work at this place had got better and better quite rapidly, he reflected, as he strolled along the shop floor amid the constant din of shoes being made, which led to the car park and the relief of fresh air and sunlight. How long could the upward trend continue? Anything going well in his life had a nasty habit of suddenly changing direction.

He could sense the hostility in the flat from a mile away as he made his way back to it. As was so often the case, a large chunk of the previous evening was a blackout, and how he had arrived at the state he woke up to at about four a.m., and with the door wide open, didn't bear thinking about. And as he came through the front door, bodies started leaping out of armchairs as the delights of the six o'clock news bellowed from the TV. The fear set in, as his enemies were contained herein, and once again, there was more of them than there was of him. In other words, more than one. As forever, he stood alone against the world and its mates.

In the often unfortunate state of sobriety, such as this one, any kind of hostility or the expectation of it, habitually interfered with his breathing. And now was no exception, as he panted his way to the sanctuary of his room. But now, more than ever, it felt that this most engrained of syndrome with in him needed to be fought. And he tried, with some self-psychoanalysis. In order to speak, one also needs to breathe. And speech was considered by many (himself included) to be a necessary requirement for hostility, of the kind he was expecting to begin at any moment. But the combination of impaired breathing and speech did not sit at all comfortably with each other. So, with that in mind, he asked himself: was he required to speak at all? No. Perhaps not. Maybe, therefore, he should forget about speech completely, without even rehearsing any such verbal defence in his mind, and just try to breathe normally and concentrate only on that, in the time it takes for the presumed committee of hate to appear. And then just let them say what they want. Mmm!

Now calmer, Jonathan switches on the kettle in the deserted kitchen. The owner of the flat, and sadly one of its residents, now stands in the doorway, with the predicted look of loathing and revulsion on his face.

'What are you? Look at the state of your room,' he says , pushing open the lockless door to Jonathan's bedroom. 'It stinks of piss!'

With every word the man uttered, he turned to look at the faces of his two other male tenants who stood behind him, and somebody's girlfriend who stood behind them, all nodding their agreement. Why was it that his critics always had a handy team of nodders close by?

On the drive back there, he had considered apologising for what he had done, or might have done that he didn't know about. But no, not now. This had too much in common with his Sheffield schooldays for any apologies. The man spoke with the confidence of someone who knew that any violence would be keenly assisted by his reliable team of nodders. Who, if the truth were told, probably didn't like the owner/resident either, but, keeping up the pretence of the opposite, was more of a survival mechanism in these cramped, claustrophobic conditions in which the enforced company of others was quietly endured.

'Well, aren't you gonna say anything?' His mocking smile was duplicated by his assistants as he turned to them once more.

Jonathan tried to get through the crowd with his cup of tea, knowing he was unlikely to succeed. Still clinging to his self-psychoanalysis while trying to concentrate on the simplicity of his need to breathe in order to live. Something he could usually barely achieve at such moments. When he finally spoke, what he said was practical, honest, and almost void of hatred or any other pointless emotion. And with something like normal breath.

'I'll look for somewhere else.' Slowly approaching the open doorway to his room, with cup of tea miraculously still intact.

'Well, you've got a week to find somewhere else and then you're out!' he heard through the now closed door, to jeers of approval from his cohorts.

Well, that was OK in a way, because although a week in this flat was similar to ten years in the salt mines of Siberia, he couldn't afford to go anywhere until he got his next wages in a week's time. Instead of appealing against his sentence, he took an almighty swig of his tea, for which he was gasping and grateful he still had.

If it wasn't for his now quite responsible job, he would get out of here now, as the overnight accommodation his car could provide was surely preferable to this. But he knew how much he needed this new job to go well, if only for his immediate security. And how possible was that, when you've spent all night jiggling about fully clothed, aimlessly trying to find a comfortable position on the back seat, with the arm rest sticking in your back?

He rose early the next morning, and fortunately, the rest of the flat didn't. He did all the necessary things as quietly as possible to avoid the awkwardness of human contact, in the narrowest of corridors where two such humans couldn't pass each other without one of them giving way. Such was the tension in the place, that violence could have suddenly erupted merely by the accidental touching of shoulders in the confined space. As always, relief on leaving the place to the now joy of the outside world. Cup of tea and bacon and sausage sandwich in canteen was heavenly, despite the passive listening to an unfunny joke which didn't deserve the ridiculous amount of laughter which followed. Such was the usual when the canteen was occupied by others, and it wasn't possible to get the timing exactly right to avoid them.

Mr Montague (now Vic) got Jonathan and Sadiq to load up the lorry with boxes of shoes to take to the warehouse. Jonathan drove, which was OK despite his young passenger, who fortunately didn't speak too much English, so he could concentrate fully on the matter in hand. To drive a vehicle of this size was one thing, to make conversation while doing so, was another. He spent most of the day at the warehouse, some of it alone, as Sadiq had to go back to the main factory and pick up more stuff to bring back to the warehouse, leaving him to grapple with the forklift truck. Surely, he needed a license of some kind to operate this thing and was in breach of safety regulations by operating it alone, he wondered. But the solitude was a blessing as he tried to get used to the machine before lorries arrived. When they did, he apologised frequently, explaining his inexperience to the drivers when he rammed the truck against their trailers too hard when loading them. Things ticked along merrily until the dreaded moment of leaving, or 'going home', as it was often referred to as. He became acutely aware that this place was home, and life would be so much easier if he didn't have to leave at all; as every time he did, the problems seemed to start. But alas, he did his usual walk through the noise and electric light of the shop floor, past long queues of South Asian men with clock cards in hand, out into the open air of the car park.

He scoured newspapers and shop windows for accommodation ads once more. He rang up one, a bedsit that was en route to work but a little closer and arranged a viewing with the landlord for the following early evening after work. The word 'bedsit' had suddenly become attractive, as it implied less sharing, less obligation to socialize. His mind occasionally wandered back to what he now remembered as the *paradise* that was Jan's place. He was depriving himself of a visit there, largely, to avoid hearing about any further visits they may have endured from the police. Right now, he was untraceable, and would rather remain so. But also, fearing that he may be invited to go back there, which was way too tempting and sure to end badly for all sorts of reasons. His 'dependant personality' was the most hazardous kind of super-glue, that had to be controlled. Although her spare room was otherwise 'needed', Jan loved a good chinwag, even if it was constantly interrupted by all manner of chaos with the kids. Her husband on the other hand, was a man of few words. Hence, her need for other adults in the already overcrowded house. So the dependency was, in part, mutual.

Jonathan was pleased with the afternoon's achievements in terms of moving on and felt almost comfortable as he entered the flat where his enemies were preparing food in the kitchen. His comfort stemmed from the fact that there was absolutely no need for speech, as far as he was concerned. He was no good at it and didn't have to indulge in the usual mandatory grappling for the perfectly timed and delivered scathing insult; something that forever eluded him. But could sense that he was about to be spoken to.

'You know you've gotta be out of here by next Monday, don't you?' the owner/resident said. Now not smiling and showing twinges of anxiety. Just confirming what he had said last night, only now with more of an emphasis on effective communication rather than show business.

Jonathan remained silent, squeezing past the man as he made for his bedroom door and went in.

'Hey, I'm talking to you!' came the stern voice through the now closed door.

Jonathan wedged a doorstop against it, in case it was opened. The nearest thing to a lock that was available. He revelled in the fact that his silence was causing irritation. Probably the same amount of irritation caused by the perfect put down, if one could be found. A lesson in there somewhere. He had realised the benefits of silence, perhaps only ever previously realised by monks or other members of spiritual or religious communities. At some point, it may be necessary to speak about his weeks' notice. But not tonight.

He hated this early evening time of day. Too much traffic on the road, people milling about, nonsense being spoken; the news and soaps coming out of tellies at such volume forcing the passive listening of those that would rather avoid it. He played some loud rock music on his portable tape recorder to try and obliterate it, now it seemed unlikely his unpopularity with the neighbours could sink any further.

'We've got a special treat for you today,' said a smiling Vic, as his driver arrived for work. Jonathan made a joke about forgetting his cyanide pill, and his boss laughed. He had a sparkling wit for someone of his youth which flourished in the company of people like Vic, who he knew were not going to laugh at him. The idea of people laughing with you, but not at you, was a strange new one that this young adult was slowly becoming accustomed. But a 'treat' it would turn out to be. Johnsons had bought out a small shoe factory on the other side of London, bordering with Essex. Vic laid out the plan.

'Go there on your own. Get loaded up with machinery and anything else they've got and come back here with it. That'll probably take you all day.'

With Jonathan's severe lack of experience, the full extent of which he had so far managed to keep secret, 'the other side of London' sounded like 'the other side of the world'. And involved much flicking through the A to Z, before, and at just about every red traffic light along the way. But a great opportunity to improve. Another lovely day, and a welcome distraction from the current perils of rented accommodation. How long could this last? It was unreal!

He saw the bedsit. A lot of foot traffic would be going past his door. Not good. But room was OK, with a sink. Window overlooking the bustle of a one-way system, that he imagined himself enjoying sticking his head out of. Was he going to get anything better before the end of the week? Unlikely. He told the landlord he wanted it but didn't have the money for it. That didn't go down too well. But he would have it on Friday when he gets paid. The landlord sort of agreed not to give it to anyone else before then.

'Don't let me down!' he said, in a gruff manner, pointing a finger. Did such people ever say anything in a non-gruff manner? he wondered. Presumably, the words 'I do', at the altar or registry office, were said in similar fashion.

Next day at work, to his delight, same as yesterday's. Only today was easier as he now knew how to get there, with just the occasional glance at the map as a reminder. Just how good was this job going to get? It couldn't last, surely.

He sat, parked up on the one-way system, trying to familiarize himself with it, as it seemed they were about to become neighbours. Thank God for junk food, he thought, as he took a bite from a double-cheeseburger, unaware of the tomato ketchup escaping onto his trousers. It eliminated the need for preparing food in the shared kitchen: a potentially perilous place full of dangerous objects like sharp knives, frying pans and boiling water. Possibly lethal in the wrong hands. And the wrong hands were all over it as usual at that time when he came through the front door. What were the odds, he wondered, that he would be stabbed, scalded or something similar, if he barged into the tiny kitchen right now to make himself a cup of tea amongst the enemies already in there: chopping, frying, boiling, chatting? Yes, perilous places indeed. Best avoided. He waited until they had settled in front of the telly with their meals on trays, trying to talk with mouths full, while being entertained by reports of the latest suicide bombings in the middle east. Only then would he attempt to make tea. They seemed blissfully unaware of his presence as he returned to his room with it and shut the door, doorstop wedged against it. Peace at last.

He was slowly coming to the inescapable conclusion that he could no longer afford to keep the car, despite its usefulness as a source of emergency accommodation. His initial dream of a comfortable middle-age being spent restoring the thing and taking it to classic car shows where it would turn the heads of fellow Cortina admirers, had been scuppered by more urgent matters of survival. The MOT was due, and God knows what needed doing to get it through that. And with all this 'deposit and rent in advance' going on, was Friday's wages going to cover it? But then he would need the car to move his stuff, wouldn't he? Ho Hum! Such were the complications of poverty, desperately trying to cling on to what little you had.

Early next morning, he packed some of his stuff in the car in readiness for his final farewell. But the current uncertainty surrounding the *where* and *when* of it, bothered him. Naturally, he would prefer an early morning departure to avoid the *tears on the doorstep of fellow residents!* As he drove, he noticed a hardware shop, but more importantly, a pristine Triumph Herald and Cortina Mark 2 parked in the small yard next to it. He stopped and got out to investigate further. The cars were secured by a tall iron gate, chained and padlocked. An interesting sight at any time, but especially now, with his vague plans of getting rid of the car. But not just to anyone; to somebody with a keen interest in such relics. Who could possibly be found in the hardware shop? He would have to wait and see, as it was closed. But, after work that day, just about managed to get himself in it before it closed again.

Was the gentleman the owner of those two lovely cars and was he interested in his Mark 3? 'A Mark 3!' the shopkeeper said with a touch of high-pitched interest. But the enthusiasm was short lived as he gave it a thorough examination with a slightly pained expression, especially when kneeling down to inspect its less visible ailments. And with the man's pushing and pulling of various bits of the bodywork, made an anxious

117

Jonathan wonder if they may come off in his hand. Which would signify it was all over.

Although trying not to appear desperate, Jonathan felt it, and wondered whether he should surrender, change tactics, and ask the bloke for a small space in his yard where he can park it and live in it. Such was the ordeal of trying to keep a roof over your head; and right now, it felt more like he was in the process of parting with that, rather than a means of transport. When they got down to business, it was essential that Jonathan bore the man with talk of his situation and the urgent need to get something for it. Without begging. If possible. He asked to use the phone. Permission was granted, as the shopkeeper continued his inspection. He rang the landlord, who, to his relief, still had the room, and confirmed their already arranged meeting there on Friday early evening after work. Jonathan assured him the money would be there, even though the expressions on the face of the shopkeeper made that seem increasingly doubtful.

'See you then,' was the landlord's unenthusiastic ending of the conversation, well used to dealing with poverty-stricken youngsters and their flimsy assurances.

Jonathan complimented the shopkeeper on his obvious talent for restoring old cars, thinking it might help sway him in the right direction.

'Yeah, but there's only so much you can do,' the man pointed out with a frown.

Eventually, a deal was reached and £80 and the car keys changed hands. He didn't bother with any immediate mental arithmetic to determine if it was enough. It was all he was going to get. The troubling issue of moving house; that had already begun with half of his possessions now in the boot, remained.

'Leave it there. I'll come round with it to your flat on Saturday morning and we'll pick up the rest of your gear and take you to your new gaff. That's the best I can do,' the shopkeeper said, with a tired look on his face, as if it was now more of a charity donation than actual business. Jonathan thanked him and left. He had to trust him. What else could he do?

At least he was a bit more confident that the move was approaching the more definite phase. He rang the landlord again from the nearest phone box in an excited fashion and used the word 'definitely' twice in the same sentence. Much to the landlord's annoyance who was having his tea.

Now pedestrianized, he walked home, and on the way stopped for a breather as much of it was up hill. He was relieved at the recent developments. But had that relief somehow made him pause for breath outside The Ship Inn, with its aroma of booze and fags wafting into the street from its open doors? The relief was often his cue to celebrate with a drink, as he stood outside the pub trance-like with contemplation. But with the terror still fresh in his mind of the last time he celebrated something in such a way; which was largely responsible for the complications he was wading through now, he carried on walking. Was this progress?

Back at the flat, the now alone, and increasingly nervous owner/resident, realizing that he needed a response from his victim to the weeks' notice he had given, was a little more polite. Just to try and get some co-operation and quell the anxiety his tenant's silence was causing. He had re-advertised the room and had calls from interested people. But couldn't give any firm assurances to, until the toerag currently occupying it was gone, and the room was back to its former glory.

'Are you going? A week will be up on Monday,' he said, now with a more pitiful look, as if he were asking for a favour. Such was the change, now his cohorts were absent.

But Jonathan just stared at him with a knowing grin. The matter was in hand, but he was not going to elaborate and risk putting the man's mind at ease about it. He would just have to wait and see. Silence had power. What a revelation!

Friday, and he got a bus to work, and afterwards back again as far as the bedsit, where he paid the landlord with his new found £80 plus most of his wages, and left there with the keys to his new abode. Luckily, he spotted the Cortina's new owner just leaving his shop, who luckily didn't scarper upon seeing him, and assured him that he would be outside his flat at ten o'clock as agreed, the following morning. Job done. The Crown Jewels were safely back in the tower, and sleep may now be possible tonight.

Next morning, gentleman shopkeeper and old car enthusiast is on time and waits outside in the Cortina. Jonathan gathers the rest of his stuff, watched closely by owner/resident who has recovered a bit of confidence now his cohorts are close by. All united in their hatred of one thing. Him.

After leaving his key on the window ledge he walks towards the front door carrying the last of his stuff.

'Key.'

Jonathan ignores him and continues towards the car. 'Key!' This time louder.

But silence prevails, and when all is safely gathered in, he instructs the shopkeeper to drive on, despite owner/resident now running towards the car. Off they go. Regret that he never managed to slash the mattress with a Stanley knife as a parting gift, as had been planned before a more concealed, early morning getaway. But maybe it was for the best, as he was already keeping one eye open for any trace of the would- be psychopath, nurse/bouncer, on his travels. Not to mention the police. His enemies seemed to be piling up to an unmanageable level.

After much chat on the journey about their shared loved of old cars, how Jonathan had acquired his and the sad situation of having to part with it, the now more sympathetic shopkeeper assisted him with his stuff at the other end. Awkwardness on the stairs as the not exactly friendly neighbours struggled to pass them as they came in and out laden with suitcases and boxes.

From the pavement outside, he waved goodbye to them both: the shopkeeper and the car. The latter with a sense of mourning, as if the keeping of such a luxurious item could only have ever been a temporary one for someone of his fragile predicament.

Elusive Sanctuary

When at last there was nothing more to unpack, he lay on the single bed propped up by pillows due to the lack of comfy chair. Window open and noise of traffic. He didn't mind it. It was predictable, constant, and impersonal. Unlike the sudden, unexpected slamming of doors, followed by loud conversations that may as well be going on inside his room. Before peace would again be restored, until its next sudden disturbance.

He felt the satisfaction of having accomplished two great missions. Now, living without the pills he had expected to take for the rest of his life; such was his dependency. But, having stuck to the plan rigidly, he was no longer dependent on them, anything, or anyone else. Also, the move away from Sheffield; to what he predicted would be, a place where he could bury the past humiliations of his schooldays. Where there would be no time to think about it. And there wasn't. But the memory still lingered subconsciously, especially in his recent contact with others.

He would avoid the shared kitchen as far as possible. As ever, the combination of strangers and lethal weapons was unsettling. He had a small kettle in his room, a good supply of tea, coffee and pot noodles, a sink to wash and piss in, and numerous places to get a takeaway of some description on the one-way system. What more could a man need? Headphones for his tape recorder, to escape to a blissful world of musical privacy. He had them too. He risked keeping some bread and cheese in the kitchen, wishing he could chain and padlock it to something large and heavy that you would have to take with you if you decided to nick it. He was lonely, missing Mr Ramaj, the Ghanaians, and other former sources of gaiety in what had been the social whirl of Rockerfellaz. But back to work on Monday would surely be a distraction from the melancholy.

The other tenants were all young couples, except one. Tracey, single, about ten years his senior, who drank and smoked heavily, was noisy, and in the room above him. As he made himself a cheese sandwich while making the most of the empty kitchen, she walked in, and they found it quite easy to chat. He was invited to bring his sandwich up to her room, where she put a record on. She was short and fragile in appearance, but aggressive, and any contact with strangers was conducted as though a job interview to determine if this were a suitable friend that meets the necessary requirements: if they came up to her standards of rebelliousness. He detected something in her that was not quite right, a bit odd, which, almost unbeknown to him, was one of *his* requirements. They had similar taste in music, and what luxury to listen to it when you're actually in the room where it is being played, he considered. Hence, without the muffled dirge as it vibrates the walls when you're underneath it. She had taken a bit of a shine to him it seemed, giving the impression of someone who didn't smile without good reason, but was smiling now in his company. She often had 'little gatherings', she explained, in her room after the pub shuts. The evidence of which was all around, in the form of empty cans and bottles littering the already overcrowded, confined space.

'Do you drink?' she asked.

Only a yes would suffice, that was obvious. Umming and arrghing, he felt like he needed a few days to prepare an honest answer but was barely permitted a few seconds before her impatience was apparent.

'Well, either you do or you don't.'

The question raised the most complex of hypotheses. If he said that he didn't, she would surely go off him which might be for the best but wouldn't cure his loneliness. He would then be condemned to endure the noise of her after-hours piss-ups from the solitude of his room. Not good. (Maybe she was just trying to get on the good side of the next victim that had the misfortune of being in the room underneath her, he wondered. Maybe the skeleton of the previous occupier of his room who had dared to complain, was still in a wardrobe somewhere being kept as a souvenir. Such was the hint of menace in the woman's eyes.) But, if he told her he did drink, he would then surely be invited to said piss-ups, which in a way was good, but was it going down a previously well-trodden road to more chaos? More than likely. Like every respectable politician, he did his heroic best to avoid a yes or a no.

'I'm trying to cut down. I've had a bit of trouble with it lately,' was his tentative final answer. A compromise, that he knew would prevent him from being considered an absolute bore. A bore perhaps, but not an absolute one. She smiled. *Oh good*, he thought, as if he had passed some kind of test. But an *Oh dear* quickly followed it. He wasn't quite sure which thought was the most appropriate at this delicate, early stage of their friendship. It felt as though at any moment a buzzer would go off, meaning that the time that he was given to impress her had expired. And then, with the same authority asserted by the likes of Queen Elizabeth I and Margaret Thatcher, he would be dismissed as one of the many who were deemed unworthy of her attention. And, if his assumptions were correct, here was somebody who was only ever impressed by excessive drinking, smoking, shouting, screaming and swearing. He himself was not averse to such pleasures, but now it felt like severe penance would be paid for any such deviation from the straight and narrow.

He felt happy and uncomfortable in her company in equal measure. He felt sure she could, and probably would, become an arch enemy, and his mind wandered into idle thoughts of savagery. Should he kill her now, just to save time, while he had the opportunity of being alone with her? Fearing that when the time came when it was absolutely necessary, he wouldn't. But she was a fellow struggler on the margins of society, and so it could be said they were kindred spirits. Who knows, life may be a lot easier if he *was* dismissed as a bore. But right now, being governed to an extent by loneliness, he didn't really want that. While at the same time, secretly dreaded attending one of her late-night gatherings. He needed privacy with the right woman, not chaos with the wrong one, and as many of her hangers-on as could be crammed into her room at any one time. Oh, the turmoil of indecision!

He became worried that if he didn't leave the room now, he never would. The music played, the lights were low, she started swigging something out of a can and he felt sure he was about to be offered some. He hadn't made a conscious decision to abstain from booze, but the severity of his last indulgence had shocked him into avoiding it for the moment. He made his excuses and left but promised, when awkwardly pressed on the matter, to attend one of her 'gatherings' one night. While feeling like he had just promised to attend the 'stocks' on a medieval village green, to be pelted with the traditional rotting food by one and all.

'Make sure you do,' she said sternly, pointing a finger, with the wickedest of smiles.

He liked her, but very often such opinions of people had proved hazardous. His new neighbour, the female of the couple in the room next door, gave him a disapproving stare as they passed each other on the stairs. Tracey was the enemy it seemed, and he had been spotted leaving her room: clear evidence of fraternization. Internal politics he didn't need after the endurance of the last place. Oh, to be Robinson Crusoe on your own island! But with a helicopter bringing your every need in from the mainland, he thought to himself before falling asleep.

Work continued to be great, and more of a sanctuary with every minute spent at it. Still more stuff to be picked up from the small Essex shoe factory. A lot of it was machinery, and a major operation to load onto the truck. Conveniently time consuming, as Vic had given him all day to do it. And in another stroke of luck, he was the only driver being told to do it. Sadiq wasn't keen, which suited Jonathan down to the ground. Increasing the variety. So much better than looking at the clock in the packing department just for the faintest bit of excitement of finding out how many minutes had passed since you last looked at it! Also, his skills with the forklift truck were gradually improving. This made time for casual chat with drivers about their lives and the perils of the job, instead of their usual swearing and exasperated tapping of wrist watches, after yet another pallet of shoes had ended up on the floor! But the information gathered was priceless to Jonathan, who was veering in that direction with his occupational ambitions.

At the bedsit, life ticked over OK during the week when he had the essential intervals of going to work and spending most of his waking hours there. Essential, not just financially, but spiritually. Work was becoming more like home, and his dependency on it increasing rapidly. No crummy bedsit, or room in shared flat could compete with it. But with no work at all at weekends, it was often a challenge getting through it with sanity intact before returning to work on the Monday.

There was a bus stop across the road from which he could enter another world and do his usual clockwise walk around the centre of London. This would take all day, a large chunk of his otherwise awkward weekend spent avoiding the neighbours. Starting with a cup of tea at Hyde Park, then along Piccadilly to a church where he would kneel in prayer (often in desperation during one crisis or another), with at least some of the reverence instilled in him by his Catholic childhood remaining; despite the mayhem of life since. Homeless men took advantage of its much needed shelter, stretched out and snoring in the pews of the otherwise empty and silent church, and he thanked God that he wasn't one of them. There was often a market in full swing outside the church, full of the charm of ageing, eccentric types selling their antique ornaments and jewellery; and sometimes wearing them, along with the more outlandish of home-made knitwear. A Chinese meal somewhere around Chinatown, in a cheap restaurant where he didn't feel too out of place as a solitary diner. Always keen to avoid the louder, more alcohol-infused kind of places. Chinese chat was more tolerable, he found, as with no idea what was being talked about or laughed at, it was less of an invasion. From there to Trafalgar Square, smartly dressed people queueing outside theatres along the way. Then the relative peace of The Mall: a big wide road with hardly any pedestrians or traffic, probably due to the lack of shops and restaurants. Only usually busy here when royals displayed themselves on the balcony of Buckingham Palace, or long-distance runners in the London marathon finally reached the tape. Large, ancient, government buildings on the right, while towering statue of Queen Victoria gets closer. This tree-lined avenue seemed to feed his passion for history. Imagining the noblemen of the 1700s in their wigs and breeches, coming out of their now blue-plaqued houses overlooking Green Park, for the afternoon ritual of a casual wander. When they would put snuff up their noses, probably sneeze, and then return home where their maids would curtsy and say things like, 'very good, sir'. Here, he could forget who he was and the fragile existence at wherever he was living. For a brief moment it paled into insignificance. St James's Park on the left, for sitting in a deck chair and enjoying the very British spectacle of a brass band playing on sunny days. Along past the railings and high walls of Buckingham Palace to the subway under the Wellington Arch, where pictures of past rebellions, jubilee celebrations and the Great Exhibition adorn the walls, while beggars beg and buskers busk. Back to the tranquillity of now dusk in a deserted Hyde Park, with nothing but the gentle sound of ducks and swans skimming along the surface of the lake. Then, it was time to re-join the struggle of his life. But what an escape! And how he needed it.

In his room one Sunday afternoon, with head sticking out of the open window getting the polluted air and noise, he sees Tracey crossing the road with shopping. That would explain the peace and quiet of the last few hours. But lonely, he felt like he could do with another invitation to her room but did not feel he knew her well enough to simply knock on her door. On hearing the footsteps of others vacating the kitchen and walking past his door, he then subtly positioned himself in it, predicting her imminent arrival laden with bags of shopping that he could help her unpack. And as he did, the possibility of sex was somewhere at the back of his mind that he dare not bring to the front. But sufficient was the lust, that it impaired his judgement in risking such close contact with the deadliest of females, if it were offered. After unpacking the shopping, they went upstairs to her room with mugs in hand. As quietly predicted, their mutual attraction felt like it had to be surrendered to, and they had the clumsiest of sex that involved zips getting stuck and tea being spilt, amongst the general clutter of her room. What had he done? There would surely be dire consequences. The usual. Commitment, or feelings of rejection when there wasn't any. Were they now 'a couple'? The thought of it was terrifying. Her room was bigger than his but with less space, due to the piles of records, magazines, junk mail and ornaments that had fallen off shelves onto the floor, never to be returned to their proper place. She was obviously a hoarder of things, and people, judging by her description of her late-night gatherings – the thought of which he was still dreading. Where would he sit if he attended? Maybe the piles of records were used as makeshift seats. She was strangely silent, which didn't help to alleviate Jonathan's feelings of guilt. Sex was largely a guilt-ridden pastime. And guilt was never too far away from much of his sober thoughts. Maybe his Catholic upbringing had something to do with it. He blamed it for a lot. Anything but himself. Had he taken advantage? Did she think he had? She lit a fag, as if miles away and unaware of his presence. It was like waiting for a firework to go off. But maybe her silence was his cue to leave, he wondered. So he said goodbye and just managed to get another wicked smile from her as he left. Later on, when back in his room, she put a record on in hers. Easier to passive listen to the unidentifiable grind, now that it was coming from the room of a (friend)?

The relentless upward trend at work continued, as Jonathan alternated between the toing and froing from the warehouse, and the removals from the small shoe factory, and the occasional day in the packing department when they were short staffed. Splendid. Being so familiar with these jobs and enjoying the variety of all three. His popularity with Vic was soaring for some strange reason. Mildly unsettling. What goes up had to come down. And always did. The driving of the 7.5 tonner came almost natural to him now; larger than the usual, as most of its time was spent carrying non-heavy items. Shoes. Of which, vast amounts could be carried without overloading it. Well aware that his means of earning a living were limited, as were his talents, he considered whether to push the driving of large vehicles to its limit. Maybe he could drive articulated lorries, he wondered. But his insomnia and anxiety would surely get in the way. Was it a disaster waiting to happen? He wouldn't know until he tried, but trying was a costly business, and therefore, not a disaster about to occur anytime soon.

He had acquired a telly, which kept him busy trying to get a decent signal with the ultimate technological sophistication of a coat hanger secured with blue tack substituting for an aerial. Right next to the window became its permanent home, after much experimentation. And he made sure it had a headphone socket, essential for drowning out the din from the rest of the house. Many a happy evening was spent plugged in, oblivious to what was going on around him.

Late one Saturday night, he was woken by the unavoidable racket of what was surely an army coming up the stairs. But no. It had to be, the dreaded, much-hyped, 'little gathering' about to commence above him. The combination of his near-death experience in the well, his more recent near suffocation in the hospital, and numerous beatings in between, had left his nerves in shreds. Sudden noise and movement was distressing, and he was in the wrong place for avoiding both. He braced himself for a loud thump on his door at any moment as the invading mob passed it. But no. What sounded like stampeding warmongers when you're stone-cold sober, which they obviously weren't, continued past his door and up the next flight of stairs. But then, he heard Tracey's voice shouting to him through the closed door.

'Come on Jonny. We're ready for you!'

There wasn't even time for a feeling of impending doom. It was already here. But nice to be wanted, in a way, he supposed, as he got out of bed and started grappling with his trousers. The music started thumping, increasing his anxiety. What were his options? He didn't want to drink, and there was no chance of any sex up there, so what was the point? But then again, he wouldn't be able to sleep through it down here, so he might as well go up there. He knocked on the door but couldn't be heard, so just entered to a cheer from Tracey, raising her hand with bottle in it. *Don't bother with introductions!* he pleaded internally, as it was impossible to be heard. But introduce she did, and Jonathan attempted a smile to each face in turn. Was this *really* better than being alone, listening to it from downstairs? Or being subjected to all known forms of medieval torture in one evening?

Jonathan found himself being stared at by a young friend of Tracey's with squinting eyes and a puzzled expression on his face as if all was not as it should be. How often had he caused such bewilderment in those trying to make sense of him. Maybe on this occasion, it was his sobriety and demeanour of reluctance at being here that was making him stand out as something different. But whatever it was, he could sense that he was about to be subjected to the most annoying conversation. And one that may possibly start with another: 'What are you doing here?' Something he himself was also wondering.

'Where are you from?'

Another, what to many, was a simple question. To which he couldn't quite give a straight answer. 'Well, Sheffield, really.'

'You don't sound like you're from Sheffield,' the man disputed, looking increasing troubled. 'Did you go up there to uni or something?'

'Umm. Yeah, in a way,' Jonathan replied, hoping it would satisfy the curiosity. 'Sorry I didn't bring any booze with me, Tracey,' he continued, irrelevantly, trying to change the subject and distract the inquisitive stranger off the scent.

The 'wacky backy' was being passed around and the booze flowed. He just about managed to avoid both, with Tracey now too drunk to notice his non-participation. A quick glance at the would-be interrogator slumped on the floor next to Tracey, showed him to be dangerously close to asking his next question. And so, as the music then resumed after its short pause, he shouted his phoney excuses of having to work the next day and a goodnight to whoever was listening. To which Tracey gave him another cheer and raised her bottled hand once more, seemingly satisfied with the duration of his presence. Well, he had shown his face, he thought; like a reluctant parent who'd just escaped from a PTA meeting, as he walked down the stairs. Deep sigh when eventually back in bed, thinking that he *must* get some earplugs at the next opportunity. The whole experience had made him feel very boring, as if on the cusp of middle-age. A time when life ended, and boredom began – so he was led to believe.

That was the one and only time he attended one of her piss-ups. Such was the pretence of enjoyment required that he couldn't quite manage. He wasn't morally offended by surrounding behaviour; it was just that life was now going in a different direction, whether he liked it or not. And he had to go with it. In Sheffield on benefit, he would have loved it. But now, it felt like even the easiest of jobs driving large vehicles was still a responsibility, which the further he advanced with, may end up being an incentive to stay sober. *If* that's what he wanted. Which he was *almost* sure that he did. He had found something besides washing up that he could do to earn a living, and that was nothing short of a miracle. For him, booze and work were on a collision course, and he knew it.

Jonathan was now an ex-friend, a disappointment, who she ignored when they passed on the stairs. His new-found unpopularity was inevitable and had to be surrendered to. Fortunately, she wasn't Tudor royalty, and he wasn't about to be beheaded, but the more she felt rejected, the louder everything got up above; including the thump of whatever was passing for music, knowing that he was underneath it trying to sleep. Not a good situation, but one that he almost predicted after their first meeting. But still fond of her, he wondered why it was not possible for them to have something like a 'normal' relationship (whatever that was). As underneath all the nonsense, the fondness was mutual. But all this to do with her cronies at the pub and after-hours gatherings was a deep complex issue. A more subtle form of hostage taking. And in the cruellest of ironies, the twisted nature of the woman, of which he was currently a victim, was probably what had led him to gravitate towards her in the first place. Him being unable to relate to the more 'together' female, with the more orderly psyche.

One Sunday morning after a sleepless night of tossing and turning when the partying went on above him until dawn, he felt dangerously close to the edge. He went to the kitchen to make a cheese sandwich, and due to the current hostilities and possible strangers still in the building, thought it best to lock his door while he was out. But the kitchen was occupied, and his bread and cheese were missing. All part of the delights of 'shared' living. He asked the door-slamming couple next door; who'd been giving him dirty looks and were now cooking, if they knew anything of the said missing ingredients. But his words ignited what seemed a seething hatred of him. Possibly, he was being mistaken for one of the all-night party goers that had kept the whole house awake, rather than, as he was, its main victim. But for whatever reason, they didn't like him anyway.

'Who d' ya think you're accusing? You fucking piece of shit!' came the *delightful* response.

A scuffle then ensues with the bloke of the couple arming himself with a frying pan, while being eagerly encouraged by his missus at ringside. A collision with a saucepan full of boiling carrots results in Jonathan's trousers being soaked and right leg scalded. When other residents enter, and for reasons unknown, immediately take the couple's side in the matter; thus increasing the antagonism towards him further, he storms out of the house from hell, to cries of, 'Don't come back!'

He got a double-cheeseburger from the usual place on the one-way system and walked with it in the direction of a cemetery nearby, feeling a panic attack about to engulf him. But, as most people in the graveyard were dead, and therefore unable to harass him further, it must surely be possible to dine there in peace, he predicted. Luckily it was, and in the nearest thing to countryside for miles around, he found peace among the twittering of birds and occasional mourner laying flowers. And some comfort, on remembering that he had locked his door, so at least his room and its contents were safe from the enemies there-in. But the comfort was short lived.

On his return, he tries to put the key in the lock, only to discover something solid in it. Like concrete. He rings the landlord who says he's 'off duty', but eventually appears with a step ladder and a look of venom in his eyes. The lock is then examined.

'Super-glue,' he says gruffly, with absolutely certainty, as if it were an occupational hazard he had previously endured. He then looks straight at Jonathan, as if waiting for an explanation. In the conversation that followed, it became obvious that Jonathan's role in all this was to now bear the brunt of the man's frustration at his Sunday afternoon being disturbed. He put up with it for a while, before pointing out the obvious: that it wasn't him who put super-glue in his own lock with all his belongings inside!

While the landlord is in the street outside making casual chat with neighbours, Jonathan hears muffled laughter from different voices, coming from the room of the frying pan-wielding enemy in the kitchen; who had invited his mates along for added protection it seemed, and were trying to control their sniggers at having locked their victim out of his room. Jonathan stands motionless outside the closed door, thinking until it hurts about his next move. Justice would be performed by lobbing a petrol bomb through the window or knocking on the door armed with the sharpest knife he could get hold of from the kitchen, before shoving it in the jugular of whoever opens it. The thought of which, was not only tempting, but almost a sensible course of action under the circumstances. But of course, would screw up the rest of his life. Was that a life worth worrying about? His attempts at creating a decent one for himself were futile, it seemed.

'Are you gonna help me, or what?' landlord shouts from the front door.

Maybe the man's words had saved him, and the jokers in the room, bringing him out of an almost hypnotic craving for revenge.

The landlord explains that he can't get a new lock fitted straight away but has got another empty bedsit a few miles away, and they can take his belongings there once they've got them out of the room. Jonathan, now well and truly sick of the place and its inhabitants, wasn't about to object. The landlord positions the ladder on the pavement and Jonathan climbs it, and then through the open window of his room. In frantic, chaotic fashion, as if so full of emotion it was almost impossible to focus on the practicalities required, he packs his stuff. Bit by bit, he passes it out the window to the landlord, who, between sighs, stares anxiously below at a group of curious children that had assembled, as he descends the ladder laden with suitcases and boxes.

The precarious two-man chain continues until everything is out; minus the telly (for safety reasons, with the miniature audience still below enjoying the spectacle), and in the landlord's car. The man still seething with the comparatively high-class problem of having to abandon the barbecue he was doing for friends and family in his garden. Jonathan tells him of the laughter from the room of the chief suspect, but the man just shakes his head with a frown, having far more important things to think about than the petty squabbles of his tenants. At the new place, the

131

landlord gives him a key and leaves, promising to forward the telly on at a later date. But the lack of one at his new home was the least of Jonathan's worries.

Alone, he could hardly regain control of his breathing. Had he breathed at all in the last few hours? It had felt like a blackout of panic and rage while trying to carry out the landlord's instructions. After a bit of unpacking, realizing that some essentials were missing and his head miles away from the task of replacing them, he threw his bedclothes on the bed and got in it. But there was really no point in attempting sleep. After the day's avalanche of problems, all he could do was mull over the avalanche of questions that remained. Unable to focus for more than a few seconds on each.

How was he going to get to work tomorrow? Where was he exactly? The 'few miles away' as described, was an understatement. What bus should he get and how many of them? Would he be able to get to work? If he did, would he be able to function and drive the lorry? Should he just go back to the house and start a fire that will kill everyone inside and then wouldn't have to think about such things?

After another sleepless night in what felt like a second wave of cold turkey, he didn't attempt the journey to work. But that didn't improve things psychologically. He was off the beaten track of what was familiar. He couldn't get himself up in order to buy food and so didn't eat, and the endless stream of questions piled up once again. He hadn't been to work and hadn't contacted them as he didn't have the phone number. It was written on a piece of paper which he now couldn't find. How could he explain why he hadn't come to work? Would he get the opportunity to explain? Would they sack him? The torture went on. In the chaos of his mind where everything was intensified and exaggerated, it felt like just one day of unexplained absence from work was enough to get him sacked. His job was like a rubber ring to a drowning man lost in the ocean. He was doing so well there. To lose it would be to drown.

Without really knowing why, he then rang the hospital where he had come off the pills, in a hopeless attempt to speak to the nameless doctor there that had been so helpful. But ended up speaking to a different one, who predictably, told him the tablets were not addictive, but as he had made the 'foolish' decision to come off them, his illness had returned. This, the doctor said, proved that he needed them, and he should get some more and start taking them immediately. They had their bullshit of promoting the product and deflecting any blame away from themselves, down to a fine art. But he was at his most vulnerable, in no position to disbelieve what he was being told with the advantage of a rational mind. And it intensified his suffering, plunging him deeper into confusion. The same confusion he was riddled with at the hospital. Not knowing what else to do, the pointless, desperate phone calls continued; the small change accumulated for such now littering the floor of the phone box. This time, to the doctor's surgery to try and speak to Dr Thackeray, only now he was in no fit state to scale the wall of disapproving lady receptionists. After a lengthy and precise account of what had happened to him, one such female with a fondness for administration seemed to delight in informing him, that as he had now moved, he must register at another surgery and was nothing to do with them. This was the final nail in the coffin, and he slumped to the floor in the phone box, head in hands, receiver dangling in mid-air, and sobbed like a baby, oblivious to the impatient queue outside that was clamouring to get in. After all he had achieved in getting rid of it from his body, if somebody was standing next to him now with the poison in hand, he would have taken it. Anything to alleviate the agony. But thankfully, they weren't, and he didn't.

After the world's longest panic attack and some three nights without sleep, Jonathan managed a bit on the fourth. And in a tentative return to normality, the physically wrecked young man made his way to a bus stop the next morning where he asked the queue for directions to whatever bus should be got for the big retail park near the factory. Two buses later and an hour late, he made it to work and spoke to Vic. He couldn't get his words out quick enough to apologise and try and explain his absence. 'I didn't have the phone number. I'm sorry Vic. I'm sorry. I'll take it now!' Fumbling around frantically for a piece of paper and a pen as if life depended on it.

Vic obliged, but seeing the state of him, was now concerned for the safety of both truck and driver, should he allow him to drive it.

In this panic-attack state, honesty was everything, where all had to be

133

explained accurately and precisely in the hope that somehow, all would be well again. Incapable of the usual falsifying of physical illness as used by the masses on such occasions, he rambled on, giving too much information on his chaotic private life, that his boss hadn't a hope of keeping up with. Much like a drug addict of illegal medicine, frantically trying to give out the hard luck story and get sufficient sympathy to get sufficient money for their fix; and get back to normal. But in this instance, Jonathan's fix was Vic's words that it was more removals from the small shoe factory that was required of him today, if he was 'feeling up to it'.

'That's fine. That's fine,' he insisted, feeling his panic easing rapidly with the mere suggestion of doing something normal that he was used to.

'Are you sure? 'Cos we don't want you and the truck ending up in a ditch off the A13 do we now!' said Vic, with the usual down to earth-ness, tinged with humour. Despite that quality being currently stretched to its limits.

'Yes, no problem, Vic. I'm fine. I'm fine. Honestly.'

And now, with his fix of normality obtained and security restored, he *was* fine.

On his way back to the factory, as usual, with more stuff from the smaller one, the panic and confusion was long forgotten despite the severe lack of food and sleep for nearly a week. The relief of being able to function and not being unemployed had transported him back from a nightmare. He now had the weekend off, during which, he could hopefully catch up on sleep. By Sunday evening, thanks to the absence of Tracey or any other weekend hell-raisers above, below, or next door, he had. And was rationally thinking that although his new home was a breath of fresh air compared with the last, it was too far away from Johnson's now he didn't have a car.

At work the next day, the warehouse, full of shoes but gloriously empty of people, had never felt so much like home. Later, when the usual queue of lorries eventually dispersed, he locked the place up and walked to the local shop for supplies for the warehouse and spotted an advert in the window for a bedsit/room of some kind. He rang up straight away, and as it was just down the road, arranged to go round straight away. And so, with an almost unstoppable force of enthusiasm due to its close proximity to work, he did; while temporarily forgetting that he was actually at work. He was greeted at the door by an old lady who led him to her long garden, at the end of which stood a vision of loveliness: a sort of one-roomed, self-contained granny flat, with a single bed in it and its own small bathroom and toilet. And with nothing above, below, or next to it, despite his incurable pessimism, he couldn't help but wonder if a miracle had been graciously bestowed upon him. His imaginings of idle sun-bathing in a deck chair while perfectly secluded between wall of granny flat and fence surrounding the garden, had already begun. The lady appeared to be doddery and confused, so just to be certain, he asked if she was sure that it *was* actually vacant and available at the very reasonable rent she was asking. Almost for confirmation that he was actually conscious and not dreaming. She assured him it was.

Yes, he would take it, and as she told him one week's rent in advance would suffice, he just about had that on him and handed it over eagerly to secure it. He told her he would be back later with his stuff and asked if he could have a key. After aimlessly searching a few drawers, she told him that she never goes out now due to her ill-health, and so would be here when he returns, and they would then look for the key. He agreed and couldn't believe his luck as he ran most of the way back to the warehouse, just in case his absence had been discovered.

How was he going to shift his stuff? No car. Why didn't he think of that?

The warehouse phone rings. Vic tells him that there should be no more lorries this afternoon to load up.

'Just have a tidy up round there will you, mate. It needs it.'

Vic was the last person he wanted to deceive, but he had no choice but to use the truck he had driven round to the warehouse, which had to be back at the main factory, with keys hanging neatly on its hook, before he clocked out at six p.m. It was now or never.

He locks up the warehouse and sets off for the bedsit some six miles away, where his belongings currently sat; most of it still unpacked after the move from the house of horrors. Avoiding the route that takes him past the main factory in case Vic pops out for a fag and spots him whizzing by. Once found in amongst the maze of unfamiliar streets, he parks as close as he can, slightly over zig-zag lines at a pedestrian crossing and a lot over double yellows with hazard lights flashing. Quick look for traffic wardens and in he goes and up the stairs, with similar intensity to that of a bank robber.

135

Parking tickets placing him at the scene could well re-induce the uncertainty over his employment. The trauma of which he had so recently recovered, leaving him in no doubt as to his dependency on his employer. Stirred by this fear-induced adrenalin, all his stuff is out and in the truck in ten minutes. He knocks at the old lady's door.

'Oh, it's you,' she says, as if surprised. 'The chap's already here.'

'Ah,' he responds. He doesn't know what she's on about, but it doesn't sound good. Hopefully, 'the chap' was a figment of her imagination, or possibly himself, that she couldn't quite remember leaving. 'Well, I'm the chap about the room, and I've only just got here.' With a smile, and the faint hope it will make things all right again.

'Well, who's that in there then?' she asks, pointing in the general direction of her garden. 'Oh, this is most confusing!'

He considered his options. Should he start crying, commit suicide or grievous bodily harm? 'But I came earlier and looked at the room, if you remember, and you said you wanted one week's rent in advance and I gave it to you,' he explained, still somehow remaining calm.

'Oh, that was you, was it? Well, there's a chap in there now!' she says, with increasing irritation. 'Oh look, can you come in and sort it out with him? I can't be doing with all this. I'm eighty-six, you know.'

She wasn't the only one who couldn't be doing with it. Jonathan goes to the granny flat which looks even more charming now it was shrouded in mystery as to whether he's actually going to live in it. And sure enough, she was right about one thing: a chap *was* in there. In the latter stages of unpacking his stuff, and looking at him with a knowing grin, as if he had just overheard his conversation with the old lady.

'I came here last week and gave the woman two week's rent in advance, but told her, I couldn't actually move in until today,' the man explains.

'What woman was that?'

'Oh no, not her! A younger woman. I think it's her daughter.'

'And did that woman give you a key by any chance?' Jonathan asks knowingly, with a touch of Sherlock Holmes in his voice.

The man holds up his key and smiles. Suddenly, all is beginning to make horrible sense. He returns to the old lady's lounge, head bowed, not even beginning to think what he's going to do now. She's on the phone.

'Well, there's another chap here now. Yes! I don't know!' she explains to somebody, as if it were a sci-fi movie in which 'chaps' were suddenly multiplying all around her with terrifying rapidity.

Jonathan anxiously waits to talk to her about the £60 he had given her, but then sees a tin on her sideboard where he remembers her putting it. He opens it, it's there, he takes it, doesn't bother to wait for her to end her call, and scarpers, just in case she doesn't remember him giving it to her and calls the police. A wise move. But as he does, coming the other way down the path is another woman who stops and stares at him with concern for the old lady's safety, as he runs past her, leapfrogging over the gate. This type of quick getaway, usually associated with escape from crime, only in this case, complete innocence, and more than likely, catastrophic misunderstanding, was strangely familiar.

Seeing the truck outside brings him back, all too painfully, to the reality that he's at work and all his stuff is in it. He frantically turns it round to escape the woman's suspicious gaze and get it back to the warehouse before anyone notices that he and it are missing. Luckily, it's still locked up and the area deserted as he had left it. He unlocks the warehouse and immediately searches it for a suitable large hiding place. Which takes him up a flight of stairs, where he sees several empty rooms, consisting of nothing more than bare concrete walls and floor, and spiders. He puts all his stuff in one of them, safely out the way, then looks at his watch. Just enough time to lock up and get the truck back to the main factory where the familiar, portly, grey-haired figure of Vic is outside with the big doors half closed.

'I'd nearly given up on you,' he says.

Jonathan examines Vic's face for any rare traces of seriousness. Any signs that he was possibly aware of the shenanigans that had taken place that afternoon. It didn't seem so.

As usual, he reverses the truck inside the building with Vic guiding him in. Keys to truck and warehouse are safely back on their hooks in the office, and he allows himself to breathe again. What a day! Time to go home, he thought. Before realizing that he didn't have one.

He assessed his options. He could go back to the now empty bedsit, which was paid for until the end of the week. At least there was a mattress there. But, after rummaging in his pockets for the key, discovered it was gone. He must have left it there and shut the door behind him. Brilliant! He was officially, and completely, homeless. Once again, he couldn't risk a night in a B&B. Every penny was needed for his next attempt at settling somewhere. And although he now had a far more responsible job, his wages didn't reflect that. And so, the increase from what the agency had paid him for five days in the packing department, was undeservedly minimal. But it was now autumn, and definitely not the weather for camping without a tent. He assessed his options further. Two buses 'home', for the luxury of a mattress, *IF* he could get in the place without a key?

A compromise was reached. After clocking out, he got a few puzzled looks as he walked in the wrong direction: back towards work rather than freedom. But fortunately, an explanation wasn't required; as was so often the case, when words had to accompany the madness. He got his rucksack from his locker, found the remotest of Ladies toilets in the deserted warehouse of the building and settled down in a corner, with rucksack placed on top of his boots as a pillow. Far safer than the Gents, he considered, where there was the slim chance of a stray night-shift worker having to relieve himself, a bit out the way, where a concealed fag break could also be enjoyed. As far as he knew, there was no nightshift at the warehouse in the factory, only on the shop floor, and more importantly, no ladies among its workers. So hopefully, no unexpected visitors.

The constant grind of machinery would go on all night of course, but in general, far more agreeable than listening to one of Tracey's all-night piss-ups. He had a choice of toilets close by and a sink to wash himself in the morning, if no towel, and he guessed that Johnson's were too stingy to employ overnight security guards. At least, not inside the building. Thoughts of himself now living up to the description of someone who 'belonged in a sewer' (as quoted by Alan Marsden) were quickly dismissed. He didn't. This was just unavoidable practicalities en route to better things. But those better things had better come soon.

Despite the bizarre circumstances, Jonathan was OK in his head. Being at work when you shouldn't be, was preferable to not being at work when you should be, and unable to contact work to explain why. Work had become home, and vice-versa. It was official.

He survived the night with only chronic pain in his back and just about everywhere else, and thankfully, hadn't set off any alarms with his presence. And at least he was already *at* work, thus avoiding the journey to it. Every cloud had a silver lining. Yes indeed, that was one less problem, he thought, as he tucked into a large, proper English breakfast in the canteen. The sight of the food in front of him stirring almost delusional cheeriness, as he hadn't got round to eating since the sandwich yesterday lunchtime.

'Haven't you got a home to go to?' the lady canteen worker asks, as she sweeps the floor around him.

The question leaves him momentarily stunned by its accuracy. How did she know that? Did she know that? And it triggered acute self-consciousness. Was he eating his breakfast too fast as if he was starving, like the animal he was becoming? Did he look as though he had no home to go to? Seemingly harmless comments like this could easily set off the panic and confusion and fill his mind with questions. So often, his circumstances were unusual and ridiculous, like this one, and could never be realised by the person making such a comment. Maybe, he considered, she just assumed he was a night-shift worker who didn't seem to be in a hurry to leave. As it was, he was a day-shift worker who had voluntarily spent the night in the Ladies loo, but she wasn't to know that. Somehow, the food, tea, and lack of other customers in the canteen was keeping him calm, and he managed to give the lady a smile which seemed to pass for normal behaviour, and she smiled back.

Luckily, he was over at the warehouse again today, and spent much of it alone while waiting for lorries to appear that were expected but delayed in traffic. After flicking a few spiders off his belongings upstairs, he freshens up with the luxury of his toiletries and a towel which makes him feel a bit more human. He then locks up and walks to the local shop for milk. With tea-making facilities but no fridge at the warehouse, this was a frequent and justifiable journey. Any such absences were a blessing and had to be taken advantage of when necessary. Often providing opportunities for the doing of quick, non-work related essentials. Without realizing it, his crazy domestic situation was gradually turning him into a creature of petty deceit.

During a quick peek through the window of a junk shop a few doors down, he feasts his eyes on a tatty old sun-lounger chair. He enters the shop and as he suspected, the thing unfolds out to the required flatness. He felt the excitement of knowing that this humble object would be supremely useful, without knowing yet how. But just the fact that it may be an alternative to the floor of the Ladies loo, was something to get excited about. He gives the shopkeeper the few quid required and carries it and the milk back to the still deserted warehouse. Kettle on, while he takes his new find upstairs, out the way of prying eyes with the rest of his treasures. And as he does this, he hears the rattle of an approaching diesel engine from outside, a lorry, causing him to put his new purchase aside, and attend to it.

He was getting good at knowing what shoes were what and what goes

139

where in the warehouse, and took the driver's piece of paper and loaded him up accordingly and quickly. The sudden work-related activity felt like a return to sanity, and almost a relief to be doing what he was supposed to, for a change. The kind of luxury normal employees took for granted: that of simply carrying out the requirements of their employment, rather than having to utilize it in order to bolster an otherwise flagging existence.

Lorry departs, and he's back upstairs and unfolds the thing flat, puts his two pillows at one end and lies on it. Wonderful. Tempting to have a nap now while in such comfort. But how was he going to get it into the main factory and into the loo without being noticed? And even if he did, where would he hide it during the day? That option being fraught with complications, turned his thoughts to what was possibly a far better one. The sun-lounger staying right here, in this, his new bedroom in the warehouse. But how was he going to achieve that with the keys having to be back on the hook in Vic's office every night? It wasn't worth thinking about. Was it?

As he drove the 7.5 tonner into Safeway's car park on his way back to the main factory, he was completely unaware that in his increasingly bizarre world, it had become a replacement for the car, essential for his ever-increasing personal requirements. His mission: he had a vague notion that there was a key-cutting kiosk in the supermarket, and if so, he had to find out if they could cut him duplicate keys to the warehouse. There was two keys, one that raised the shutter, and another that turned off the alarm once you were in. Was this wise? No. But right now, what choice did he have? None. Yes, there was a key-cutters, and yes, they could cut new keys, and they did. Was the cocky young key-cutter absolutely sure it was a one hundred per cent accurate duplicate, and it would work?

'Nobody's ever brought one of mine back,' he said, with a proud grin.

Vic waits by the big doors to guide him in and take the necessary keys off him as usual. Jonathan obliges, being careful not to make the mistake of giving him the wrong keys he had just got cut. There was no room for errors. And despite having what he hoped were the keys to his new home in his pocket, this was as ambitious as he was prepared to push things that day. Thus, conceding to another night on the toilet floor. But, with renewed hope of better things to come.

Last night's bit of sleep in the same back-breaking circumstances had obviously been a fluke, as tonight was impossible. As he struggled to get his boots and rucksack in perfect coordination for maximum comfort, he cursed himself for his failure to smuggle in a few pillows. There just wasn't time to think about everything that needed thinking about. But at least his belongings had never been so secure, under lock and key and alarm, he reflected. There was surely other keys to the warehouse dotted about among the hierarchy, he assumed, but was confident that nobody ever went upstairs to the squalid, empty rooms – with the possible exception of pest control operatives. Everything work-related happened on the ground floor. And this was going to have to be his last night on this floor, or he may find himself unable to get up off it without assistance.

Still wide-eyed and horizontal, he anticipated the near-constant flow of caffeine that would be necessary to get him across London to the small Essex factory if he were unfortunate enough to be given anything so demanding to do tomorrow while in his current sleep-starved predicament. Despite the progress being made with his accommodation issues (he hoped!), right now, with nothing else to do but anticipate (or rather trepidate), it felt like he was on a rollercoaster towards insanity. But thankfully, before such feelings could be dwelt upon further to the point of panic attack, the morning approached, and it was time for doing rather than thinking and feeling.

Lucky it was, that the driving was coming easy to him. So easy in fact, that driving was possibly the only thing in life that he could cope with, he considered; as well as the irony of his nine driving tests and his father's supposed wisdom in advising him to forget it after the sixth. His survival in the adult world (with driving license) had been enough of a struggle, but where would he be now had he taken that advice?

The day began with his fears of more removals from the Essex shoe factory being confirmed. But he copes: pouring water from a bottle straight into his face in more desperate moments of fatigue while sitting at red traffic lights, and half and hour's undisturbed kip at the small factory. On the journey back, he could think of nothing else but testing those new keys. But to do so on a non-warehouse day such as this, when he didn't have the luxury of the normal keys as back up in case of any mishaps, was risky. But failure to do so today, Friday, would mean what? A weekend in the toilets *without* the cover of being at work? Trespassing? (as only occasional maintenance work was ever done at weekends.) And the possibility of needing medical attention on Monday? The complications multiplied the more he thought of it. There was nothing for it; he would have to call in at the warehouse and test them; for better or worse.

Late afternoon, the warehouse is locked and deserted, just as he likes

141

it. First bit of good fortune gratefully received. And, as always, it is conveniently situated, as its entrance is invisible from the main road or any other premises close by. With heart thumping, he puts the key in the lock and turns it. Shutter opens. Alarm sounds, as normal. Relief. But now, and even more crucial, was that the second key which turns the alarm off would also work, as he now had twenty seconds to do so – so Vic had warned him. Or 'the old bill will arrive', and he can then add unemployment to his list of problems, and a possible conviction for breaking and entering.

His hands tremble with the tension as the alarm continues blaring, and he makes his way to its box. It's all too much and he wants his mummy. Cocky young key-cutter had better be right. He puts the key in the alarm box. Turns it. Alarm goes off. As normal. Relief, sweating like a bomb disposal trainee on his first day. But the fun wasn't completely over just yet. He looks at his watch. 5.50! Just enough time to lock up and get back to the factory without pausing for breath. He turns the key back, alarm sounds. Twenty seconds to exit and get the shutter down. Turns outside key back. Shutter lowers. As normal, as if he were using the normal keys currently hanging on their hook in Vic's office. And once again, he's got to get back there quick to avoid suspicion. No time to think. No time to park up at Safeway and give cocky young key-cutter a big kiss!

With almost disbelief at his luck so far and the prospect of a blissful night on the sun-lounger, he tries to remain focused on the drive back. He *MUST* remember to only give Vic the keys to the truck, and *NOT* the new keys to the warehouse. After the pandemonium and sleep starvation of the last few days, this would be an easy mistake to make, as it was *always* the usual procedure to hand over the keys to both when coming back from the warehouse. But on this occasion, he had been there illegitimately with his own keys, and was therefore only supposed to have keys to the truck on his person.

'What time d'you call this?' Vic asks.

An anxious glance at Jonathan's watch shows it to be 6.10. Followed by an equally anxious and more prolonged look at Vic's face.

'Sorry, Vic, traffic's diabolical out there. You wouldn't believe it.'

There was the, what-had-become usual tension at the uncertainty surrounding what Vic did or didn't suspect.

'Oh yeah, course, it's Friday night, innit. Almost forgot. It would be.'

To Jonathan, his boss's words with their familiar air of casualness, could not have been more soothing, and with that obstacle safely passed, Vic guides him in as usual. Jonathan hands over the keys to the truck as usual and wishes his boss a nice weekend. Job done. He then walks speedily through the grind of the shop floor, rummaging in his pocket for the key to his locker to get his rucksack. Vic follows, calling him. Jonathan turns, to see his boss in the distance holding something high. At which, in his exhaustion, he concedes defeat, without bothering to think or search himself for the precious new keys to the warehouse. It was surely over.

'Have you lost something?' Vic shouts.

Jonathan exhales in surrender as he slowly walks towards him. The moment he'd been dreading. The game was up. Was it? No. Vic was smiling, it can't be. He'd dropped the key to his locker, while fumbling about with other keys. Fake nonchalance was the last thing he felt capable of, but it had to be attempted; and he rolled his eyes with self-deprecation and smiled as he took the key from Vic. He then walks the rest of the way with hand in his pocket, surrounding the important keys to his new home, just for safe keeping. Would he have a nightmare tonight about being chased by a giant key, or buried alive by a swarm of millions of small ones?

One question remained. Why was he not the proud owner of a priceless diamond or a ton of gold bullion after today's efforts? Now, at last out of the building, he stands perfectly still, savouring the relief and fresh air of the car park, and freedom. Could he really, possibly, now, just have the simple task of the half-hour walk to his new abode, where a tub of Pot Noodles awaited him? Surely not!

An Accidental Nudge in the Right Direction

After the harrowing events surrounding his super-glued lock, he considered it appropriate to seek professional help in his quest for a stable existence without the dreaded psychiatric pills. But also, in a more rational moment of thought, that such 'help' must not consist of the taking of any other medicines, the contacting of a GP, or being admitted to a mental hospital. And so, a compromise was reached in the form of a counsellor who specialized in the withdrawal from addictive substances prescribed by the medical profession: tranquillizers and anti-depressants mainly. What miracles he expected the lady counsellor to perform, he didn't know, but such was the severity of recent panic attacks that a crutch of some kind was needed, without returning to the clutches of the psychiatric establishment.

When he rang her office, he spoke to a receptionist, to whom he explained a bit about his circumstances. But this particular receptionist was unusually intense with her questioning. 'Do you drink alcohol?' she asked.

This felt like one enormous and intrusive red herring, as it was prescribed medication and the withdrawal from it, that was the subject matter. But he attempted an answer nonetheless. 'Well, yes. On and off.'

'And what's the name of the tablets you were taking?'

Jonathan reluctantly gave the names, with an overwhelming feeling of his time being wasted. Now, behaving a bit more like a normal receptionist, she told him that the counsellor was away on holiday, but the message would be given to her on her return. He rang again a short time later, to be told that the elusive counsellor was insisting that he must attend a meeting of a well-known organisation that encourages the sobriety of alcoholics.

'Why?' seemed like the obvious question. As in his mind, he didn't, and had never had, a problem with alcohol. Such was his denial of the obvious, and amnesia of past mayhem.

'I'm just passing on the message, sir,' was the slightly agitated reply.

The constant switching from the downright bizarre to normal receptionist like behaviour, was annoying and unsettling for Jonathan. But strangely familiar, with feelings of deja vu from being made aware of the merits of homosexuality and 'coming out' by a psychiatrist who was not going to take no for an answer.

'Look, can I speak to the counsellor herself?'

'I'm afraid she's in a meeting.'

Aren't they always, he thought. The classic receptionist cliché.

'When?' seemed like the next obvious question.

'When what?'

'When do I have to go to this meeting?'

'Meeting?'

'The meeting she's insisting I gotta go to!'

'Oh yes. Well, now. As soon as possible, because she won't see you until you do. Ring back when you've been to a meeting, and we'll be glad to give you an appointment.'

A bewildered Jonathan hung up. What was this? Trickery? Some kind of devious receptionist ploy? Or just apathy? The most elaborate form of passing the buck he had ever heard!

But later, he considered his position with more seriousness. He still needed professional help, and as the lady counsellor's reputation was deemed exemplary (as advertised on the leaflet with her name on it), he proceeded to find such a meeting; and attended it, with the reluctance of a dental patient about to have several teeth removed. And absolute certainty, that at some point during the evening, he will be asked, 'What are you doing here?' or told, 'You are in the wrong room,' or something of that nature. Thus, bringing back painful memories of further education, basket weaving, and many other instances of being in the wrong place at the wrong time, on possibly, the wrong planet. But, if such torture satisfied the lady counsellor, so be it.

A white-haired, slightly dishevelled looking man of a few years past his sell-by date, instructed him to find a seat. The man wore a trilby hat with feather at the side, polka-dotted bowtie, faded suit with slightly grubby white handkerchief in breast pocket, and unmissable large white trainers on his feet: somehow at odds with the rest of his non-sporty image. And a little unsteady on his feet, although, presumably, sober. The man was

145

clearly eccentric, and that impressed an otherwise sceptical Jonathan, who it felt, had been starved of such people since his departure from the Tea Bar at St Mary's. But also, after listening to all that had been spoken, was staggered by the similarities to his own drinking, thoughts, and feelings. Suddenly, it felt OK not to be OK. There were others in the same predicament. Was there some concealed wisdom in the intentions of the lady counsellor and her messenger? Or just a case of mistaken identity in an administrative cock up?

Oscar, his new eccentric friend and retired journalist, described his drinking career over post-meeting cups of tea in a local cafe. Vastly different to his own, with a lot if it being international, in between the interviewing of film stars and the like, in all-you-can-drink, free-of-charge, 'courtesy binges for the press'. Obviously, someone who had inhabited a very different world to his own, but significantly, as his friend pointed out, they had both ended up in the same one. And in Oscar's case, as he explained, that was after the devastation of being treated as an outcast by his siblings and father, when he suddenly appeared out of the blue for his mother's funeral. After which, he was refused entry to the reception where alcohol was being served, something that hastened his descent into 'madness'. And when Jonathan described his pursuit of oblivion: the frantic consumption of all he possibly could before last orders, the intense feelings of antagonism towards others stirring an almost other-worldly, uninhibited, craving for violence, (among many other drink-fuelled psychological trauma) it prompted continuous nodding with eyes lit up and a knowing smile from his new-found friend. It was a revelation that there were others in the world like himself. Everything seemed to make sense to Oscar, and others, even though they may not have experienced the exact same thing. And everything they said, made sense to him. And to someone for whom being misunderstood had become an accepted regular occurrence, the understanding here was astonishing.

Oscar became a firm friend, and Jonathan was a regular visitor to his humble bedsit; not unlike one's he himself had endured. While on occasions, just managing to stop short of all-out begging for shelter in his more desperate moments. He knew his friend would strongly disapprove of him taking up residence in the warehouse, without realizing the extent of the desperation; and so, didn't tell him.

After a period of regular visits to his friend and mentor, after which, the two men would walk together to the meeting close by, an increasingly frail looking Oscar revealed a diagnosis of cancer. The visits soon transferred to an oncology unit at a hospital, followed by a hospice. In the last of which, there were no words, just the touching of hands. And when Oscar's hand lost any kind of grip, Jonathan left, assuming his beleaguered friend had gone to a better place.

But a huge chunk of Oscar's wisdom managed to get through to the young man. His words of warning about alcoholism progressing even after long periods of abstinence, Jonathan himself had experienced. The shaking and general terror that followed his last celebration, being far more severe than on previous occasions. Something that, at the time, he had put down to his recent withdrawal from the pills.

'We tend to blame everything except the booze,' Oscar had said in response, with another knowing smile. Followed by, 'Make it your last, please,' with no smile, and absolute sincerity and concern in his eyes. A special man.

Jonathan's attendance of meetings became far more irregular after his friend's passing, as the desperate avoidance of homelessness took over his life. But Oscar and his message had found a permanent place in his heart and mind, and a decision was made to never touch the stuff again. Partly, out of self-centred fear for his own well-being, but also, in honour of his dear, departed friend.

He forgot all about the lady counsellor and the appointment he had been promised after attending a meeting. But she had nudged him in the right direction; intentionally or accidentally, he would never know.

Crashing Down

Now safely inside the strangest of home environments, it was peace at last, as he swivelled on the battered and torn office chair eating pot noodles, with a bag of chips from the shop to accompany it. The general dirt and grime of the place was more apparent than ever, as his brain made the transition from it being a place of work to suddenly being home. Time for a clean-up, he figured, without overdoing it and arousing suspicion in the process. There would be complications, which up until now he hadn't given any consideration, having been too busy with the complications that had brought him here in the first place. The lack of heating for one. But it was rent-free, no landlord, and after the recent struggles with neighbours, the sudden lack of them was bliss. Life seemed to be pushing him in a direction where only a solitary existence was tolerable.

With the feeling that it was all too good to be true, he looked around for any technology that couldn't be identified. Motion sensors that set off alarms when they detect movement after working hours, that kind of thing. But at Johnson's, fortunately, everything was done on a budget (although sadly, that included the payment of its employees) and he could find no such mysterious, high-tech security devices. The place was generally left to look after itself by the hierarchy at the factory, with only the occasional visit from Vic. So, as long as there were no unexpected out of working hours visitors, his future, he considered, was safe. All he could do was cling to his suspicions that nobody at Johnson's was keen enough on work to do so.

It was Friday night. No work tomorrow. And for a change, a blessing, as there was much home improvement to be done. Perhaps weekends would become a pleasure in his new home, he wondered. So much in the habit of dreading them, a time when all manner of domestic strife was likely in the confined spaces of his over-populated recent abodes, and often with booze as its catalyst. And no work to escape to. But here he was, in a luxurious amount of space all of his own.

Exhausted, he goes upstairs to get his bedroom organised, unprepared for the lack of electricity. And in almost pitch darkness, fumbles about until at last he's horizontal on the relative comfort of the sun-lounger, with duvet over him, pillows to rest his head, and about ten glorious inches between his arse and the concrete floor! Albeit fully clothed due to the lack of heating. The challenge of the task ahead, suddenly all too obvious. His mind flickered across all kinds of essentials that needed to be bought from shops nearby if this was going to work. And it had to.

Despite the primitive surroundings, there was a feeling of utter contentment as he took refuge in what had become more like home than anywhere else. He felt safe and slept. The silence, lovely as it was, caused him to wake up startled when it was disturbed by the occasional flutter of a pigeon's wings or the scampering of a mouse. No windows, but columns of glass bricks dotted about the building, and wonderful, after a good night's sleep, as the Saturday morning sunshine came through the ones in his bedroom wall. Lying there on the sun-lounger, he felt a peace, stillness and safety of the kind that hadn't been felt since his childhood in Horsham.

After washing himself in the tiniest of sinks downstairs in the loo, he sat in the office writing a long shopping list. But then reminded himself of the lack of transport to shift it, and so, would have to be restricted to what he could carry. With the contentment of knowing that keys, shutters and alarms were behaving as they should, he sets off to the shops on a Saturday morning – much like a normal person with no psychiatric history, who hadn't just moved into his place of work without his employer's knowledge.

He returns, ladened with: pot noodles, toilet rolls, milk, bread, cheese, dustpan and brush, feather duster (for the cobwebs), insect repellent, torch, batteries, battery charger, a book to read, bedside lamp and four electric extension cables. All to be plugged into each other, and hopefully long enough to bring electricity from the only socket in the office, up the stairs and into his bedroom. An electric heater he had seen would have to wait until he's got wheels on Monday. As winter was fast approaching, it would be difficult to limit the usage of such an appliance: his only source of upstairs heat. Would his electric bill be separate from that of the factory? Would there be an increase? If so, would it be noticed? He realised that he may have to treat all this as a temporary arrangement. But also figured, that in the time he had here, he should be able to save a bit of money due to the lack of rent and bills, and eventually, be able to be a bit more selective in his choosing of future accommodation. At least, that was the plan. Assuming he still had a job when his time of living here was up, of course.

Now with the glory that was electricity in the bedroom, bedside lamp sitting neatly on top of a suitcase next to the sun-lounger, life had returned to something like normal.

On the Sunday, he treated himself to an impromptu visit to Jan's place while remembering her words that he was 'welcome to call in and visit anytime'. But, as so much had happened since then, namely the police turning up at her house looking for him, followed by him declaring his true feelings for her, (albeit in a more practical, non-romantic fashion) he realised this may no longer be the case. Both of which he had forgotten about until now, due to more recent traumas. But perhaps all needed to be put to the test, as he was desperate for some company and home comforts the warehouse couldn't provide (mainly a comfy chair!); even if just for the afternoon. Being the creator of his own destiny, he would just have to face the rejection if that 'welcome' had been finally outstayed.

Long walk, but much needed exercise. To his relief and feeling of unworthiness, the forever tolerant and accepting Jan was pleased to see him. And as was usual in their marriage, if she was pleased, so was Steve. The sight of a potential babysitter on their doorstep may have had something to do with it. Jonathan was, of course, happy to oblige, with a conscience now eased by making himself useful. Despite his crazed antics after the 'missing' Cortina, and subsequent departure to a mental hospital, they were trusting people. And a brief pep talk on the dos and don'ts was deemed sufficient to leave him in charge of their five children. He kept them amused as best he could, and when settled in front of their favourite TV programme sucking thumbs and dummies, he risked making the most of a proper bathroom and stripped off for a proper wash. Parents returned with their garden centre supplies, and Jan cooked a lovely roast dinner. Over which, they assured him that no further visits from the police had been endured in his absence, so the matter of his 'assault' on the chef was surely closed. Once again, it would be difficult to leave the domestic bliss of their home. The feeling of tranquillity he had right now was almost dangerous to the incurably dependent.

He avoided the topic of his current housing, feeling sure Steve would suggest some kind of illegitimate transporting of shoes out of the place. Almost hearing him say the words, 'golden opportunity', with eyes lit up. Possibly, with the wrongful assumption that that was Jonathan's reason for being there in the first place, unaware of the ridiculous complications in the life of his ex-lodger. It was enough of a challenge just living in the place without being noticed, without adding to it by nicking its contents. Jonathan's capacity to be misunderstood was vast. Even Oscar and fellow broad-minded ex-drunks would have difficulty getting their heads around his current (sober?) choice of accommodation. Which of course, in the reality that only he knew about, was Hobson's choice[9] in a desperate world.

The walk back to the warehouse now felt shorter and easier after the much-needed company and laughs. Once again, he had been truly humbled by Jan and family, from whom, he seemed forever embroiled in a doomed struggle to establish his independence. It's dark when he returns to the warehouse, and he does the necessaries with keys, shutter and alarm, while thinking to himself: *am I really getting away with this?* Colder nights would be tricky, and this was one of them. Never mind. Must get that heater. Tomorrow.

Work the next day, and he sets off for the walk to the main factory after making sure no evidence is left lying around, with more than a touch of obsessive compulsive disorder about it. Toothbrush and toothpaste removed from toilet, empty food containers disposed of, and most importantly, trail of extension leads unplugged from office and safely stored upstairs. As he walks, puts his warehouse keys (now cautiously on the end of a chain that is attached to his belt loop) safely in back pocket of trousers which he then buttons, in readiness for the possibility of being given the normal keys. The two sets of keys getting mixed up needing to be avoided at all costs. The normal ones having a distinctive logo on the leather key tag, and his, not. Had he just murdered someone in an episode of *Columbo* and was now meticulously covering his tracks? It felt something like it.

The sight of a large green, curtain-sided 7.5 tonne lorry entering the car park of Safeway, and its driver taking up four parking spaces with it,

---

[9] no choice at all.

was becoming a familiar one to shopworkers enjoying an outdoor cigarette break. After getting more provisions from the supermarket, he makes the short walk to the electrical shop where the heater is on special offer.

Queue of lorries at the warehouse! Disgruntled drivers snarling and tapping their watches as he arrives. All he could do was hope that Vic wasn't informed of his absence. Just enough time and room to conceal his purchases in the cab of the truck. He apologises to the waiting drivers now gathered in conference, telling each other they've got to be at such and such by such and such, and conferring on the best way of avoiding the traffic. Jonathan gets on with it as quick as he can. No slouch when there was work to be done. Seated on the forklift truck, he wades his way through the queue without stopping for the next four hours. His ability to cope alone with these mad rushes seemed to have led to the decision by some *wise*, overpaid person at the factory, that the running of the warehouse was a one-man job. The fact that it contravened safety regulations (as who would know if that one man had had an accident while working alone with a fork-lift truck) was never going to compete with the juggling of Johnson's finances. But, alas, a decision that worked in his favour, as his young Asian colleague's absence was more of a blessing than anything else right now, giving him more time to concentrate on the home-making that was currently going on there. So, with today's supplies safely tucked away, he locks up, takes the truck back to the factory, clocks out, and then walks back as usual.

Late one evening at the warehouse, hunger forces him to risk going out. For every exit/entrance, the whole procedure with keys and alarm had to be done, and the enormous shutter raised and lowered on each occasion. This, he would rather avoid, after initially getting himself safely back in there, but tonight, the lure of fish and chips was too strong. There was another small 'fire exit' door permanently padlocked, its key permanently hung up in the office next to the fire alarm. But it was decided that, although tempting as a far less visible means of exit, it was best left alone and seemed bound to cause more complications if opened. But it was a noisy and nerve-wracking experience to raise the shutter out of hours when nobody was supposed to be in there. And impossible to check that the coast was clear before doing so, as there was only one window in the place, that didn't open, and so filthy that only a lorry in daylight could be seen from it. Another good reason for the regular checking of Vic's face for any sign that his suspicions had been aroused.

But raise the shutter he does, and once again, relieved at the sight of the deserted concrete area outside, he sets off for the walk to the chippy. As he returns with dinner in hand, he hears what sounds like the beeping of a car horn at regular intervals. As he continues walking it gets louder, confirming his fears that it must surely be coming from said, usually deserted, concrete area outside the shutter. He stops walking, with the anticipation of what could be the end of both home and job. From behind the seclusion of the side wall of the warehouse, he peers round the corner and sees a car with interior light on and windows steamed up. Difficult to make out anything else, except now, a pair of feet sticking up with the rest of the body invisible. The car shakes and lets out another beep of the horn when obviously, a part of someone's anatomy accidentally comes in contact with it.

He breathes a deep sigh of relief, realizing it is fellow seekers of privacy and solitude, in the form of a courting couple in the advanced stages of courtship. He waits for them to leave, and waits some more, fish and chips now eaten with the unscheduled entertainment. All is quiet, cigarettes being lit in car, but no sign of departure. Now freezing cold, he has no choice but to continue and walk past them towards the shutter, keys in hand, causing a severely startled man to turn round and stare out the window. The relief, that their presence was nothing at all to do with his, as previously feared, was overwhelming. Then, with key poised ready to raise the shutter, he hears conversation from the car.

'Who is it?'

'How should I know?'

'A peeping tom?'

Followed by a shout of 'Oi, perv!', after alarm is turned off and shutter slowly makes its welcome descent to the ground, shutting the world and its ignorance out. Jonathan resisted the urge to shout something equally offensive back, while trying to look as much like a security guard with legitimate reason for being there, as possible. But too risky to keep popping out after dark, he concedes, while making a cup of tea, relieved to still be able to enjoy it in the privacy of his home.

The night was another cold one, and the heater's not working. Shivering, he resists another urge to give it one almighty kick, and instead plots the tricky procedure of tomorrow's return visit to the shop for a replacement, and, getting it up the stairs to safety. He pondered his luck so far, with so much falling conveniently into place and his movements going unnoticed, while wondering how long it could last.

He manages to fit in the necessary visit to the retail park the next day on his way back from the Essex small factory, carrying the large faulty appliance across the car park, to the amusement of the usual outdoor smokers. But there's a bit of a queue in the shop, and no time to get the replacement back to the warehouse where it belongs. Straight back to the main factory he must go, hiding it as best he can behind the passenger seat. Another night of shivering, but a mere triviality, he considered, compared to the recent horrors of more communal living in bedsit and shared flat.

Eventually, he got some heat in the room and made many more improvements to it, including a thorough clean up. He began to take pride in his bedroom, the one place that was his own and wouldn't be seen by others. Things ticked over quite merrily for a while, and he saved a bit of money. Still just about managing to use the truck as a replacement car for all his personal requirements. On one such occasion, after successfully getting a month's dirty washing down to the launderette in the truck, he soon cursed with frustration as a lorry passed by that he recognized going the other way en route to the warehouse. After the quickest three-point turn ever performed in such a vehicle, he returned to the warehouse to load up the offending lorry, with washing left spinning happily. Then whizzing back again to retrieve it, shutter up, shutter down, back to the factory, reverse in with seconds to spare. This kind of pantomime during a day's work was becoming normal, without him realizing it. The truck being whizzed here and whizzed there like a Ferrari, or a beloved Mark 3, as driven in *The Sweeney*. Not what could ever be described as a 'boy racer', just someone juggling with an increasingly complicated life, frantically trying to catch up with it. And one in which, he only ever had the luxury of a vehicle during working hours so all must be done in that time. But despite all this, for a while it seemed like he had got it made in his rent-free existence, and with no evidence of suspicion from anybody.

One late afternoon, in similar fashion, he drives the truck into Safeway's car park as usual for more provisions and hears the most almighty

THUMP! The truck stops dead, and for a few seconds he wonders if he is also, while paralysed with the shock of hitting something invisible so hard. The thump came from somewhere above his head. Eventually, regaining the ability to move, he gets out of the truck and to his horror sees the top of it smashed right in by some kind of bright yellow bar.

Suddenly, the size of the thing, with which he had been popping here and there, doing what many normal folk did in their cars when they're off work, was all too apparent. The craziness of his life was staring him in the face. Still with no idea what this thing was he had hit, or what the hell was going on. But then, reading something above it, numbers, of feet and inches, all becomes horribly clear. It's a height-restriction barrier, and a brand new one at that, or he would have hit it before on one of his many previous visits. It was mainly these visits in a vehicle deemed unsuitable for their car park, that had prompted the decision of Safeway to erect such a devastating obstacle.

The humiliation went right through to his bones, as people come out of shops to see exactly what kind of destruction had taken place to make such a noise. The Safeway workers laughed and applauded on their outdoor smoke break. This was sheer terror of unimaginable proportions to someone who had so meticulously tip-toed around his life in the last month, desperately trying to avoid drawing attention to himself and what he was doing. An intensely private person who never stood up to school bullies for fear of supplying regular playground entertainment to one and all. Here he was, entertaining these scum, giving them an added bonus to their smoke break.

He now had the task of trying to reverse it, with cars now queueing behind him and what looked like two suited, manager-types emerging from the supermarket and walking towards him. As if to inspect the damage incurred by the first victim of their new structure.

Making conversation with strangers on such occasions was not one of his talents, and so, moving speedily, he just about avoids the chat and gets the wreckage back to the factory where Vic is open-mouthed at seeing it bent right back and a big part of its roof seemingly not attached to anything.

The sight of his usually smiling boss throwing his arms up in the air, shaking his head in disbelief as he storms off in the opposite direction, was a gut-wrenching one, reminding him of his dad's reaction to past catastrophes of his youth. He reversed it inside the building as usual, but this time without Vic guiding him. It didn't seem necessary as there wasn't a lot more damage that could be done. But word had spread rapidly, and the spectacle was attracting visitors from all over the factory. By the time Vic returned with one of his superiors, Jonathan had surrendered to his new-found unpopularity and whatever consequences were to follow. He quickly developed a thick skin, throwing the keys to Vic with a -*shove your lorry up your arse*- kind of stare. Comfort was being taken by something that was emerging from the furthest reaches of his mind: the notion that oblivion would once more be pursued tonight in the nearest pub, in suicidal fashion, like never before.

Jonathan had had the good fortune of two of the best bosses in the world, in his short working history to date. And had somehow managed to make enemies of both. First Mr Ramaj, and now Vic. Both had been more like friends. Although he was now the lowest of the low in his current boss's eyes – and if not yet, certainly would be upon the discovery of his residency at the warehouse to accompany his demolition of the truck – he was a good bloke just trying to tackle the obstacle course that was life. But try explaining that to a comfortably off middle-aged man from the suburbs. Poverty was a scary business and didn't he know it, despite himself originating from the ranks of the seriously comfortable, in a long-lost time on a different planet. Wasn't one supposed to start off poor and work one's way up? Typical Jonathan, doing everything back to front, in such a way that was unacceptable to the masses.

He walked out of the place with no thoughts of clocking out, whether or not he would ever walk back in again, or where he was going to sleep tonight. Complete abandon. And after so long of caring too much about everything, only for it to all come crashing down around him, that felt good.

He entered a pub at six o'clock, and proceeded to drink as if life, or in this case death, depended on it. Usually, a dangerous time to commence, giving him a good five hours of consumption, only shortened in the event of an earthquake. But then, it would solve more than a few problems if he didn't wake up tomorrow. Thus, eliminating the concept of danger from the equation. But sadly, wake up he did, in a cell in a police station, in a state of sheer terror like never before. Shaking violently, while trying to hold his trousers up with belt missing.

156

Blood on his hand as it touched his swollen face and big lumps on his head. How they got there and how he got here was a mystery. He had to expect the worst, that during the course of the evening he had killed somebody and his life was over; even though, sadly, it wasn't. Not completely. It could almost be described as a failed suicide attempt.

Suddenly, he remembers Oscar, his words, and his face, as if it were looking down on him with disapproval. How could he have let his dear friend down? What was going on?

After hours of agonizing thought, pointless speculation and uncontrollable shaking, a copper enters with a small amount of breakfast which he declines, feeling as though his intestines had been tied in knots. Luckily, this was a kindlier sort of custody sergeant, who had no better idea of why Jonathan was there than he did, having just started his shift. But assured the prisoner that he would know if it was serious, which did much to calm him.

They had a brief chat, after which the copper remarked, 'You're quite a sensible chap aren't you, really. What are you doing here?'

This prompted some deja vu from the basket weaving department of the madhouse when the same question had caused much turmoil. Another one of those questions that needed a few days to answer, if he knew where to start. But whatever he had done after nine p.m. the previous night, to his relief, he wasn't being prosecuted for. But was warned that he would be if he was ever found in a similar state again.

Off he went, back to the chaos of his life as he had left it, but knowing he had had a lucky escape, and vowing once again, that no matter how bad life gets, this *will be* the last ever drink. Suicide, if necessary, would be attempted sober, with far more certainty of a successful outcome.

A working day, he was now two hours late, if he was still employed. Should he just assume he wasn't? In the street, there was chronic indecision as to what to do or where to go. He couldn't bear the thought of going anywhere near the factory or warehouse, despite the craving for a bar of soap, toothbrush and toothpaste and other such luxuries of his former home.

He could feel himself about to enter an abyss of panic and confusion, when he spots Jan going by in the car, laden with children. A sight for sore eyes. A tonic when one was needed more than ever. He shouted to her, and there were tears in his eyes as she pulled over. He ended up in the park in the sunshine, experiencing the healing that was pushing the children on swings and roundabouts and playing football with them. The sound of their laughter making him forget what he should be doing, if he was anywhere near deciding what that was. Jan of course, noticed his appearance, with it being strikingly similar to that of the hospital patient she and the family had previously visited, but said nothing about it, or anything else to do with his life, choosing to keep to herself the thoughts that her ex-lodger was a deeply troubled soul. Perhaps more so than previously imagined.

His life was now a maze of insecurity and uncertainty, unbearable to even begin to try and make sense of. And impossible it seemed, to make even the simplest of decisions about; just in terms of which direction to wander aimlessly in. And as such, came within an inch of begging Jan to let him come back, after all his previous rational talk about why it was best that he didn't. But the few grains of pride he still had left stopped him. He knew it would put her in a difficult position, and he wasn't sure if he could cope with the rejection of a 'no' right now. And why ruin a light-hearted, blissful afternoon with her and the kids, with such serious talk. But as he waved them goodbye, watching them slowly disappear in the distance, in this, his hour of desperate need, it felt as if he had just parted with his only hope of anything. If only Steve would just die a painless death, or run off with another woman and let him take over, so he could surround himself with the warmth of being looked after by Jan. His luck would never change in that department. He was sure of it.

He got fish and chips from the shop and sat on a bench eating it, feeling like once again his disfigured mouth needed a straw for its intake, and pining for the good old days in the hospital when he had one, and nurses to look after him. Weary, and craving a lie down on the sun-lounger, his tired brain contemplated the ridiculous: going 'home' and doing just that. Thinking that by now the coast would be clear, he made his way there, and attempted the usual entrance with his keys. Nothing. Won't turn. Locks had been changed. After yesterday's destruction and today's unexplained absence, he guessed it had prompted one of Vic's rare visits, and his bedroom and belongings discovered. Maybe he'd left the chain of extension cables plugged in downstairs and its trail followed upstairs or left some other vital bit of evidence lying around, he pondered. But whatever the reason, it was damning and final, and led to a surge of self-pity at the new-found homelessness. Should he have just gone in late this morning, apologised, and begged for mercy? Thus, perhaps, allowing the precarious situation of him living there to continue undiscovered a while longer! In his present condition, it was all too much to get his head around, and anyway, what was the point, it had happened! And until the day arrives when technological wizards discover a way of rewinding not only live TV, but life itself, the past has to be accepted as done and irreversible!

Discovering an abandoned settee close by, he pushed and prodded it as if choosing a three-piece suite in a showroom. It was reasonably dry, and he positioned it in the shelter of a small gap between the warehouse and a neighbouring building and did his best to settle down for the night. Exhausted, and shivering uncontrollably, but better than nothing. Thank God for small mercies and fly tippers!

In his time of fork-lift driving at the warehouse, he had had several chats with drivers from the local haulage firm of Armstrong's, who were frequent visitors.

'I wanna get my HGV one day,' he had said frequently, 'but it costs a fortune, doesn't it?'

'Go and see Jim in the office at our place. He'll sort you out. They've got smaller ones as well. He'll start you off on them and if you do all right, they'll pay for your HGV. Trust me. He's a good bloke is Jim.'

The no-nonsense advice, which suggested he would live happily ever after once he had met the great man, was accompanied by nods of agreement from fellow drivers, who presumably, had also had the pleasure. At the time he had nodded his enthusiasm, but alone in private thought, knew this was way beyond him. And to throw away the security of his job at the shoe factory for such a drastic change? But now, as that security was surely no longer there, and the thought of coming face to face with Vic or anyone else at Johnson's was too unbearable to contemplate, maybe the giant leap forward was the answer, and therefore, in the absence of any other option, had to be attempted.

He shivered his way through another seemingly endless night, while pining for the toilet floor in the main factory with the warmth of its radiator close by. The fact of previous hardships now being thought of as luxuries giving him a disturbing feeling of rapid descent. But, as a bright morning emerged, he smartened himself up (as best a man could who had spent last night outdoors on an abandoned settee and the one before that in a police cell) en route to Armstrong's in a public loo. While grieving the loss of toothbrush, hairbrush, razor and other essential items for such, currently under lock and key and alarm in a warehouse he no longer had access to. But nothing could be done about the battered face without make-up artist or plastic surgeon. Lucky it wasn't a modelling job he was after, he thought, as he looked at himself in the mirror with disgust. 'Jim', who, contrary to the generous description of his faithful driver, almost putting him on a par with Florence Nightingale in terms of rescue of the downtrodden, was a charmless haulage boss of the worst kind. He hadn't smiled since 1972 when a substantial win on the pools afforded him his own business.

'Can you start on Monday?' was one of the few questions a desperate Jim, currently submerged in staff shortage problems, asked him.

Jonathan needn't have worried about his appearance. His potential new boss rarely looking above the paperwork on his desk, with obviously far more important things to do than inspect a future employee. And conveniently, it meant that Jonathan's prepared story of falling down the stairs to explain his facial injuries, hadn't been necessary.

'Yes,' he answered, feeling sure he was now sacked from Johnson's. And so, what other choice was there?

'Right, see you Monday at six then.'

That was the immediate future dealt with. The recent past would surely be more difficult. He had to think about Johnson's, and his belongings, presumably still in the warehouse with its new locks. Preferably, without thinking himself into a frenzy of confusion. It seemed an impossible task. But here goes: the new job had eliminated the need for a visit to Johnson's to find out if he was sacked or not. But Vic was someone he would want to at least try and be straight with, and visit, in order to explain. If there was time for ethics, which almost certainly, there wasn't. The new locks implied they had seen his bedroom, which implied they knew he had been living there. Was that a criminal offence? Would they think it was? Vic seemed the kind of person more likely to avoid the police, rather than inform them of someone else's wrongdoing. But he had superiors, who may be only too keen to have the law, whatever it was, enforced. Especially, after the costly damage to their vehicle. How badly did he need his belongings? If he went to see Vic, face to face, man to man, would he get them back? And if so, how would he transport them, and to where?

The avalanche of complications eventually brought him to a decision to forget Johnson's, Vic, the warehouse, and his possessions which could be replaced in time. Maybe one day he would return to the warehouse triumphantly, in an articulated lorry with 'Armstrong Haulage' written on the side, to be loaded up with shoes, and all would be forgotten. But right now, with only the dirty clothes he stood up in, it would surely help matters if it were possible to go to a launderette, strip off completely, chuck your clothes in a machine, sit there as nature intended while watching them spin, and then get dressed, without hassle from either fellow launderers or the police. His underpants were now, questionable. Ho-Hum!

Jonathan's sudden departure from the Sheffield comprehensive school in degrading circumstances, had somehow set a recurrence in motion for the future. A quick getaway being essential when everything turns to shit. As it had done, so publicly, at Rockerfellaz and now Johnson's. For someone with an inferiority complex and enormous ego constantly running parallel with each other, the humiliation of these failures was felt intensely, with only the prospect of a sudden, permanent, departure as a partial cure.

As it was, Vic had had time to grieve the loss of his wayward, but indispensable worker, who he had been told by his superiors, was definitely *NOT* coming back, should he dare show his face again. But who had run the warehouse single-handedly and professionally; if only he hadn't made the bewildering decision to live in it! A complete mystery to everyone, except Jonathan, who was miles away, mentally, and now physically, from recognizing any such achievements. Once again, he had failed miserably, and an escape was needed, and quick.

Although, in anybody's life, the ability to break free of all things negative could be regarded as an asset, his need to get out quick had become more of an unhealthy, almost disturbing trait like a creature

161

scampering between one unhappy ending and the next. He had had great times at Johnson's when everything else was bad. But as usual, there was no time to dwell on it. The show must go on.

He moved himself into a B&B establishment with money saved from his rent-free days at the warehouse. If his assumptions were correct, years of over-indulgence in mind-altering substances had taken their toll on the ageing landlady. Pale faced and wrinkled, with a chaos of long hair, she didn't seem the type to pay too much attention to *his* scruffiness and unusual lack of belongings. Or much else that was going on around her. As long as he could pay the rent, which, with new job, he assured her confidently, he could. With more than a touch of enforced optimism for the sake of survival.

Day one at Armstrong's: in the morning he helped out in the warehouse and got on well with fellow warehouse workers. But by lunchtime he was itching to get out on the road and wondering would he ever. There was no mention of warehouse work at his 'interview', just the feeblest of promises that they *would* pay for his HGV license, if he 'proved himself', without mention of what that entailed.

After lunch, he put his head round the office door to ask when exactly he would be driving. To his delight, 'in about half an hour' was the reply. And so, off he went in an aged 7.5 tonner in the afternoon. No power steering, almost in a standing position for any awkward manoeuvring and sharp bends. Heavy stuff, mostly multi-packs of bottled water and booze to shops. But not many deliveries and not much mileage, and he finished work with the elation and relief of his dreaded first day being over. And, having pulled off another amazing recovery, without looking at the shaky evidence supporting it too closely. For a brief moment he kidded himself that he had moved on to better things. Once again, a new life, with no time to dwell on the catastrophes of the previous one.

But in the days that followed, it became obvious that slavery actually hadn't yet been abolished, contrary to popular belief, as a pattern of his working day started to develop. Once again, told to assist the warehouse workers from six to ten a.m. During which, he noticed a sharp decrease in his popularity with them. He had been spotted going out in a lorry, meaning that he was obviously not *one of them,* as had been previously thought: a matter of crucial importance to the sensitive youthful workers.

How familiar was that! Not one of us, one of them, or one of anybody! The story of his life.

Ten o' clock, and the warehouse workers, now his enemies it seemed, start loading him up with a ridiculous amount of 'drops'. The usual heavy stuff, lots of it, long distance, loaded in the wrong order, and in such a way as if pre-planned to capsize as soon as it went round a bend. In short, minimum cooperation from everyone around him. Six p.m. or later, he returns to the depot exhausted with about half the drops done. 'Unacceptable' to charmless Jim.

This daily itinerary continued consistently, with him stretching himself to the limit to try and keep it going, as if about to fall into a pit of poisonous snakes if he didn't. As hopeless as a 'Round the World' Yachtsmen, who had lost his sail.

It didn't help matters, that although he now had perfect knowledge of how to get from the shoe factory to the smaller one in Essex, just about everywhere else was a mystery. But all the same, Jim was a bloodsucker of a businessman who wanted a continuous flow of it, if he was going to pay for anybody's HGV license. Whose expectations would have exceeded many an experienced driver's capabilities.

At the end of the second Friday, to his relief and despair in equal measure, he was sacked. He left there with his exhaustion, minimum wage, and charmless Jim's parting words repeating over and over in his head. 'You're no good to us!'

What Now?

With memories of Oscar, and the horrors of his last drink very much in mind, the drowning of further sorrows in local pubs was resisted after his sacking. But also, there was some doubt in his mind as to whether the latest bad news *was* actually bad. His last brief place of work, being of the type that causes many people to pursue unemployment enthusiastically, and therefore, maybe he was better off out of. He had one almighty hangover from an overdose of work. But not just the doing of it. The thinking about it, the trying to live in it, the false promises motivated by greed, the full, mind-bending circus of it. And now, once again, some unashamed 'scrounging off the state' seemed fully justified.

He got up late and had breakfast late that morning at his new abode, 'Pam's Guest House'. It was the cheapest of non-cooked breakfasts, and Pam had left everything out for him and he ate it, as usual, in her absence. And, due to the apparent lack of any other paying guests, alone. He desperately needed a holiday but had the uneasy feeling he was on one right now that he couldn't afford, and dire consequences were to be suffered for any such pleasure.

He scoured the charity shops, chemists, and anywhere he could, to replace his lost belongings, and when the cheapest of clothes were bought, he at last could visit a launderette. Dipping into a large chunk of his minimal savings with the assumption that he could now claim benefit, as he had done so with ease in Sheffield, and had been sacked through no fault of his own.

This was the next thing on his list of urgent things to do.

At the DSS[10], he filled out lots of forms and explained his situation to a young lady who seemed to treat every claimant she saw with equal contempt. She sat behind a large transparent, protective screen; presumably, in case that contempt was returned. He didn't feel the need to change his story or add anything to it for good measure, as he naively thought he had legitimate reasons for being there.

---

[10] Department of Social Security, or 'the social'.

'Why did you leave your job?' she asked, while looking down at the forms he had just filled out.

'I didn't. I was sacked.'

'No, the job before that. This, urgh... Johnson's shoe...'

He gave her the full story, only to then wonder what that had to do with anything; and giving himself an unsettling feeling that he had possibly said too much to the expressionless, bespectacled female on the other side of the screen, who now looked directly at him, and appeared to have listened with interest. But said nothing. As if from nowhere, a strange tension had entered the atmosphere, similar to that that had been experienced by representatives of both super-powers during the cold war.

Up until now, his history of claiming benefit had been like the cogs of a machine, lubricating themselves with their constant movement, enabling more, glorious, free-flowing, uninterrupted rotation. At least, that's how it was in Sheffield, during his years of continuous unemployment. But once those cogs have been left stagnant for a while, try getting them moving again! They don't like it.

The unnerving silence was eventually broken as the officious lady probed further.

'So, you were not actually told you were sacked, you just assumed you had been, at this Johnson's place, is that right?'

A now increasingly unnerved Jonathan felt powerless to do anything other than nod his agreement. What had he got himself mixed up in?

With that seemingly important information gathered, the officious customer assistant returned to more robotic behaviour, delivering the rest of her spiel with lightning speed.

'Your claim will take up to 21 days to be processed. Thankyou. Goodbye. Next!'

The next morning, to his horror, Pam was present at breakfast, looking not unlike the young bedridden girl in the film, 'The Exorcist', just before the green bile torpedoes from her mouth.

'Good Morning. You look well,' he remarked, as he came down the stairs, setting the tone for the pretence that was to follow. Amusing himself with his cynicism, but dreading, what was sure to be awkward conversation.

'No work today?' she asked, as she poured him a cup of tea.

'No, not today.'

On the surface, this could be perceived as a polite enquiry about her guest's well-being. But, as she was never present at breakfast (except for the collection of rent) and now was, there had to be a more sinister motive. She reminded her guest of what it said in her advert in the shop window. *"Employed Only"*. Now, nearly choking on his toast, he told her he had been sacked. He wasn't expecting sympathy and didn't get it.

'Well, you know you can't claim benefit from here, don't you? I took you in, in good faith, as you said you were employed.'

Deep Sigh! The new complications had arrived.

He returned to the DSS and asked the assistant, who possessed a similar level of charm to the previous one, if he could come here to the office and collect his giros over the counter. He explained his recent dismissal and unsympathetic landlady, foreseeing big problems with him actually receiving said cheque, if it were sent to his address. To him, with a brain fully occupied by common sense, this seemed a perfect solution and it would save them the postage, he pointed out. But, as he spoke, it was as if he were asking for a full year's benefit, now, in advance, so he could go on a cruise to the Bahamas. As the male assistant, with a seemingly permanent sarcastic grin that only a plastic surgeon could remove, silently shook his head from side to side.

'Name? National insurance number?'

Like a judge at the old bailey who should have been wearing a black cap for what he was about to say, the assistant tells him that his claim has been rejected, due to him, 'leaving the job of your own accord.'

'I was sacked!'

'No, the job before that. You told one of my colleagues that you left that job of your own accord.'

Oh, dear god! Whoever said 'honesty is the best policy', and where are they now? Face down in a skip, with only rats for company?

Jonathan stuttered and stammered, trying desperately to respond in an appropriate manner, but couldn't find the words to do so.

'Next!'

He remained seated, open-mouthed with the shock, until the next claimant beckoned him with a snarl to vacate the seat. He knew he needed to ask the assistant something, but in the few seconds he had, couldn't

166

think what. Doubtless, he would think of it later when he wasn't here to ask it.

The next obvious place to go seemed like the agency that had originally sent him to Johnson's shoe factory. *Not* that he ever wanted to return *there* but hoped that he was still registered with them and so could by-pass the arduous registration process that involved the filling out of masses of forms, and hopefully, be sent to work elsewhere. He wasn't, and he couldn't. And the place was now inhabited by strangers.

'Well, there's a shoe factory that we often send people to, if you'd be interested in that,' a lady asked, while peering at him over the top of her glasses.

Again, his mouth opened but words didn't follow. Everything felt like a merry-go-round of madness.

'Actually, I've been there before but didn't get on terribly well.'

Was that an understatement, or not, or what? Who knows. How could he begin to put into words what had actually happened there?

'Well, at the moment, I'm afraid that's all there is. But if you give me your phone number, I'll see what...'

He stood motionless, oblivious to the rest of her sentence. Again, his mouth opened and nothing came out. King George VI had the same trouble, didn't he? So, he had something in common with the best of 'em. But said royal, didn't get spoken to like he was sub-normal when he failed to come out with an immediate, intelligible response. He then realised that he had no phone number to give her. The increasingly impatient lady, with several phones ringing simultaneously, repeated her words slowly and clearly in a patronizing fashion as if she were dealing with someone of very low intelligence. After explaining his lack of telephone, he asked if he could just come round to their office when they opened in the morning just in case they could get him in elsewhere.

'OK, you do that,' she replied, grateful that the conversation had at last reached some kind of conclusion.

So, he was now re-registered with them, which was progress of sorts, wasn't it? And, he would return first thing tomorrow, thus giving the impression to charming Landlady that he was employed, maybe, possibly.

Next morning, he endured Pam's presence at breakfast again. Again, it was not rent day, which signified that to her, all was not completely well, and she needed to maintain surveillance on her only paying guest. There was a definite hint of menace about her. Maybe her other guests were now buried under the floorboards, drained of every drop of blood, when unable to pay the rent. Most nauseating of all, was the faked friendly chit-chat, before the inevitable enquiry about his employment status. She seemed edgier than normal. Her hand shook as she poured his tea out, some of it landing in the saucer, as though a waitress on her first day of a new job at Buckingham Palace. He was perfectly capable of pouring his own tea out, but it added to the pretence that she was looking after her guest, who in reality she just wanted to interrogate.

'Any sign of work yet, at all?' she asked, awkwardly.

'Yes, I'm just off there now,' he replied swiftly, getting up from the table. This was at least semi-true, he thought, as he was going somewhere where he may be given work.

'Oh good. Umm...'

She was about to say something else it seemed, but he interjected with a loud and perfectly timed, 'thank you for the breakfast', and 'have a good day', before she had a chance to do so, and out the door he goes. He smiled at the frustration he knew he had caused. Politeness could be a fearsome weapon if used in the right way, it seemed. As well as silence.

At the agency's office was a familiar face that he now didn't want to see. The bloke that had so brilliantly got him back in at the shoe factory in his post-discharge-from-mental-hospital visit. His mind was cast immediately back to that afternoon and how grateful and relieved he was when he left. What had happened?

'Hey, how ya doing? Yeah, Jonathan, that's it. I remember,' the man said, in that young salesman kind of way that suggests that everything's permanently groovy. 'Don't tell me, Johnson's yeah? The shoe place. You need to get back in there, right?' with a point of a finger at his victim, who quaked at the thought of the conversation now horribly necessary.

'Well, no, not exactly. Um...'

'He didn't get on terribly well there, apparently,' the cynical lady colleague interjects, remembering his precise words from yesterday.

Oh god, was this awkward or what! Who needs work when you can get this much aggravation just talking about it!

'Oh, well, no, I did. I got on very well actually. I got a job there actually,' he said awkwardly, saying the word actually too many times.

The two colleagues now look at each other with increasing bewilderment as Jonathan continues his rescue attempt.

'But it didn't end very well. Well, no, actually it did,' disagreeing with himself clumsily. 'Amicably, I would say. Yes, amicably,' congratulating himself on finding a good word; albeit an inappropriate one, just in the nick of time.

Oh, the strain of trying to make anything in his crazy, farcical life, sound reasonable and acceptable to normal people! If only he could just go back to the carefree days of the Tea Bar right now, and listen to Elsie's regular catchphrase:

'I'm eighty-five-years-old, never been kissed, kicked nor trod on.'

Or Eric shouting with pointed finger, 'Now you listen here! I am God, and if you don't give me a cigarette right now, I'm gonna go out of here and lie down in the road in front of the next lorry that comes along!'

Oh, the good old days when landlords were like that. People that you could deal with. On something like the same wave length as yourself.

'Anyway, what can we do for you today, Jonathan?' the agency man asks, with a clap of his hands, feeling an urgent need to get back to the basics of now.

'Well, anything that isn't Johnson's please.'

'Do you have a driving license, Jonathan?'

'Oh, yes, yes!' almost shrieking his response, as if suddenly awakened from a deep amnesia on the subject.

'Fine, fine,' the young man repeated, as if everything was. 'Ever done any commercial driving, at all?'

'Oh yes, definitely!' Jonathan's reply was again enthusiastic, before realizing that it was probably best to avoid the finer details and say no more.

The embarrassment, he considered, would be unbearable, if the agency man ended up on the phone to Vic, offering the services of the young 'driver' sat before him. And so, he felt the need to repeat his request for 'anything that isn't Johnson's', just in case it wasn't heard the first time.

'No problem,' the young man reassured him. Thankfully, not enquiring as to why Jonathan was now so keen to avoid the place. There was only so much delicate weaving in and out of the truth one could stand before collapsing, screaming, or exploding.

169

'I'll see what I can do,' said the young man, with a contented smile as if all was well.

Did such people practice their professional smiles in the mirror before coming to work? he wondered. As well as attending seminars where the hypothesis of the non-existence of 'problem' in favour of 'welcome challenge' was discussed, with other work-related psycho- babble.

The insertion of driving into the equation had given him renewed hope of work, but by twelve o'clock there was nothing. He leaves, walking briskly through the chaos of traffic and the whaling sirens of emergency vehicles, that eventually leads to the peace and harmony of the park: with only the gentle sounds of bird life, creating ripples in the green, moss-covered pond, as they skim along its surface.

The daily ritual of no work continued. The only improvement to anything was that Pam had reverted to her usual absence at breakfast, which he could now enjoy alone. Maybe she was satisfied that all was well with her guest's employment status: a topic so dear to her, which, in reality, couldn't be further from the truth. With the discovery that he was not entitled to unemployment benefit, and his meagre savings dwindling, he had enough for next week's rent, and then that was it. Into the hands of the great unknown, with only the goodwill of a seemingly merciless landlady to be relied upon.

One morning, during Jonathan's solitary breakfast, there's a knock at the door. He ignores it, assuming Pam will emerge at any moment. She doesn't. Another knock, now louder. So he thinks he'd better open it. A long-haired, unshaven man stands there, looking a bit menacing, but then smiles, displaying a gold tooth. There was the sound of an engine running close by, and he was obviously in a hurry.

'Gary! How are ya? Long time, no see. Listen, do us a favour. I gotta run. Give that to ya mum and tell her I'll pick it up next week. All right. Ta da, mate.'

Jonathan, still munching on a mouthful of toast, has no chance to speak or time to do anything other than take an envelope from the man, who then runs away, and he closes the door. He then finishes breakfast, with vague thoughts about Pam having a son, for whom he had just been mistaken, it seemed. But still no sign of her, and with far more important things to think about, he folds it up and puts it in his wallet, thinking he'll give it to her when she appears. He then sets off for 'work'.

Still nothing, and now in increasing desperation, declares that he will do what up until now had been unthinkable and go back to Johnson's – thinking that he may find a concealed corner of the packing department to hide in. If they would have him, if that was all they had. They hadn't.

'Ah, it's all gone a bit dead down there I'm afraid. Sorry.'

He left, and now substituted the peace and harmony of the park with the registering with another agency round the corner. After which, to his dismay, the only work they told him about that they 'might' have, was too far away and the sort of hours where one would need a car. He pined for the days when he had one, that could at least be used for shelter when all else had failed. It felt as if life was now on a countdown to disaster. How was it possible for him to have been doing so well at Johnson's, getting on so well with Vic, to now this, nosedive into the ground?

Next morning at breakfast, no sign of Pam, no awkward questions. Nice. Knock at the door. Still no sign of Pam. He opens it. A different, although equally menacing looking bloke stands there.

'Hello mate, you haven't seen anything of Pam, have ya?'

'No sorry, I haven't. Not since Tuesday, I think it was.'

She was a lady who was in demand, for something. It was becoming all quite mysterious. The man frowns and wanders off slowly, looking confused and deep in thought.

With any luck, these two menacing looking blokes had already disposed of her in a shallow grave on some waste-ground nearby, and were just coming round here with their pretence of looking for her to cover their tracks. *Columbo* would never fall for that. He amused himself with idle thought; a welcome interlude from the intense, serious kind, as he finished breakfast. Pam was up to no good. He was sure of it. On the surface, it was like dealing with a traditional Landlady of deep conservative values, who strongly disapproved of anyone not working and the claiming of benefits. But this was somehow at odds with her unkempt appearance, and looking as she did, like someone who had had much to do with *The Rolling Stones* during their drug-bust period. Now, it felt more like her reasons for not permitting the claiming of benefit from her property were more to do with anonymity. Hers, and the urgent need for it to remain so. All this thought, but he completely forgot about the envelope and its contents in his wallet, now hidden amongst a load of other worthless bits of paper that sadly wasn't money.

His regular, and at times, annoying presence at the agency office, led

171

to the colleagues just giving him a sullen shake of the head while they were on the phone, on seeing him enter to ask about work. There was nothing. Neither here, nor at the other one, whose forms he had so pointlessly filled out. And once again, he took refuge in the park. Would he soon be trying to live in such places permanently? The thought of it was both attractive and terrifying in equal measure. Sadly, he wasn't a duck or a swan.

A few more days of searching local newspapers and other potential sources of immediate employment proceeded. He made an enquiry down at the phone box about delivering leaflets ('cash paid'), but the lady he spoke to couldn't give him a definite yes or no, despite the apparent 'urgent' need for people 'in all areas'; and again, annoyingly, he was asked for his phone number. Could he give Jan and Steve's number again? But when he'd rung them the last few times there was no answer, and they didn't know where he was to give him any messages. It was hopeless.

Ageing hippies, with heads full of peace and love in the sixties, had now moved with the times and become greedy bastards in the eighties. It was official. As, to Jonathan's horror, the beast had returned and was alive and well and present at breakfast, on the morning he was supposed to pay the rent for the week ahead. He didn't have it.

'I'm sorry, but you'll have to go, NOW!' she told him sternly, which was frightening. And even more so now that he was aware of her menacing looking associates, who, presumably, could be called upon to remove him from the premises if necessary. 'And I'll have my key back before you do.' Equally so. And he hands it over.

Conveniently, the only belongings he had managed to replace fitted into a small hold-all bag and he filled it up. Pam kept a watchful eye on the proceedings from her kitchen window, to make sure he had actually left. Jonathan, sensing he was being watched, desperately wanted to do something vengeful, smash something up, shout abuse, anything. But denied himself the instant, if futile, gratification. Partly out of fear of making the situation any worse. But also, in his acutely vulnerable position, his only hope of survival was from the assistance of others. Anybody. Seemingly merciless landladies included. And as such, the burning of bridges with even the most unlikely of future assistant needed avoiding. Such was the desperation.

Where to now? The park had become his favourite place of sanctuary of

172

late. You had to walk through the mayhem of the centre of town to get there, but it was worth it when you did. A good place to gather one's thoughts. But now, he had a ridiculous amount of time to gather them.

While there was still daylight, the park was its usual tranquil refuge, and kept him fairly calm as he sat on his usual bench next to the pond. Once again, with relief at having parted with the latest source of human aggravation. But the future had to be contemplated, and was terrifying. He had approximately £20. What could be done with that? Find a cheap B&B somewhere, for one night, and then starve? Or buy the cheapest of food when you can get it, search the bins, and maybe the starvation process will be slower and more gradual?

As tea-time approached, he left the park and joined a queue outside a fish and chip shop, consisting mainly of happy, smartly dressed young people in groups, about his own age but with very different lives, out and about on a Friday night of leisure. He caught sight of his reflection in a shop window. His under-nourished, 5'7 frame, now in the relatively clean but ill-fitting clothes from the charity shop. Baggy jeans, several sizes too long, having too much contact with puddles. Long hair no longer pony-tailed, as that would suggest some kind of order to his life, of which there was now none. Hold-all bag in hand, thick, padded, hooded jacket draped over one arm, purchased in readiness for the expected outdoor experience ahead. Self-preservation to an extent, but what was the point of that? Clothes would become dirtier, stomach emptier, and dignity would vanish without trace.

Despite the new, second-hand clothes and subsequent visit to the launderette during his all too brief 'holiday', he still looked hopelessly out of place in the queue. And felt it, merely by being the only lone person in the surrounding area, it seemed. He stared at others, to see if they were staring at him. There was the odd glance in his direction in the more stagnant periods of the queue, to relieve the boredom. These would surely get more frequent and prolonged.

Riddled with self-consciousness, he left with a bag of chips. With the pretence of throwing something in the bin outside, he made a quick inspection of it. Nothing edible. Only a short distance from his new home, the park, so he could pop back later if necessary. Planning for the future, which had suddenly got much more immediate. Rubbish bins outside fish and chip shops, that had suddenly become a horrible commodity.

At night, he just kept walking round and round, doing endless laps of the park as it was too cold to be still. After a while, his exhaustion prompted some sleep on a now rain-sodden bench, occasionally woken and startled by a fox or other wild animal. They had it made, he thought, living comfortably in a tranquil place where they belonged.

He had surrendered to his fate, no longer having the energy to fight it. The quicksand of homelessness; the edges of which he had precariously tip-toed around for some time, was sucking him in. Resistance was futile.

Down and Out

The full horror of his situation sunk in immediately as he suddenly awoke on the bench, freezing, wet, and still in darkness. One couldn't expect the middle of November to be kind to the homeless.

Life had been a countdown to disaster of late. This, being the disaster. He'd arrived at it. But now, it felt like he was on a countdown to another one: that of his little money running out completely and having to beg for everything. He considered ringing his parents while he still had the money to do so but squirmed at the thought of updating them on his latest failings that such an emergency appeal would require. Imagining his dad rolling his eyes in a – *here we go again, Jonathan struggling* – kind of gesture. He only really wanted to speak to them when things were going well, when he had something good to report. That wasn't too often in their opinion, so he imagined. Stuff like, freeing himself from an addiction to prescription drugs not really counting as an achievement, and nothing, compared to those of his over-achieving sisters. And besides, he didn't have an address for them to send money, so what could they do in Sheffield except worry?

The indecision was intense. Considering various options in turn, before coming to the inevitable conclusion that they were all pointless for one reason or another. Still horizontal on the bench, but wide awake, unable to decide whether to stand up, sit down or move around.

But eventually, he manages the decision to walk in the direction of what had been more like home than anywhere else since leaving Sheffield: Jan's place. The begging from friends needing to be tried before the begging from strangers actually commenced. The ones he hadn't left on such bad terms with to even consider the possibility, were few. But it was a relief to be upright and walking, with a purpose, however futile it may turn out to be. He checked the bin outside the fish and chip shop, now less inhibited, more thoroughly. It was between five and six o'clock on a Saturday morning and the streets were deserted, apart from the odd group of Friday night revellers staggering home, now lacking the energy to do any real harm. He tucked into breakfast, the remains of someone else's dinner, without self-consciousness and the worry of onlookers. A luxury of sorts, that had saved a few quid. But he needed to do something positive with his remaining cash, something that would rescue him, but just couldn't think what. What else could you do but waste it on food, and then beg for more money to waste on food? To keep yourself alive. For what?

From across the road he gazed at Jan and Steve's house. The absence of both Jan's car and Steve's motorbike was distressingly unusual. He risked a knock on the door despite the early hour. Just to sit in their house while they continued sleeping would be heavenly. No answer. The possible reasons why, were devastating to consider. Had they moved without telling him? But maybe it was a blessing they weren't there. After his surge for independence that had caused him to leave their home, how humiliating would it be to be seen in such a desperate state, craving anything they could give: food, tea, warmth, love.

Running out of ideas, he felt the same confusion and indecision he had suffered at the mental hospital, threatening to possess him completely. When you've actually arrived at the abyss, where do you go from there? Back to the park? Why? Why not?

During a prolonged sit down on a bench en route, he attracted the attention of two, small, early rising boys in the street, kicking a football.

'What are you doing?' the boldest of them asked, as Jonathan sat there, hunched and shivering.

'Sitting down,' he replied.

But his answer was obviously not enough to satisfy the curiosity he had provoked. As the boy stared at him intensely with a blank face and big eyes, lost in thought, as he tried hard to think of his next question. This was no ordinary 'sitting down', and he knew it, and wanted an explanation.

'What are *you* doing?' Jonathan asked, and the boys laughed.

'Playing football, silly!' was the reply, as they ran off down the road with their ball. Now restored to their non-inquisitive state of blissful ignorance, after their brush with one of the tragedies of adulthood.

Jonathan was sorry to see them go, such was his loneliness. Wishing he was their age again and could ask them if he could play football with them. These were children. Easily bewildered. But he was equally proficient at bewildering the adult world.

As he wandered slowly back in the direction of town, the temperature plummeted, black clouds appeared and he raised his hood. But before long, found himself walking against a strong wind with his exposed face taking a battering from hailstones. People ran to the shelter of their cars and he envied them. It was Saturday, a time when happy families went out together. Friends stood together sharing umbrellas. The piercing wind and now rain became unbearable, and he turned his back to it and just stood still. The idea of not rushing, lacking any purpose in life, being in no hurry to get anywhere or do anything was a strange one. Doubtless, an enviable one to some with too much to do, but when one actually arrives at the nothingness, life becomes terrifyingly bland. His jacket was not exactly waterproof, and his soaked jeans stuck to his legs. This turned his thoughts to launderettes, and how he was going to wash his clothes. And if he managed it, it would be a temporary luxury until his money ran out completely and then he couldn't wash his clothes. A lot of his thoughts ended with that most disturbing financial inevitability, which begged the question: what was the point in doing anything?

But he was reminded of a launderette nearby, and of the shelter such places offered at times like this. Could he get away with the comfort of a seat and temporary refuge without spending any money? It looked quite possible, as he walked towards the warming vision of its electric light. It was occupied by two separate people in worlds of their own: one reading a book, the other holding a small transistor radio to his ear with football commentary coming from it, while their washing spun. They paid no attention to him as he sat, relishing the warmth and shelter, looking out the window at water running down the hill, great pools of it forming around blocked drains. There was a tranquillity to the place. He'd been here several times before, too busy with the purpose of washing clothes in the quickest time possible to ever notice it. The warmth was making him very drowsy, as so little sleep was had last night. Now he knew the feeling the homeless men had, sleeping in the pews at the Piccadilly church, while normal folk prayed and lit candles for their loved ones. For the moment, there was a stillness in the air, his mind free of the constant pre-occupation with his situation and how he could get out of it. Such moments needed to be treasured.

The two launderers leave with their washing, leaving him alone, and he sits, killing time, with vast amounts of it to be killed, enjoying the shelter for as long as possible. A sign on the wall reads: 'closing time eight p.m. last wash seven thirty.' There's a long row of dryers as he sits opposite them. All empty, nothing moving. The noise of an unattended washing machine grinds on.

Under the dryers, there's a long, hard plastic panel, as if there to cover or protect something. But it's just propped up, nothing really securing it, only slightly wedged at both ends. He moves closer for further examination. He jiggles with the panel a little and it tips over, now flat on the ground, exposing nothing, except a lot of dust and balls of fluff and a sign that reads: 'this area must be swept regularly'. It obviously wasn't. A fire hazard perhaps, from the heat generated by the machines. But, more importantly, possibly big enough for him to fit himself in. He hears voices and approaching footsteps, and fumbles with the panel to get it back into position. Launderers enter and begin unloading the previously unattended machine, chatting away as they do. Jonathan's self-consciousness forces him out of the place before any barmy new plan for future accommodation can be experimented on.

The rain had now eased off and he wanders back to the park, hardly daring to let what he had just seen lift his spirits. Back at the almost deserted park with just the occasional dog-walker, the now reasonable weather, gentle sounds of the pond, and severe drowsiness, cause him to lay on a bench once more. But he awakens at midnight, some six hours later, disorientated and freezing. Starving hungry, but shouts from the direction of the pubs near the fish and chip shop tell him he must remain where he is. Parks being relatively safe, and of no interest to Saturday night shouters. He hadn't been this cold since his night in the priest's shed in Horsham. But that was for the trivial reason of missing the last train home. Now, he didn't have a home to get the last train back to. The lack of light at the end of this tunnel was suddenly terrifying again. Any thoughts he had had earlier in the day of appreciating things he wouldn't normally, due to the lack of reason to rush, now long forgotten.

When there was much longer intervals between the shouts, screams and laughter, he ventured out to the bin outside the chippy. Just a few chips tonight. The kind that tasted as if they'd just been discovered between the cushions of a settee that's about to be disposed of. Not that he had ever indulged in such culinary delights until now.

His relief, as daylight slowly appeared, was equally matched by his dread of the following night in the park. Was there a better place to spend it? Anywhere else would incur the hazard of the human being, or groups of them, and he didn't fancy being there after-hours entertainment. Best stick to the park with its wildlife, where he was beginning to feel like one of them. But thoughts about the panel in the launderette and the dusty space behind it, were providing a glimmer of hope. The concept of luxury, having taken on a whole new meaning.

Eleven o'clock on a Sunday morning, hunger gets the better of him, and he enters a cafe of the not too expensive but rather pretentious kind. Artificial flowers on the tables, ornate stitching on the napkins, waiting staff in uniform saying 'enjoy your meal' and such like. The sort of place to be avoided in normal circumstances, but now, the desperation for something other than discarded chips was overwhelming. A large place with only a few customers at the far end, he didn't attract too much attention. But the look he got from a waitress, and the vision of himself in a mirror when he used their toilet, made him acutely aware that his general demeanour now had homelessness written all over it. His thoughts turned to tools that may be needed for the delicate operation at the launderette, and a knife and fork was placed in the inside pocket of his jacket. It had to be attempted. Another night outside in sub-zero temperatures was more than he could stand. The meal was disappointing. Not the proper one he'd been craving. And when given the bill, it was clear that most of it was for the artificial flowers and smartly dressed waiters that he could have so easily done without. Parting with the £5 would leave him with around 10. That much closer to the impending disaster of having to beg for everything, unable to do anything until a kind passer-by hands you the money to do it. Even the new, modern public toilets had a 20p entrance fee.

Looking around the place, he notices a waiter who keeps looking at him and then turning away immediately as he looks back at him. How he would love to prove these creeps wrong in their assumptions, pay for the meal and leave a ridiculously large tip in a carefree manner. But alas, an escape had to be attempted, and they appeared to be ready for it. Trying to look casual, he examines the contents of his wallet to keep up the pretence of being about to pay, gets up from his table, and like a hungry tiger picking his moment to chase the pack of wildebeest, legs it out the door.

Despite being almost successfully rugby tackled in the process by the over-attentive waiter with lightning reflexes, Jonathan was a fast runner when circumstances called for it, and they had, frequently. He manages to get away, running through the streets to safety while being chased much of the way by the over-zealous, athletic looking waiter. And just about wriggling free of a wall of chunky pedestrians, determined to stop what they assumed was the escape of a shoplifter or mugger, and not the innocent victim of a sub-standard meal.

He made his way to the launderette, nearly an hour before its scheduled closing time. Still occupied by a few launderers, he anxiously waits for them to leave, and when they do, he only has fifteen minutes to conduct his experiment. He gets the panel off, and gently slides himself and his bag under the dryers. Now the tricky bit, getting the panel back in its proper place while lying down next to it.

After several attempts and contorting the top half of his body in the most excruciating of positions, he manages to wedge the thing in place with the help of the knife. But the other end is sticking out, and with no room to turn himself round, is going to have to do something miraculous with his feet. He shuffles himself down so his feet are close to its end, and bends the fork. Curls himself into a foetal position to put the fork between his feet, and just about manages to pull the thing towards him, hopefully, just enough for its disturbance not to be noticed.

Now drained of his last bit of energy, all he can do is lie there with head resting on his bag and wait for the inevitable visit from whoever locks up the place. Eventually, much later than stated, he hears footsteps and the rattling of keys. Hopefully, a thorough search of the place before locking wouldn't be considered necessary, as human beings were usually big, vertical things that could be found near to where their washing was going round. Nobody would be expecting a horizontal one to be hiding in such cramped conditions under the dryers. But he stopped breathing in case it made a noise, as somebody crouched down next to him and sighed, while pushing the other end of the panel back in. Without suspicion he hoped, as the thing wasn't properly secured in the first place and so probably needed the occasional push back in place. The light is switched off; he breathes again, hears the door slam shut, followed by the sound of it being locked, and Hallelujah! One night in paradise is assured.

With the foot end of the panel still open enough to let some air in, a degree of what was now passing for comfort was achieved. His body now more accustomed to having something solid like a bench or floor beneath it as he slept; or didn't. The now unattainable luxury of a mattress, fast becoming a distant memory. As predicted, once safely installed in his new home with panel concealing him, he would not be considering leaving it for any reason, for fear of the dire struggle to achieve it having to be repeated. And as such, the inevitability of peeing in the night was catered for. Having the good sense to bring a sizeable empty plastic bottle with a wide enough rim for his todger to pass through. Like a modern-day Robinson Crusoe, desperation had a habit of bringing out his ingenuity.

After some thought about tomorrow's potentially tricky procedure of getting out of here unnoticed, his final thought of the day was a positive one. Had a cure for his claustrophobia been found, and only just realised? Not so long ago, such confinement would have resulted in palpitations, and full-scale terror. But, with the now less frequent nightmares of being buried alive, and this temporary coffin being sanctuary from other more severe discomfort outside, it felt like a psychological breakthrough had been achieved. The peace and warmth were wonderful, and he was soon in a deep sleep, letting tomorrow look after itself until it had arrived.

The next morning, he's woken by voices outside his chamber, coins being dropped on the floor, retrieved, and inserted into a machine above him.

'It's getting nippy now, innit. There was a hell of a frost this morning,' said a female voice. 'Well, we're getting into the winter now, aren't we. I must do something with that panel. It keeps coming off,' said a male one.

Not now, *please*, thought Jonathan.

It was official. The owner, or person employed to look after the place, was present. The person to be feared. Now, a touch of claustrophobia returns as any hopes of a quick, unnoticed getaway were dashed. A dryer in motion above him had created some much appreciated warmth, and noise, to drown out any he might be making. But now it stops, and its contents are removed.

'Well, cheerio then, Joe, you take care now.' The lady customer departs.

Silence. More silence. Where's Joe? The door of the place was still open as traffic could faintly be heard from outside. After a while of stomach-churning anticipation, remembering Joe's words about doing repairs to his new home, which will doubtless imprison him in it, Jonathan decides to make a quick getaway. If successful, and panel replaced with no suspicions aroused, maybe the same thing could be attempted tonight. But just as his hand touches the panel to push it out and free himself, he hears footsteps, getting closer and louder, and the dropping of tools on the ground outside not much more than a foot from his face. He exhales in surrender. The game was up, and his morale plummets with the imminent return to the cold and despair of the street outside. In the cracks between the panel and its frame, he can just make out a screwdriver in a hand, and then hears a screw being turned with it.

Jonathan knocks on the panel, not too loud, thinking the shock may kill the man. Which might be a solution to the immediate problem, but one too complex to entertain. Silence. Screwing stops. Then continues. Another knock. This time louder. Unscrewing starts, fast. Panel off.

Joe is thrown backwards by the shock and screwdriver falls to the ground.

'Jesus, what d' you think you're doing? You nearly scared me to death! Get out of there!' The expected pleasantries.

'Sorry,' says Jonathan, noticing a hammer on the ground and the rage and shock of its owner, who may feel the need to defend himself.

'What are you playing at?'

Another of those short, simple (to the asker) questions, that felt like there was no point in even attempting an answer.

'Good question. Is it all right if I come out?'

The two men stare intensely at each other in anticipation of the other's next move, as Joe stands up at sufficient distance to allow his intruder to do the same.

'Sorry, Joe, I nearly froze to death the other night.' Trying to calm the situation and appeal to whatever sympathetic nature the man may have.

Joe is a well-built, bald-headed, bespectacled man in his fifties, local to the area judging by his accent. Sufficiently well-built for Jonathan to be wary of, even without the assorted weaponry with which he was about to fit a metal turn button latch to the frame to hold the panel in place. Sufficient to incarcerate any refugees or mice that happened to be in there.

'I haven't damaged anything,' Jonathan adds to the case for the defence. With the correct assumption that the perils of being a launderette owner were largely vandalism committed in their absence.

Joe stands aside with head bowed as the reason for his overnight guest becomes a little clearer, allowing Jonathan to leave.

'I'm sorry about your umm…' pointing to his all too brief home.

'Are you on drugs?' Jonathan shakes his head. 'Booze?'

'I'm not on anything, mate. Just the struggle to survive, and I'm not winning at the moment.' Jonathan makes his way to the door.

'Do you want a cup of tea or coffee? You look like you could use one.' Jonathan turns round startled, as if hearing things.

'Ah, yeah, tea please. I'd love one. Thank you.'

Joe leaves, leaving Jonathan alone, who sits in disbelief. A cup of tea wasn't one of the expected consequences if his intrusion was discovered. They both sit drinking, and he takes advantage of something hot to surround with his hands before his inevitable return to the abyss. He nervously anticipates further questions.

'How long have you been sleeping in there?'

A rare, nice, easy one to start off with, that could be truthfully answered. 'Oh, just last night, honest.'

'So you're not on drugs, and you're not working, I presume.'

Jonathan shakes his head looking at the floor. 'No. I was. I was sacked, and the social wouldn't give me any money.'

Joe looks puzzled. Not being an expert on the benefit system, he wonders if this was the usual procedure after someone had been sacked.

The conversation gets more in depth as Jonathan savours the tea, wondering where the next one in his life would come from, as they usually cost money, and his was fast disappearing. He says more about his sacking at Armstrong's, where his attempts at flogging himself to death were deemed 'unacceptable'. And his time at Johnson's, ending with the collision with the big yellow bar.

'Oh, that was you, was it?' Joe smiles, seeing the funny side of it, before realizing it was a major contributing factor to the driver now trying to get some warmth underneath his dryers. 'The wife and I live just down the road from there, and we do our shopping at Safeway. I noticed it all bent. You must have hit it with some force.'

Again, he smiles, unable to separate the humour from the life-changing consequences now being suffered.

'Yeah, I lived round there as well and eh...' Jonathan starts to explain, before his sentence fades out upon realizing that too much talk of his recent past was best avoided, and any sympathy so far gained maybe short-lived.

His tea now drunk, Joe gets to his feet, with what seems, a plan.

'I tell you what I'm gonna do, um...' he says, as if fumbling for a name for his visitor. To which the homeless young man assists.

'Jonathan. Jon.' He wasn't about to suggest the man calls him by a name with three syllables in it, after the hassle he'd already caused.

'Right. I'm Joe. Wait here. Finish your tea. I'll be back in a minute.'

Jonathan, in no hurry to return to the hopelessness of the outside world, remains seated. Relieved and grateful for the faintest glimmer of hope, of just being in the company of someone who appeared to want to help. Joe returns looking deep in thought.

'My kid brother Andy is on his way,' he announces, as if the relevance of it were obvious.

But the prospect of added company fills Jonathan with dread. By some kind of miracle, one, ordinary member of the public seemed to be convinced of his worthiness of help. Two, was never going to happen, and may jeopardize the one that had already sprouted.

'He's an estate agent.'

Definitely not. An estate agent in a time of crisis! Where was the connection? Did it need explaining that he wasn't in the market for buying a house right now?

'He won't be long.'

Jonathan wasn't comforted, and Joe didn't elaborate. But there was a sense in the air that a plan was afoot, although he didn't dare raise his hopes of any good coming from it, whatever it was. Doubtless, he had had his one and only night of shelter underneath the dryers.

'I might be able to help you, Jonny,' Joe says, now looking far more intense and serious as if with something else on his mind. 'I can't promise, but we'll do our best.'

Jonathan thanks him sincerely, just for the intention. Still with no idea how an estate agent kid brother could possibly help, and not feeling there was much point in asking. All, or nothing, would be revealed in time; of which he had loads, and the delay in finding out was at least warm.

'I had a son, you see. About the same age as yourself,' Joe explains, looking down at the floor. 'He was on drugs.'

Joe looks up, as if looking for some evidence of shock on the face of his intruder. There was none. Obviously, not something Joe found easy to admit to a stranger, but for some reason felt it necessary to do so. Jonathan nodded silently as he listened, feeling much like a priest hearing a confession.

'He was on a high, or low, it's difficult to tell. He either wanted to fly, or just die.' Tears were just visible in the eyes of the bereaved father.

Jonathan, sensing what was coming, tried to share the grief. 'Oh my god. I'm sorry, Joe. That's dreadful.'

'He threw himself off a multi-storey car park last January.'

Joe covers his face with his hands, and tries, but fails to stop himself crying. Jonathan is stunned by what he hears. It was official. Other people, ordinary, respectable people, who he didn't consider himself one, had worse problems than what he did. He moves closer to Joe in the silent, otherwise empty launderette, and nervously puts a hand on his shoulder, causing the man to flinch as if not what he wants. Jonathan removes the hand.

'I'm so sorry, Joe. That's just horrendous. I don't know what to say.'

'I should have done more for him, you know. I should have done more! And now it's too late!' Joe shouts, with a clenched fist and tortured face, looking straight at Jonathan, abandoning any self-consciousness of his tears. Obviously in agony, dealing with the past as it was, unable to be changed.

Jonathan wanted to disagree with that statement, understanding as he did, the force of addiction. But felt it wasn't his place to do so. He was, after all, a homeless intruder taking advantage of the shelter of the man's launderette.

'I'm sorry, Jonny. I don't why I'm telling you all this,' he says, wiping his eyes.

'No, don't apologize. There's me thinking I've got all the problems in the world. Have you got any other children?'

Joe shakes his head. 'The wife couldn't have any more. Andy'll be here in a minute.'

He gets to his feet, trying to regain whatever dignity he feels he may have lost, before his brother's arrival. Was Andy a messiah with the gift of healing, as well as an estate agent? Because that's what was needed, for both of them it seemed, and quick!

A customer loaded with washing enters and Joe makes more determined efforts to recover from his display of emotion and assists with change and soap powder.

'Andy!'

Joe walks over to the doorway, where a younger, slimmer man in a suit is standing, and shepherds the man back out the door for a private word. The two men now come back in, as a lady in the corner sits, staring at her rotating laundry as though in a trance.

'Jonathan. Or Jonny, yeah. This is my kid bruv, Andy.'

Andy attempts a smile while looking distracted, as if his brother's request had interrupted something rather important, and here he was, standing face to face with the distinctly non-spectacular cause of it.

Jonathan felt awkward and guilty, still without a clue as to the trick the great magician was about to perform. He felt Andy's disapproval of him. Many people had a fixed idea about the homeless, that it was a result of them being somehow up to no good, and therefore should just accept the punishment without disturbing others. At first glance, Andy came across as one of them, but it was to be expected. But in reality, the kid brother completely understood his older sibling's reasons for wanting to help another young man in distress, and it was a time for blind obedience to the bereaved father. It was all part of the grieving process the family was now enduring.

'Thanks, Andy, sorry if you've been put out,' says Jonathan.

For the moment, just grateful for the presence of anyone, who approves or disapproves. Still humbled by Joe's tragic revelation.

'That's OK, mate, we'll do what we can,' says an expressionless Andy.

Joe, at last, explains to Jonathan what will be done with him. 'Andy here, is an estate agent. I told you that, didn't I? Yeah. He often has a few houses that he's dealing with, you know, in the process of selling, type of thing, which are empty. Some have got bits and bobs of furniture still in them.'

In between the words, there's regular glances at Andy for approval at what is being said. Andy nods each time. There was a touch of mania about Joe's determination to help; something Jonathan knew all about. Dealing with his son's death and his own regrets in any way he could, without the need of a nervous breakdown.

'But it'll be a bit of temporary shelter for the moment, and a lot more comfortable than the underneath of my dryers!'

Laughter from the two brothers, which was truly heart-warming to see, even if it was at his expense. There's a look of bewilderment on the face of the eavesdropping lady customer, still supervising her washing.

'So you two run along, and Jonny, feel free to pop in for a chat and a cuppa. I'm usually around, but I've got two other launderettes that I have to keep an eye on. You know how it is. But I'd like to know how you're getting on. I'm sure you'll get yourself sorted out.'

'I will, Joe,' Jonathan says, almost overcome with gratitude, looking the man straight in the eye as he shakes his hand. 'I can't thank you enough. And you too, Andy.'

The two men leave.

'Oh, don't forget your drink. Oh, and your fork!' Joe shouts out, and Jonathan returns for his bottle of piss and bent fork.

Not exactly worth returning for, and strangely enough, never given away as prizes on any popular TV game show. But an apology needed to be made for littering the place and was. 'I'll be lost without me fork,' he says, holding the thing up, to the brother's further amusement. Anything to distract attention from the potentially horrific embarrassment of his 'drink'.

With the two useless items now safely out of the way in Jonathan's hold-all bag, he and Andy leave Joe to his work and get in the car. Jonathan says nothing of the conversation with Joe about his son but talks to Andy with the same courtesy that befits a grieving uncle. Still overwhelmed by the tragedy of it all, and humbled by the help he was receiving. Andy drives, making small talk about the recent cold snap that his passenger was all too aware of. The weather, now a matter of great importance. Something to be dreaded and feared, no longer a mere topic of idle chat. At least, not for him. But unsettlingly, there's no word of their destination.

He'd never thought of estate agents as being among his favourite people; not that he'd met many, but now, as he relished the warmth and comfort of the man's car, felt guilty for such assumptions. Another lesson in humility, and the day was only half done. This one being, that when your life is in danger, you're not too fussed about who saves it.

'Thanks again, Andy.' Jonathan breaks the silence. 'I can't tell you—'

'Don't worry about it. I owe him a few favours anyway, and I know what he's been through recently. You've had some bad luck yourself lately, so I gather.'

'Well, yes, in a way,' Jonathan replies, without elaborating. Temporarily separated from the insane desperation for money that had been his life for as long as he could remember.

'I'm taking you to a house in Isleworth that's in the process of being sold. I'll explain when we get there.'

The relief of getting some confirmation that this was real, not a dream; and he wasn't about to be taken to some waste ground and chucked in a disused well or ordered to dig his own grave at gun-point, was gratefully received. Such was the feeling of acute vulnerability. At the mercy of everyone. And anything was possible in this crazy world, it seemed.

After turning into a gravel driveway with statues of what looked like Greek gods and goddesses dotted about along its path, they enter a large, luxurious, detached house. Jonathan was speechless, open-mouthed, in awe of the place.

'Now the rules, Jonathan,' Andy says, smiling.

Warming to him a little after the laughs provided and the constant gratitude for the help. But still preferring the more formal 'Jonathan', as if some formality needed to be maintained due to the delicateness of the situation they were about to enter.

'You've got to be out of here during the day, in the week, as potential buyers will be coming to look around, and keep your stuff well-hidden so it doesn't look like anyone's living here. Now, of course, it's Monday, but as I'm certain no one will be coming round today, I think we can safely let you settle in and have a rest. But from tomorrow, out between nine and five. OK?' The thought of 'settling in' and 'having a rest' in such surroundings, was just too blissful a notion for his battered psyche to grasp right now.

'The phone works, but whatever you do, don't start ringing your relatives in Australia.' Another smile, and it was clear to Jonathan he had gained the man's trust. A vital cog in this machine.

'Now, I may have to ring you at other times as well, evenings and weekends. If I'm coming round with someone or one of my colleagues is, for you to get out for, no more than an hour I would say. But just be careful and remember if there's a car in the driveway, keep well away.

Also, when it's sold, you'll have to go, obviously. I've got no idea when; it could be next week or next month, and I won't be able to give you much notice. Sorry, mate, that's the best I can do. Just lie low and try not to look too conspicuous,' he says, with a hint of a smile, as if a comment on Jonathan's appearance already bordering on it. But for a man who spent most of his life in a suit, as he was now, his homeless acquaintance was never going to fit tidily alongside him.

'And don't have any wild parties or anything like that!' Andy jokes, easing the tension. The unshaven, weary and dishevelled looking Jonathan rolls his eyes with a smile at the suggestion of anything so outlandishly pleasurable.

They chuckle as Andy gives him the key. He agrees to everything and thanks Andy again, overwhelmed by how much he'd been helped by no more than a stranger, and his brother.

'You two have probably saved my life,' he tells him, but knowing deep down that his problems were far from over. Work had to be got, in bulk, and quick!

When finally left alone in the place, Jonathan could hardly take in what had happened. The transition from such squalor, to this, leaving him mesmerised and slightly less cautious of the impending financial doom. So much so, that he risked spending a few quid on supplies from a local shop. One of which was bubble bath, and he had the most enjoyable bath anyone had ever had without the presence of naked females. Still in awe of the luxury that surrounded him, examining the bathroom floor and the few steps leading up to the sunken bath, which he was certain were marble. The telephone may help in his quest for work. He didn't dare use it, but the number was written on it, and so, at last, he could be contacted.

His weekdays were spent frantically registering with agencies, who said they might have this, might have that, and took his number. And applied for a few permanent jobs, but predicted that even if he was successful, he may well be long gone from here by the time any decision was made; cast adrift again, and uncontactable. He stuck to the rules rigidly about being out all day every day, and managed to get himself picked up from the house twice that week at the crack of dawn by a bemused lady in a van, unused to picking up her leaflet-deliverers from million-pound properties with gravel driveways. The work was tedious and relentless, and he needed seven days of it to sort himself out, and would have done them with wild enthusiasm, but had to accept and be grateful for the two he was given. A certain amount of the junk had to be delivered in one day for one to be considered worthy of another hellish day of it. And that meant running at times up very long driveways, resulting in some close encounters with unwelcoming dogs. The leaflet, with its promise of a free pizza after you'd eaten about fifteen, often ending up in the dog's mouth before he scarpered. It was cash at the end of the day, but not too much of it; affording him a few takeaways, supplies from the shop, bus fares and coinage for a launderette. Clean clothes at last! But no little hiding places in which to set up home when his time at the palace was over.

He got himself a day's fork-lift driving in a warehouse and a promise there would be more of it, from another agency that specialized in promises. But he knew he needed a lot more than this for the next lot of rent in advance at wherever, if he was to avoid being back to square one at the end of his brush with luxury. He hadn't so far had to ring Mum and Dad and beg for help while reporting his latest failures, and wanted to keep it that way.

After a heavy day's leafleting and nursing a few blisters in the evening, he sets his alarm as usual to get himself up and out of there before nine, as per his instructions. But after an erratic night's sleep with numerous visits to the loo, he suddenly wakes at ten to the sound of a car coming up the driveway. Followed by a key being put in the front door lock and conversation between several people. To which, he leaps out of bed as if it were on fire, and frantically gathers his stuff. He makes a feeble attempt to make the bed, before shoving all his stuff and himself under it, just as the 'potential buyers' plus estate agent come up the stairs. He really didn't want to let the brothers down after all their kindness and could only hope this wasn't kid brother with clients about to come through the door. But was certain there was no trace of his presence anywhere else in the house.

'Well, as you can see, it's quite spacious despite being the smallest of the bedrooms.' It wasn't Andy. Relief. 'And, with a handy small sink in the corner there.'

That you can piss in if you can't be arsed to go to the loo for the umpteenth time!

Jonathan finishes the well-spoken male estate agent's sentence in the privacy of his mind, as he hears the sound of the running of taps.

'Oh, and, I almost forgot, a lovely view of the garden.'

'Isn't it just?'

'Yes.'

From beneath the bed, he could see feet, frighteningly close to his nose.

'Oh, what's this?'

Female client notices something on the floor and bends down to pick it up. Jonathan cringes, assuming it's something of his.

'Oh, a sock.'

Ah, for god's sake don't smell it.

'Oohwwhh!'

Too late.

'Oh, I'm terribly sorry! I don't know how that got there. Very strange.'

'That should definitely knock a few grand off the price, don't you think darling?' Much laughter between the clients.

'Well, shall we move on to the bathroom?' the now embarrassed and unamused estate agent suggests.

Yes, close contact with his socks did tend to make people want to move on to the bathroom; usually with a sense of urgency, especially after a long day's leafleting had been done in them, he thinks. Managing to see the funny side of it all, despite it demonstrating the fragility of the shelter he was currently enjoying; and of life itself. Deep sigh of relief now they had left the room, and even more so when he heard the front door slam, car leave, and then silence. He cursed the alarm clock whose battery had run out. Luckily, not a leaflet delivery day, so he hadn't missed the lady chauffeur and jeopardised any future work.

How should he spend the day? Registering with new agencies? Hassling the ones with whom he already was? Applying for more jobs? Looking for ridiculously cheap accommodation where deposit and rent in advance weren't required? Was any of it achieving anything?

With an increasing sense of hopelessness and frustration, he walked round the place aimlessly from room to room. Trying to make sense of why he hadn't so far been able to rescue himself despite the amazing good fortune of being here, and, with a telephone to assist. Andy had said this was a place where he could 're-charge his batteries', implying that all that was needed was a rest. But he needed a lot more than that to avoid the horror of returning to the same situation as before; and one where the overnight refuge of Joe's launderette would be no longer an option. Looking around at the spectacle of affluence he had found himself in, increased the sense of failure. Wondering what it must be like to own a house like this. To raise enough money, legally, to buy it. He was just passing through it seemed, on his way back to the park bench and the bins outside the fish and chip shop. But to actually own a house like this and live in it! It was incomprehensible. And in the two weeks *he* had lived in it, which had resulted in accumulating nowhere near enough money for even the grimiest of bedsit, it was beginning to feel like being on 'death row' in a five-star hotel, instead of a maximum security prison.

The phone rings, reminding him that he's not supposed to be here and therefore shouldn't answer it. But what if it's work? One of the agencies he had given this phone number. What was the point of it all if he was not going to answer the phone? He picks it up.

'Jonathan!'

'Andy, I'm sorry. I just had to pop back quickly and get something, and I'm now off out again.'

'Oh, don't worry about that now. Listen, I'm really sorry but it's been sold, about an hour ago, and the new owner is coming round there this afternoon. Can you do us a favour and get yourself and your stuff out now, have a quick tidy round, lock up, and bring the key into the office here and leave it with the girl at reception. You know where it is, don't you, in Hounslow?'

Jonathan feels the panic begin to surround him as he listens to the fateful words but finds the selflessness to thank him again for his help.

'No problem, Jonathan, and if I don't see you again, the very best of luck.'

He needed truckloads of it, and only just avoided the indignity of begging the estate agent for another house that he could possibly be shifted to. The separation from the Good Samaritan feeling like being thrown out of a lifeboat without a jacket. Back to the quicksand, which wasn't going to let go of its victim that easily.

A Rural Retreat

He gathers his stuff. There was much to be said for the wisdom of travelling light. Only have as much baggage as you can carry without too much effort, and which can be used as a makeshift pillow, seeming the best philosophy for those in his predicament. He sweeps up, empties the bins and cleans the bath out, purely out of respect for the brothers, but with a feeling of otherwise hopelessness. Just before leaving, he rings his parents. Something that now had to be resorted to as a possible source of rescue, due to the lack of anything else procured by his own efforts. And, while he had only a few minutes more to bask in the luxury of having a telephone. The timing had to be right when Dad was likely to be out and sympathetic Mum would answer. But this time, distressingly, there's no answer, and he wonders what it is he expects them to actually do, now that he was just about to leave the address where they could have sent money in the post. 'The great outdoors' was now a hopeless place he would surely be seeing an awful lot of, and he returns to it, locking the door and waiting at the bus stop to Hounslow, pondering his failure to rescue himself.

In his quest for work, he had been hesitant to present himself as a 'driver' of commercial vehicles. After that most damning of collisions at Johnson's and what remained of his confidence being finally crushed at Armstrong's, neither place would have given him a good reference as such, and it all seemed best avoided. But, having been severely punished for his lack of money, and now returning to that punishment, he conceded that the fear of failure had obstructed his efforts to get it. Vast amounts of bullshit should have been given, declaring his vast experience of anything from international politics to multi-lingual interpreting, if it would move him a few inches nearer to that most essential of ingredient for survival. Dosh! How he would perform in such jobs was irrelevant, as long as he got the money for doing them. Yes, a far more mercenary attitude should have been adopted to it, he reflected. But, as the bus arrived to take him back to the abyss, it was all in hindsight, lessons being learnt. For a young

193

man of twenty-five, with still only a few years' experience of paid work and much of that washing-up, there was so much to be learnt about the often sick, greedy world of employment, or the lack of it. Money, and the lack of that!

He leaves the key with a receptionist at the estate agent's office as requested, and now panics, and shivers, for the moment, with just the expectation of the onslaught of cold. Back to the previous financial state of having just about enough for one night's stay at the cheapest B&B, and then what? Back to the world without purpose, to the exact same state of affairs he had been in before stumbling upon the brothers at the launderette: an incredible piece of good fortune that hadn't been capitalized upon. One person he now didn't want to see was his saviour, Joe, remembering his words, 'I'm sure you'll get yourself sorted out'. And how he yearned to do just that. But by his own efforts, and preferably, without any giant leaps backwards, to things, places, people, that he'd previously been chronically dependant on, but had managed to wrestle his way free of. Mum and Dad, Sheffield, pills, hospital, Jan and Steve's house. But could he afford to be that fussy?

The panting for breath and chronic indecision was gathering pace, as he stood in the street wondering should he go in this direction or that. Once again, it didn't matter, and once again, it was terrifying. But the sight of an empty phone box reminds him of his failed attempt to contact his parents, and he walks to it, almost running out of the physical energy and mental will to keep himself going.

'Mum!'

'Jonathan, how are you? We've been worried about you.'

She would always speak on behalf of the family and felt duty-bound to report on the well-being of its entirety in one phone call. Making an immediate start on it before her son has a chance to answer the original question.

'Uncle Sam's back in hospital with his knee, again! I keep going round there doing what I can, tidying the place up, but really—'

'Mum.'

He looks anxiously at the amount of change he has left to shove in the phone and the now assembled queue outside.

194

'Oh, and Becky's graduated from medical school with a PhD! Can you believe it? A doctor in the family!'

'Mum, I'm gonna have to go in a minute.'

'OK, love.'

'I've been homeless. Well, I am now, again… Ah!'

The pips. The repeated bleeping that prompts the fumbling for another 50p.

'Mum! Mum! Are you there?' he asks frantically, as if they are both in separate life boats while the Titanic is sinking.

'Yes dear. I'll ring you back. What's the phone number? Hang on a minute, let me get a pen and paper.' Continuous tone. Jonathan curses.

There was growing unrest in the queue outside and he had little choice but to exit and join the back of it. He had a bit more change to continue after it had dispersed, if Mum was still there. At least he managed to get the word 'homeless' in, so the chances are she would be. But what could she do anyway? Money, possibly, to Jan's? But how would he get it, as there was still no sign of them?

'Mum, it's me again.'

'What's all this then, about being homeless?' as if it were a petty crime.

'Ah, I had loads of different places, bedsits and stuff, after I left hospital, and then I was sacked. It's a long story, but I'm back with nowhere to go again. Sorry.'

It was an endurance to say these words, knowing he sounded like a lost cause. His voice was filled with cynicism and anger, knowing she had a long history of listening to his tales of woe, and all he could do was give her another. There would surely be groans at the dinner table tonight when she reports her findings to her weary husband.

'So where are you going to sleep tonight then, dear?'

'Well, I was gonna see what they've got at the Hounslow Hilton, but if not, in the park, I suppose.'

'Well, you know they've forecast snow, don't you?' she reports, as if he had a choice in the matter. 'Just wait there. I'm going to ring your Auntie Pauline, and I'll ring you back.'

'I thought she was dead!'

'No, that's her husband. He died last year.' Continuous tone.

A queue of one outside. He reluctantly vacates the box again and

195

waits outside. 'Mum, it's me again, could you ring me back now? I've only got one more 50p.'

He reads out the number with intensity, as if a coded message being given to fellow soldiers behind enemy lines, and then hangs up. Even the first telephone call ever made after the thing was invented must have been easier than this one. Five minutes passed by. Ten minutes. Nothing. Any minute now the assembled queue will return, as if commissioned to turn up at such moments.

Eventually, the phone rings. 'Mum!'

'Have you got money for the train fare to Auntie Pauline's? It's Aylesbury you need to go. Buckinghamshire. You really need a holiday, love.'

When you're homeless, only a home is going to sort it, not a holiday. Difficult for Mum or anyone else to understand that, he knew. He wondered how this was going to improve the situation apart from giving him shelter for tonight but was in no position to argue. He had rung her for help, and she was doing her best.

'Yeah, I think so,' he replies, solemnly.

'Get on a train to Aylesbury today. Ring Pauline when you're there.' She reads out her sister's number slowly and clearly.

'Every cloud has a silver lining', as the saying goes. Even queues outside phone boxes it seemed, as due to his lack of pen he turns and spots one, in the breast pocket of the jacket of the one person now in the queue outside and asks him politely if he can borrow it.

'Are you still there, love?'

'Yeah, Mum. Give me that number again. I've got a pen.'

He scribbles it on the outside of his hand. The stationery facilities in the phone box being well below par. Now, all these things that were once trivial were now crucial: getting the number exactly right, as it could make the difference between a warm bed and a frozen bench in Aylesbury – if he managed to get there at all.

'I'll do that. Thanks a lot, Mum. Take care. You too. Bye.'

Despite needing some tranquil time in the park after his telephonic trauma, he bypasses it and proceeds to the station where he gets his first taste of begging, as he's a few quid short of the price of a ticket.

'Excuse me, sorry to bother you,' is repeated with every passer-by.

Five of them walk straight past without a glimmer of recognition.

Everything about it was horrible, but as he seemed destined for a life of it, figured that the more experience he gained the sooner an immunity to the rejection would develop. But, with the only train of the day leaving in ten minutes, all seemed hopeless. Until at last, the goodwill of a stranger prevails, ticket is bought and a mad dash to the platform is made, gasping for breath as he boards the train. And as it pulls away, he relishes the warmth and comfort of the carriage, and once again, the tranquillity of being nowhere: escaping from one catastrophe before arriving at the next. And relief, at discovering he still had his hold-all bag of belongings, despite putting it on the floors of phone box and station toilets with a brain overloaded with information and uncertainty. But his arrival at that most feared of predicaments: of having no money at all was scary, as he went forth to place himself at the mercy of a relative he wouldn't recognize if he bumped into her in the street.

Reversing the charges for the call (one of the few luxuries a penniless public phone user could enjoy in 1989), he immediately apologizes for doing so, and Auntie Pauline explains that her neighbour, 'an elderly gentleman', has a car and is coming to pick him up. Such efficiency. Such was the bond between Mum and her sisters. Gratitude is expressed repeatedly to both chauffeur and Auntie; once again, feeling unworthy of such treatment. After the rare delight of a proper meal, he went to bed in the most comfortable and peaceful of surroundings, with only the gentle sounds of wildlife and weather from outside.

He thanked her again for her kindness and sympathized greatly for the loss of her husband; able to turn on the respectful charm when the need arose, to which she told him she was pleased to have some company. But for every minute that went by, it felt like he was on a very expensive taxi ride with the metre ticking over rapidly; ever reminding him that something had to be done to get money and so far hadn't. He asked her about possible locations of places of work nearby. But she was vague in her response and repeated his mother's futile but well-meaning words about him needing a holiday, as if the mere mention of paid work were an unnecessary complication. She was a small, polite, quietly spoken lady of frail appearance, who had never had children. Of similar good, but often misguided intent, to her sisters. But lacking the robustness of her younger, more down to earth sister, Mrs Piper.

Her nephew's presence was filling a gap in the life of the bereaved

197

Auntie right now. But, with no agreed duration for his stay, he was only concerned with regaining his independence and not outstaying his welcome, always considering himself a burden to others.

While in her garage looking for something she needed, he spotted an old bicycle, lying flat, abandoned, and covered in cobwebs. With similar excitement to that of whoever discovered Tutankhamun's tomb in the 1920s, he gets it out for further examination. Junk, and its potential usefulness had always stirred the adrenalin from within. Was it the answer to his prayers? Transportation, if he had the strength to ride it. Despite its rust, and looking like it hadn't been ridden since World War II, it was rideable and had no punctures; which was lucky, as how to repair them was a distant memory of his youth. Could he borrow it for the afternoon? Yes, he could, and he left without saying where he was going. He didn't want to burden his auntie with details, and he wasn't too sure of them either. To look for work was as much as he knew right now, and at last, with transport to do it, was at least trying to do something about the imaginary taxi metre.

After cycling a few miles in near deserted countryside and gathering as much information as possible from the few pedestrians that were around, he eventually stumbles upon a big farm with a few factory-type buildings. They didn't have any vacancies but had people there who were 'from the agency' in Aylesbury. This sounded promising. He wrote down some finer details on a piece of paper, thanked the hair-netted informant and headed back to Auntie Pauline's which was now mostly uphill, and he was suddenly aware of how severely and inconveniently unfit he was.

Although he insisted on cycling to the relevant agency the next morning, his auntie insisted it was too far and sent him round to the elderly gentleman neighbour to ask for a lift. He felt like he had inconvenienced the old man enough, especially now, as it sounded like he was grappling with a large dog, stirred into a frenzy by the sound of the doorbell. He stood patiently on the doorstep expecting to be shouted and barked at by both occupants, human and canine, when it came to the door eventually being opened. But surprisingly, the gracious neighbour; with apologies for the disturbed creature he was trying to restrain, agreed, and off they went with now quiet Alsatian on the back seat, but unsettlingly free to roam around as it wished on the journey. During which, old man neighbour explained his accidental acquiring of the dog, when a spot of dog-sitting for a friend who then 'sadly passed away' while on holiday meant he was permanently lumbered with it. But, that it was what the late friend would have wanted, and they had since grown 'rather fond of each other'; patting the animal's head with his one free hand as the other one rested on the steering wheel. Such were the gentle goings-on of the locals in this seemingly gentle world, far removed from Jonathan's own, where people were not constantly submerged in a desperate mission to keep a roof over their heads.

His ambitions for employment, although essential, were stretching the boundaries of good fortune to the limit, it seemed, as they went through the narrow country lanes. Would this agency have any work? A lot of them didn't and were keen to get people's phone numbers, as if collecting them for some other mysterious purpose. Although he had his auntie's phone number, he wanted to avoid the dubious business of giving it out, with or without her permission. And if they did have work, it would have to be at the vegetable processing plant that he had stumbled upon. At only three miles away it was surely the nearest place of work to him, just close enough for him to cycle there and back without needing medical assistance. Thus, not having to commandeer the services of the elderly neighbour any more than he had already, despite his auntie's almost peculiar insistence that the man must be called upon when any transportation was needed from her remote cottage. Would it not be easier to just rob a bank, or use the dog to 'demand money with menaces' while they were in Aylesbury, to cure his financial ills?

To his amazement, they did have work, and, at the place he had stumbled upon, and he could start there tomorrow, and then simply ask them if he was required to continue from then on. A timesheet would have to be put through their letterbox at the end of the week, with hours worked and a signature on it, 'if you want to be paid'. But, to his joy, that seemed to be the full extent of the complications, and he wasn't forced to give out his auntie's phone number. Wow! What progress had been made, he thought, with a rare feeling of contentment on the journey back to the cottage, where dinner was ready and the birds twittered merrily.

The cycle ride in the morning was mostly a nerve-wracking descent down the narrow country lanes, looking closely for any signs of ice. With the occasional swerve into a hedge to avoid collision with oncoming cars, going dangerously fast round bends in the 'rush hour'.

After being given a hair net, which 'must be worn at all times', and struggling to get his long hair secured inside it, he set to work chopping different vegetables, cleaning them, and mixing them ready to be frozen. Tedious work, but as his biggest fear right now was inactivity, which meant no money, which meant homelessness, he was happy. The mean looking supervisor was either an ex-sergeant major, stuck in a groove of reliving old habits, or a would-be frustrated one, who'd never had the chance to scream in the ears of young soldiers at six o'clock in the morning, as craved. So his little team of vegetable sorters were his makeshift army. With the occasional clap of his hands and motivational shout of, 'come on now, let's get a move on!' as he walked up and down, overseeing the general fiddling with the veg.

On the wall, a chart with various dates on it was displayed showing the rate of productivity, with slogans written next to it, designed to encourage and inspire the worker to greater efforts. And it soon became obvious that the supervisor was in competition with other supervisors, as to whose 'team' was working the hardest. The man's prestige was at stake. Which made Jonathan feel relieved and grateful for his 'temporary' status in such an atmosphere. That his was not a life sentence. And he yearned for the day of his escape. With the necessary dosh, of course.

Tomorrow?

'Yeah, I don't see why not. Eight o'clock. Sharp!' Now the uphill struggle home.

How relieved he was to be working; at last, on a mission to better things. How difficult the stagnancy would have been to just be around his auntie all day, with his two choices being to stay there permanently and give her nothing for his keep, (if she agreed to it!) or just leave there and continue the homelessness in Aylesbury. He tried to explain to her why he needed as much work and money as possible; without it sounding like greed, so something like normal life could be continued in Hounslow, on his return. But her continued use of the word 'holiday', and how other members of the family would come and stay for such pleasure, told him that she didn't understand. Which was fine, as long as the work continued and she didn't ask for any rent. Although she may consider it justifiable and reasonable to do so, now he was working, he worried. Thus, throwing one almighty spanner in the works. Ho-Hum! The precarious dependency on the goodwill of others was something he longed to break free of.

Crucially, the work did continue; he gradually got fitter and the cycle ride felt a bit less like the Tour de France, and he now had a packed lunch made for him by his auntie. Better than staring longingly at crisps and chocolate secured behind the glass screen of a vending machine, for which he had no money to access. A long week of arduous grind went by, in which he had worked there every day, including the weekend: when the increased hourly rate had to be taken advantage of. It was tough, but he set himself the task of continuing the same for at least another week. By then, he predicted, he would have sufficient funds to return to Hounslow, where rent in advance/deposit on a bedsit or such like would have to be paid. He didn't bother to ask about work the next day, feeling like there was more chance of them finding use of him if he just appeared in front of them. And if they didn't, he would just have to go home. But thankfully, that never happened.

En route to the plant one morning, he stopped for a breather and a prolonged gaze at the most exquisite of boozers; if just the outside appearance was anything to go by: white painted, a thatched roof and hanging baskets with colourful flowers all over the place, in the middle of a long, straight, deserted country lane. As though it had somehow been put there to lead him into temptation. His mind wandered off into thoughts of it being the perfect venue for a final day's celebratory drink, triumphantly having raised the necessary cash in order to leave. And to his confused imagination, drunkenness out here would surely be far easier to get away with, especially if cycling. One being likely to end up in a ditch at the side of the road, with face in the mud, and back wheel sticking up in the air. The only complications that could occur, were if a passer-by thought you needed rescuing. But these were idle thoughts, riddled with denial, triggered by exhaustion and a need for comfort. And luckily, intercepted by the powerful memory of Oscar, bringing him out of a semi-trance, causing him to cycle on with renewed gratitude for what he had, rather than the endless pursuit of what he wanted. Sensing the great man smiling at him as he went.

There was a slight improvement in the supervisor's overall opinion of him, as the man fell under the misconception that the new member of his team was as keen on work, fitness and self-discipline as he was. As he had seen Jonathan arrive for work in all weathers on his bicycle ten days out of the last ten, and that sort of dedication was to be admired. Even though he was just an agency worker, not a full-timer: an important factor to any keen observer of the pecking order, which the supervisor most certainly was. But Jonathan was none of the things that he was being perceived. His exertion was purely out of having no choice if he wanted to be surrounded by bricks and mortar and a roof above him when he slept at night. And his humble means of transport was no attempt to lose weight or keep fit, but simply a by-product of the same desperation. Something that was beyond the realms of understanding of most people, it seemed.

He was feeling evermore guilty for not giving his auntie anything for his stay. She was by no means a millionaire having lost her husband at a relatively young age and did sewing and alterations to the clothing of locals to help keep herself and the cottage going. But he was on a very tight budget, and knew he was never going to wrestle free of his current predicament if it wasn't stuck to. So in his mind, the best thing he could do for her was to try and make his stay as brief as possible. Especially, as he'd overheard her telephone conversation with a friend one evening after he'd gone to bed, in which she revealed some concerns about him. The untidiness of his room for one, and his snoring for another! After the shock of criticism had died down, he harboured no ill-feeling, and it made him more determined than ever to give the lady back her space, as soon as possible. The fact that that looked like being as soon as the coming weekend, was nothing short of a miracle. Caused mainly by the periodic abundance of different types of vegetable; at the moment cauliflower, so he learned, creating plenty of work and his determination to do it.

After twelve days of working every day, he was exhausted but fitter from all the cycling. And content that every day's relentless activity was moving him nearer to recovery and further from the threat of homelessness that had dominated his life for so long. But he had to get somewhere half-decent and affordable to live, back in Hounslow, if that was possible. The area couldn't exactly be described as home, especially after his estrangement from Rockerfellaz and Jan and family's disappearance, amongst other previously good things that had tragically ended. But a permanent geographical change, he felt, would complicate things further, creating more decisions to be made. But he would certainly miss the countryside. On his journeys to and from work he would often stop for a brief rest at the side of the road and enjoy the peace, stillness, and silence; only disturbed by wildlife, in the mist of the early morning or the fading sunlight of late afternoon.

After supper, amid the clatter of pots and pans from downstairs, in a rare moment of rest, he sits down and examines the contents of his wallet. It had become like sitting on a lump, with it being in his back pocket. Now, a good few centimetres thick, bursting with odd scraps of paper of one sort or another. And just the small amount of wages amassed so far from his first few days of work; vital to the cause, that had thankfully remained undisturbed, due to Auntie Pauline's kindness and the lack of buses and launderettes. And suddenly, the *great* memories of Pam's Guest House came flooding back when he notices the envelope he was given by the menacing looking visitor on her doorstep. He had forgotten to give it to her, and was slowly becoming quite glad of his error, as he examines the scribbled note inside it with curiosity and amusement.

1g mand
2g wiz
1g ket
4 x 150 mg 007

What could this be? Whatever it was, it was in some sort of code. 'Wiz', he'd heard mentioned at Rockerfellaz. Slang for 'speed', possibly? Which was probably slang for something else. He knew about mg's; his anti-depressants were 50 of them. But 007? Apart from the obvious secret agent, he hadn't got a clue. Rhyming slang for heaven, perhaps? His experience and knowledge of non-prescription drugs was limited. His experience of anything to do with leisure was a distant memory. But in his rare exposure to the news on other people's radios and TV, he'd heard stuff about the so-called 'rave' culture, ecstasy, the closing of illegal warehouse parties by the police and such like. Maybe this was something to do with it. Outside of the confines of his poverty-stricken world, people were enjoying themselves, and this was the latest way of doing it, it seemed. He remembered the gold-toothed man's words.

'Give this to your mum and tell her I'll pick it up next week'.

He had suspected she was up to no good, and that she had, or had had, a strong association with drugs. Looking at this, it seems he was right on both counts. But then, what a risk the gold-toothed man took in giving it to him in the first place! And to give to his mum? It was baffling. His memories of it were vague. So much had happened since. He turns his attention back to the task in hand, and the disposal of the more useless contents of his wallet. But this was not one of them, and who knows, some self-gratifying revenge may be achieved with it. So, it went back in the wallet among the bits of paper for which a decision was pending.

His time was nearly up here. One more day's work at the plant and he will have completed his mission of fourteen day's work in two weeks. Thus, giving him what he hoped would be sufficient for his train fare back and rent in advance/deposit somewhere. Auntie Pauline offered him money, which he only just declined. He still had his principles; for now, until such time as he would have to sell them. And figured, that it was he who should be giving her money, either for rent, or compensation for the snoring, untidiness and general inconvenience. But if he did, it would just delay his departure while he accumulates more money before leaving; with it being crucial that he has enough to put a roof over his head when he gets there. And underneath all the pleasantries, he sensed that was what neither of them wanted. Only when he had a certain amount of savings could he risk leaving. A delicate, precise situation, which only he understood. And one with pride and self-respect in it somewhere, with the all-out begging from wealthy parents forever being resisted.

The usually gruelling cycle ride and work the next day was far easier, energised by the relief that it was the last. It was late Sunday afternoon, and even the supervisor's enthusiasm for the job was waning. He pointed to the mess on the floor where Jonathan had been working, that he would normally sweep up before leaving.

'It's all right, you can come in early and do it tomorrow morning. But make sure you do!' the supervisor ordered, sternly as ever.

He had got used to seeing Jonathan on a daily basis and assumed this would continue for evermore. Jonathan nodded, told him he wouldn't forget, and enjoyed deceiving the man immensely. The fake courtesy continued, just up until the crucial moment of getting the supervisor's signature on his timesheet; thus, authorizing the wages to be paid. As he cycled away with signed timesheet safely in his inside pocket, he threw the hairnet off his head in celebration, having grappled with the thing and his long hair every morning for the last fortnight. The litter of it remained on the ground, prompting a suspicious glare from the supervisor. One of his soldiers had gone AWOL, and slightly mad, it seemed. Jonathan returned the glare as he cycled away to freedom.

The next morning, elderly neighbour plus dog are again summonsed for the trip to the station. Jonathan smiles as he apologises for his *alleged* snoring and untidiness, causing an enormous blush to the face of his auntie, who eventually laughs and dismisses it with a downward stroke of her hand. He kisses her, thanking her sincerely for everything and promising to make it up to her somehow, without the vaguest notion of how that could be achieved. But resists the further promise of returning soon for a visit, as he couldn't foresee a time when the money for the train fare (even if he could get it) *could* actually be spent on such a frivolous luxury. Social visits and holidays were a normal part of life for her and the rest of the family, but nothing at all to do with his.

Elderly neighbour and Alsatian are thanked and stroked respectively; the latter being of good temperament with just an aversion to doorbells and the ringing of telephones, the neighbour explained. Jonathan shared the dog's feelings. Luckily, the agency in Aylesbury was close to the train station, and he popped the timesheet in an envelope marked 'URGENT', through the letterbox. Hopefully, this week's pay would grace his almost empty bank account next Friday as planned, without any hiccups, as he wouldn't be around to sort them out. And who knows what chaos would be occurring next Friday, for which, last week's wages would probably be the only cure.

He now had the rare luxury of just sitting there, by the window, as the world whizzes by in the sunshine, with the last of the early morning frost diminishing. Would arriving at twelve thirty give him enough time to find a new home before dusk? That was the big concern. He hoped so.

That was all he could do.

Fighting Back

Back in Hounslow, he made his way back to the familiar territory of bedsit-land with its memories of the pre-warehouse trauma of shared living, and its many cards in shop windows advertising such. It was a necessary evil, and him now being unemployed would surely prove to be a severe handicap in his search.

But he was quick in at least finding himself on the doorstep of one such potential resting place. A courteous, seemingly good-humoured man from the West Indies showed Jonathan a room at the back of his house, that had a nice view of his garden. Wesley, in his sixties, explained that he had recently retired from his job at the airport and needed extra income to finish off paying his mortgage. Everything looked OK, but he didn't have a crystal ball to look into which would have been handy at such moments of big decision. How many times had things looked OK, and then plummeted after he'd moved in and somehow put the kiss of death on it?

But what money the man wanted for it right now was more than what Jonathan had. After he explained briefly about his recent employment history and subsequent failed attempt to claim benefit, Jonathan cursed himself for being too honest. And then waited in anticipation for Wesley's words that only an employed tenant was acceptable. Instead, the man spoke of his nephew who had got an 'emergency loan' from the DSS but didn't go into details about his nephew's circumstances, or how many continuous backward somersaults one had to perform in order to get it.

Wesley wasn't prepared to reduce what he was asking for. So Jonathan left, reluctantly, regretting the time wasted, feeling that bit closer to what he was desperately trying to avoid. But Wesley didn't seem the type to either sniff glue or put it in the lock of anyone's door, and there was only one of him. A nice number, when it came to the amount of people in a house to whom it was necessary to get on with. And as such, Jonathan had assured him that he would try and find a solution and may be back later. An emergency loan from the DSS? That didn't raise too many hopes (despite him being a more than suitably qualified recipient),

206

but he paid them another visit nonetheless, while increasingly anxious about the time and how much of it remained for him to find a home. Preferably today, as he'd just heard from Wesley's TV that sub-zero temperatures were again expected tonight.

He explains his case to a male assistant, who thankfully seems a bit less of a bureaucratic zombie than others so far endured. He tells of his recent claim for benefit being rejected due to him leaving the 'previous previous' job of his own accord.

'The previous previous job?' the assistant queries, with a look of bewilderment.

'Yeah, the one before the previous one,' Jonathan explains, while somehow feeling foolish, despite trying to convey the complexities of DSS policy to one of its employees. Policy he was now all too aware of having been a major cause of his recent homelessness.

He then explains his current desperate circumstances, and that he has come to find out about the possibility of having an emergency loan. As he said the words 'emergency loan', he expected to hear laughter from somewhere. As if he was asking for something wondrous. Something too good to exist. As if he were in the fictional world of 'Charlie and the Chocolate Factory', asking for the actual chocolate bar that contains the elusive 'Golden Ticket'; thus, giving him entry to the factory, and freedom to gorge himself on its contents. Something you had to climb several mountains bare foot, and swim in shark-infested waters to obtain.

No laughter. Just the craziest and sickening of ironies.

'Well, to get an emergency loan, you would have to be receiving benefit already.'

'If I was getting benefit already, I wouldn't need an emergency loan, would I!' Jonathan responds, his exasperation too much to contain.

'Look, I'm just trying to help you. Now you said that you had made a claim. What's your name and address?'

His name he knew, but what was his address? A potentially trick question when you didn't have one. And if it was known that you didn't have one, you would be surely contravening some other regulation. Thus, being not only in a physical abyss, but also a bureaucratic one. And one where, any financial assistance for the desperate would be ceased before it had started. Even if you were now living on the moon, you had to make absolutely sure the address you gave was the same one that you gave when you made the claim in the first place to avoid further unnecessary complications, and the possibility of freezing to death in the park tonight. He would have to do it from memory.

'Jonathan Piper. Pam's Guest House. 16 Walpole Road.'

'Well, Jonathan, good news. A giro was sent out to you yesterday.'

His mouth opened in disbelief and remained so while his body collapsed backwards, suddenly remembering there was no back to his seat to stop him falling. But struck by a sudden attack of amnesia about all else. It was weird. He stared at the assistant intensely, as if trying to read his thoughts from his face. And began to wonder, unsettlingly, if, in the confusion, he may have already admitted to being homeless in his initial account of his desperate circumstances: trying desperately to be deemed worthy of the so-called 'emergency loan'. Thus, no longer residing at 'Pam's Guest House', as stated, or anywhere else. And if he had, was this a sufficiently kindly assistant who would pretend he hadn't heard it? The man's longish hair, beard, chunky, thick-framed glasses, and overall appearance being similar to that of a presenter of BBC 2's Open University, suggested it might. But the jury was still out on that one; and may never come back. And there was other stuff, that was equally baffling.

'But they said before that my claim was rejected,' he said, his sentence gradually rising to a peak of exasperation while trying to make sense of the trickery. So-called 'good news' about giros being sent out to failed claimants, was not to be believed without a thorough investigation.

'Well, it just gets suspended for so many weeks, if there are any discrepancies.'

'Discrepancies?'

'Yes, like you leaving a job of your own accord, which you told us that you did,' the assistant explained with a smile, as if the half-witted claimant was failing to grasp what was painfully obvious.

Slowly, the minefield of claiming benefit was beginning to make some sense, now he had the good fortune of speaking to, what was surely the only person in the building who was prepared to give out the tiniest of useful information without being tortured.

'How much is it for? The giro.'

'I'm sorry, but regulations forbid me to disclose the—'

Deep sigh! It was inevitable that the assistant would occasionally return to the spouting of the bible, for which, the protective screen in front of him was necessary.

This stunning revelation raised too many questions for him to grapple with in the few seconds he had. It *was* potentially good news, but a final decision on that couldn't be made without a meticulous rummage through the facts. The more basic of which, now flickered past his brain. How was he going to get that giro? Was it worth getting, as he didn't know its worth? Should he tell the man to stop sending any more giros to that address, as the task of retrieving them from what felt like a lion's den seemed a hopeless one and may end up providing a second income for its most undeserving occupier? But how was that helping the immediate, desperate situation? What other address was there to give? A bit premature to give Wesley's.

'Will giros keep being sent there now? I mean, to me, at home, at my address, there now, please?' Jonathan asked, clumsily, his words descending pathetically into not much more than a squeak towards the end. As if in danger of the truth spilling out in a catastrophic mess if he didn't stay focused, while at the same time attempting to clear up said mess, just in case it had already spilled out previously. As it had done so horribly, with his admission of leaving the previous job of his own accord, despite, at the time, not being fully aware of having done so, or, that it was an actual 'discrepancy'. For which he would be punished.

'Yes, unless you tell us of a change in your circumstances.'

Again, he wondered if had already done so, but either he hadn't, or the man wasn't paying enough attention to notice. He suspected the latter. Something that was universally common, when someone was giving the horrific details of their misfortune to someone else, who wondered what they were going to have for tea tonight or about the boil that had suddenly appeared on their bottom. And so, the almighty changes in his circumstances that *had* taken place since his departure from 'Pam's Guest House', were strictly off-limits for conversation, in light of the new facts being obtained. He seemed to have regained control of the situation, somehow, in a manner of speaking, if he dare come to such a positive conclusion while at the DSS. The benefit system had to be played carefully, with a limited, controlled distribution of the truth, if any at all. In the hope that something could be squeezed out of it when at one's most desperate.

'Can I come here to collect the giros in future, rather than them being posted?'

Back to that most wonderfully obvious and simplest of solutions that would effortlessly bypass so many obstacles. It was worth a try.

'I'm sorry, but because of current regulations—'

At least *this* assistant did appear to be sorry for once again raising the wall of bureaucracy, rather than glorifying in it. But Jonathan doesn't let him finish his excruciating sentence and decides to cut his losses, thank the man and leave, having obtained far more useful information than he had ever dreamed possible. And in a moment of the merging of madness and gratitude, puts his hand out to shake the assistant's, only for it to hit the protective screen, and they both smile, awkwardly.

How he was going to get future giros was thinking too far ahead. His brain, struggling to cope with the enormity of getting this one, that may or may not be at Pam's Guest House. But obviously, a visit was needed, and with precise timing. Preferably, after it had actually arrived but before it had found its way to her rubbish bin, if that was possible, which he increasingly doubted. One thing was certain, there would be no cooperation from the merciless landlady. A brown envelope with his name on it going to her address was something he knew would be treated with venom and scorn.

With his newfound (wealth?) and dusk fast approaching, he decides to return to Wesley's to see if the room was still vacant, and if it was, to use whatever charm and deceit that could be conjured to secure it. To his relief, it was, and after some empty promises were given, an agreement was reached for him to pay what he could now, and the rest of it would be handed over by Wednesday. How, was another matter, as today was Monday, and he wouldn't get last week's wages until Friday. But that bridge would be crossed when he came to it. And so, he handed over what he had, which got him the luxury of a key and the chance to at last put his belongings down on the floor of his own room. Deep sigh of relief. Mission, sort of accomplished.

After some intense mental arithmetic it was deduced that Friday's wages from Aylesbury agency wasn't going to be enough to get him completely over the hurdle of two week's rent in advance plus the same in deposit. Despite him agreeing to pay the lot by Wednesday!

Everything hinged on that giro. He had to get it and it had to be for a reasonable amount. That left the small matter of what he was going to eat until he did; having given everything except some loose change to a somewhat sceptical Wesley to sway a decision in his favour, but that was mere trivia in comparison.

Next stop must be Pam's to recover the elusive giro, that he could only hope was there and still in one piece. He must expect maximum resistance of course, as she had already made it clear that no such claim was to be made from her property. He walks in her direction, brain whizzing so fast he can hardly catch up with it. There was much to speculate in the expected confrontation, but also, the note in his wallet the gold-toothed man had given him occupied much of his brain. The more he thought of it, the more it felt like the 'Golden Ticket', that, rather than gaining him entry to the chocolate factory, was getting him closer to that giro. Which, he could sense, that if he didn't get, would seriously affect relations with new landlord. A nice man, but one with an intense financial mission of his own going on, so it seemed.

He suddenly changes direction, deciding that he's being too hasty. It wasn't enough for him to just turn up on her doorstep and confront her with his assumptions as to what was written in the note. Cold facts needed to be obtained, and one exciting one stood out from the rest. What was the usual jail sentence for a convicted drug-dealer? He knew he had to decipher the note properly, with hopefully the aid of a book from the library, to gain some knowledge of drugs with which to arm himself.

Lady librarian looked him up and down a bit, making a few incorrect assumptions as to his motives for asking for what he was asking for. But led him to where there might be books about 'illegal drugs', and he got stuck in. After an hour of searching and creating an untidy pile of books that were of no use, he gained some useful knowledge that could be thrown at the suspected drug-dealer, if it was necessary, which he was certain it would. Now dark and freezing cold as he leaves the library, he must accept the day's limited achievements and return to his new home. The confrontation with the enemy would have to wait until the morning.

He avoided the new landlord as best he could, which seemed appropriate as he was possibly in the process of deceiving the man, depending on the outcome of tomorrow's giro hunt. The avoidance was made easier by the fact that the telly from Wesley's private lounge blared out so loud, he would never have heard his lodger coming in and going up the stairs, even if he were accompanied by a brass band.

From the comfort of his room, Jonathan looked out the window at the

211

falling of sleet illuminated by a full moon. He counted his blessings that he was not outside in it for the night, certain that his morale couldn't have taken another overnight stay in the park wishing he had stayed at Auntie Pauline's for just a little bit longer. He hardly slept, with hunger, and the anticipation of what was to follow. Part excitement, part anguish, part going over facts obtained from the library as if rehearsing for a forthcoming lecture.

In the morning he sets off, having resisted the almost uncontrollable urge to help himself to anything that was Wesley's in the shared kitchen. Such was his hunger, and thirst for tea. But, just like all great detectives, was spurred on by the mystery before him that had to be solved and walked briskly onwards to face the enemy.

He knocks at the door, grappling with a mixture of fear and excitement at the thought of presenting her with the facts, and embarrassed at the extent to which the woman had control of his emotions. Hoping, but also dreading, that it was her who would open it. Someone else would surely complicate things further, and there would be no time for the construction of a plan B. And the consequences of nobody opening the door, were too painful to contemplate. He tries to regain control of his breathing as he waits, as in *this* potentially hostile of situations with so much to be explained, silence wasn't going to cut it. Speech was essential, and it had to be clear.

The door opened and Pam appeared, looking as always like she had just got out of bed and was being blinded by the daylight; something that had been the demise of many a vampire. He thought it best to start off polite and then work his way down, if necessary. Which it would be.

'Hello, Pam, sorry to bother you. I know you said not to, but I'd already made a claim at the social, 'cos I was sacked from my job. I had no choice. But they rejected the claim, so they told me. But I've just been back there now, and they say they've...' He became aware that he was talking way too fast, desperately trying to cram it all in before she slams the door in his face, as if he were a door-to-door salesman of used toilet roll, or a Jehovah's Witness with bad breath. But his efforts were wasted, as she does just that, forcing him to continue, much louder, through the letterbox. Determined to be heard.

'They've sent a giro here! Anyway, you've got a son called Gary haven't you. 'Cos there was a bloke—'

Suddenly, having said the magic word so it seemed, the door opens again, and he now has her full, undivided attention.

'What's that gotta do with you?' she asks.

'Hello mate, how ya doing! I'm Gary, pleased to meet you.'

Jonathan jumps out of his skin. Fearing the worst at hearing a male voice, and that of her son, whose name he had just shouted. A wide-eyed, some would say, over-friendly young man with a very loud voice suddenly appears in the doorway and shakes his hand. Looking about the same age as himself, and much like himself, height, build, hair length, colour. There really was a likeness here, and he could see how the mistaken identity on the doorstep with the gold-toothed man had occurred. At first, Jonathan suspected that the unexpected friendliness and exuberance of the young man was caused by his possible fondness for the "007's", or something similar that induces the 'increased empathy levels' (as listed in a library book as being one of the medically recognised side effects of Ecstasy).

Despite his obvious tension, Jonathan finds it in himself to return the cheeriness. 'Hello Gary. Nice to meet you to. I'm Jonathan.' They shake hands again, much to the irritation of Pam.

'Gary! Come away, go and sit down,' she ordered.

Her words, and her son's now solemn face, made Jonathan realise that this was not a case of drug-induced friendliness, and that although they were of similar age, Gary had the mind of someone a lot younger. Not a problem to Jonathan, and it made a nice change to speak to a friendly person. As right now, it felt as though Pam and the DSS were in danger of becoming his social life; and he wasn't entirely sure which was the most unpleasant.

'So, what's all this about Gary?' she asked sternly, as if about to get violent at any moment, now her son was safely away from the scene.

'Well, when you were not here one morning, a bloke knocked on the door. He was in a rush.'

'Hang on, what's all this gotta do with giros coming here?' she asked, getting more impatient and agitated, and he could sense the door was about to be slammed in his face again.

'This bloke called me Gary, and gave me an envelope, and said, can I give it to my mum, and that he will pick it up next week.'

A blissful silence now prevails, as Pam listens attentively, and for once appears incapable of speech, or movement. And to his further amazement, after a pause to catch his breath, he realises that the way is clear for him to continue; and he does, now speaking slower and clearer, looking directly at her, like he's got all the time in the world.

'In the envelope is a bit of paper, and on it is a list.' He goes through it from memory. '1g ket. Now, that's short for Ketamine. A gram of Ketamine.'

He examines her face. Cold, expressionless. But her Adam's apple gives it all away, as it twitches nervously at the mention of the drug.

'1g mand,' he continues. 'That's "mandy", which is MDMA, or Ecstasy in powdered form.' He deliberately said the word 'Ecstasy' with a bit more volume, at which, she looked beyond him and roundabout, nervously. And a new, previously unseen Pam, started to emerge.

'Look, do you wanna come in a minute?' she asked, now quietly and much more polite.

'Ah, no.' He nearly faltered there. What may have happened to him once he was in there, with someone who clearly wanted his silence? Who knows. 'Well, it looks like you're supplying a class A drug, doesn't it?'

Only his recent visit to the library had made him able to say that with the confidence of a drug squad officer, and still with increased volume at the important bits.

'So, what are you gonna do about it?' she asks, with a defiant smile, regaining a bit of lost confidence.

'Well, nothing, if I get that giro, but I must have it. I've been sleeping rough and everything since you chucked me out.'

That didn't prick her conscience, as was intended. Not even slightly. 'And if I don't give it to you, or it's not here?' she asked coolly.

He was flummoxed for a second, at her words, 'or it's not here', with a flicker of doubt as to how he would know if it had actually arrived here or not. But quickly realised that any dithering or hesitation must be avoided.

'I'll be straight down the police station with the note and tell 'em all about it,' he answered.

'Well, do you wanna come in and get it?'

Was this a trap?

'No,' he replied firmly. 'If you've got it, you bring it out.'

The conversation had now descended into something out of a

spaghetti western between two gunslingers, staring straight into each other's eyes, trying to call each other's bluff.

'It's not here.'

That silenced Jonathan, and he took a deep breath. He felt like he needed a ten-minute consultation with himself if she wouldn't mind waiting. But eventually, came up with some sort of a plan, which sadly involved the asking for her assistance.

'What time does your post come?'

There was a lengthy pause in which she considered whether she could stoop low enough to give it an answer.

'About ten, usually,' she said, without emotion. But he could almost hear her teeth being gritted, at being forced to discuss such trivialities with a low-life 'guest', or ex-guest, on her doorstep.

'I'll come back tomorrow at twelve. Make sure you're in,' he said, with a point of a finger and the sudden confidence of a serial blackmailer. Almost frightening himself in the process.

She shut the door, quietly this time, making no response. And as she did, he heard the loud voice of Gary from inside saying, 'He's a nice man, Mum. Maybe he'll come back.'

To have the mind of a child in such a devious world, felt like not such a bad thing to be lumbered with.

What was going on? A few nights ago, he was sitting in Auntie Pauline's front room with a cup of Ovaltine, calmly watching her doing crocheting with her cat asleep on her lap. And now, blackmailing a drug dealer? (Even if the drug dealer was an ageing female). But if ever there were a new film entitled, 'The Godmother', a sort of early politically correct sequel to the 'The Godfather', the real life Pam would be perfect for the title role.

He had no choice but to take her word for it. The man at the DSS had told him that it was sent out 'yesterday'. But the yesterday in question was Sunday, wasn't it? That didn't exactly fill him with confidence that said giro actually existed in the first place. If ever he gets time to write an autobiography, he will call it, 'Clutching at Straws', he mused. And the stingy buggers sent everything second class, didn't they? But tomorrow would have to be as much time as he was prepared to give it. Wouldn't it? Oh, the indecision!

He bumped into Wesley in the hallway and said an awkward hello and assured him it was getting sorted with the money. Despite the man's jovial exterior, he sensed that he wasn't going to tolerate too many broken promises regarding rent. Such was the need to get that mortgage paid. He went up to his room and lay on the bed after a mentally exhausting morning. He turned the radio on, and in a rare moment of appreciation of past good fortune, reflected on his auntie's kindness. She had given him the small appliance saying it was her late husband's and she didn't need it. Its tuning dial wasn't working and it was permanently stuck on Radio 3, but Debussy's Clair de Lune while staring out the window at bird activity in the garden was a tranquil combination.

In bed at night, his thoughts and worries were about avoiding Wesley, as tomorrow was payday; and the preparation of a convincing story for his absence should one be needed. And also, the expectation of Pam having some assistance, as she knew he was coming and at what time he would be there. It seemed natural to assume that a female-drug dealer had male accomplices, associates or customers. Like the two menacing looking ones that had visited in her absence. Concerned for her well-being for one reason or another. And now, she could plan ahead, whereas today she was off-guard due to his surprise visit. How important the element of surprise was in such matters. Again, he didn't sleep too well, tossing and turning with a brain full of questions and insecurities. Was it blackmail? All he was doing was trying to get what was rightfully his! A proper blackmailer would demand other niceties. A cooked breakfast for a start! Something that had eluded him during his brief but troublesome stay with the meanest of landladies.

Oh, the pining for a cooked breakfast, or one of Auntie Pauline's suppers! It had been two days now since he'd had anything other than a packet of crisps and a bar of chocolate, with the wonderful smells of Jamaican cuisine wafting up the stairs to his nostrils. Was the starvation affecting his brain as well as his stomach? It must, surely. Was he out of his depth with all this giro blackmail nonsense? Yes, definitely. But what choice did he have? He had to make the most of the good fortune of that bit of paper falling into his hands. Was Pam going to part with that giro without the extortion? Not a chance.

Pam didn't suffer fools gladly. But in her opinion, everybody except her was a fool, so she didn't suffer anyone gladly. Since the hippie days of her youth when she first smoked cannabis, she had grown it, extracted resin from it, campaigned for the legalization of it, and supplied it. Not always for money. Sometimes just to return a favour. But she had wandered into supplying for the new 'rave'/'acid house' scene almost reluctantly. It was a new thing she wasn't quite sure about and had been persuaded that a killing could be made in Ecstasy and other such party drugs, by a more big-shot drug dealer: a friend of a friend who had acquired rather a lot of the stuff and needed to offload it. And so, the usual procedure of leaving your order with son Gary if Mum wasn't around, needed to be reviewed, (especially now, as the odd Class A drug was being ordered) but never was. Was she out of her depth? Just a bit.

With a burning desire to avoid Wesley and the subject of money, and an equal curiosity about Pam's postage, he sneaks out of the house at eight o'clock. With the intention of hovering around the 'Guest House', and hopefully, stumbling upon her postman or woman. And the knowledge, albeit probably unreliable, that he or she will appear at 'about ten, usually.' But he got there much earlier, just in case, and it was a long and tedious hover during which he got a few suspicious looks from locals. Until at last, postman is spotted, and he positions himself at a non-threatening distance from No.16. Much innocence, fake nonchalance, and general charm would need to be displayed for the task ahead. Postmen not being in the habit of doing favours for loiterers, regarding the mail they were about to deliver.

Just at the point where the man is close enough for it to be obvious he is about to deliver to the all-important house, but not too close that it's occupant overhears a suspicious conversation from outside, he addresses the man.

'Excuse me, sir. Can I ask a quick question before you deliver those? It's a bit urgent.' The man turns, immediately alert to whatever was about to happen.

'It's OK, I'll stay over here,' Jonathan assures him, taking a few steps backwards, giving his best casual, innocent, harmless smile.

The man stares back unamused, and Jonathan risks his next sentence. His voice as hushed as he can possible get away with, while still needing to be heard.

'You know the ones you have there in your hand. Is one of them addressed to a Jonathan Piper, or a J Piper, for No.16, by any chance?

'If there is, it's going in there,' was the postman's gruff reply, pointing to the letterbox of Pam's Guest House, and taking another defiant step forward to it.

'Oh, absolutely, no problem,' says Jonathan, raising his hands in surrender. 'But if you wouldn't mind looking, I'd be ever so grateful.'

The man sighs, flicks through them, holds one of them aloft, and points to it. 'This one. OK!' Before shoving the lot through the letterbox.

It was a beautiful moment, and the postman is thanked sincerely for his minimal efforts of cooperation. He wasn't going to be a multi-millionaire after all this, but just to be a bit further from the threat of homelessness right now was priceless. Slightly sickening, yes, to see the possible treasure disappear into enemy territory, but another bit of useful information with which to arm himself at twelve o'clock, as planned.

Luckily, he still has some loose change and the phone number on one of many scraps of paper in his wallet. And so, contrary to arrangements, at 11.55 he rings Pam from the phone box just the other side of the road from her front door. It was busy in the street. A lot of potential witnesses milling about. A comfort of sorts, as long as none of them wanted to use the phone. He wasn't too sure what he was doing, but it felt a lot safer right now than knocking on her door. With her having had the time to arrange the unexpected for when he does.

'Pam, it's Jonathan. Is it there?'

He knows the truthful answer to that of course but braces himself for a deceitful one. 'No, it isn't.'

A tricky one. His biggest fear right now was her hanging up, leaving him dangling in mid-air. He could surely stitch the woman up somehow with his knowledge of her activities, but he desperately needed that cheque. He would just have to chuck everything at her, bullshit included, and hope for the best.

'Yes, it is! I saw it this morning before the postman put it through your door. I got the address of the drug squad just in case, and if you don't come out here to the phone box outside your front door, now, with that envelope, I'm going straight down...! Hello?'

Silence. Continuous tone. She hung up, just as he was gathering momentum. But not before he had a chance to get much of his informative rant in, he suspected. It was a quite magnificent performance, with shades of Michael Caine in *Get Carter* about it. Except for the 'Hello' at the end.

It was a nail-biting moment, and he felt like he was about to collapse under the strain of it. If he gets it, it'd better be an actual giro, and not one of their – jargon-ridden, specially composed so that no living person can understand it – letters!

To his relief, her door opens, and out she comes, and crucially, alone. She walks towards him, envelope in hand, with the now familiar grimace that didn't quite conceal her rage, which told him that everything was as it should. He stands outside the phone box and opens the door as she approaches and tells her to throw it inside on the floor; looking around intensely for any predators or anyone approaching who looked like they may want to use the phone. He should have looked at it first, he knew, and scolded himself for his laxity. But it was brown and rectangular.

'Note,' she says, holding out her hand, glaring at him with contempt.

Suitably prepared for this, he gave her the one he had scribbled down earlier. Not the original. That was in his wallet for safe keeping. After a quick glance at it, she turned to leave, while looking unusually nervous, vulnerable, and confused, like she was about to say something, but didn't. Maybe – *please don't tell the police* – seemed to her, the obvious request at that moment but couldn't stoop low enough to say it.

'There may be a few more. I don't know. Then that'll be the end of it,' he said, clumsily, doubting whether he would have the nerve to go through this again, even if there was. But difficult to predict how desperate he was going to be for money in the weeks ahead. She glared at him with disbelief as he said it, and her mouth moved as if about to say 'fuck off'. But said nothing. Her suppressed anger was a joy to behold, signifying victory, tranquillizing his whole body better than any benzodiazepine[11].

As she walks back to her front door, he opens the slightly sticky, possibly tomato ketchup-stained envelope frantically. It's condition suggesting she had just retrieved it from her rubbish bin, and he had got to it just in the nick of time. And to his joy, his efforts are rewarded. A giro for £150. It would do the trick, and he got swiftly away, feeling the need to put some distance between himself and the crime scene, and get to a

---

[11] name of a group of medicines for the treatment of depression, anxiety and insomnia.

Post Office to cash the thing immediately. Before some other catastrophe prevents him from doing so.

Sickening to have to hand over just about all of it to Wesley, after the ridiculous struggle to get it. But the roof over his head was now secured, for the time being. Some proper food could be eaten and tea drunk, and it gradually dawned on him that he had single-handedly administered something like justice to someone who needed it. Who had chucked him out, the minute he didn't have the rent, condemning him to full-blown homelessness; fortunately, for just two nights, and one in a launderette, and only with something like divine intervention had he avoided it from then on, it seemed.

There were millions of others like her; untouchable, wealthy property owners, giving out the orders: 'no pets', 'no DSS', 'employed only', 'references required'. Thus, helping to make his life a dire struggle. But the mighty had fallen, and this one was now at the mercy of an ex-tenant who now sits at his table in a cafe, wondering if he should be a *responsible citizen*, and inform the local drug squad of the police.

Revenge was sweet, and he was slowly but surely getting a taste for it.

A British Refugee

The bloke at the agency described it as a 'peach of a job,' which usually is a cast-iron guarantee that it's a bruised, rotting banana of a job for which he can't get anyone to fill. But on this occasion, he was right: Bristol and back every day in a 7.5 tonner, Monday to Friday. To some, tedious, but to someone on the brink of homelessness whose daily survival had been the most intricate of small-scale financial operation, a godsend. And sheer bliss, as the steady trickle of money entered his bank account, causing him to risk cancelling his claim for benefit, thus ending a troubled association with the DSS before all his hair turns grey and then falls out. A late morning start and late evening finish, he managed to avoid Wesley much of the time who, he suspected, needed his mortgage paid off far more than he needed company in the house.

After all the dire experience of living in someone else's property, this was a new one. Late one evening, unusually, Wesley was still up as Jonathan returned from work, and reported that some of his stuff, valuables, wallet and cards, were missing from his room. He was not happy, and it soon became clear who the prime suspect was, and even more so now that Jonathan reported that nothing of his was missing. And him pointing out that he hadn't got anything worth nicking, apart from a wallet which was in Bristol with him at the time, wasn't doing much to deflect suspicion away from himself. Wesley's thinking seemed to be, that because he had a front door key, he could have easily lent it to some burglar friends for the afternoon. Understandable suspicion perhaps, as they knew virtually nothing about each other. And in reality, didn't want to know. Simply providers of each other's desperate needs, living in awkwardly and regrettably close proximity.

The police were called and he was questioned, but in the end they had no choice but to believe that he was just as puzzled about it as they were. He added that he had forgotten to shut his window before going to work, but as they were three storeys up, wasn't expecting Spiderman or any other wall-climbers to be visiting. Eventually, it blew over, but Wesley's initial suspicions never fully left his mind. His lodger, and prime suspect, was probably more likely to commit mass murder than petty theft of this type. Yet another example of Jonathan's unwavering ability to be misunderstood. Forever a figure of mystery that could never be comfortably placed into this category or that, which the human brain had a seemingly programmed need to do so.

A few days later, unused to dealing with tail lifts on the back of lorries, he got his thumb trapped in one. And then proceeded to hop up and down in the yard like a bull in a rodeo that had already unseated its rider, before being whizzed to hospital with thumb half hanging off. Now beginning to feel like his life in Hounslow (that he was perhaps unwise to return to) was under some kind of a curse, he sobbed a little when he thought he was alone. The unsympathetic nurse who attended to him must have thought he was the biggest wimp that had ever set foot in the casualty department. But it wasn't just the thumb he was sobbing about. It was the full, mind-blowing, head-banging struggle of daily survival that he could tolerate no longer. The mangled thumb had somehow released a catch from within, that's usually in place to contain his emotion.

Soon after recovering, from both suspicion of burglary and the sewing back on of his thumb, raging toothache caused him to go to a dental college where students removed his four wisdom teeth in one afternoon. It was free, as they needed patients they could practise on. During the extracting, the laid-back students discussed their holiday plans with each other in great detail and how the weather might affect them, with the occasional 'how ya doing?' to the patient, who grunted his reply with a mouthful of the fearsome articles of dentistry. This in turn, caused Jonathan to be told by similar unsympathetic nurses at the same casualty department later that evening, that he 'must wait in the queue!' while howling in pain with the left side of his face like a balloon. Which in turn, caused a straight-faced, inquisitive small boy to turn to his mother and ask, 'Mummy, why is that man making all that noise? Is he mad?'

After the traumas of burglary, thumb and teeth in quick succession, the peace and contentment of regular work and income resumed. And what a paradise island Bristol was becoming, purely for the fact that it was somewhere else, an escape, where the problems of living didn't exist.

After being 'tipped'[12], he would habitually settle down to eat his Clarke's Pie[13] and chips with bum on passenger seat and feet on dashboard, outside the chippy, where his only concern was that the bored and devious looking, council estate gangs that loitered nearby, might replace his wheels with bricks if he risked falling asleep afterwards. Predictable work, with one day being much the same as the next, but the money was also delightfully predictable; something that had been lacking in his life for so long.

Having at last got his feet on firmer ground, there was now time to reflect on the chaos of his recent housing crisis; and 'Pam's Guest House' had been very much a part of that crisis. His mind flickered over memories of her ban on the claiming of benefit from her property when it was desperately needed. Her ruthlessness in ordering him to leave, immediately, after just one missed payment of rent. The look of contempt on her face that had accompanied her words, 'So, what are you going to do about it?' And there was only one course of action that seemed appropriate. The party drug shopping list the gold-toothed man had given him was stapled to a blank piece of paper, on which he wrote the necessary details of how and where he had acquired it. Adding that, he had 'confronted' (which sounded so much better than 'blackmailed' he decided) his ex-Landlady with her activities, and that her response suggested she was completely guilty.

After some painstaking research, he then posted it to the headquarters of the regional drug squad of the police, recorded delivery, with the satisfaction of knowing, or at least hoping, that he was stitching someone up who thoroughly deserved it. Any such opportunities to do so that fell into his lap, to the incurably mean and merciless that happened to cross his path, had to be relished and acted upon. And this one was. Making him feel a little bit less like someone put on this earth as a pin cushion for others. But there were other examples of it where no such opportunity had arisen. Like being stuck in a hole in the ground, covered in the piss of those that had put you there. The lack of justice administered for that was like a knot permanently residing in his stomach.

---

[12] Unloaded.

[13] A shortcrust Bristol delicacy.

As his daily trips to Bristol came to a peaceful end; and with it, the luxury of steady money, it was back to grim reality. But he scraped by, experiencing the delights of early morning supermarket cleaning, struggling to keep control of a floor-buffing machine that had a mind of its own. This supplemented whatever other work he could get from the agency, resulting in a year of just about avoiding further collisions with the DSS.

Life was bearable at Wesley's, but there'd been a sharp increase in the rent, and he suspected he would be terminated just as soon as the man's mortgage was eventually paid off. So, not in desperate need of a change of address, but thought he'd have a peek nonetheless, after spotting a card in a shop window for a bedsit down the road. He was greeted at the door by the most beautiful and charming of middle-aged South Asian female, wearing a long, colourful dress and speaking to him with such courtesy. Surely a case of mistaken identity, he wondered, as he was neither Cary Grant, or the local M.P that she was possibly expecting. The lady belonged in a Bollywood movie, or the Taj Mahal perhaps, but definitely somewhere more exotic than a terraced house in the dingier end of Hounslow. Not great English, but she beckoned him in with a 'Come! Come!' and directed him to go and view the room upstairs alone. Almost self-contained with a small fridge, large sink and two-ringed Belling cooker, he liked it. This would definitely do. He expressed his keenness to the lady who said she would tell the landlord Mr Hubbib, and that he should come back tomorrow and discuss business with him. The man apparently occupied the room next door to Jonathan's if he was to take it. Oh! The news was devastating to someone already struggling with similar close proximity to a landlord, which had turned ugly when stuff went missing. He guessed that Mr Hubbib would not possess the same beauty and charm as the lady who lived downstairs with her teenage nephew. But nevertheless, he returned the next day to check the man out.

The landlord seemed bearable. Hopefully, not the sort that would be knocking on his door every five minutes trying to detect any undesirables he may have stashed in his room: females, non-paying overnight guests, electrical appliances that increased the bills, that sort of thing. But the pleasantness of the room and blissful lack of shared kitchen, eventually swayed a decision towards money and keys changing hands with a strangely optimistic feeling that the wind was possibly blowing him in the right direction. Back at Wesley's, he decided to move himself and his stuff down the road immediately. His deposit, that he had struggled so hard to get, would be sacrificed. But bearing in mind, rent would now have to be paid on the new place even if he didn't move in immediately, there didn't seem much point, financial or otherwise, in hanging around. And sudden departures were very much Jonathan's forte.

Wesley was out. In different circumstances he would have liked to have said goodbye and wished the man the happy retirement he so surely deserved, but the type of desperate world he inhabited rarely allowed for such normality. And since the burglary incident, (if there *had* actually been a burglary, which was still shrouded in mystery) Jonathan had somehow felt like its creator, despite his innocence. With its raising to the surface of any racial tensions that may have been lurking beneath the pleasantries.

The plan was to get everything out, (his stuff only, not Wesley's!) leave a brief note of explanation and apology, lock the door and put the key through the letterbox. But, with typically awful timing, prompting clumsy, awkward explanation, Wesley walks up the pathway.

'Sorry about this, Wesley,' he apologizes, mainly for blocking the doorway with his stuff as he clumsily tries to move it out the way so the man can pass. 'Em. I'm off. Ah. I've seen a bedsit down the road which looks like it might be suitable for me, and I've had to pay for it straight away so I don't miss it, sort of thing. Sorry.' Always more comfortable with the brief-note method of explanation rather than speech.

Wesley's unrestrained hostility was unexpected, to someone who always considered his departures as being more of a cause for celebration to those he was leaving, thus, getting out of their way. But this one, had slightly derailed plans for a blissful, mortgage-free retirement. 'I don't like you very much,' Wesley says, putting his face up close to Jonathan's.

'I don't like you much either,' seemed an appropriate response, to someone in the middle of the mayhem of moving house, lacking the energy for more articulate conversation.

'You've lived here all this time and you don't like me!' Wesley was astonished by what he perceived as a shock revelation. A million miles away it seemed, from understanding the kind of pressure his lodger had been under to get somewhere in that afternoon after leaving Aylesbury, and subsequent blackmail of previous landlady to get the money to pay him in full. There was certainly no time for morals, if that was the man's suggestion now that he surely didn't have any. Shelter needed to be got, and quick! *Obviously*, he was the only person in the world who'd ever been in such a desperate situation. Was he? Surely not. But it often felt like it, and now was one such time. Jonathan made his way to the gate, carrying too much stuff, having unwisely abandoned his previous philosophy of travelling light.

'I'm gonna report you to the Race Relations Board!' were Wesley's loud parting words. Jonathan, almost tripping over his large suitcase as he and it are both squeezed through the narrow gateway, had run out of conversation. Sometimes it just wasn't worth the effort.

In their rare conversations not about the weather, he imagined that Wesley had been in England for some time, and therefore must have experienced the horrors of signs in the windows of boarding houses stating things like: 'No blacks or Irish or dogs', when he first arrived in the *promised land*. So, perhaps his bitterness was justified. Jonathan had had more than enough trouble himself trying to keep a roof over his head, even without the colour of his skin, his nationality or pet ownership being an issue! Any more issues on top of the ones already endured, didn't bear thinking about.

Onwards he staggers, occasionally dropping a saucepan or other such embarrassing article that makes a loud clatter as it hits the pavement. Only to then have to put everything down on the pavement to retrieve it. The psychological disturbance of the hostilities on the doorstep, somehow increasing the precarious, chaotic nature of the removals. But fortunately, only a short distance. Not quite long enough for the potentially amusing spectacle he was creating to attract much of an audience in the street.

On his arrival, the charming and beautiful lady again smiles warmly and bows as though an air hostess on an Air India flight greeting a passenger, as he enters with his clutter, her usual courtesy unwavered by the shambolic vision on the doorstep. Teenage nephew stares at him like the moustached keyboardist from the seventies pop duo *Sparks*, from behind a doorway. When ordered by his Aunt to assist the British refugee with his belongings up the stairs, he quickly disappears in the opposite direction.

The coupling of his complex personality with the right place to live was never going to be an easy match. At least, not until such time as money was literally pouring from the sky on top of him, and he could buy his own island with an army of servants attending to his every whim. But this was about as close as it was going to get. There was a generous supply of spicy dishes from the charming lady downstairs, which he would take up to his room on a tray. Teenage nephew continued peering at him oddly with a mixture of fear and fascination, when there was a wide enough gap between door and door frame to do so, or with a twitch of a curtain as he came and went. Charming lady had two equally charming and beautiful daughters (both married of course!) who would visit and were equally as courteous to him as their mother. The antidote to all this charm, beauty and courtesy, was of course, Mr Hubbib: a sort of South Asian *Rigsby*[14].

One freezing February day when he knocked on his door to give him the rent, Jonathan was treated to a bizarre energy-saving demonstration. The man was sitting up in bed wearing a thick jumper and gloves, refuting the need for heating, be it electric or central, dismissing it as 'unnecessary' as he flicked ash from his cigarette onto a saucer. Doubtless, hoping his tenant would follow suit in order to keep the bills down.

Jonathan bought an old Datsun car from him, having seen the man depart and return in it day after day, with seemingly no trouble. For that reason alone, a good buy, he thought. But, as if he had put a curse on it, the problems multiplied under its new owner.

'All this time I've had it, and no trouble, and now you...' Mr Hubbib told him, shaking his head in dismay instead of finishing his sentence. As if accusing his tenant of ruining the beloved machine, that Jonathan had only just managed to push to safety, alone, on a particularly perilous three-laned section of the Great West Road with only hazard lights for protection. Mr Hubbib had his charm but kept it well concealed.

When it was running, the car served a useful purpose, getting him to a paint factory where he got himself a permanent position as a van driver. He delivered paint, which was fine and interesting much of the time, but spillages were a major cause for concern, the shouting of expletives, and at times, a source of amusement amongst colleagues. Tins of paint not being the easiest of things to keep still in transit, but surely the messiest

---

[14] the miserly fictional landlord of the 1970s TV sitcom *Rising Damp*.

when spilt.

There were pros and cons to permanent jobs, he learned. The same people day after day. Some being enjoyed, others endured. He laughed with the usual crowd who were mostly older than himself, in whose company he felt safe. And to him, laughter was an essential part of life. Without doubt, 'the best medicine'. But just like at school, there were others who regarded him as something to be laughed *at*. Many people, it seemed, could only find amusement in someone or something that they consider to be far beneath them; laughter being purely a conditioned response of superiority. Perhaps in the same way as medieval royalty had first laughed at their fool or jester, the idea of which was then carried down through the centuries. And Jonathan, with his unconscious talent for providing laughs, often found himself in such a role when he least wanted it.

Also, the same problems occurring day after day, which could be cured by this or that being done, but never would, was one of Jonathan's particular favourite cons to internally moan about. Or externally if anyone would listen. But, at the paint factory he acquired a useful road knowledge of just about everywhere in the south-east of England, and did his job efficiently, if at times, obsessively. And at home, to compliment his new-found 'yuppie' lifestyle, he got a telephone installed in his room. No more phone boxes! Almost too much of a frivolous luxury to take in.

Now settled in his new home, and his struggles with accommodation (or the lack of it) seemingly behind him, it was time to replace them with those of acquiring an HGV license. With his track record of failing driving tests, it would surely be just that. His experience of which was like repeatedly smashing one's head against a wall in the hope that one glorious day such insane levels of persistence would be rewarded and could then be celebrated with a glass of water and an Aspirin. The thinking being, that as driving was possibly the only thing in life he could cope with, best push it to the limit. Especially as other options of ways for him to earn a living were not exactly vast. Did he think he could drive an articulated lorry? Yes. Did he think he could pass a driving test in one? Probably not. But it was something that had to be attempted and endured.

At this time of relative comfort and progress, letters started appearing from old mate and ivory-tickler Dennis, which brought back some fond memories of a by-gone age. Mainly of full-time leisure, music, and crazy conversation in the Tea Bar; in the days when he had a social life, however bizarre. Having been invited round for tea by Mrs Piper at some point in the distant past, Dennis must have got his address from her, he assumed. But the occasionally psychotic musician was now in Plymouth, with a council flat, and a piano in it! Jonathan wondered if his former friend had had another of his delusional episodes in which it was assumed the people of Plymouth were expecting him and would be there waving and cheering on his arrival. Thus, steering him in the direction of Plymouth psychiatric services, thus, making him top priority on the council housing list. A scenario that seemed to have been repeated throughout the man's adult life. But maybe it wasn't delusional after all, and the council *had* actually put a piano in the flat, in preparation for the great man's arrival. All puzzling and intriguing.

Jonathan's life was becoming more and more dominated by work, stirred by an assumption that the security he so desperately craved would eventually be achieved with it. After his fourth HGV test failure and lack of funds to continue the torture, Mr Hubbib got him a weekend job at a 'cash and carry' type-supermarket with contacts he had in the local South Asian community. And so, with grim determination, a gruelling itinerary of work commenced: the usual *work* at the paint factory Monday-Friday, and *work* at the cash and carry place Saturday and Sunday, in order to get a *work* qualification. Somewhere in the back of his mind when he had time to think or feel, the recent contact with Dennis had stirred a pining for the good old days; that in reality were troubled and full of anguish, like so much of his life had been. But, with some larger-than-life characters, a musical accompaniment, and delightfully, no *work* at all.

Feeling like a mountaineer who can at last stick his country's flag in the ground at the summit, he passes an HGV test. The Ministry of Transport was a good deal richer from his numerous failures and determination to continue. An emotional moment in a life rarely blessed with success, and feeling the need to share it with someone, rings his mum. But after explaining that his new conquest was something to do with the driving of large vehicles, it prompted an unusual silence. During which, she realised that the safety of other road users and the public at large was something else she now needed to start worrying about. Such was her confidence in the son that seemed to have the exact opposite of the Midas touch about him. A daughter with a PhD was cause for celebration and the subject of much proud conversation. But a son with an HGV license was something she wasn't quite sure she wanted to broadcast to the neighbours and extended family. At least, not just yet, until a period of time had passed during which there was no loss of life.

He continued at the paint factory, but now driving the company's only HGV, with a miserly pay rise to reward his efforts. A 'rigid', 17-tonne lorry, and to him, frighteningly heavy when fully loaded with tins of paint. But his quest for progress continued with a decision to leave the paint factory, as he would not be gaining any experience there of driving the articulated lorries that he was now licensed to drive; due to the inconvenient lack of them. So, he returned to agency work and early morning cleaning, and eventually got his reward in the shape of a day's work on 'artics' at a chilled food establishment. While doing his preliminary checks on the vehicle and trying to remember the important bits of the expensive but inadequate training he had received, he looked about as sure of himself as *Frank Spencer*[15]. All eyes were upon him it seemed. As he spots the now disgruntled looking, hair-netted figure of the Manager-type person, now talking to someone on the phone while observing his activities with a look of concern through the office window. Probably talking to the agency that had sent him here, he assumed, for some assurance that all was as it should. This being the kind of work where one was expected to be an expert from the word go. Where any whiff of a beginner was treated with dread, fear and suspicion. Was he ever going to escape the intense scrutiny and claustrophobia of this depot in a lorry?

Eventually he does, with a quick look in the mirror to check that he wasn't being chased by anybody from the depot trying to stop him. The day improved greatly from then on, ending with an enormous sense of achievement. An easy day by most driver's standards: two journeys to the same place about fifty miles away, but a challenging one to the most inexperienced. No disasters, but sadly, a one-off that would never be repeated. The agency regularly sent drivers to another place for the driving of artics, but to his frustration, was repeatedly told that he couldn't go there as he didn't have the required two years' experience. It was beginning to feel like the only way he was ever going to get two *days'*

---

[15] the main hapless character of the 1970s TV sitcom *Some Mothers Do 'Ave 'em.*

experience, was in the event of an administrative cock-up resulting in mistaken identity, or the outbreak of some incurable disease affecting the local lorry-driving population, to which only he was immune. Until one day in the middle of November, with Christmas-mania looming and an increased sense of urgency regarding supermarkets supplying the nation's festive over-indulgence, he gets a bewildering phone call telling him to get straight down to said depot.

'But I haven't got two years' experience, as you keep telling me!' Worth pointing out, just in case he is told to go home as soon as he arrives.

'Ah, don't worry about that. Just get down there as quick as you can.'

With trepidation, he does just that, wondering whether his luck had changed or was about to get much worse. But he survived, and from then on, a steady stream of work flowed, and the lack of catastrophe enabled him to just about blend in with the crowd in the chaotic pre-Christmas frenzy of the depot. But it was a close run thing, with him frequently unable to disguise his blundering inexperience. Something regarded as almost a crime in the modern, fast-paced, impersonal world of supply and demand of HGV drivers. Where the reputations of salesmen, assorted 'charmless Jim' replicas and other office-types with a sense of their own importance, were at stake. It had all looked so easy in the busy despatch area at Johnson's as a spectator.

Another sober Christmas came and went, with much satisfaction at the progress with work that had been achieved in the year. But had workaholism replaced alcoholism?

There was disturbingly little work in January, and he began to question his motives for leaving the security of the paint factory. He rang the agency with increasing desperation.

'Is there no work down there now?' he asked, referring to the place of work he had been going almost on a daily basis for the month leading up to Christmas.

'Well, not for you.'

'What do you mean, not for me?'

'Well, you haven't got two years' experience, have you?'

Deep sigh. Followed by a moment of silence while Jonathan tries to take in the parasitism of it all.

'But you lot sent me down there. I've been going there for weeks now!' Jonathan pleaded, just in case there was some kind of mistaken identity going on, and this one not working in his favour.

No answer, and he could hear the keyboard of a word processor being tapped in the background, suggesting the man was too busy to continue the conversation. It was all becoming clear. The usual, strict (safety?) regulations, previously abandoned due to the Christmas rush, had now resumed, in a cold, grey, workless, January.

He avoided Mr Hubbib as he struggled to pay the rent. Not an easy task, as the man occupied the room next door. The confusion and panic began to set in once more, as the speed with which his fortunes had changed and returned him to roof-threatening poverty was overwhelming. Due to the lack of rent, Mr Hubbib suggested a deal where his old Datsun was returned to him as an equivalent of two week's rent as it had been performing a bit better recently. A solution, but one that felt like the beginning of the end for Jonathan, the start of a possible drift back in the direction of the quicksand of homelessness, and the traumas of grappling with the bureaucracy of the DSS. There was even a lull in the early morning cleaning, as he struggled his way through the ever-increasing culture of casual 'as and when required' type of work. And he now had an added handicap in his quest for it: no transport. Had anyone ever been so punished for their sense of ambition? At least, not since the last assassinated U.S President.

After the first letter he received from Dennis, he had feelings like: this was someone from his ancient past who he wasn't sure he wanted to resume contact with. So much had changed since then and he had moved on, he thought. But now, it was with pure irony that he asked his old friend to rescue him from the life he had made for himself.

Did Dennis have a spare room? No, but he had a large settee.

Would he mind if his biggest fan (forever grateful for the piano-playing!) slept on it, until he found somewhere else in Plymouth? No, he didn't mind at all. That was settled.

The perils of work, money, the lack of both, and the DSS, would be faced in Plymouth at the appropriate time.

More and more it had seemed like he was approaching the end of the line in Hounslow. What little that had remained of a social life, his once dear friends, Jan, Steve and family, having disappeared without word. Perhaps unable to contact him to say goodbye during his chaotic struggles with housing, or, for whatever reason; and painful for him to consider, preferring not to. He wouldn't have been content with the stagnancy of staying at the paint factory and driving the smaller lorry for evermore, with no experience of artics gained. And as such, was somehow destined for further upheaval, insecurity, and a possible reuniting with poverty. He desperately needed a holiday. Something with which his mum would surely agree. But such delights were forever out of his reach. And so, it felt like he was doing the next best thing; a change was as good as a rest, as had often been said.

As he prepared to leave, he wanted to thank the lady downstairs and her daughters for their charm, beauty and courtesy that had so enriched his five years there. But that wouldn't have been considered normal, he predicted. And trying to arrange such feelings into words that sounded normal was always a challenge. So he thanked the lady for all the South Asian cuisine he had enjoyed instead, and kissed her cheek. Possibly not the done thing for those of such different cultures, judging by the slight embarrassment it caused. But this was a rare special person, in amongst the sea of the otherwise indifferent or hostile, to whom, gratitude of some kind needed to be expressed.

Surprisingly, Mr Hubbib insisted on giving him a lift to the train station and carrying some of his stuff to the platform once there. They waved as the train moved off, the landlord as expressionless as ever. But he had eventually warmed to his English tenant, and his unpaid assistance now in getting him and his stuff to the station was proof of it. As emotional a gesture as his manner would allow.

Dennis was on the platform at Plymouth when he arrived, just as he had been ten years ago in Sheffield when he departed. Jonathan dropped his belongings to the floor on seeing his smiling face and now greying hair, and the two men hugged.

'So, how d' you get on in Hounslow then?' Dennis asked, with the usual casualness when in non-psychotic mode.

'Oh! Don't ask,' Jonathan replied, with a roll of the eyes, a smile and shake of the head.

A Return to Frivolity

At Jonathan's new home, a musical evening was enjoyed with much reminiscence about the old days, the Tea Bar, and the many characters there in. Several of whom, Dennis did his usual, hilariously accurate impressions of, in between some old favourites being thrashed out on the piano. And by the sound of it, there was a few characters in Dennis's life now.

Wherever he went, it didn't take long for him to establish himself in the local psychiatric community, largely due to the essential visits to a hospital for the injections that kept his usual, witty, laid-back demeanour going, and the playing of pianos once there. The instrument, usually in abundance at such places, but sitting silently and neglected in a corner of the room. And his ability to quickly transform such a room, got him noticed. Even by the most unappreciative of audiences.

'Has anyone got any requests?'

'Yes, bugger off and take your piano with you.' Laughter.

'No, apart from that one.' More laughter.

Jonathan fitted into any psychiatric, eccentric, or otherwise slightly off-centre community like a hand in a glove. Dangerous at times, like his hand was superglued inside that glove and would take one almighty wrench to get it out. The same kind of wrench that eventually got him out of Sheffield. Amongst the increasing leisure and apathy he was once again partaking in, (after its ten-year interval) was the disturbing and inevitable awareness that employment of some kind had to be found; despite Dennis's recommendations that he just 'join the club'. 'The club' consisted of long-term benefit claimants with handy diagnoses like 'paranoid schizophrenia' which, as well as being something that can seriously mess up one's life and other people's, had also been known to make the claiming of benefit go that much smoother with the submitting of regular sick notes from a doctor not required. The more he hung around with his musician friend and got to know various other members of said club, the less chance there was of him finding employment. Especially, as this most unusually casual of landlords wasn't exactly breathing down his neck for the rent.

At one particular weekly psychiatric social group that Dennis frequented and played the piano, and was only too happy for his friend to tag along, Jonathan felt a bit like he was trespassing. As if there under false pretences, as some far more disturbed characters came and went with the occasional slamming of doors and shouts of the nonsensical. And as such, as if to ease his guilt, would help the assembled staff and voluntary helpers put things out, and later put them back in again: chairs, ashtrays, table-tennis table, cups and saucers, that kind of thing. And so, was often mistaken for being one such official helper and treated accordingly: the patients telling him their problems in detail without looking at him or paying any attention to him as a person. To which, he tried to give helpful advice where he could and very often succeeded, having had first-hand experience of a lot of their ills: problems with medication and hostile neighbours to name a few.

While there, Jonathan began to notice and miraculously chat with, an outgoing, attractive lady helper about his own age. With each week they got closer, seemingly drifting towards the inevitable arranging to meet up somewhere else. She also assumed he was an official voluntary helper of the non-psychiatric variety like herself, and therefore safe to chat, and on occasions flirt with. And it was, whoever Jonathan was or wasn't. For a brief moment, it felt like he was possibly on course for love and romance. However, it was common knowledge that Dennis was a patient, and therefore, not an official civilian musician from outside; like some others who had entertained the troops for small remuneration. Once it was established that Jonathan was not only a close friend but lodger of his, the patients became far more relaxed with him and began to see him as one of them, someone they could have a laugh with. All quite refreshing. But sadly, the same revelation caused the staff/helpers, including attractive lady helper, to move swiftly in the opposite direction, becoming far more distant. Which hurt, and she stopped flirting and he stopped helping. The kind of complex, delicate, social situation governed by strict, unspoken, and almost unrealised regulation, to do with the all-important issues of belonging, not belonging, and distancing. And very much the story of Jonathan's life. Forever on the fringes of everything, without actually belonging to anything, who, when finding himself drifting in the direction of normality, is suddenly and abruptly redirected.

When more serious concerns were put aside, he relished the constant sightseeing of being in a new place. Constantly discovering, as he travelled everywhere on foot or the top deck of a bus. And all with the constant accompaniment of the squawking of seagulls, and much fresher air than could be inhaled in London and its surroundings. The settee, despite its foam stuffing escaping here and there, was just as comfy as a bed, and the regular live music as he lay on it was a cure for much of his ills. For a time, it felt like his move west had breathed new life into him, with previous work-related ambition all but faded into nothing as more leisurely pursuits took over.

At another such event of music and occasional mayhem, with Dennis in full flow on the piano and staff/helpers attending to every whim of the outpatients, a lady enters the room looking flustered, fumbling with an umbrella. Slightly older than Jonathan, now approaching his mid-thirties, and much younger than Dennis, twenty years his senior, who gives her a broad, cheeky grin, suggesting he knows her quite well.

'I'm sorry I'm late, everybody!' she loudly announces, as if she were some kind of pre-booked entertainment.

But her words are ignored, as the regulars are too engrossed in the music, card games, table-tennis, or just staring out the window, to notice her. Seeming completely oblivious to the lack of attention, she smiles affectionately at the room, like an opera singer at the end of her performance about to be presented with the customary bunch of flowers. Much of her clothes, including her hat, are knitted or crocheted, and she possessed a charming, infectious eccentricity, a pretty face and a lovely figure, and was a magnet to Jonathan's eyes.

Dennis sat down on his interval where Jonathan was sitting and lit a fag, and the newly arrived knitted lady, presumably here in her capacity as a fellow ex-patient, joined them.

'Hello, Jenny. How ya doing?' Dennis asked, in his usual softly-spoken comforting way.

'Oh, plodding on, you know. Who's this?' she asked Dennis, but looking straight at Jonathan, smiling. He smiled back, amused by her childlike honesty and directness, and her question prompted the rarity of an almost formal introduction from Dennis.

'This is my friend Jonathan. He's come to live with me from London.'

'Oh! Very nice too, I'm sure,' Jenny said, laughing loudly, as though hinting at the unintended homosexual connotations of Dennis's words. 'Are we gonna be hearing the sound of wedding bells, I wonder.' More laughter.

It was obvious, she was the kind of vivacious, if slightly unhinged girl, who could find the sexual connotations in a laboratory full of white-coated chemists concocting a new liquid for unblocking drains. And possible reincarnation of a turn-of-the-century, music-hall artiste.

Dennis laughed and did his Kenneth Williams impression in the most camp way possible. ''Ere, stop messing about!'

Much laughter.

'Oh no, I'm on the settee.' Jonathan thought it necessary to confirm.

More laughter, especially from Jenny, now attracting the attention of others in the room due to its volume.

'Cor blimey! Does the News of the World know about all this?' she joked. 'You know, you two must come and see me on my boat sometime,' she added, with a sudden and bewildering change of direction.

Jonathan waited for the laughter, expecting her last sentence to be treated as a joke, as everything else had been up until now. But no laughter, and the subject is immediately changed again, as Dennis and Jenny natter about various people they knew. Jonathan had so many questions about said 'boat' he would have loved to have asked if he could have got a word in. Would she be lying on the front of it in a bikini? That was one of them. He fancied her; there was no doubt about it, and was anxious not to appear boring. Not easy, while in the company of such an extrovert, apparently boat-owning, comedienne, and a gifted piano-player and impressionist.

She turns her attention back to Jonathan.

'So, what am I gonna call you then?' she asked.

His mouth opened, about to reply, keen to say something spellbinding but was beaten to it. 'I can't call you Jonathan. It's too much of a mouthful. If I keep saying that I'll end up with more wrinkles on my face. I'll call you Jonny. Is that agreed?'

Her words were accompanied by a deep seductive stare into his eyes, as if so natural, she was unaware of it.

237

'And if you ever leave me, I'll sing, *"Jonny, come back with my heart, for only in death must we part..."'*

Adding more fuel to Jonathan's overall suspicion that here was another such character whose natural drift in the direction of show business had been diverted into one of mental illness, the lady bursts into a rousing rendition of a song of lost love known only to herself. A beautiful voice, reaching the high notes with ease and a beaming smile, while beckoning Dennis to the piano to accompany her, who shrugs his shoulders in ignorance of the said tune before turning to Jonathan with the familiar mocking-yet-affectionate grin at the weird and wonderful. But his young friend was enthralled by her and couldn't remember the last time he'd had so much fun spectating a conversation; of which he was so much the subject but had hardly managed to participate.

He felt the full force of a strong, mutual (he suspected, unless he was dreaming) sexual attraction here, to which, only the presence of others in the room was stopping the immediate and frantic shedding of clothes. Her words were as if they were about to commence a long association, and he was flattered that she considered him important enough to warrant a debate about what she should call him. Although keen to inject some of his own repartee into the conversation as if to prove himself worthy of her interest, 'I'm on the settee' was all he'd had the chance to say, but somehow, even that dismal contribution got a laugh. People like Jenny, he thought, who could laugh so easily without the aid of alcohol, needed to be preserved, or at least their brain retained in a jar for closer examination long after the rest of them had gone. There were similarities to the long-lost Bridget here, which he adored.

So one sunny afternoon when Dennis showed him around the harbour, the obvious question was, 'where's Jenny's boat'? And there she was, hanging out washing on the deck of a small vessel, surrounded by others in the square harbour. It was a smart looking boat, which apparently she had recently inherited from a deceased uncle, so Dennis explained.

'Ah, chaps!' she shouted, now struggling to remember their names, after all the furore about Jonathan's.

'We can come back later if you're busy,' said Jonathan, half expecting to see a male companion come out on deck to see what the fuss was about.

Her marital status had been much on his mind but thought it best not to quiz Dennis about it, having barged in enough on his friend's social life over the years.

After a guided tour of the boat, which she obviously lived in, judging by the extent of her belongings scattered about all over the place, the visitors were treated to a lovely cream tea which she prepared down below in the tiny kitchen and brought up to them on deck. Jonathan felt like he'd gone to heaven prematurely, and the usual worries of employment, how he must get it and return to something like the real world, were far from his mind. As he partook of the refreshments, he tried his best to stop looking at her smalls and imagining her wearing them, as they blew about in the wind on the washing line. Jenny was still her cheery self, just as before on their first meeting, but now seemed a little distracted. She suddenly notices something on land, starts the engine and frantically unties the ropes holding the boat. Then moves off without explanation, bashing into other boats and only just getting it out of the harbour, with washing flapping about furiously. Jonathan and Dennis look at each other, puzzled, with slight concern for her well-being and their safety.

'Are you all right, Jenny?' Dennis asked, calmly as ever, rescuing a jam-covered scone off the floor.

'Yeah. It's OK. Don't worry. Just saw something back there. We'll go round a bit and come back later. You don't mind a bit of a cruise do you, chaps?' she asked, regaining her usual chirpiness.

'No, not at all!' Jonathan piped up, with mostly fake nonchalance. Trying to grab any opportunity not to appear boring, thinking it may ruin his chances of getting to know her more intimately, as hoped.

For the guests, it was a rare treat, as long as they didn't dwell too much on the possibly disturbing reason for it. Jenny seemed far away in thought as she steered. She was a skilled, if frantic, boat handler, who hopefully, wasn't in the habit of hallucinating, as she wasn't telling what it was she saw at the harbour that had caused such panic. And her passengers hadn't noticed any dinosaurs, or similarly fearsome creatures that would warrant it. Whatever the reason for the escape, Jonathan doubted its connection to sound practical logic, and so considered it best not to ask. Jenny seemed the type to be more influenced by the spirit world than the maritime one. A charming quality in any human being, if not especially in the person in charge of a boat you found yourself travelling in.

Dennis puffed on his fag, gazing at the scenery, showing no sign of concern, even though Jonathan remembered from their days in Sheffield that he couldn't swim, and there was no sign of lifejackets on board. Fairly soon they were in the estuary of the River Tamar with the mighty bridge towering above them and a train passing over it, and to his left, Jonathan could see the outside of a pub all painted like a union jack. Once again, the joy of seeing lots of lovely things for the first time. A precious moment.

Suddenly the engine stops.

'Oh shit! Petrol.' She bangs her hand against her head. 'I'm sorry, chaps.'

'Don't worry, Jenny. Worse things have happened at sea,' Dennis tells her, with hushed tones, as she stares despondently at the floor, while looking at Jonathan and smiling, with another look of affectionate mockery of the weird and wonderful that used to be reserved for the clientele of the Tea Bar. But now, stranded in an unpowered boat a fair distance from land, surely warranted a more serious look. Apparently not.

Jenny called out to passing vessels for assistance to no avail. Jonathan, keen to do something useful that will increase his popularity, volunteered to swim to the nearest land and search for fuel, carrying an empty plastic petrol container she had on board. So often in his life, what great pleasure had been experienced was quickly followed by equal pain, and this was no exception. A quick swimmer when he had to be and had to be now to avoid other boats whizzing by. The plan was to get petrol and return; sort of swimming one-handed with full-up petrol container in the other, he supposed, if that was possible. After which, the gorgeous Jenny would fall into his arms saying something like, 'Jonny, my hero!'

It took a while. Once safely ashore, but with no special boating pumps visible along the river side, as an optimistic Jenny suggested there would, a petrol station, usually for the fuelling of road vehicles, was the only other option. He eventually found one, filled up his can and caused much amusement as he joined the queue inside, with water still dripping off the few clothes he had on. Only for it to dawn on him that his wallet was in his jacket on the boat, which, despite feeling like a disaster, *was* actually a blessing, as it would be sopping wet if it wasn't. After loud, panic-ridden explanation, a kind person in the queue paid for his five litres.

And off he went, back in the direction of where he thought he'd left them, somewhere near the Tamar Bridge. He shouted and waved his arms about from the water's edge, but no sign of them, or any kind boat owners to give him a lift and help with the search. And when all seemed hopeless, he walked along endless roads, barefoot, with socks now torn to shreds and disposed of, and shoes left behind on the boat, thinking they might weigh him down while swimming. Following the coast around as best he could, but with numerous obstacles forcing him further in land, he could only hope he was moving in the general direction of the harbour where they started out, and only hope that his friends had somehow managed to do the same. He asked a few passers-by for directions without much success. A now mentally unstable looking man with long wet hair and bare feet, carrying a plastic container clearly designed for the storage of petrol, was best avoided.

Eventually, and close to collapse, he made it back to the harbour, wondering if he was the lucky one with his friends now possibly adrift somewhere in the ocean. But, to his joy, sees them on deck in the distance. It may have had something to do with his injections doing their job, or his addiction to nicotine being satisfied, but Dennis was not a man who was easily ruffled. As Jonathan got closer to them, he could see him chatting away to Jenny, still dry and smiling, as if nothing had happened. Maybe it hadn't, and this was all a dream, he wondered, as he walked towards Jenny's boat. Then, with equal relief, they see his bedraggled figure approaching with now full petrol container in hand. Jenny gave him one enormous, prolonged, silent hug, before any explanations could be made. And after the most memorable of hugs came the most memorable of kisses on the lips, as if the mayhem of the last three hours had at least succeeded in cementing their friendship as he hoped it would. But after the unrestrained affection, to his dismay, there were no immediate explanations. Just the two friends resuming their intense chat about all things trivial, as if absolutely nothing had occurred since the spreading of jam and cream on scones earlier in the day. An exhausted Jonathan sat there in silence leaving them to it, examining his blistered feet, at last reunited with their shoes.

Dennis paid for a taxi home, after his weary and blistered friend insisted he would have to be carried to the bus stop. And on the way, he managed to get some sense out of Dennis as to what had occurred. Apparently, a passing Good Samaritan sailor had towed them back to the harbour. They had to accept the help, not knowing whether or not he had been successful in his mission to get petrol, or if he would ever return with it.

'Is she on the run from the Mafia or something?' Jonathan jokingly asked, referring to the earlier quick getaway from something presumably horrific either seen or imagined.

'No. Her son. Well, she thinks it's her son.'

'Her son!'

Jonathan no longer had the energy to make further enquiries. That was it. No more questions, and no more crazy answers, today at least. He ended the day exhausted and bewildered, but possibly in love with a woman who it felt should be branded with some kind of government health warning. And, like a glutton for punishment, couldn't wait to see her again.

'What tranquil, soothing tune would his lordship appreciate this evening before he retires, may one enquire?' Dennis jested, sitting at the piano. As Jonathan lay on his settee, surrounded by duvet, already half asleep.

'Chopin. The rain drop one. You know.'

'Sonata?'

'Yeah, him as well.'

'I did it my way?'

'Yeah, that'll do.'

It was the dreaded day of signing on and showing his form/diary full of mostly fictional details of what he had done to find work. As it was now known as 'Job Seeker's Allowance', the job seeking bit was taken rather seriously, so it seemed, even though the place looked a lot like a social club for people with piercings in strange places and malnourished, depressed looking dogs. He enquired about a job displayed on one of the many cards advertising the grimmest of work at the minimum wage, as it was at least something truthful that could be put in his diary for when next inspected. And if he indulged in any more cream teas, cruises and musical evenings, the grim reality of job-seeking would be just too unbearable to be faced.

The assistant rang the company who said he could go down there straight away. With a sense of impending doom, he did. He didn't like the sound of it one hit Long distance parcel delivery in a van, was about as much information as could be grasped, before the 'interview' reached its horrific conclusion.

'So, when can you start?'

He was cornered. If he backed out now, they'd be straight on the phone to the social which would result in no benefit for six weeks: the usual punishment for 'discrepancies', like not accepting a job when you've been given one or leaving a job of your own accord. The latter, he was now something of an expert on, and had cautiously refrained from admitting to another recent case of, from the paint factory in Hounslow. And that punishment, would in turn lead to him, not only being a non-paying guest at Dennis's, but having to scrounge off his friend as well. Something that needed avoiding at all costs, as he was already troubled by his growing dependency on the man.

'Monday,' he solemnly admits, as if arranging an appointment to be castrated. They had HGVs, including a few artics, which was his only attraction to it. And promised he would be first in line for promotion to HGV once a vacancy arose, despite his minimal experience. But he'd had more than enough experience of the empty promises of such people, and his suspicions of the contrary proved to be correct as time went on. After nearly a year of 5 am starts, driving about 100 miles away in a van, then delivering around one hundred parcels in that area before returning home, he gave himself an early Christmas present and chucked it. But fortunately, in his defence, was the rarity of an understanding GP, who surveyed his patient's messy psychiatric history and medication prescribed for it with a shake of the head and a frown, and gave him repeat sick notes until the glorious day he didn't have to send them in any more. Thus, promoting himself to the rank of claimant of 'Disability Living Allowance', which Dennis also received. Thus, giving him membership of 'the club', which his friend had so strongly recommended he joined. As if he had any say in the matter.

'*Aaahh*, you've joined the club. Congratulations,' said Dennis, with an arm around his shoulder, as if welcoming a new member to the weirdest of religious cults. With his usual cynicism, but misguidedly believing that all Jonathan's troubles were now over, now he had. For the moment they were, but Jonathan could feel that superglue in the glove on the verge of setting. With no diagnosis on his records any more severe

243

than the odd 'personality disorder', or 'dependant personality', the authorities were never going to be far away. And in his peculiar, topsy-turvy world, had gone from being an aspiring workaholic in one place, to a 'work shy scrounger' in another, in a relatively short space of time.

A period of regular and blissful visits to the post office with benefit book in hand commenced, with no sick notes having to be submitted and no visits to the much-feared 'dole office' to be inspected, scrutinized or snarled at by fellow claimants. But a now world-weary Jonathan knew when something was too good to be true. It was much like being trapped in a large closet with only the world's most poisonous snake for company who, for the moment, was nice and friendly, and liked nothing more than to curl up next to its human friend for a kip.

Such insecurity, coupled with a flicker of ambition, steered his thoughts in the direction of a possible return to the driving of artics. And for that, a car would be needed, as the depots that needed to be got to for such driving were a good distance out of town, and as such, inaccessible by public transport. Eventually, with the aid of some 'cash in hand' labouring work, supplied by the brother of a friend of Dennis to supplement the continuous DLA, a car was bought. Where would he be without Dennis? And once again, the dependency was frightening, even if this particular example of it was assisting his movements in the general direction of independence.

But once the car was bought, the labouring was abandoned with the minimum of explanation, much to the frustration of Dennis's friend's builder brother. An awkward situation, but the 'benefit fraud' of an officially-recognized disabled man humping great sacks of cement about before mixing it and keeping the workers well supplied with bricks, and being left peacefully alone to get on with it, was another of those things that was way too good to be true, as far as he was concerned. Judging by his history of struggle with the benefit system to take advantage of it legally and honestly, the trauma of being discovered doing it illegally and dishonestly didn't bear thinking about. And so, with the newly acquired jalopy, was able to slightly reduce the feeling of growing dependency on his friend by transporting him to various piano-playing bookings. Mostly in old people's homes, as pianos in pubs were all but extinct having failed in their competition with jukeboxes and karaoke. And the aged audiences varied from the oblivious not knowing what was going on, to welcoming Dennis with open arms and beaming smiles, with cries of, 'Have you

244

come to play the piano?' and, 'He's come to play the piano!'

The Ford Sierra was badly dented and scraped, and well into the autumn of its years. But because it moved, he often found *it* and himself being invited to various things by some of the many new friends he had acquired via Dennis. Things where car transportation would be very useful to one and all. And as Jonathan appreciated all things second-hand, including car boot sales, he agreed to take Bernie to one such extravaganza of junk.

On his arrival at the man's terraced house, was invited in. As he entered, it became immediately obvious that this was the home of someone in the advanced stages of *collectomania*. Obvious to anyone with eyesight and a brain, except the *collectomaniac* himself, who had sound reasons for not being able to find an electric mains socket on the wall, that was 'there last week'. A hoarder of one thing in particular it seemed, due to the vast piles of them everywhere: records, singles, LPs, Eps and 78s, all stacked on top of each other in precarious towers. But Bernie was a cheery sort, with most things he said being accompanied by a cheeky grin. Even when an avalanche occurred, caused by the annoying but essential movement of humans in the house, with great piles of the stuff collapsing onto other piles, it prompted no more than a minor expletive without much volume.

'I see you've got a good system going here, Bernie.'

'Oh, don't you start!' Suggesting there were others who had expressed an opinion.

Jonathan soon realised the hidden genius behind his invitation. That a car could be used to enable his friend's addiction and get him to car boot sales further afield, where the records had so far not been scoured. And of course, unlimited amounts of the gems could now be bought, with a car to get them safely home.

'You don't want a cup of tea, do you?'

Maybe the kettle was buried somewhere after one such avalanche in 1976 and hadn't been seen since.

'We can get one when we're out, can't we?' Bernie further encouraged, with a smile.

'Yeah, don't worry. I'm fine. I wouldn't say no to steak and chips though,' Jonathan added, with the feeling that he'd let Bernie off a bit too lightly with the inhospitality to his chauffeur.

Prompting a stern look from the host, before realizing it was a joke. They laughed at the ridiculousness of the request. As it didn't look as though even a sandwich had been successfully made in the kitchen for some time due to the records taking up whatever available space there was, no matter what domestic necessities were being impeded.

Suddenly, the obvious question, but which had so far eluded Jonathan, was asked. 'Have you got a record player?'

There was a pause, in which Bernie stared at him intensely with unusual seriousness, as if trying to think of an acceptable answer that might fend off what felt like the most threatening of sensible questions.

'What?'

'You know, something to play them on. You do play them sometimes, don't you?'

'Oh yeah, yeah, course I do! Ummm, it was round here somewhere. I've seen it. I know I have.'

All of a sudden, Bernie had lost the confidence and humour that was so much a part of him, as if confronted with the madness of his activities, and there was no way out. With vague memories of playing records swimming about in his brain, but the insatiable need to get more and the problems of then storing them, had invalidated any such leisurely pursuits.

Jonathan commented on the beauty of a lady in a photo on a shelf, who a somewhat younger looking Bernie had his arm around.

'Ah, she left me, didn't she.'

'Did she get sick of sitting on piles of records?'

Jonathan realised he had touched a very sore nerve, and so quit with the jokes, that weren't really jokes. More, observations of the obvious chaos, which was too easy to mock.

But soon, Bernie's eyes light up and the confidence returns.

'But there's this other really gorgeous bird who I've got chatting to a couple of times at one of the boot sales. I think I'm in there.'

The optimism seemed ridiculous for an overweight man well into middle-age with thinning hair, whose only visible asset was a house that he apparently owned. And would be just that, had its purpose not been redirected to that of a storage container. Jonathan was the exact opposite of Bernie, with little optimism and no idea whatsoever about chatting up women. But one thing they both had very much in common, was their proneness to mania and obsession. Of very different things perhaps, but

246

with equal intensity, Jonathan was no stranger to all manner of psychological malady, either witnessing it in others, or experiencing it himself.

So off they went, and on arrival went in different directions arranging to meet up later: an increasingly intense Bernie choosing to be alone for the task of scouring the place like a hawk in pursuit of his prey, during which there would be no time for idle chat with his chauffeur. On the way home, Bernie's excitement at what he had bought was clear. Some of it was quite rare, he was sure of it. Various singles in their original sleeves 'could be worth a few bob'. Back at the house, the equally intense unpacking of the day's catch and the challenge of finding a new home for it commenced as Jonathan passed his friend records, with them both standing knee-deep in the sea of vinyl.

At times, Jonathan conceded to an almost moral duty to give advice to his beleaguered friend who was blissfully unaware that he was. Finding it impossible to avoid sounding like a health and safety inspector as he spoke. Especially when anyone needed the loo, which was upstairs, and involved treading very carefully between the piles of records at either end of each stair. God help anyone who misplaced their feet slightly on descent, he thought, but then again, their fall would probably be cushioned by the LPs at the bottom. To which, Bernie explained his 'system' whereby only singles fitted on the stairs, so that space was sensibly reserved for them; doing his best to make it sound organised and controlled. But Jonathan noticed that the odd 78 had found its way to the stairs and slightly overlapped them, limiting the foot space even further. Which he chose not to mention.

It was too easy to criticize and Jonathan tried to avoid it, having had similar obsessions of his own and been far less amiable than Bernie during them. It brought back memories of a flawed DIY challenge that had got out of control and had reduced his Sheffield flat to a similar state of chaos to the one he was witnessing here. With the settee being used as a work bench, sharp tools, planks of wood and sticky substances everywhere; their lids lost among the debris, there was no longer anywhere to sit or lie, and even putting one's foot to the floor was a risk. And with himself ravaged by the horrors of perfectionism, had been unable to divert his attention to the much needed clearing up, or any of life's other essentials. So, he was in no position to judge.

Bernie treated his guest to a quick look at the garden, which was a welcome break from the claustrophobia of the house. And, Jonathan assumed, a record-free zone. However, not exactly a horticultural paradise, it was mainly occupied by two large sheds and a washing line. Each shed was crammed full of filing cabinets, and each filing cabinet was crammed full of LPs. This was a disturbing enough sight on its own, but somehow increased when Bernie asked his advice on where cheap sheds and filing cabinets could be bought, as if planning to get more. And, whether or not he had a roof rack on the car, as it would surely be needed for the transportation of them. Doubtless, it would all be explained as a sensible way of easing the congestion in the overcrowded kitchen, where cooking, and tea-making it seemed, were now impossible.

'They're just the right size, you see. Perfect.'

Bernie demonstrated the perfection, pulling a draw out of one of the few cabinets he could actually get to, displaying the LPs neatly fitting inside ready to be flicked through. Just to prove there was method in the madness.

Jonathan left without giving any more advice, as it was like trying to stop a train by waving a feather at it, so it seemed. Nothing short of imprisonment would do the trick. So what was the point? Perhaps a team of world-renowned psychologists should be drafted in to determine what it was the records were a substitute for that was so lacking in his life. But Bernie was happy in his own way, with a purpose, however barmy it may look to others.

Jonathan hovered around the harbour at a safe distance, hoping to catch a glimpse of his beloved, armed with a box of chocolates just in case he did. Just to say thank you for the lovely cream tea and cruise; pre-running out of petrol, which would not be mentioned at the risk of disturbing the ambience of serenity that it felt needed to be created. Was that a respectable enough charade for him being where he was, with the carnal intentions he had? He hoped so. He had to see her again, but as usual, was terrified of the slightest hint of rejection. And doubted whether him being alone without Dennis, even with chocolates, warranted the disturbance of the peace of not much more than a stranger. But at the same time, something inside him (that probably couldn't and shouldn't be trusted) told him that it was inevitable they would be having sex on her boat soon, but not with Dennis in attendance. And so, for that reason, it made perfect sense for him to be where he was, alone, didn't it? Oh, the indecision! Suddenly, he saw her come up on deck. She saw him. He felt like a peeping tom and turned away.

'Jonny!' she shouts, beckoning him to come over, enthusiastically. The relief that she remembered his name was overwhelming.

Once again, he was greeted with an almighty kiss on the lips. During which, it felt like even a nuclear missile couldn't harm him. She offered him a can of lager, which was *so* difficult to decline at such a carefree and wild moment that he desperately didn't want to risk destroying with such caution. But just about managed it, accepting the offer of a cup of tea instead. And as the kettle boiled, they looked at each other silently, smiled simultaneously, and moved slowly towards each other. And that moment of surrender; with its confirmation that what had been going on in his head since their first meeting wasn't just crazy fantasy, was sheer bliss. As was the fast and furious undressing of each other, passionate, clumsy (as always when Jonathan was doing it) sex, and prolonged laying in each other's arms afterwards, with a chorus of seagulls overhead.

Later on deck, with his mission so blissfully accomplished, they sat holding hands in the late afternoon sunshine with Jenny smiling at him in her usual seductive way, in between the occasional nibble of the chocolates he had brought with him.

But just as it seemed that life couldn't get any more tranquil, he noticed a fearsome looking young man striding in their direction who didn't quite fit with the surroundings. And as the man then turned towards the pontoon to which the boat was moored, and suddenly remembering Dennis's words about 'her son', he alerted Jenny. At which point, he half expected her to start the engine and attempt the same disappearing act as before. And almost wished she would, as the man's stare left him in no doubt as to his intended destination. But not this time. Just before her ashen face disappeared below deck, she instructed Jonathan to tell the bloke that he had just bought the boat from a lady. That he was now the new owner and had no idea of the whereabouts of the lady he bought it from. All was said so quickly he could only just catch her words but grasped the basic idea. Sure enough, the young man marched straight onto her boat, after having leapt on and off the decks of other boats to gain access with disturbing athleticism, staring straight ahead the whole time, at Jonathan, as if ready to kill.

'Where's my mum?'

Miraculously, he obviously hadn't seen his mum on deck just a few seconds previous, and unusually, there was nothing on the washing line to indicate female presence. Hence, the planned charade could be at least attempted, and hopefully, giving him a few more minutes to live. Something for which it felt, whichever god it was that had divinely intervened, would be worshipped, vigorously, when there was a bit more time.

'Er, I don't know. I don't know your mum.' Still seated, trying to appear calm, despite feeling the urgent need to get up and at least prepare to defend himself, with water so close behind him.

'Oh, you don't! Well, this is her boat, so you're trespassing,' the surly young man continued, as if about to start the removal process of said trespasser, as he moves a few paces closer.

'No, I bought this boat this morning from a lady. Maybe that was your mum.'

Jonathan's look of fake bewilderment and slight concern for the missing mum and attempt to sound like someone who was in the habit of buying boats regularly, was showing vague signs of success. As it silenced the young man who began to walk away, but then suddenly turned back with a point of a finger and a prolonged stare.

'You'd better not be having me on.' His words were hushed, but the stare more than substituted for the lack of volume. This man had one hell of a grudge about something.

Jonathan was frozen with fear, as he wondered what on earth he had got himself involved in. Not daring to move a muscle, just in case it prompted a search of the vessel for the elusive mum who he hoped had managed to escape through a trap door, if boats had such things.

The young man left, hopefully for good, but he guessed not. And as all went quiet, Jenny emerged and beckoned him downstairs so they were out of view. There were tears in her eyes as she gave a long explanation of how she had given birth to him all alone in a park and then left him in the doorway of a hospital. Her actions having caused a childhood of children's homes and failed foster homes, with the boy later being abandoned again, by a foster mother he had guided in the general direction of a nervous breakdown.

'I was sixteen, Jonny! My head was all over the place! Somehow, he's found out where I am and he's gonna kill me. I'm sure of it.'

Her desperate words sounded very much like a request for protection. And uncomfortably, as he had partaken of such pleasure with her, and liked her, a lot, felt duty bound to do what he could. Which would probably amount to no more than being a human shield for whatever vengeance the man had in mind to throw at her. Her son was at least half a foot bigger than him in all directions, and right now, ten times as angry. Unarmed combat without the aid of ridiculous amounts of alcohol, was something he had never been comfortable with.

All was quiet in the harbour as the more well-heeled, boat-owning neighbours had other homes to go to, and as it approached dusk, she asked him to stay the night. Very much with protection in mind rather than sex. Which unusually, was also the last thing on Jonathan's mind, as that and sleep were two pleasures he definitely wouldn't be indulging in tonight now he had accepted her invitation. As they tended to make one a lot more vulnerable to visiting monster sons who didn't have the courtesy to tell them what time they'd be arriving.

She took some pills from a bottle marked 'Lithium Carbonate[16]' and swigged them back with water, reminding Jonathan of someone from his distant past whose flat had been littered with empty bottles of the same stuff, amongst other things. Who spoke with the same wide-eyed exuberance when in full flow, as if being powered by a motor; just like Jenny had been at their first meeting when he couldn't get a word in. Whatever Eric had suffered from, so, presumably, did this most fragile of mothers. The pills seemed to do the trick, as despite the current insecurity, she slept soundly, alone in the single bed. With her guest wide awake, sat in an armchair, listening out for her son's footsteps up above on deck at any moment. At which, he must be ready to leap into action. Of some sort. His unease not helped by the lack of key to the cabin, and the lock she had 'never got round to' replacing.

She awoke refreshed, smiling and affectionate; beckoning him over to her bed for a cuddle, as if now unaware that she even had a son, or any other problems. But a sleep-starved Jonathan was nervous for her, as she later climbed the stairs to the sunlight of the deck with amnesia of yesterday's events. Still below making tea, he suddenly hears the heavy

---

[16] for the treatment of manic depression/ bipolar disorder.

footsteps he had been dreading all night, followed by a scream from Jenny. He leaps upstairs, and suddenly finds himself grappling with her son in the middle of his matricidal rage, dangerously close to the edge of the boat. The young man swings the sort of punch that is deadly when it makes contact but throws the puncher seriously off balance when it doesn't. And in this case it doesn't, as Jonathan loses his footing just at the crucial moment, sinks to the floor and avoids it, as the boat goes up and down like one lost at sea in a storm; forcing the son overboard as he to loses balance, smashing his head on the side of another boat just before he enters the presumably shallow waters of the harbour. But not so, it seemed.

'I can't swim!' he yells, flapping his arms around like crazy, unable to grab hold of anything on the boat he had just collided with, to save himself.

This gives Jonathan seconds to make a very difficult decision. What was he supposed to do, save the man's life so he can resume trying to end theirs? Or was it just a ploy to get him in the water so he can drown him? The sudden and drastic reverse of the situation, with the invading monster now apparently helpless and at *their* mercy, was almost beyond belief.

Jenny starts screaming at him to rescue her son, and he rummages around the boat frantically looking for something to throw to him; thinking that was a less suicidal approach to the situation. But there was nothing, and just as the young man's head is about to go under, he prepares to chuck himself in. But Jenny beats him to it and drags her son to the boat. Unable to haul him up while standing on deck, Jonathan then enters the water, and the two of them desperately struggle to get the lifeless human lump back on the boat, by any means possible. Who at least now, looked genuinely incapable of doing them any more harm once he was. All three of them are now safely on deck, sopping wet and gasping for breath, and the sight of her son laying on his side coughing and spluttering, begins to stir some lost maternal instinct. She cradles him in her arms, stroking his head and rocking him gently from side to side which has a remarkably healing effect on the young man, whose breathing gradually returns to something like normal.

'What's your name?' she whispers in his ear.

'Terry.'

'Ah, Terry. That's lovely!'

Her eyes lit up as though a mother being passed her first new-born baby. And just like a baby, monster son then starts crying uncontrollably with complete abandon, at being in his real mother's arms, and at last wanted, some eighteen years late.

'It's all right, Terry. It's all right. We can be friends now, can't we?' she whispers, as the emotional spectacle begins to attract a puzzled and curious audience of onlookers.

Apart from the obvious regret at failing to bring a towel and some dry clothes with him (again!), which hadn't seemed necessary at the time of arrival, Jonathan had never been so undecided as to what to feel. Partly relieved to be still alive, partly happy for them and to have played a part in their reuniting (without being quite sure what that part actually was), partly jealous of the attention formerly monster son was now getting; and also, strangely invisible.

As neither seemed aware of his presence, he thought it best to leave without disturbing their peace with a goodbye.

The Anti-Climax of the Century

It was an apathy-filled evening with Dennis far away in thought in his armchair, and his lodger, already in pyjamas and covered in duvet, reclined on the settee. Noise from the outside world was gathering momentum, and with it, worrying thoughts began to invade the otherwise peaceful atmosphere. Sadly, it was no ordinary evening but New Year's Eve. Not exactly a favourite time of year for a now long-time sober Jonathan, or, for a forever tee-total Dennis (due to lack of enthusiasm). And sadder still, no ordinary New Year's Eve that could happily be ignored with the aid of cotton wool in the ears and the lack of TV in Dennis's flat, but the sort that only comes round every hundred years. Outside, a river of alcohol would be flowing, causing inhibitions to be abandoned and strangers being embraced. An atmosphere that often led to the unease of those whose lives didn't include the partaking of. And thoughts of which, eventually led to some movement in Dennis's front room.

After much debate as to whether to do something memorable to mark the occasion (and if so, what?) Jonathan got dressed, declaring an intention of going out to look at fireworks that had already started blasting like gunfire in the neighbourhood. If one was to be subjected to the noise pollution, it made sense to go out with eyes pointed to the sky, and hopefully see a few. Dennis, in a similar state of indecision, followed, and the pair drifted in the direction of the 'hoe'. Not only the place where Sir Francis Drake had allegedly played bowls as the Spanish Armada approached, but also, one that commanded panoramic views, and hopefully, ideal for the viewing of fireworks. It sounded idyllic, but they soon found themselves in the most enormous crush of people, as if an order had been passed making it mandatory for everyone, everywhere, to evacuate their homes simultaneously. In which, the continued blasting of fireworks could be heard, but only the backs of people's heads could be seen. And Dennis, who had followed the back of Jonathan's head for as long as physically possible, had now vanished. Impossible to know in which direction you were moving but having no choice but to keep doing so and just hope the cluster you found yourself in wasn't about to fall off the edge of a cliff. When there *was* the briefest of clearings in the crowd, specially commissioned and increasingly hostile 'bouncers', physically moved people in the direction they wanted them to go. All probably similar to attending the 'poll-tax' riots of ten years previous, or the painfully named 'Pitchfork Rebellion' of even more previous, or any other such violent outbreak of public disorder. And perhaps, the nearest experience a human being can possibly have, to being a farmyard animal.

Exhausted and flabbergasted, the pair are eventually reunited at the flat, without a flicker of excitement at being in a new century, with Dennis's wallet now missing in what had been a pickpocket's paradise.

Not until the next morning was a smile managed, when Dennis returned from the shop with fags and newspaper, proclaiming that H.M. The Queen had had a similarly disastrous evening. As on its front page was a picture of the grim looking monarch, cross-armed with P.M Tony Blair in the middle of 'Auld Lang Syne'. Possibly wondering if this was as horrific as things were going to get, or, whether she should make a run for it before an outbreak of the conga.

Chaos Amongst the Vinyl

Never one to be comfortable with dependency, but often finding himself falling into a chronic state of it, his relationship with the most casual of landlords bothered him. And in this case, he predicted, eviction was only ever likely to occur in the event of one of Dennis's much-heard-about-but-never-actually-witnessed 'episodes' of psychotic delusion. But others had, so it seemed, and when the subject was raised in Dennis's absence, it prompted a troubled frown from even the most frivolous of acquaintance. So the current relaxed attitude to the rent, regular piano and comedic-based entertainment, coupled with the continuous, uninterrupted flow of DLA[17], at times felt a little too good to be true. Grim reality was out there somewhere and would have to be faced sooner or later. And with that in mind, he had looked for alternative accommodation periodically, solely to satisfy a need for independence from his friend. In his quest, he had seen bedsits of the type where, if you had the faintest of suicidal tendencies when you went in, you'd never come out alive. The sort of places that made John Christie's[18] bleak abode in the film *10 Rillington Place* look like a holiday camp; the money required for such domestic misery was extortionate. All, the exact opposite of life at Dennis's when the landlord was his usual charming self. Not an easy place to remove oneself from.

But eventually, after a long time on the council housing register, a solution to his dilemma appeared to have been found. He was offered a flat, albeit in a 'dodgy' area of Plymouth, and sadly, only informed of the full extent of its *dodginess* after he'd accepted it. It satisfied the need for independence but not much else. On the other side of town from Dennis's, but despite his lack of work was just about hanging on to the car which could just about get him there for a visit and back again. Dennis's flat had become like a rubber dinghy in the middle of an ocean, something he didn't want to stray too far from.

---

[17] Disability living allowance.
[18] The post-war serial killer.

But at least here at the new flat, his employment or financial status was nobody else's business, and he wasn't having to share a bathroom and kitchen with strangers with personal hygiene or thieving issues or listen to the afterhours piss-ups from the flat above. Just the regular blast of *Coronation Street* from the TV of the hard-of-hearing old lady next door; but fortunately, the only programme she ever watched, and the sudden vibration of the walls at seven thirty became a comforting signal that she was still alive – with her being the most painless of neighbours one could expect in these parts.

It was the sort of place where decay was everywhere you looked: abandoned mattresses left outside to rot, bicycles still padlocked to railings with both wheels missing and the occasional burnt-out car. He often looked out the window and worried for the safety of his car. Not exactly a boy-racer's dream that would appeal to the locals, but something that could be happily smashed up when there was nothing else to do. The usual crowd of hoodlums were on duty most evenings in their chosen bus shelter, always on the lookout for those under their suspicion of being poofs, weirdos or paedophiles. Or anyone sadly lacking the regulation track suit bottoms, one of the select few accepted brands of training shoe and vicious looking dog: who were probably all three of the former. Political correctness had yet to arrive at the shores of this island of iniquity.

Convinced they could smell a computer from a fair distance, Jonathan kept his inside a broom cupboard and put a mortice lock on its thick solid door. A shelf was put in, acting as a desk for it to sit on, and a small swivel chair just fitted underneath that, giving him surely the smallest but most secure and concealed of offices in which this most desirable of latest technology never left its hiding place. But a white extension lead cable went into it under the locked door, suggesting something electrical and interesting inside. So he painted it red, the same colour as the carpet, to camouflage it, hoping that would fool any uninvited guests. Fully prepared for an invasion.

Just like his departure from Jan and Steve's, moving away from accommodation that equally served the purpose of social life, was never going to be easy. Soon he found himself submerged in a solitary existence of non-stop painting and decorating. The flat on his arrival looked like it had been the venue for an indoor football tournament, with graffiti (mostly obscene) being scrawled all over the walls at half-time. And so, with very little time for cross-town visits to Dennis or accompanying him to psychiatric social groups or piano- playing venues, felt a tad isolated in his new life. But at least he had a telephone, which rang occasionally, and just about kept in contact with his support system (Dennis) in times of distress.

But it was the other way round one day when Bernie rang, determined not to lose contact with his supplier of transport. A vital cog in the unstoppable record-buying machine. He could tell by the man's words that something serious had kicked off or was just about to. And in Bernie's world, that could only mean one thing.

'Jonny, how ya doing?' He didn't wait for an answer. 'Listen, I've got a crisis. Well, I'm not sure really. It could turn out to be the opposite. But I need your help.'

Jonathan immediately erected a wall of resistance in his brain. He had a habit of being persuaded to help a friend in need, or somebody else's friend in need; usually with a lift or removals, and often regretting it soon afterwards. And a friend in need with an addiction, had added powers of persuasion. He knew he had to get work before the *nice* people at the DSS got it for him, and to finish the seemingly endless decorating before that. So the last thing he needed was to get involved in another time-consuming project that didn't involve the seeking of regular, steady employment, or the making of huge sums of money so one didn't have to.

Bernie continued, with the usual mania gathering pace in his words as if describing a new escape plan from Colditz[19]. 'I got chatting to a bloke at a boot sale the other day. He had loads of records, and he gave me some useful tips on what to look out for. Like, what might be valuable. There was a few Beatles ones that I haven't got, but he reckons there's a Sex Pistols single, 'God Save the Queen', on the A&M label, that's now worth a fortune. Thousands! The thing is, Jonny, I know I've got one, somewhere. I know it was A&M! I can picture it! It was one of the first singles I ever bought, years ago, when I didn't know what I was doing.' Which implied that now, he thought he *did* know what he was doing. And Jonathan could sense, that the details of his expected participation were imminent.

---

[19] German prisoner of war camp of the second world war.

'Could you come round and help me look for it, Jonny? If we find it, we'll go 50/50 on what we get for it. That's a promise. We'll shake on it when you come round. How does that sound?' It sounded like the denial of an addict, well-versed in the art of the understatement.

'All right, I'll be round Sunday,' Jonathan agreed, reluctantly.

'Ah, well, Sunday, I was gonna ask you to take me to a new sale out Tavistock way, and we won't have time to go there and do the search on the same day. D' you know what I mean?' Jonathan knew what he meant. Figuring the likelihood of not having time for the search in the same week. And tried to draw the man's attention to the quantity of records that could easily obstruct the search for an item of furniture, let alone a seven inch disc!

'Well, d' you think you ought to lay off buying any more 'til we've done the search?' Silence. Laying off buying any more? Was that possible?

'Can you make it Friday, Jonny?'

Deep sigh! 'OK, see you then.' So much for sensible suggestions, and his wall of resistance. Bernie had a habit of making him feel like the Archbishop of Canterbury, or other such dignitary revered for their sensibleness, despite him being nothing of the kind and regarded by many as a fully-fledged buffoon in his own right.

So, it seemed like his Friday and Sunday were to be occupied in the pursuit of records. But it would provide some company, which was gradually becoming more of a rarity. And he had a passion for records also, if not as great as Bernie's. Dating back to childhood, when his parent's radiogram/record player could be set to automatically play a pile of singles one after the other, much to the boy's fascination. But he would surely be sick of them by the end of Friday, he predicted.

He did some research on the computer, with the certainty that it wouldn't be as straight forward as his optimistic friend was expecting. Even if they found it. And that was a big enough if. It was indeed valuable. But apparently, had been re-issued at various times since, and trying to spot a worthless re-issue from the real thing may prove an equally difficult task. And one that would surely require the assistance of overpaid experts to determine. He read about fake labels and sleeves, and all sounded much like the world of art forgery or counterfeit money, and generally, something like what benefit claimants in council flats shouldn't be wasting their time investigating.

Jonathan noticed an advert in a local paper.

'HGV Class 1 Driver. Liskeard depot. Nights out. Early starts'.

He had seen similar ads but managed to talk himself out of it before getting to the stage of picking up the phone. He was no good at early starts but it was a necessary evil, and wouldn't normally consider 'tramping'[20] in the vehicle, as his insomnia; exacerbated by frequent night- time urination, (in this case done on the ground outside the cab in all weathers!) would surely make it an accident waiting to happen. He put the newspaper on top of an ever-increasing pile of other bits of paper, for which a decision was pending.

'Right, 50/50. Deal?'

Bernie spat on the palm of his hand and put it out ready to be shook, with a self-deprecating grin. But the tired look on his reluctant assistant's face told him that the exchange of saliva wasn't necessary, and he wiped it clean on his trousers and they shook.

'Synchronise watches?' Bernie jested, looking at his.

'Let's just get on with it, eh.'

As the rummaging through the jungle of vinyl commenced, Jonathan reported his findings off the internet trying to get his friend suitably prepared for the obstacles that lay ahead. But Bernie wasn't listening.

'Look for a Beigey sort of Grey label on the record, with large brown A on the left and large brown M on the right,' he instructed.

'Beigey sort of A and large Brown Grey… What?'

Jonathan repeated the instructions back to himself, like a confused Bob Hope[21] as the inept travelling dentist taking instructions from the local townsfolk on how to defeat their most feared gunslinger.

They grappled their way to piles of records in far corners of rooms, blocked off by other piles. Disturbingly unable to keep any kind of structure to the search, as avalanches occurred around them. After about four hours of grappling and swearing, with still no luck and no tea-breaks, they made their way to the welcome fresh air of the garden, and a vital question. Was Bernie sure that the filing cabinets in the two sheds

---

[20] The sleeping in the cab of the lorry between shifts when too far from home depot to return to.

[21] In the film 'The Paleface' 1948.

contained only LPs? Jonathan hoped the answer would be an affirmative 'yes', thus completing the search.

'Well, as sure as I can be.'

As that sounded like a jazzed-up version of 'I don't know', the search of the filing cabinets commenced; at least the ones they could get to that weren't blocked in by others. He noticed Bernie getting increasingly agitated as the search continued, into a state that he hadn't seen him before. And the more they searched, the more they found singles in the place supposedly reserved for LPs, confirming their fears that all must be searched. But again, it was too easy to criticize, so he didn't. But insisted on resting, hoping Bernie would see sense and do the same, as the sunny afternoon heat approached the 80s in Fahrenheit. Jonathan lay there silently on what bit of grass remained.

'I know it's here. I know it's here! We'll have to break down these sheds.'

'What d' you mean? Smash 'em up?'

'Have you got a better idea?' Bernie asked, with an unusually aggressive tone.

'Well...' Jonathan shook his head in dismay, lacking the enthusiasm to finish his sentence.

The filing cabinets, that would have been empty, light and movable when they got here, however they got here, were now full up, heavy and immovable. At least without a sack truck, which of course they didn't have. Leaving them with an unenviable choice between dragging each one out of its house or just smashing up the house that surrounded it. Although equally unpleasant, the latter was decided upon, and the demolition of sheds commenced.

Bernie, still trying to keep a lid on his anxiety, borrows a hammer and crowbar from a kindly next-door neighbour. Jonathan starts off, although in two minds as to whether to walk out on his possessed friend and do something more worthwhile with the rest of the day. Bernie supervises the demolition. With first shed now an untidy pile of wood on the ground, they scour its contents of twelve cabinets. No luck. And one shed unnecessarily demolished, as the search scarily approaches the point of no return. As Jonathan catches his breath, Bernie starts demolishing second shed, exerting more energy than a man of his age should. And after a while of this, suddenly stops, clutches his upper chest and appears to be choking, with face now crimson.

'Bernie, Bernie!'

After realizing the futility of calling to his friend, Jonathan goes back indoors, frantically trying to locate the phone. No luck with that either. So he alerts the neighbour who calls for an ambulance. The peculiar scene of destruction in the garden, with its abundance of standing filing cabinets and discarded records, could have passed for a carefully arranged piece of modern art to be found in only the most underground of galleries. And the paramedics glanced at it with curiosity in between transferring the patient to a mobile stretcher. But luckily, kept their questions to themselves, and wheeled Bernie away with oxygen mask over his face, leaving Jonathan alone with the debris, still in shock. But eventually, manages to get the grass clear of records and back in their cabinets, before leaving the place unlocked due to the lack of key, and going home, vowing to visit Bernie in hospital the next day.

On arrival back at the flat, a letter from the Department of Employment ('regional medical team') is there to greet him.

'Dear Mr Piper, you are required to attend a medical examination to determine your ability to work.'

It was inevitable, and everything he'd been dreading, but it prompts him to ring the number on the ad for 'Class 1 Driver, Liskeard Depot' and accepts the offer of an interview for next week. Liskeard was a fair distance for himself and the car to drag themselves to on a daily basis. But, if he got the job, and if he coped with it, he could then afford to upgrade the Sierra. But that was two almighty ifs. His mind was racing, unable to slow it down after the day's events at Bernie's.

To his relief, Bernie is conscious and manages a smile when he sees his partner in madness. The doctor confirms a mild heart attack.

'Can I ask a favour, Jonny? Can you just have a bit of a tidy up as best you can. See if you can get one of them... ah...'

'Sack trucks?'

'Yeah, that's it. You know, on two wheels. One of them would be perfect for moving the cabinets about. Just so we can get them indoors.'

Bernie's words were unusually sensible, before descending into madness again in that last sentence. But now was not the time to enquire how anybody was supposed to do that without the immediate disposal of at least a thousand records. And the mere suggestion of it may be enough to finish him off.

'Just forget about the search, OK,' Bernie surrendered, in a rare moment of inspired wisdom.

'Yeah, no problem. Just rest and try not to think about it. Oh, where's the key to lock up when I leave?'

'You mean it's unlocked!'

'No, I mean… Look, don't worry. I'll get straight round there now.'

'On the mantel piece in the lounge in a cup.'

'Mantel piece in the lounge in a cup. Got it. Don't worry. Rest.'

'Thanks Jonny.'

He really didn't need all this now with all the hullabaloo about to kick off with work, interview, medical etc.

Bernie's unlocked home was more likely to have been the victim of vandalism rather than burglary, unless the intruder needed a few tons of records on the quick. And arson didn't bear thinking about, with as much black gunge only ever previously seen on the set of a science-fiction film. But fortunately, all was intact and in the same mess as he had left it. And alone, he had the afternoon to 'tidy up' with the aid of a new sack truck; for which he would be sure to get reimbursed when his friend had sufficiently recovered to start worrying as to the whereabouts of his wallet. Deciding that he may as well finish the demolition of second shed to get it into a manageable pile of wood ready for disposal, he sets to work. After which, he completes the search of its contents, opening draws, flicking through mostly LPs just to make sure there are no hidden singles among them. But there is one. And it's the one. His heart misses several beats and he kisses it with relief. Then remembers that it's likely to be worthless, for a whole variety of reasons, but just that it was one crazy mission accomplished before the next one begins, was worth a moment of celebration.

A JCB or a magic wand would have been an appropriate aid to clear space in the kitchen for some of the cabinets that needed to come in, but he did the best he could with neither. The kitchen was at the back of the house, the nearest room to the garden and therefore the only possible place he was going to get them 'indoors'; as per his bed-ridden leader's instructions. But indoors, after his efforts to clear space, a lot of the piles were now no longer piles, more like a sea of records that it now felt appropriate to consider other forms of transport for human movement in the house, other than the usual two-footed kind. But a lot of the cabinets were now safely inside, and the others secluded as much as possible in the garden. The kitchen sink was now completely inaccessible, and its cold tap constantly dripped as though in need of a new washer. A disturbing sight that somehow symbolized the beginning of the end for Bernie, but the inevitable result of his wishes being carried out. The mass debris of wood was then carried in numerous journeys from the garden through the narrow confines of the house, and into his car, ready for a visit to the local tip. He remembered to lock the door, and of course, take the elusive 45 with him for further examination.

Now at home, and with the aid of technology, he could hopefully compare it with an original, from descriptions of markings and the like that he had previously read about on the internet. Fully prepared for the likely disappointment, he spent hours searching for information. And gradually, to his amazement, the black vinyl with 'beigey grey label' he had, *was* fitting the description of the genuine article: one of the very few that were pressed during the brief coupling of the Sex Pistols and A&M records in 1977. And, being the eternal pessimist, he was thorough in his investigation.

'Only a handful of them left'. Could this really be one of them?

'Expected to fetch about £10,000 at auction', was a quote from somebody, prior to a previous selling of another of the few.

And another miracle was the fact that Bernie couldn't find his record player, as the black vinyl looked almost untarnished by stylus. And despite being kept in a garden shed, it being sandwiched between LPs in the full-to-capacity drawers of Bernie's filing cabinets, was probably the best place for it. Jonathan *could* find *his* record player but resisted the urge to play it for further proof that he wasn't dreaming, and that it was, actually, The Sex Pistols version of the national anthem that could be heard when it was. Just in case he put any scratches on it and halved its worth in a second.

During a telephone call to arrange an appointment with one of a few auctioneers whose details he found, he happily gave details of the item to be sold, but was hesitant when then asked for details of himself while wondering how it was relevant. Politely refusing to give his address, just in case the front door was kicked in soon after. Irrational fear perhaps, of someone totally unused to handling anything of such value, and, who almost had a sixth sense for when something was too good to be true.

'Good morning, sir. I understand you have a "God Save the Queen" for us, that you "think is genuine". Is that correct?'

The 'expert', of conventional appearance and an air of superiority, quoted a snippet of Jonathan's initial words to the receptionist with what appeared to be a hint of mockery. Appearance and presentation had never been Jonathan's strongest assets, and as he sat down in the man's office it felt as though it was himself who was being examined for authenticity. After what seemed a thorough examination of the disc, the expert shook his head with a mixture of amusement and frown.

'I'm afraid, sir, that what you have here is a re-issue, from about, ooh, I'd say late 80s, early 90s. They did a lot of them around that time. You might get a couple of quid for it at a car boot sale.' After the expert analysis came a patronizing smile.

Up until now, he'd never been a fan of the internet and computers. And had only got one for the internet dating; which someone had (foolishly?) recommended, and the prospect of finding the girl of his dreams, who, if she existed, was probably on the other side of the world with profile displayed on one of the many 'local' websites with such slogans as, 'find love in your area'. And with its shortcomings regularly plastered all over the news: 'cyber-bullying', child porn and the suicides of its more 'respectable' viewers, and the broadcast of live executions, the internet seemed like something to be avoided. But right now it was paying dividends, in that he had managed to arm himself with vital information to do with markings and serial numbers, for when confronted with the almost inevitable, 'you might get a couple of quid for it'. But despite those words being delivered with casual confidence, their speaker seemed in no hurry to give 'it' back.

'OK, thank you,' Jonathan said calmly, holding out his hand for the record to be put back in it.

'Well, if you like I can hang on to it and just see what we can get for it at our next auction, but there's no guarantee, I'm afraid,' the man said glibly, with the pretence of an urge to do something charitable.

Of course, Jonathan was out of his depth, and despite the research he had done was in no way qualified to start arguing about it. But he quietly suspected his research was correct, and an attempt at a very subtle form of theft was taking place, and just followed his instincts.

'No thank you,' he replied, with hand still held out, and after their eyes met briefly with the expert's now showing signs of unease, eventually, the record was put back in it.

'Ah, excuse me!' the man called out, as Jonathan was close to his car.

Again, he stayed close to his instincts, ignored the man and left, with intentions of trying the other auctioneer whose details he had. An expert on antiques he was not but had a pretty good idea of the perils of human nature.

After an informal interview with a man who wasn't quite as unpleasant as had been expected, he got the job at LH Distribution's Liskeard depot. (Not the usual kind of interview where one's personality and appearance were taken into consideration. And, with an increasing shortage of qualified drivers, employers were operating a more anyone-with-an-HGV-license- will-do- policy.) He wasn't optimistic of the success of a sudden transition to very full-time work, after so long out of it. But, having endured his 'medical examination' a few days previous, with a doctor who looked like he was on a God-given mission to push work-shy scroungers back in the direction of work, it now seemed like a wise move to be at least attempting it.

At the second auctioneers, keeping a tight grip on the treasure as he sat in the waiting room, he eventually met with a less pretentious type of expert, who, to his relief, didn't call him 'Sir'. Which, although a sign of respect in the early twentieth century, seemed to have re-emerged as a concealed lack of it in the early twenty-first. After examining the disc with a magnifying monocle, the man then sat back in his chair and examined the face of its minder, in silence, with a look of amusement and wonder. As if wondering whether the tired looking, ill at ease man, with an air of deprivation about him, actually knew what he had in his possession, but with none of the devious overtones of previous expert. And his face then broke into a broad smile, to which Jonathan allowed himself something similar. It was one of those beautiful, silent moments when words were unnecessary, and facial expression said it all. The most beautiful in fact, that non-romantic ones ever got. But financial ones were almost as good.

'Well, I think we've got a winner here,' said the expert. 'And nice condition as well.'

To hear such an esteemed person describe something that had lived at Bernie's for so long in such a way, was almost unreal.

'We've got an auction coming up in a few weeks' time and I think we can just about squeeze it into that one. And we'll give it a reserve price of £10,000 if that's OK with you, Mr... ah?'

'Piper. Jonathan.'

It was all going swimmingly with the mention of £10,000 and the added, 'if that's OK with you', but he now had to ask the most embarrassing of questions which made his ignorance all too clear. And, as had been so apparent with previous expert, that meant vulnerability.

'What's a reserve price exactly?'

What he had learnt from the internet was minimal in terms of what he should know to successfully conceal the fact that he was a pauper, totally unused to dealing in antiques, and currently being hounded by the DSS and their 'regional medical team'. But thankfully, there was none of the expected amazement and humour at his question.

'It's the lowest price you're prepared to accept. So the bidding will start at that figure. These things have sold in the past for a bit more than that, so I think we can be fairly confident with ten.'

Jonathan's breathing seemed to get easier and slower with every word the man uttered, sounding like he knew what he was talking about, and just spelling it out, without any added bullshit or deviant trickery. He already knew what the other few identical pressings had sold for in the past, so no great shock, but relieved nonetheless at having it confirmed by such an authority.

'Dare I ask where you acquired such a gem? Only, you don't look much like a record company executive. No offence intended.' They both smiled. 'Because they never made it to the shops, you know. So, technically, only A&M employees would have them. Or their offspring, perhaps?'

'A car boot sale.'

Once again, as so often in his life, that was about as much of the truth that could be revealed without creating a circus of misunderstanding, during which, the police may be alerted.

'A car boot sale!' Expert makes an amused, sharp intake of breath with disbelief. 'Incredible. And how on earth did it get there, I'd love to know. But alas, we never will, I'm sure,' the expert continued with a smile before they parted.

The jovial nature of the conversation made a weary Jonathan at last able to see the fun of it all, now the obstacle course of finding it (with its one casualty recovering in hospital) and getting it to auction was near completion.

He drove home, minus the record, and the carefully examined receipt now took its place as his most precious possession. Or rather, Bernie's most precious possession. But the owner's hopes mustn't be raised just yet. And certainly not in his condition.

To his relief, he got through the first week of the new job without being fired. But it was touch and go. On one occasion getting lost in rush-hour traffic, during which, he managed to get out of a barmy situation when confronted with a low bridge he suspected he wasn't going to get under. Stopping just short of it in the nick of time to do some metric conversion, much to the *delight* of surrounding motorists. But, with the help of a kindly off-duty trucker/pedestrian, managed to turn the thing round, taking so long and causing sufficient chaos for it to be described as an 'incident' on local radio traffic news. Luckily, no damage and new employer none the wiser.

He found himself having to ask colleagues for general assistance and directions to places. Some were a bit reluctant, but one in particular, Tony, was always helpful and seemed to be a fountain of knowledge on a wide range of subjects. But even without the useful tips on anything from changing the oil in one's car to the most effective treatment for athlete's foot, Tony's friendly manner was priceless to Jonathan, who, having veered in the direction of full-time employment, was entering a comparatively strange, alien world, to the one he had become so accustomed to since his arrival in Plymouth.

When he got home one day, on the doormat was a letter that was 'pleased to inform him' (sadists!) that he had passed the medical and been declared fit for work, and therefore, his Disability Living Allowance would cease to be paid, immediately. This would have been seriously distressing news, but now, daring to feel secure in his new job, he let out a deranged cheer of celebration as if now immune to the kind of aggravation that comes in brown envelopes. He told Dennis of his employment, disturbing result of the DSS medical and subsequent non-membership of 'the club'. And as he did, he may as well have been declaring an intention of emigrating to Australia. As the more he improved his lot, not by any real sense of ambition other than that of survival, the further away he seemed to drift from his old pal.

Dennis was entering a new period of disillusionment with the piano, frustrated that his talents hadn't given him what he deserved. And after Jonathan had made several visits across town to see him, and instead of the usual entertainment on the piano, found himself watching the six o'clock news on his friend's newly-acquired TV, and being told to 'Ssshhh' during the 'important' bits, he stopped visiting.

In another, unsettlingly officious-looking envelope, came the rarity of the most wonderful news. The elusive Sex Pistols single had sold at auction for £14,000, and could he contact them to discuss payment.

'Warrrgghhh!'

It was too much to take in. All that insane, back-breaking effort had been worth it. People like himself and Bernie just didn't sell things for five-figure sums unless they were dreaming.

This turned his thoughts to his hospitalized friend. Which right now, were strangely muddled and conflicting. It had of course crossed his mind that he could say nothing of ever finding the record, Bernie would be none the wiser, and himself much much richer; instead of just much richer (the proceeds no longer having to be split between them). But that didn't seem right, with Bernie being a fellow downtrodden person. Even if much of the treading had been done by his own feet. And he so wanted to share the good news with him as he lay in his hospital bed. But at the same time, suspected his friend would not be the easiest businessman to deal with once the good news was shared and so may need reminding of the 50/50 arrangement. Imagining Bernie then reminding him, that they only shook on it, and never actually spat on it, or some other such lunacy, with humour of course. But at times, that humour was very fragile. Somewhere amongst the chaos of thought was a decision to tell Bernie of their good fortune, but with caution. As money was not only 'the route of all evil', but probably a major cause of heart attacks, as could be argued in this case.

After arranging a bank transfer with the auctioneers, with the fear that

269

a cheque may get lost in the post or somehow intercepted by the locals, the glorious day arrived and the money entered his account, although somewhat reduced to more like £13,000 after various charges were taken. He rang the hospital to check on the whereabouts and condition of his friend. Still there, and 'doing well'. He then wrote a cheque for £6,618 and took it, with the letter which proved it was half, to the hospital. This seemed the best way, leaving as little room for discussion as possible.

Bernie was sat upright in bed and had recovered a lot of his usual optimism and chirpiness but had yet to be reunited with the chaos at home. And now increased chaos, at least indoors, as many of the previously homeless filing cabinets had been housed. He had tried to leave gangways but Bernie may have to lose a few pounds to squeeze through them. Was this a suitable domestic situation for a recovering heart patient to be discharged to? But Bernie's thoughts were far away with all things futile.

'There's some gorgeous nurses in here, Jonny,' he said.

'How's the ticker going then?'

He was still wired up to a monitor that gave out a slow intermittent bleep. 'All right, so they tell me. They've done tests and everything.'

'Bernie, I've got some news for you.'

'So have I mate, so have I!' he shrieked.

Was he about to announce his engagement to one of the said gorgeous nurses? As that was the only thing Jonathan could think of that would warrant the jubilation.

'I'm being discharged in two days!'

Was that a reason to be excited? Bernie obviously thought so. Possibly, as his hospitalization had caused a disturbing lull in the record buying.

'Oh, that's great.' Jonathan did his best to agree. 'No, what happened was, I found the record.'

Jonathan's words were bland, as if announcing that he'd found the lid to a tube of toothpaste. Thus, avoiding any excess of emotion in his friend.

But Bernie looked puzzled, as if suddenly struck with amnesia concerning all matters of the outside world, before waving and smiling at a female nurse who passed his open door.

'You know, the Sex Pistols, God...'

'Oh yes, yes!' He was now wide-eyed and seriously paying attention.

270

'So, I took it to an auction place, right, and they sold it for 14 grand. But now after—'

Bernie stopped listening after the '14 grand' hit him like a bullet, and his face was in total disarray as he tried to take it in. Should he be happy, angry or sad? Had he been helped or deceived? But then, as Jonathan produced a cheque from his pocket, let out one enormous roar of approval, with the incorrect assumption it was a cheque for the said amount, for him. It just wasn't like him to remember minor details like a 50/50 agreement, shaken not spat on, or otherwise.

'Now, because of our agreement about going halves—'

Bernie's mouth suddenly opened wide and he clutched his chest just as he'd done before, as if unable to breath, and the technology he was wired to confirmed it with a continuous wailing. Jonathan ran out of the room to alert the medics who were already running towards him. The patient's head was now slumped forward onto his chest as if there was no life supporting it.

They sprang into action doing chest compressions before getting the electrics out, but it was too late. They then turned their attention to him, a little too intensely he felt, as if he were under suspicion of something. He wasn't sure if they'd heard Bernie's roar of elation, and mistaken it for a roar of something else, caused by his visitor.

'I don't know what happened. One minute we were talking, the next, this.'

His words seemed to be accepted, and the room then fell into silent acceptance of what had occurred, as Bernie's head was covered. Jonathan touched the blanket-covered body as a final farewell.

There was only a brief moment to grieve, before his brain was invaded by a lot of worrying concerns about the immediate future. Bernie was not much more than an acquaintance who he knew very little about, apart from the obvious love of records that had overshadowed all else. And as such, had been about to ask for the man's full name to write on the cheque before being horribly interrupted. He had no idea what close friends or relatives he had, if any, and assumed the staff would have a piece of paper on which the patient had written the name of a next of kin. He hoped it wasn't his, but worried that if it was, would make him legally responsible. For something? And him still having the key to Bernie's house; the contents of which would have to be disposed of, by somebody, was right now making him feel a lot closer to the deceased than he wanted to be. The dealing with Bernie's affairs, especially the round ones with holes in the middle, didn't bear thinking about. He now had a time-consuming job which had to be maintained, where the overtime wasn't optional: you finished when you finished, whenever that was.

But nothing was said, and the staff did the usual preparations for the patient's journey to the morgue, as Jonathan moved himself quietly towards the door, hoping his exit wouldn't be noticed. As if with something to hide, but without having the time to work out exactly what.

Once out of the room he walked briskly down the corridor, when he heard a female voice call out to him.

'Excuse me, sir, are you a relative?'

'No,' he replied firmly, and just kept walking, and then running, picking up the pace as the lady continued with cries of 'Sir! Sir!'

Not how he wanted his association with Bernie to end, degrading as it was. But just couldn't face the awkward explaining of the unexplainable. Now safely in the car, he breathed a sigh of relief, tore up Bernie's cheque and drove home with a muddled mixture of sadness and pleasure at now being twice as wealthy as was originally thought. But predicted, that it wouldn't be long before a good chunk of his riches would be needed to rescue himself from some future catastrophe that wasn't far away. Sadly, he was spot on, only much sooner than expected.

On his return to the flat, he discovered that all the windows had been smashed, graffiti sprayed all over the walls and the place trashed, ruining the painstaking decorating he had spent months perfecting. The familiar rage and desperate need for revenge was almost overwhelming, occurring before he'd had barely a moment to grieve for the loss of Bernie, or rejoice at his financial gain. But what was he supposed to do, beat up the prime suspects when they next appeared in the usual bus shelter, despite some being technically children? He swept up the glass, while listening to a disgusted elderly passer-by blaming the parents, the government, and the abolition of national service and the death penalty. All the while trying to conceal the rage that was brewing inside him. And, as predicted, parted with some of his new-found wealth getting a 24-hour glazier out, who implies he's not the only victim, with the remark, 'we do a lot of work round here'. Only one consolation, his (some would say) bizarre efforts to secure the computer had paid off: cupboard still locked, with its handle now snapped off. Probably with some bastard's frustration at not being able to gain access.

He hardly slept that night wondering if his car was about to get the same treatment, half prepared for a quick exit in dressing gown and pyjamas to defend it. The next day, he was glared at as he passed the smirking, bus-sheltered, ensemble of youth, as if inviting him to come and avenge, and in the process screw up his life. As they were young and 'vulnerable', would doubtless have an army of professional do-gooders and sadistic older relatives looking out for them if the nasty man lost his temper. Now, there was a real sense of urgency to get out of here.

Tony had become a priceless commodity at work, who, when told about the recent destruction of the flat, came up with a possible solution: an old, run-down cottage with a 'For Sale' sign outside. It was situated on a narrow country lane about a mile from where he and his wife lived, out in the sticks on the outskirts of Liskeard. Tony always passed it on his way to work, he explained.

'Where me and Sharon are now, it was in a right state. We got it cheap because of it. I pretty much did all the work myself. Might be worth checking out. I can help with the work and a bit of advice if you needed it.'

It sounded a wonderful idea, but if he knew Jonathan a bit better, would have replaced the 'a bit' with 'a lot', and the 'if' with 'when', in that last sentence. Jonathan was embarrassed to let on how little he knew about all the things one needed to know if one was to make it in the adult world. Tony was a proper man, whose wife loved him, parents were proud of him, and who'd never set foot in a mental hospital. Jonathan felt like he was trying to do a passable impression of the same. Always trying to conceal the more incomprehensible components of his life.

Having fallen deeply in love with the surroundings of the deserted cottage in several curious, solitary visits, Jonathan made an appointment to look inside, doubting very much whether he could afford it. On entry to the place, it became clear that money would not be the only obstacle, as he looked around at the seemingly endless work that needed doing to it, while wondering if he was up to the task of transforming it, and, keeping himself and the driving job going. Even with Tony's 'help' it was a tall order. How he wished his friend was here right now to advise but had resisted the urge to beg the man to accompany him, sensing he was already in the early stages of another chronic dependency. Admittedly, it was surely the cheapest detached property money could buy, being as much of the dining room floor was missing, and various door frames had rotted so badly there wasn't much holding the bricks up above them; 'Ideal for renovation', as so eloquently put by the estate agent. Some kind of adrenalin-infused mania, expert advice and super-human strength was called for. But then, something similar was now required at the flat if he chose to stay there and attempt the clear-up operation, with the nagging feeling that an armed 24-hour police presence was needed to prevent the same thing happening again.

He loved the remoteness of the cottage, with only the sound of running water from the river at the end of the garden to be heard. And somehow, could picture it after its restoration to former glory, and himself and the elusive girl of his dreams living happily ever after in it. And so, with a bit of help from the late Bernie and the Sex Pistols, a sizeable mortgage, and generous donation from his father, he bought the place. His dad was pleased that his now middle-aged son was at last veering in the direction of normality and home ownership and offered some financial encouragement. But fortunately, was too far away to see what that money was being invested in, which would have led to the usual doubts as to his son's sanity.

The decision to buy, with more than an air of Hobson's choice about it, had now placed absolute urgency on the continuation of two things. His physical well-being – *to do the work* – and employment – *to pay the mortgage*. He had moved up in the world at an alarming rate. But could he stay up there, defying gravity, and the direction in which his life had so often gone?

With everything he possessed that had survived the invasion now safely packed into a hired van, he locked the front door for the last time. Not that there seemed much point, as it was also locked at the time of invasion. But all, blissfully, no longer his problem. As he crossed the road to go to the local shop and say cheerio to its Pakistani proprietor, he noticed the forever snarling or smirking duo of teenagers that had glared at him previously, and, as far as he was concerned, guilty in some way of the trashing of his flat. He watched as they came out of a flat on the second floor of a low-rise block and locked its door, and then, as they got in the boy-racer mobile and roared away.

Once in the queue at the shop and looking around at the various items for sale, he suddenly has the most splendid and greasy of ideas. He takes three bottles of cooking oil to the counter, pays for them, and bids his South-Asian friend a fond farewell. With the duo's car still absent, up the stairwell to the second floor he goes, and when the coast is clear, empties the slimy contents of the bottles outside the front door and through the letterbox of the flat he had seen them exit. Constantly looking around for potential witnesses and listening out for the ping of the lift from which they could emerge. Thus, creating a nice greasy lake for the thugs to return to, as a parting gift. Chucking the empty bottles on top of it, which float about on its surface. But then, as he makes his way back down to the van with a sense of almost spiritual fulfilment, passes the offensive duo on the stairs. He immediately recognizes the infernal din of their laughter, but they remain blissfully unaware of who exactly is scurrying past them in the dimly lit stairwell. And after the initial, sudden fear of being so close to his victims as they pass, realises the perfect timing of it. After hurrying to the van, he reverses it to be close enough to get an earful of the reaction, and in another rare but beautiful moment smiles peacefully as he listens to what to him is the equivalent of the first cuckoo in spring: the deafening rage and profanity from above, as the empty bottles come flying over the balcony. Not exactly mass murder as he would have liked, or forcing them to drink the stuff at gunpoint, but better than nothing.

The Beginning of the End

Tony's first viewing of the cottage's dilapidated interior was a crucial moment. Jonathan looked anxiously at his capable friend's face for the verdict, as if trying to work out from it whether he'd been foolish or not for buying the place, and just how much of a miracle worker his trusted advisor would be. And although Tony was shocked, he tried to conceal it, aware of the desperation that had brought his beleaguered friend here. But a highly sensitized Jonathan noticed the shock, and felt clumsy and stupid for buying it. But the only possible cure for that now was relentless work at every opportunity to do the impossible when he wasn't otherwise fully engaged in the task of earning a living.

After a while, several miracles *had* been performed with Tony's help and advice as promised, spurring Jonathan on in the pursuit of more progress while at times grappling with near self-destructive levels of perfectionism. And without the luxury of alternative accommodation, it wasn't the most comfortable of places to live while the work was being done. But the regular night's out in the lorry provided at least some respite from that.

Inevitably, he had fallen into state of chronic dependency on Tony, whose visits, also served as the only means of socializing available to him. All contact with Dennis and his psychiatric friends having been lost. But the pair managed a few laughs in between the giving and receiving of education, and Tony was a rare breed of teacher who was never patronizing to his pupil.

Tony commented on Jonathan's weight loss, more with concern than compliment.

'Well, I haven't had much time to rest,' Jonathan explained the obvious, with a faint smile. His determination to carry out the instructions from Tony's last visit as soon as possible, had become like a well-oiled machine. With the 40-foot lorry regularly parked as near to a local DIY superstore as possible for the gathering of supplies, so there was no time wasted on his next day off from work and could get straight on with it.

But the hardship was a suppressed form of joy at moving that little bit closer to a dream.

A visit to the doctor was not something he relished, but had already made two because of stomach pains: an annoying inconvenience and waste of precious time on his day off. A variety of non-prescription remedies were failing to shift it. He assumed it was something he ate, and told the doctor this, explaining that hygiene standards and his attention to 'use by' dates had slipped a little recently, due to the current DIY mania at home. The doctor rarely looked at his patient, considering his computer screen a far more valuable source of information. Failing to notice the weight loss or any other symptoms, and with a full waiting room to be seen after Jonathan, he happily let the patient do the diagnosing and prescribed some tablets for food poisoning and severe indigestion. They didn't work, and neither did antibiotics a second doctor prescribed.

He desperately wanted his days off to be clear of other distractions, so the cottage restoration could continue undisturbed. His thinking being that it had to be done, and the sooner it was, the sooner he could enjoy the comfort of his new home. And, with the satisfaction of knowing he had doubled or trebled its value. Thus, eradicating poverty from his life, once and for all. Whatever was going on with his health, if anything was, it could wait until the work was completed, when there would be far more time to deal with it. And it certainly wasn't affecting his energy levels. If he *had* lost weight; as now observed by several concerned parties, it was surely a result of rushing around, physical activity, and possibly a sign that he was getting fitter. Not a bad thing for a man in his early fifties, he considered. But, after another bad night of stomach and now back pain, which seriously impeded the next day's home improvements, another blood-churning visit to the doctor's was unavoidable.

The great female wall of the doctor's surgery reception was as sturdy as ever. Jonathan's popularity had sunk to new depths, as they had had the misfortune of seeing rather a lot of him recently. Feeling like he had already been diagnosed as a hypochondriac or 'attention seeker' (as previously misdiagnosed by regal lady consultant psychiatrist), he just managed to find a seat in the crowded waiting room. Not so long ago, men had been criticized for not seeking doctor's advice and not talking about their ill health. But now, in the twenty-first century with its increased workloads and patient numbers quadrupling, it felt as if such lack of concern for one's health was something the NHS would be encouraging. Just to keep their waiting rooms a bit less congested. Jonathan felt awkward and out of place as he sat among the OAPs and young mothers with small children. Genuine patients, who were fully justified in taking up the doctor's precious time. Late middle-aged men who nobody else cared about, were definitely not, it seemed. But take up the medic's precious time he did, once again, with extreme reluctance and so much to do at home. This doctor was disturbed by a yellowing of the patient's skin, but chose not to mention it, until a scan was done. So now, hospital appointments were to be the next distraction that would delay the restoration project even further.

Being ill (if he actually was), now beginning to feel like a full-time job in itself, Tony once again came to the rescue. A fellow driver at LH who also had to find time to earn a living, but suffering from a recurrence of sciatica, was now off work with it and covered by a sick note. But luckily, was now feeling 'a lot better', and needed something to supplement his now insufficient income. And so, Jonathan started paying him to undertake the work at the cottage alone, while he grappled with his increasing medical appointments.

'Go and see your GP to get your results,' were the instructions from hospital staff after his scan was done. The chances of seeing 'your GP', or anyone else's, on your day off work, were similar to that of seeing the second coming of Jesus Christ and a total eclipse of the sun, at the very same time! But after some adjustment to his shift pattern at work, just managed to disturb the medics once more. It was a large building, seemingly only occupied in part by the surgery. And he pondered with exasperation, the benefits of squatting in it, due to its close proximity to the surgery where he had become a regular visitor.

Still miles away in thought over the deeply troubling subject of the dining room floor at the cottage, or lack of it, his name is eventually called. He knocks on the door and then enters, to be greeted by a smiling young female doctor looking directly at him as soon as her door is opened. Not what he was expecting. She offers him a seat. Still smiling. This was getting weird. Either the smiling stops or he leaves. Luckily, it was the doctor behaving this way and not the receptionists, which would have not just been weird, but terrifying. Was he in love with her? Was she in love with him? Was it love at first sight for both of them? Was she a born-again

Christian? On Prozac? He wasn't quite sure what was going on, but hadn't experienced such courtesy from the medical profession since Dr Heinbecker had invited him to play squash with him and a few of his psychiatric colleagues. And it had been all downhill since then. Something was wrong. He was just beginning to sense it. Her high cheek-boned smile collapsed somewhat as she began to refer to the results of his scan, and it felt as though the reason for her initial friendliness was about to become clear.

'Well, Mr Piper, your results have come back. Some small tumours have been spotted in your pancreas. That's what has been giving you the pain, and I'm sorry to have to tell you that they are malignant.' He waited for a 'but'. There wasn't one.

Malignant. What was that? He had heard of it. But as it was nothing at all to do with the restoration of run-down cottages, his brained struggled to adjust, before the obvious question came from his mouth.

'Cancer?'

'I'm afraid so. We need to do more tests to determine if it has spread elsewhere, and if it hasn't, then surgery is an option.'

She touched his hand and smiled, relieved that there was at least some faintly good news she could offer. But Jonathan didn't feel it, stunned, with time suddenly coming to an abrupt halt and standing completely still.

He left the surgery a completely different man to the one who went in. But his thoughts turned to Oscar and his wise words: 'At first I thought, "why me"? and then I thought, "why not"?' He couldn't remember whether his deceased friend was referring to his alcoholism or cancer when he had said them, but their message of anti-self-pity seemed particularly appropriate and comforting now. Still in a daze as he sat in the car, he wondered what he should do now. She had given him a prescription for strong pain killers, and he would wait for another appointment at the hospital to be posted to him. Less of an annoyance now he knew what was going on. More of a tragedy.

Tony was still more of a colleague and DIY advisor than close friend, but a thoroughly good bloke nonetheless, and currently all he had, and so shared the news with him when he returned to the cottage. It was difficult not to, with the man commenting that he looked like he had seen a ghost as he came through the front door. Tony was up a step ladder with a tub of something in hand, but for once, Jonathan was oblivious to what he was doing or what still needed doing to the place. The urgency of it all had suddenly gone. He had the basic essentials for survival here. That was all that mattered for the moment. After the expected words of sympathy, Tony reminded him that the hired cement mixer was being delivered tomorrow. Jonathan nodded slowly without taking much of it in. Tony touched Jonathan's shoulder before leaving him alone, sat in a chair in the lounge. Something Jonathan had rarely allowed himself to do up until now.

Apart from the painkiller-induced drowsiness, his energy levels were not really affected. So he carried on working, with the mortgage still having to be paid and him not wanting to add homelessness to the list of problems. But also, it felt as if something familiar and structured needed to be maintained to keep himself moderately together. He continued paying Tony for his efforts, but his own involvement in improvements to the cottage were now postponed until he got the results of these new tests he was supposed to be having; and quietly dreading. Figuring that if he was now riddled with inoperable tumours it was pointless, and any strength to continue would soon desert him. He chose not to tell Mum, as word would travel around the family quickly. What could anyone do except worry? And nothing was definite yet. Although best not to indulge in any optimism, he conceded. Having been exposed to the wisdom of acceptance in his brief stumbling upon 'the fellowship', whose teachings had somehow kept him sober for so long.

But he grieved the loss of Dennis and his psychiatric friends like never before. Them being fellow strugglers, now suddenly meant something again. There hadn't seemed much point in telling them where he was now living. From the moment he bought the place, he was purely focused on the work that needed doing there and nothing else. And the only people he needed in that work were an assistant and advisor, and he had that. Anything or anyone else had become irrelevant. He had been forced to take a path in life that was very different to theirs. In their small world, the other side of the Tamar Bridge was the other side of the world. At times, he was close to ringing Dennis and telling his news to get some comfort. But then remembered his old friend's parting words at the station: 'Sometimes you've got to move on and see what's out there'. Was that moving on, to contact someone you'd willingly parted with for the sake of sharing bad news and getting a shoulder to cry on? One of a load of troubling questions his diagnosis had brought up. None of which he really knew how to answer.

He had made regular trips to Wakefield recently, which involved tramping. In the late afternoon on one such return trip, at the location of his overnight stop, he found himself in a queue at motorway services on the M1. There were a few local newspapers on display and one of them was the Sheffield Telegraph. It stirred memories from when his childhood was comparatively normal and he delivered them as a paper boy. And from a distance, he could just make out a familiar name on its front page. 'Kevin Porter'. Without losing his place in the queue, he reaches over, grabs a copy, and takes it back to the cab for further examination.

'Construction Boss Donates 50K to Hospital Appeal'.

There he was with self-satisfied grin and greying hair, flanked by admiring, mostly female hospital staff. But was it the same one?

'Kevin Porter, 53, (same age as himself) CEO of KP Construction in Sheffield.'

The sickening reminder of the past left him with a mixture of shock and rage. Especially, as it seemed, *this* Kevin Porter was some kind of local hero. *'Kevin Porter gets life'. 'Kevin Porter dies of cancer'.* Those were headlines he *could* stomach.

Picturing the leering smile of the boy in his head, he remembered the two upper front teeth in disarray as if having grown at slight angles away from each other, creating a visible gap between them. With a real sense of urgency to determine if this was the middle-aged version of the boy that had made his life such a misery, he scoured the shops for a magnifying glass. No luck. He would have to wait and use the one he had at home. He lay on his bunk, fully reunited with his schooldays and being stuck in the hole in the ground in what he had thought would become his tomb.

With the help of the painkillers, he slept but also dreamt, and for the first time in decades, about being buried alive. Still haunted by the incident in the well and how it had set him on a path to further incidents of trauma and struggle, he continued his journey back to Liskeard the next day; and while trying to talk some sense into himself, realised that there was no point in thinking any more about this particular Kevin Porter until he was certain it was the same one. And if it was, then what? But he couldn't help doing so. If this Kevin Porter was anything like the adolescent one he had had the misfortune of knowing, then he was holding that hospital donation above his head like a trophy, in a – haven't I done well – gesture.

Despite the tiredness and pain as previous painkillers had started to wear off, on his return home he couldn't resist rummaging through drawers for his magnifying glass. However, as he did, it occurred to him that a man of such stature and wealth would have probably had the wonky teeth surgically realigned or false ones implanted, so perhaps the search was futile. But not so, it seemed, as with the optical aid he could at last see clearly the still-crooked gnashers in the colour photo as Porter smiled, soaking up the glory. This spurred him on to search the internet for more information on the enemy.

'Porter makes bid for United', was a previous headline in the Telegraph.

'A local boy. Sheffield through and through, he grew up in Ecclesfield...'

Location of the well. That confirmed it if any more confirmation was needed. It was him.

Tony's insistence that he should be having chemotherapy by now, although well-meaning, made him feel once again like he was failing to grasp the obvious. There was so much he should have asked the doctor at the time but didn't. The sudden switch from trying to make sense of all things DIY, to now medical, was all too much. And with a feeling of increasing hopelessness about everything to do with *his* life, his investigations into the adult life of Kevin Porter were at least some distraction from it. But painful. Reading of the man's entrepreneurial conquests was sickening, as was the general adoration for the rich man giving headline-grabbing amounts of money to charity. Revenge was somewhere in his mind, without the vaguest notion of how it could be achieved. But the fact that the man was a public figure, of whom, details were easily accessible on the internet, seemed to provide a flicker of hope, of something.

'KP Construction. How can I help you?' The cheery female voice sang her introduction.

'Hello, my name is Ryan and I work for a company called

Plasterboard Direct. We supply all types of plasterboard direct to the trade, to company premises or direct to building sites where construction work is taking place.'

Jonathan had read something on the KP website about 'reliability and affordability' with plasterboard suppliers having been an issue at some point. Amongst other issues, which it said, KP himself had 'fought tirelessly to overcome in his battle to get KP construction to where it is now. The top!' In other words, possibly still an issue which hadn't yet been overcome.

He waited for the continuous tone that would signify that he had got as far as he was ever going to get with this.

'Oh yes.'

Relief. She was still there. He took encouragement from that. How much he would love to come face to face with the school bully once again, and that keenness was somehow giving strength to his bullshit. What had he got to lose? Not much, it seemed.

'Well, we were wondering if Mr Porter would be kind enough to spare fifteen minutes of his precious time, so one of our representatives can have a brief chat and leave a few of our brochures with him. And we promise to cut by a third, what he is currently paying for plasterboard.'

'I see. Well, all I can do Mr erm…?'

'Ah, Walker. Ryan Walker.'

'All I can do Mr Walker is pass this message on to his secretary, and if she can give you an appointment with Mr Porter, she will contact you. Is that OK?'

It was about as OK as it was going to get for the moment.

When fully focused on something, Jonathan was like a train moving speedily with determination to achieve his goal. Just like he had been with the restoration of the cottage. But that particular train had been stopped abruptly by the recent discovery that he may not live to see its completion. And this new train for the great Mr Porter's demise, was stirring, but hadn't quite left the station. And may never do so. In the modern world, if a company could not be successfully googled, it didn't exist. And as such, his fragile bluff could so easily be called.

He gave the lady his phone number, including the area code for Liskeard. Then, with a sudden awareness of the Cornish town's distance from Sheffield, made a clumsy, spur of the moment explanation, that despite the company's location, due to its recent expansion were now 'able to branch out in other areas of the country'. After which, it felt like his polished performance thus far, had just fallen down the stairs. He hung up, not expecting to hear any more. But what he didn't realise, was that the wall of efficiency he presumed he was up against, had some serious cracks in it.

Jonathan attended his next hospital appointment, followed by the dreaded doctor's appointment for the results. He had to expect the worst as his only means of defence. It was the same young lady doctor as before. Again, after the initial pleasantries and warm smile, the scaffolding holding it all up gave way, and he could see the future in her face.

'I'm very sorry, Mr Piper, but the tumours have increased in the pancreas and have now spread to the liver. There really is no more we can do.'

He stared at the floor. No great shock now, thanks to the first bit of bad news he'd already received. This was the first time the fairly recently qualified young doctor had had to pass sentence of death, and it clearly affected her. But she had braced herself for this occupational hazard, and was determined to hang on to some professionalism.

'Possibly six months I would say, depending on how you respond to chemo,' she answered her patient's predictable question, with continued defiance of her emotion.

After questioning the doctor some more about the side effects of chemotherapy, and she described the nausea, fatigue, and hair loss, he didn't immediately commit himself to it. Much indecision followed while the doctor insisted that if he were to have the treatment it should begin now. However, with a brain still veering more towards the criminal, he considered that if he were to be rewarded with an appointment with the school bully turned entrepreneur, he needed energy, and to vaguely fit the description of the slick salesman that he had impersonated on the phone. But was that a hope worth hanging on to? And if he didn't get the appointment, was the nausea, fatigue, and hair loss worth it, just to prolong a worthless life a little bit longer?

'How do you feel now?' the doctor asked. 'Are the painkillers working OK?'

'Yeah. Not bad.' His answer had the vagueness of someone with other things on their mind. 'Knocking me out a bit, but I suppose it's to be expected.' She nods her understanding.

He needed to keep the doctor at arm's length. Still officially employed, he had so far said nothing to his employer, and Tony had promised not to. If she learned what he did for a living, she would surely insist that he did, and employer would in turn insist that he no longer drives their lorries. The job and the travel involved may still be useful to him, and he didn't want to give it up until he was sure it wouldn't be. And the thought of being stuck at home, alone with his deterioration, no longer employed and without the strength or motivation to transform the cottage, seemed too much to bear.

The doctor assured him that he would be visited and 'monitored' by a nurse, and a place at a 'charming' hospice would be reserved for him when necessary. She also gave him a few leaflets to do with benefits that could be claimed for the terminally ill. His mortgage was safe, so it seemed. At last, money, that he had spent all his adult life accumulating and meticulously planning his survival around, was no longer a problem due to his lack of future.

The phone rings. 'Can I speak to Mr Walker, please?'

As a few weeks had passed since his initial chat with a lady at KP Construction, he had more or less given up on it. So the call came as a complete surprise, and his response was not ideal. 'Who?'

'Mr Walker.'

'Ah, yes! Ryan. Umm. Sorry. Yes. I'll just get him. Could you hold on one second, please?'

He pulled the phone away from his ear and put a hand over the mouthpiece in case he did any more damage. He exhaled while he had the chance, heart pounding with anticipation. His brain needed a moment to reorganise itself. *KP Construction were the only people who knew about Ryan Walker. Yes. So it must be them. Great.* With that established, he needed to disguise his voice a little, to continue the charade of now being someone else.

'Hello, Ryan speaking.'

Now a little higher. He decided against doing a foreign accent, as it may need maintaining for longer than he could cope with.

'Mr Walker?'

'Yes! I'm sorry about that. My colleague was a little confused. He only knows me by my Christian name. Mr Walker here. How can I help?'

'Regarding your request for an appointment with Mr Porter.'

'Yes, indeed!' Jonathan said, eagerly and excitedly.

'Well, Mr Porter would be interested in seeing you or one of your representatives, briefly, about your offer. If you can make it next Tuesday at nine a.m. at our Sheffield headquarters. It will have to be brief though, as Mr Porter will have a full day's schedule.'

'Oh, yes, definitely, definitely! It will be brief, of course. And I will leave a few of our brochures with the great man, and he can caruse them at his leisure.' He chuckled, finding it difficult to contain his excitement.

'We'll see you then, Mr Walker.'

'Absolutely, I will be there myself, and thank you again for the call. Goodbye.' *Caruse! Was that a word? Well, if it wasn't, she didn't seem to notice.*

Managing to sound slicker than an oil slick and twice as greasy as if having just emerged from the longest ever seminar on positive thinking and speaking that any living person had previously been exposed to, he now faced the challenge of having to look the part before next Tuesday. Revenge, in the grisliest form possible was now foremost in his mind, but had to be prepared for it not being immediately possible as soon as he entered the place. The charade would have to be played out until it was. And that required his clothes and words to be spot on, in order to get close enough to the enemy to carry out his devious intentions without arousing the faintest of suspicion.

The forthcoming appointment had breathed new life into the dying man. For the first time ever, he enters a gentleman's outfitters, and with plucky excitement and humour, says the first thing that enters his head.

'I've got to try and look like a slimy salesman.'

The sales assistant looked confused. As though he were exactly such a thing, and therefore did not easily associate the words 'slimy' and 'salesman' being next to each other in the same sentence. Helpful, informative, intelligent perhaps, yes. But 'slimy', no.

'I need to look slick. Do you have a suit that can do that, do you think?' Jonathan asks, as though he were Mr Benn[22] in the fancy dress shop, hoping to be transformed for his new adventure.

The sales assistant looked troubled. The customer was obviously not a frequent suit-wearer. Something he was not used to dealing with in his shop.

'Any particular preference? Double breasted, single? Material?'

Jonathan shakes his head. The man was talking another language. 'I've no idea.'

It was beginning to feel as though this new-found adrenalin was all that was keeping him going. All he could do was hope that he still had enough of it to get him to Sheffield by nine a.m. next Tuesday, and do whatever damage he possibly could.

---

[22] Animated children's TV programme of the early 1970s, in which the man enters the world for which he is dressed.

School Reunion

Jonathan started early with the packing of essentials having decided to drive up to Sheffield the day before the appointment. His Monday night's stay at an 'exclusive' five-star hotel close to KP construction HQ, already booked. The usual frugality abandoned for what was surely his last night of freedom.

But the one essential not so far packed or decided upon was a weapon; which ideally, needed to be small, easily concealable and lethal, without too much effort. And his quest for such a thing, led him to a camping and outdoor living shop where he examined the 'hunting knives' on display. He managed to get the plastic safety cover off the blade of one, and with the faintest touch on his fingertip it drew blood and was deemed more than adequate.

He then grappled with different options as to how such a weapon should be carried, which involved mostly pointless prediction about what may or may not occur at the appointment. He was firmly set on a briefcase that he would open with the bogus intention of getting some brochures out for KP to look at. But then noticed a leather sheath with a short belt, presumably to tie around the arm or lower leg; and took a moment to visualize a perfect violent scenario occurring with it. Some strange looking experiments then took place, overlooked by a bewildered and increasingly nervous shop assistant. To determine if knife would go in sheath, and if so, could sheath be buckled around his forearm so knife sits comfortably upside down on the inside of it. Bearing in mind, that the width of his forearm had considerably reduced along with everything else, due to the recent, cancer-induced weight loss. And if so, how easily would the knife stay there when it was upside down, so as to be easily accessible when concealed under a jacket sleeve.

'Excuse me, sir, we don't allow customers taking the knives out in the shop.'

'OK, I'll do it outside the shop.'

'You'll have to buy it first.'

'Shut up! I'm buying it!'

Since his diagnosis, along with the reduction in a lot of other physical things, so was his tolerance for petty nonsense. But, as there were other customers now looking alarmed that knives were out of their packaging and voices were being raised, he stands outside the shop to continue his experiments. With feelings of deja vu from the 'threatening-the-chef-with-a-knife' incident at Rockerfellaz, and how easy it was for those that didn't like you to slightly distort the facts a little to their advantage. And as such, sensing he was making an enemy of the young shop assistant, peers through the glass of the door anxiously to see if the youth was possibly on the phone reporting a knife-wielding maniac in his shop.

He'd always had an unorthodox, 'fertile imagination' as a teacher once described it, and a habit of using things for a purpose other than its intended one. And as such, his ability to aggravate orthodox shop assistants was the stuff of legend. On one such occasion, an assistant had spieled off the virtues of a fridge: its free delivery, guarantee, and not having to be paid for until next year. But all Jonathan was interested in (apart from its ability to keep things cold) was the size of it, which had to be exact. And as such, had busied himself with his tape measure, oblivious to the gibberish being spoken, before causing further annoyance by asking the man to assist by putting his finger on the other end. After which, having satisfied himself that the appliance was a centimetre too wide, left the shop in silence, causing exasperated assistant to turn to his colleague with a roll of the eyes and a raising of arms in despair. On another similar occasion when a lady shop assistant had commented on the beauty of a table Jonathan was seen examining in her shop, he promptly declared the intention of sawing its legs off and using it as 'a sort of platform'; but again, alas, its dimensions had to be exact, and sadly were not. All nowhere near the levels of buffoonery achieved by many of his past acquaintances, but still placing him firmly at odds with the mainstream of society and what it considered normal.

Due to his now inconveniently thin forearms, he comes back in the shop and makes another hole in the belt with a tiny screwdriver he spots sitting next to the till among some pens, to the increasing annoyance of the young man who then threatens to call the police if the customer doesn't pay for the goods he had now 'damaged'. To which, Jonathan asks him politely for an elastic band to further assist the experiment. This causes a silent moment of eye-to-eye contact, with a smile from Jonathan and a grimace from the young man, who reluctantly obliges. Eventually, his arduous experiments all prove positive and he buys the weapon and holder. But all would have been far easier if the knife and sheath were sold together, as they fitted each other perfectly; a point he raises with the shop assistant. But the young man only worked there on Saturdays, was completely disinterested, and had already dismissed his customer as a weirdo. As was so often the case.

He was still hanging on to full-time employment by a thread, despite comments of, 'he doesn't look well', as soon as his back was turned. Sadly, this Monday and Tuesday's activities in Sheffield had fallen on working days, so he had to ring in sick on account of a 'bad cold'. This didn't help to quell the rumours of his assumed ill health of a more serious kind.

With the car packed and new suit hanging up above the rear window still in its cellophane, he set off, trying to tolerate the pain without reaching for the painkillers. They would surely slow him down, despite the supply of energy drinks and bars of chocolate to counteract their debilitating effect. But now, being seated in the car seemed to aggravate the tumours even more.

As he drove, there was much rehearsing and speculating. And the ifs and buts going on in his overloaded brain were threatening to cause his body to grind to a halt with indecision. If the cancer hadn't succeeded in doing so first. So much so, that he was in danger of losing track of what he was doing and why he was doing it. It all needed re-assessing. Leaving the consequences aside, all he had to do to achieve his goal was turn up with a sharp knife to an appointment with someone who was unlikely to be also armed and stick it in him. Justice will have been done. And for that privilege, he reminded himself, the subsequent incarceration for the brief remainder of his existence was without doubt, worth it. Also, something to keep in mind, was that in the unlikely event of him being greeted by a smiling ex-school bully turned decent human being, justice must be done. This was the person who imprisoned him in a narrow hole in the ground and urinated on his head for the purpose of amusement, and how lucky was he to now have this opportunity to avenge it. Counting one's blessings always seemed to do the trick, (even if these ones were a bit out of the ordinary) and he continued the journey with renewed composure.

On arrival at the tranquil surroundings of the hotel, he collapsed on the bed and allowed himself two painkillers. Only to awake three hours later in a daze, with initial confusion as to where he was and why he was there. He could see from the window, his comparatively ancient Sierra looking painfully out of place in the car park alongside top-of-the-range Jaguars and BMWs. And as such, thought it best to return to reception and make them aware that it belonged to a guest of the hotel, and hadn't been abandoned in their car park. Any unexpected hitches the following morning involving wheel clamps and tow trucks needed to be avoided. But after he pointed out the potentially offensive vehicle to a bewildered receptionist, there followed a clumsy mess of misunderstanding, so typical of Jonathan's experience. During which, the anxious-to-please young lady of Chinese appearance apologised profusely, saying she would arrange for it to be removed immediately. Only after he vigorously explained that it was his car, and he wasn't complaining about it, did he get an assurance that it would be safe in their car park.

Now regretting having drawn such attention to his and his car's presence, in light of tomorrow's activities, his unease extended to the abundance of CCTV cameras dotted about the place. Especially the one in the car park that had a nasty habit of moving, as if with a mind of its own.

A restless evening was spent alone in the hotel room, much of it pacing the floor with a mind constantly wandering in and out of further speculation of the unknown. During which, he considered that at least some rehearsal was appropriate. But for what? Would Porter be sitting and himself standing, or the other way round? Or should he just plunge the knife straight into the man at first sight, whether or not he was alone, upside down or back to front, and just let himself be apprehended? The indecision was rampant. And as he attaches the knife and sheath to his left forearm, is forced to consider the likelihood that just one penetration of the enemy with it, may be all there would be time for. The raising of it above his head ready to stab, with his intentions clearly visible for any more than a second, may result in a scream, a shout, somebody else intervening, the wrong person being stabbed? And if all that was finally achieved before being apprehended was the wounding of the man, it simply wouldn't be enough. A wasted opportunity.

Now clothed as he would be for tomorrow's appointment in something of a dress rehearsal, with knife upside down in position, he realises it's in a far better position for horizontal slashing than vertical stabbing. And so, with the aid of a shower curtain and its coloured pattern of wavy lines, he stands in the bathroom practising his aim with repeated release and slashes. As he slashes his way along one particular thin wavy line and then another, with a step forward with each swing of the knife, he allows himself a smile as his accuracy increases, and a sporadic moment of excitement and joy at the prospect of tomorrow's downfall of the high and mighty. His murderous ambitions were giving purpose to an otherwise pitiful, depleted life. Keeping self-pity, and a whole range of other negative emotion caused by his condition, at bay.

An unsettled night was spent unable to stem the adrenalin flowing like Niagara Falls within him, until a much needed painkiller at five a.m. puts him into a deep sleep, making the noise of the alarm clock at seven thirty feel more like an electric shock. Immediately his heart races with excitement and anticipation. He gets into his sales rep disguise and looks in the full-length mirror. It was a smart suit that concealed all that was going wrong with his body. But from the neck up, it was impossible to hide the gaunt face and tired brown eyes that looked like they had seen it all and much of it unpleasant. Despite the usual ponytail, there was too much greying hair for any conventional salesman keen to make a good impression, he considered. And as such, feeling the urgent need of a change of image, clumsily puts the knife to his hair and starts to remove chunks of it, before realizing he's about to make things worse and end up looking like the sort of unhinged person who would cut their own hair before an appointment. With the knife back in its sheath, secured against his forearm and concealed with jacket sleeve, he stands in front of the mirror and has a last few practice slashes with it. After which he puts the elastic band around the knife to keep it in place, pressing its handle against the skin of his forearm, thinking that it may need a bit of explaining if it suddenly fell from his sleeve on to the floor at the wrong moment. He clears up the mess of what remains of the shredded shower curtain before it arouses any suspicion, and stuffs it into his luggage. Better to pretend you never had one in the first place, he decides. A final anxious glance in the mirror and he realises he's forgotten to have a shave, before telling himself to stop fussing. *You're supposed to be a plasterboard salesman not a bridegroom! Just get on with it!* were final stern words said to himself before closing the door and leaving.

With a mixture of excitement and anxiety, he found himself in a waiting room with several other legitimate salesmen and women, eagerly awaiting their brief opportunity to persuade the almighty to part with his money. He sat with a small modest briefcase on his lap. In it were a few miscellaneous brochures, which he considered may be needed to create a distraction. As he stared intensely at the wall opposite him with unblinking eyes, he had a nagging feeling that he'd forgotten something. Something he hadn't so far been asked for. Identification. A card with his and the name of his company on it, which he now suddenly and belatedly presumed was the norm. He scolded himself for his error, and his brain did a few somersaults. Was he about to be asked for it at any moment? Who was he again? Ryan Walker, of course. For god's sake, don't introduce yourself as Jonathan Piper. Not for the moment, anyway.

'You can go in now, Mr ah, Walker?' The words had brought him out of a trance.

'Yes, that's right, Walker,' he confirmed to the receptionist, and himself.

He knocked at the door with a nervous smile at the ready, trying to compose himself, as though an actor about to audition for his first west end stage musical having lost his voice. *Smile, be polite, but remember this is vermin you're dealing with,* were stern words he gave himself just before entering.

He needed the hatred and anger alongside him, but those two emotions were difficult to function with when any meticulousness or care needed to be taken. Balance was essential. And despite the pep talks to himself about disregarding the consequences, now, he really needed to get away with it. Not so much out of fear of being locked up, but the need to avoid becoming a victim himself. With memories of Porter victimising him many times before and easily getting away with it, now it was his turn to do the same. As if, *him* now getting away with it, was all part of the justice being administered. And for that to happen, care needed to be taken.

The much thought about and dreamt about ex-school bully is now a man wearing dark grey immaculately pressed trousers and a white open-necked shirt with sleeves rolled up as if ready for action. Alone, he stands at his desk, off guard, while looking downwards at a list of names on a clipboard with a troubled expression on his face, as Jonathan enters, wondering if an early opportunity had presented itself. Should he act now? Too late. Porter turns to face him.

'You are Ryan Walker of...?'

The broad Sheffield accent was all too familiar, if a bit deeper. 'Plasterboard Direct, sir.'

Porter put his hand out. Jonathan wasn't sure whether it was an invitation to shake it. It wasn't. 'ID. Well! Do you have a card or something?'

Porter's manner was impatient and patronizing, talking to him as if he were sub-normal, taking Jonathan right back to his schooldays. And in a brief moment, remembered looking up at the vision of the leering boy Porter from inside the well, as he unzipped his trousers ready to piss on him. At least his conscience would have no trouble disposing of the man, should he get the chance. But Jonathan was disorientated at this point, not focused on the physical damage he had come here to do. Thrown off course by the whole identity card crisis. But managed to recover with some settling words for the beast, to get him more relaxed and off guard. Waiting for what his brain would tell him was the right moment for the slaughter to commence.

'I'm really sorry, sir. I was just outside in the waiting room there and realised I must have dropped my card on the way here. I really won't take up much of your time, sir.'

Porter was well used to people grovelling to him, especially salesmen, so the sound of the repeated 'sirs' and apologies eventually have the desired effect.

'You mean they didn't ask you for one at reception when you arrived? Porter raises his arms in exasperation. 'OK, let's just get on with it!'

Jonathan, having passed the first potentially catastrophic of hurdles, felt a little more assured. And for the knife to make sure it was still in place. It was. He was yearning to say his real name and see the look in the man's eyes. But that was a luxury he forbade himself for the sake of trying to avoid raised voices, and with it, the possibility of somebody else entering the room. All needed to be normal, until the moment it suddenly wasn't.

'So, you're going to cut by a third what we spend on plasterboard,' said Porter casually, quoting Jonathan's promise as he sat on the edge of his desk with a smile of mockery displaying the familiar oddly arranged front teeth. 'That's what it says here, so that's what you're gonna do,' he continued, pointing at his clipboard. As if relishing his power, and the fear he usually injected into visiting salespeople.

But his words ignited the spark of aggression Jonathan needed to continue. And for once, the hatred, anger, and courtesy, were in perfect balance.

'Absolutely, sir. No question about it. I have here a few of our brochures if you'd care to take a quick look.'

Still standing, not having been offered a seat, he opens his briefcase and lays them on the desk. Porter now standing, looks down at them. Jonathan takes a step back, poised, hand on knife, awaits the inevitable: Porter looking up again, angry at being made to look at camping accessory and holiday brochures. And at last, feels a rush of confidence and excitement at having the opportunity to put an end to the charmed life this man must have enjoyed, since walking away from that disused well with his two cohorts.

'What is this?'

'Jonathan Piper. Remember me?'

Now, full of power and revelling in it, he allows himself the joy of giving his victim the briefest of reminders of the past as he stares deep into his eyes. A second later, he releases the knife from its sheath, and in an almost 180 degree swing of his arm, hits the jackpot. Right across the throat of his victim, who collapses backwards. Jonathan guides him to his swivel chair, blood squirting from his neck. Just to avoid the thump as the lifeless body hits the floor.

'Jonathan Piper.' He whispers his name again into the man's ear, desperate to give him one final piece of information, in the hope that he's just conscious enough to take it in.

He felt absolute peace and joy as the blood drained quietly from his victim. But not as a vampire or sadist, just someone who had achieved what they had set out to do; and despite all the uncertainty, it was happening right now. The almighty had been toppled. Porter was untouchable as a schoolboy and untouchable as a businessman, until one day, today, when he was well and truly touched.

He waited patiently, until a vacant, lifeless expression took hold of the face of the still seated Kevin Porter. Silence was crucial to his escape. He was fully aware of that from the moment he entered, with the reception and waiting room being so close outside. If he had mistimed it or missed his target, thus allowing his victim to let out any noise audible from outside the room, someone would have surely entered it and sealed his fate. But, as all had occurred so quickly and quietly, he was able to rearrange himself, put the brochures and knife back into his case, and thank the receptionist with a smile on his way out. And then leg it. As fast as any cancer victim could move, down three floors via the stairway. Outside in the main car park, his escape was assisted by a mass of people generally milling about having just alighted from two coaches, and he weaved his way through them unnoticed to his car. He sped off down the road, and when it felt safe to do so, let out an almighty shriek of joy. Mission accomplished. He had got away with it for now. But was suddenly brought down to earth when he noticed blood spattered on his face and the collar of his shirt in the rear-view mirror which he then frantically tries to remove with a cloth and some water, while still speeding away as fast as he can without attracting attention.

Having found a deserted spot, he changed clothes quickly into the non-bloodstained casuals he had arrived in yesterday, disposing of the suit, knife, and anything else incriminating, in amongst some bushes and trees. But as he set off again, realised that he had lost his bearings completely, and could only drive on until he saw a sign that might give him a clue. Not one to trust the technology of a Sat Nav, and too risky to stop for some prolonged map reading. But eventually learns that he's somehow gone under the M1 instead of joining it for the quick getaway he'd hoped for and was taking the scenic route in the wrong direction through endless small towns and villages. And worse still, while on the outskirts of one of them, notices the engine running unusually lumpy and uneven, and a lit-up exclamation mark then appears on the dashboard.

'A fucking lot of good that is!' he screams at it.

As he had checked all the basics before leaving home, it had to be something more serious that he knew nothing about. He had breakdown cover but was still way too close to the scene to think about seeking help.

It had to be the end. He was feeling weaker as the day went on. Driving like crazy and going round in circles had taken its toll. As the complete breakdown of the car (and himself) seemed imminent, he directed his efforts to getting it anywhere out of the way of anything or anybody. And when it finally conked out for good, those efforts had seemingly paid off. An ideal spot. For a picnic, yes, definitely, but sadly, not an option. He got out in the small, deserted car park, feeling a lot calmer for the tranquil surroundings and silence, and surveyed the scene. On a slight downhill slope with a lake of what was hopefully deep water at the end of it, his brain got to work. No houses nearby, but several cars and a tractor had passed the car park infrequently while he'd been there. It was risky, but so was everything. He got his essentials out of the car that could be carried, before letting its handbrake off and giving it as much of a push as he was capable of. Just hoping it would have enough momentum to clear the uneven ground and clumps of long grass before the water. Off the end of the concrete and onto the grass it went, going slightly off course, dangerously close to a low bit of hedge. Fearing that the hedge may end up being its final resting place, he chased after the car, and put all the strength he could muster behind it, giving it one last almighty push. After which he lay on the grass, face down in the mud, temporarily paralysed, panting and heaving for breath. But the car continues rolling to its desired destination, over the bit of hedge, somersaulting as it enters the water and slowly sinks without trace. With its owner still horizontal and wheezing, oblivious to where it had ended up.

Now, without much needed transport, but feeling far more anonymous and invisible, he starts the long walk back in the direction of the last village he had passed through which, he was forced to consider, may end up being a crawl. He staggered along the narrow country road with his bag, having to squeeze himself into hedges for safety on its bends, and stick his thumb out at every passing car. Now with severe pain, he rested on some grass and swigged down a few painkillers with energy drink. The getaway was beginning to eclipse the challenge of the actual crime. But then, to his relief, a car approached and slowed right down, just as he no longer had the strength to raise a thumb to request it.

'Excuse me, are you all right?'

'I'm not feeling too well.'

'Yes, I can see that. Can I give you a lift?' asked the lady driver.

'Oh yes, please,' he said, almost in tears of gratitude.

She got out and helped him into the passenger seat. Suddenly, the full insanity of what he was doing was terrifyingly clear.

'My car broke down back there, and I realised I'd left my mobile phone at home,' he told her, doing his best to make everything sound normal, like that was the full extent of the problem. 'I'm sorry to trouble you.'

'Don't mention it. I really think I should get you to a hospital though.'

'Oh, no, no, that won't be necessary. I'll be fine.' His words were instinctive, but his resistance to the heavenly idea of being looked after in hospital was weakening rapidly. 'Just somewhere I can get on a bus, perhaps, if you wouldn't mind.'

Eventually, they arrived in a small town and he spotted two very useful things close to each other, the sight of which rejuvenated his escape: a cash machine and a taxi office.

'That'll be fine. Just here, ah…?'

'Trisha.'

She gave him a big smile as she said her name, with a warm feeling that she was helping a most deserving person in distress. Not a knife-murderer make his escape.

'Are you going to be OK now?'

'Absolutely.'

'Are you sure?'

'Oh yes, I'm feeling a lot better now, Trisha. Thank you so much.'

With an uneasy feeling that he may be about to be taken hostage by the most well-meaning of hostage-taker, he says all the right things to get her to stop the car and let him out. Which needed to be right here, while still in staggering distance of the taxi office and hopefully a chair to sit on if he had to wait for one. She obliges, and in a determined effort he gets out of the car unassisted, sensing her watching him closely, as though it were a test to prove he was well enough to be set free. With relief, he waves to her as she drives away. She had been pivotal in resuscitating the helpless lump at the side of the road, thus enabling the show to go on.

After much needed refreshments in a cafe, he took £200 from the cash machine and soon was in a taxi bound for Chesterfield, having asked for the nearest big train station.

'Are you all right, mate? Only you look a bit under the weather.'

He was going to get a lot more of this type of questioning before he pops his clogs, of that he was certain. But funny how a suit, collar and tie, seemed to make such a difference to the general perception of one's health, he reflected, as there was no such questioning this morning in his sales rep disguise. Maybe he just looked a bit more pathetic in his now dirty jeans and kagoule, he wondered.

'Oh yes, thanks. Bit of a long day. Be glad to get home.'

Fortunately, the taxi driver was satisfied with the normal sounding response to his question and says no more. He turns his radio on to break the silence, and together they listen to local news.

'There's some nutter on the loose, apparently.'

'Oh, yes,' Jonathan replied casually, failing to grasp the connection between himself and the 'nutter'.

'Yeah, this morning. Boss of a big company, knifed in his office.'

Jonathan now trembled with fear, wondering if he was about to be taken hostage in another vehicle for a very different reason. But did his best to keep up the show of normality. 'Really. What's the world coming to? It's not safe to go out these days, is it?'

'Or stay in, by the sound of it!' the taxi driver retorted with a laugh.

'Yes, of course,' Jonathan nervously agreed.

Driver turns up the radio, increasing Jonathan's tension. 'Here it is now.'

The radio takes over and they stay silent.

The voice of a high-ranking policeman can just be heard above traffic noise and passers-by. 'We're looking for a man who—'

Jonathan deliberately coughs repeatedly at the crucial moment, prompting a concerned look at him by the driver in his rear-view mirror. Two unacceptable things for passengers to do on their journey were dying and being sick, and this one seemed a possible for both.

'Are you sure you're all right, chief?'

'Yes, I'm fine. Think I got something stuck in my throat,' he says, rummaging through his bag for a bottle of water. Forever having to fend off suspicion with displays of normality, it seemed.

'—and was driving a Ford Sierra. Anyone with information should—'

Now the copper's words were replaced with crackles.

'Arrghh! I must get that aerial seen to,' the exasperated driver mutters to himself.

Jonathan was traumatized, wondering how accurate the description of the 'nutter' he had obliterated with his coughing actually was, and if it was safe to go anywhere. In none of his pre-murder philosophizing had he prepared himself for this. At last, they arrive at Chesterfield train station, and thankfully, not its police station, and he was free to go.

'Here we are then, chief. Have a safe journey. Mind how you go.'

In something of a trance, he just manages a 'thank you' in response and gives the driver a generous tip, just out of relief at being released into the open air. The taxi feeling like the nearest thing to custody he had experienced so far.

Too exhausted and drained for any real positive feeling about what he'd done, he desperately needed to get home. And allowed himself some optimism that maybe he was now safer at the densely populated train stations of the Tuesday night rush-hour, than driving the now publicized 'Ford Sierra'. He put on sunglasses and raised the hood of his kagoule. Suitably disguised for the boarding of trains and sitting on platform benches waiting for them. With confidence that at least he looked nothing like the beige-suited, pony-tailed man that he was earlier in the day, just in case the news was giving out CCTV images of one.

He now had plenty of time to think, and with it came doubt. Although the car was safely disposed of, the fact that its make and model had been so accurately described must surely mean its registration number and therefore address of its owner, was also common knowledge. By going home, was he going exactly where they were hoping he would, and would be there to greet him? Anything was possible. The intense speculation had given him a headache to add to his other aches and pains, and he swallowed more pills before conceding that go home he must, for better or worse. No way was he in any condition to go on the run.

Now nearly midnight and his taxi from Liskeard station moves slowly along the narrow country lane as it nears the cottage, with a tense Jonathan bracing himself for the possibility of police presence. Listening out for any noise other than the usual water running and owls hooting, he leaves the taxi at the top of the driveway and walks down it quietly in pitch darkness. Half expecting spotlights to be switched on and armed police telling him to lie down at any moment. But to his relief, there was no such intrusion, and he unlocked the door to what was now a palace. Never had he been so satisfied with the place, in its dilapidated, forever unrestored condition. Just that it provided peace, solitude, and running water for a much needed shower and cup of tea. And then, after these comforts, during a rest in an armchair, slowly but surely a feeling of enormous achievement re-emerged, having lost it this morning somewhere in the chaos of the getaway. After you've just slashed the throat of your childhood abuser while masquerading as a sales rep; just to get close enough to him to do it, the last thing you're going to concentrate on as you make your escape, is where you're going, it seemed.

At one a.m. he goes to bed with peace and contentment at the day's extraordinary achievements. Oblivious, that tomorrow, which was now today, was a working day for which he was due to rise at two thirty a.m. After the rarity of a good eight hours' sleep, the next morning he rings work, full of apologies, reporting that his cold was no better. But after listening to his bosses' exasperation at not being told yesterday, gave up the charade and told the man of his cancer and borrowed time.

'Why didn't you tell us before?' was the predictable response.

As if that would have made everything hunky dory if he had. In his experience of transport managers, they liked to think that any problem, however severe, can be solved with a quick phone call to them; and they are all powerful from their swivel chairs and computer screens. Not this one.

'I'm sorry to hear that, Jonny. We've got to let you go, of course. But come in and see us before you urgh... urgh. Well anyway, we'll have your P45 and that for you. OK?'

His boss clumsily searched for the right words, doing his best to make the said tax document sound like something to look forward to when in the last few months of life.

He picks up a note on the doormat from a 'Cathy'. Nurse of some kind, who had been given the task of monitoring him and was 'sorry to have missed you'. He was sorry he had missed her. It was rare for him to get the chance to enjoy the company of females. Or anybody else for that matter, now Tony's visits had come to an end, but especially females. And after a brief flash of deranged, Bernie-style, female-related optimism, that this may be the elusive girl of his dreams, he reminded himself of why she was visiting. And as such, would be rather cruel timing if she was. After what he'd done, it didn't seem appropriate to arrange another visit.

A letter from Mum had also arrived. How was he doing? He hadn't told her of his cancer. She would feel duty bound to come and see him, and she had enough to deal with, what with the ailments of her geriatric relatives. He would also have to conceal his murderous activities. Or perhaps she already knew if she had been watching the local news. Either way it was awkward. She had always been the giver of unconditional love, no matter what. But her only son coming all the way to Sheffield to kill a respectable businessman, and not bothering to visit! He wasn't quite sure which of these two crimes would be considered the more severe in his mother's opinion, or if he had stretched the boundaries of unconditional love to its limit. And was too scared to ring her and find out.

He was mentally prepared for the inevitable: a knock at the door by the police. Of course, they had no way of tracing Ryan Walker or Plasterboard Direct. But the receptionist had seen him close up and would have given a detailed description, and, the Liskeard phone number he had given for him to be contacted. So all they had to do was match that phone number with a name and address. Or do the same with the registration number of his car, doubtless picked up on CCTV cameras somewhere on his travels before it ended up at the bottom of a lake. When the police want information on somebody, they get it, without being obstructed by mention of the 'data protection act', or having to wait in a queue and endure the – *if you want this press one, if you want that press 2s* – like the rest of the unfortunate population. No, they wouldn't need to get Sherlock Holmes out of retirement for this one.

But a few days went by. Nothing. Then a week went by. Even more nothing.

Slipping Through the Cracks

South Yorkshire Police liaised closely with staff at KP Construction, who were just beginning to emerge from a state of shock. Work had ground to a halt the day Jonathan left there with a big smile and the blood spatter of the chief executive on his face, and not a lot had been done since. That day was chaos, not only for the assailant in his escape. Salesmen and women with appointments after Jonathan's, some sitting in the waiting room bewildered, others just arriving, as a steady stream of emergency service personnel invaded the place. A traumatized receptionist had made the grim discovery after Mr Porter failed to communicate with her via the intercom after his appointment with Ryan Walker. And eventually, after remembering the job she was supposed to be doing, announced to the visitors that Mr Porter would not be keeping any more appointments today, without giving any specific reason. But it was generally perceived that her scream and the subsequent wailing of sirens from outside had got something to do with it.

In the eyes of the local media, with his recent hospital appeal donation, Porter had transformed himself from just another rich person who wasn't quite rich enough to buy a football club, to a hero, credited with almost single-handedly rescuing a hospital under threat of closure. So now, with huge public and media interest, the pressure was now on for a quick result on his murder. And that was something fully expected by the hierarchy of the local police, who had almost promised it, in their overconfident statements to the press thus far.

How difficult could it be, with the aid of technology of the sort that any modern, successful company would have at their disposal? CCTV, and all phone calls logged and recorded 'for quality and training purposes'. But there was glaring incompetence within the company.

Security had been unconsciously relaxed to the point where just about anyone could get an appointment with the big chief to sell their wares, even if they didn't have any to sell; a lapse that Jonathan had taken full advantage of.

Detective Inspector Marshall was the man with it all to do. And as someone who'd been in the thick of it for as long as he had, wasn't prone to sudden bouts of optimism, as his superiors seemed to be when confronted with the media. Clear headed and down to earth he most certainly was, and a wealth of past experience had taught him to expect the unexpected. And not one to rely too heavily on technological gadgetry to get quick results. Which was just as well, as his first viewing of the company's CCTV images of the outside of the building on the morning of the murder proved less than encouraging. 'Bird shit on the lens' was deemed the likely reason for the camera that pointed at vehicles as they arrived in the car park revealing nothing at the relevant time. And when a much clearer image was obtained from another one, it revealed a coach, annoyingly positioned right in front of what was suspected of being the assailant's car, as a man could be seen walking speedily in its direction at just before ten a.m. that morning, before it roared off at speed from behind the coach. And as it did, the make and model was just about visible, but not much else.

Then, after close examination of their telephone records, it emerged that all calls received and made in a two-month period had been 'accidentally' deleted. And among them, the one from Ryan Walker and the one returned to him giving him his appointment. So, no recordings of them, or phone numbers logged. So the lady whose job it was to deal with calls as they first came in and redirect them to other departments if necessary, was top of Marshall's list to be interviewed. And according to her colleagues, it was she who was deemed to be the culprit of the deleting, having been under a lot of stress with her preparations to emigrate. The truth was, those preparations had been going on at work as well as at home, and as such, had made many personal calls on the company's phone which she then attempted to delete. And was successful. But sadly for the police, a whole load of other calls went with them.

'So, where is she now?' Marshall asked, with increasing curiosity.

'Australia,' the former colleague, who seemed to know all there was to know about the place, answered. Without a trace of expression, as if such complications were a perfectly normal part of daily life at KP construction.

'Ahhh. I see.' Marshall smiled with a roll of the eyes. This case was rapidly turning into one of those unexpected ones that must be expected.

But there was more to come. Marshall then asked for the name and contact details of the company's telephone service supplier, who would surely have a record of such calls, even if the company didn't. But even that was an issue filled with complexity. He was treated to a story of how Mr Porter had been in dispute with the telephone and broadband provider, and after finally losing patience with them, suddenly switched to an alternative one. And so, was given the details of the previous provider before the switch, to whom, KP construction were still 'just about' customers of, at the time of the all-important Ryan Walker calls. The inspector's head was now spinning with all the information. Having just about got to grips with the Australian connection, he gave up halfway through the latest barrage, conceding that it was a matter for more junior colleagues to make sense of.

Although not one to rely on quick fixes to solve major crime, such as the matching of telephone numbers with the addresses of suspects, he had to admit, that in a case of this magnitude, it may come in very handy. And as such, on his return to the station, gave the necessary details of the relevant telephone/broadband provider to a trusted junior colleague, with the instructions, 'Get that phone number, ASAP!'

Not much had changed in the personality of the late Kevin Porter, between him leaving his boyhood victim in a disused well and last Tuesday's appointment. The bullying loud-mouthed boy became a bullying loud-mouthed man and being a bullying loud-mouth was well paid, so it seemed. Now, of course, adored by many, who never knew him but read newspapers. But for the many unfortunates who *had* crossed his path, to know him was to loathe him. One of the few exceptions to this, was his forever loyal, inner circle of buddies: a must for a man who was forever 'one of the lads', who adored the company of his own sex. Like himself, keen golfers, many also had their own businesses, were originally from Sheffield and made of much the same stuff as himself. Tread on whoever you must to get to the top, was their collective motto. And Porter had done more than his fair share of treading. And so, wading their way through the man's enemies may prove to be a challenge for the inspector and his assistants. But this was something Marshall was already prepared for, as it was not his first encounter with Porter. He had interviewed him some years ago when an accusation of embezzlement had been made by a former colleague. Who then suddenly vanished without trace.

To Marshall's quiet dismay, there was to be no quick fix with the telephone number of whoever was passing themselves off as Ryan Walker being obtained, and leading them to his front door. As a dejected looking WPC returned with the news that, in the general disturbance of the recent telephone/broadband provider switch, the old provider no longer had a record of calls made from KP Construction at the relevant time, as its boss had unceremoniously terminated the contract, and payment, prematurely. Again, the inspector smiled and rolled his eyes. Luck was definitely not on his side, but he remained philosophical: that this case, although obviously about to take longer than expected, would be far more of a personal victory once he had cracked it. He just hoped his superiors would be of the same opinion. Up until now his record was almost exemplary, and as such, promotion to DCI was imminent; or so he'd been told by those in the know. Although definitely not one to absorb such rumours with any enthusiasm, he quietly, desperately, wanted to keep things that way.

Over lunch, he digested the morning's complications; and steak and kidney pie and chips. He was swayed in the direction that one of Porter's business enemies, or possibly a bereaved loved one of the vanished former colleague were responsible. Both urgently needed looking into. But one thing he was sure about: some old-fashioned, proper police work would have to be done to sort it out, now the cameras, computers and admin staff had failed so dismally. And with such annoyances at last put aside, was determined to crack on with it.

'Well, it seems our Mr Porter was a bit of a lad. Had a few other things going on apart from charity donations. Not exactly Mother Teresa, you might say,' Marshall mused out loud, while he and his sergeant drank tea.

DS Hennessy was a deeply conservative young man in comparison. The philanthropic nun was a little before his time, but he got the general gist of the insinuation, of which he didn't approve. This was only their second time of working together, and they were like chalk and cheese. Shackled together purely at the convenience of their superiors, longing to be somewhere else, with someone else.

'With respect, sir, I don't think that's fair,' Hennessy pipes up, having reluctantly succumbed to an unspoken obligation to sit with his inspector at lunch, partly due to the lack of other available seats. Finally plucking up the courage to vent his feelings, he wore his opinions like a knot in his stomach. And on this occasion, they duplicated that of the media's, and much of the local population that had absorbed it: that Kevin Porter was a hero, even more so now he was dead, and criticism of the deceased was not allowed. But such opinions had to be controlled if he was ever to climb the precarious ladder to police aristocracy: something he yearned for.

'Fair! Since when has anything been fair?'

Marshall didn't have to elaborate further. But did, on account of the fact that it may be easier to catch the killer if there was at least some harmony of thought between the two men given the task of doing it.

'Look, all I'm saying is, just because a man gives a large chunk of his dosh to a good cause, doesn't mean he's Sheffield's answer to Santa Claus! And doesn't mean that we should be looking for a deranged nutter, as only someone not in their right mind could do such a thing to a kind, loveable, pillar of respectability!'

Marshall's speech turned into a rant as it gathered pace. The frustrations caused by the ridiculous bad luck the pair had experienced so far with this investigation were beginning to come out. Marshall tried to get his point across, while choosing for the moment to remain silent about his previous meeting with the alive Kevin Porter. But he had a gut feeling then, that Porter was in a big way responsible for the ex-colleague whistle-blower's disappearance. But sadly, needed a lot more than gut feeling, and so it was dropped. He was now reliving that frustration all over again, as well as enduring the current ones.

'Look, we need to keep an open mind, OK?' Marshall continues, now calmer, with the feeling that the sergeant just needs a bit of guidance, as he himself had done and received many times. Irritated by the local media's seeming love affair with the victim since his headline- grabbing hospital donation, he now foresaw the increased pressure on him because of it. Hennessy on the other hand, was more seduced by it. And had a bit more to say on his superior speaking ill of the dead but conceded that it was one of those moments when best not to.

As this was a high-profile case and now considered far more of a challenge than first predicted, Marshall was assisted by a large team of mostly strangers. He clapped his hands once, loudly, to get their attention.

'Right, ladies and gentlemen, with our efforts to trace phone calls and car registration numbers having failed, we must get our heads down to some serious work. Kevin Porter, I want to know all about his business activities as far back as possible. KP Construction is only five years old. What was he up to before that? I want names of people and companies he either worked for or had dealings with. Anything of interest, that could possibly create enemies, I want to know about it.'

Marshall had a head start on his team, having reminded himself of the finer details surrounding his previous interview with Porter, but without telling them. Just in case he was accused of being over-influenced by it. And figuring, that if they were doing their jobs properly, would tell him.

'Also, we have a Julia Braithwaite who was the receptionist who spoke to a man on the phone, who presumably gave his name as Ryan Walker when he asked for an appointment with Mr Porter. Because Ryan Walker was the name listed for that appointment slot, when the victim was killed. Now, of course, that's unlikely to be his real name, so we won't bother looking in the telephone book. But did he give any other bits of information about himself in that phone call? And as you know, we have no recording of it or any other phone call, so Mrs Braithwaite is a vital witness. She's now living in Australia.'

Groans from the assembled team. They had been completely attentive and respectful to his every word, until the final sentence which turned it into a pantomime.

'Yes, I know. It's a hard life, innit? You'd think she'd have the decency to be just around the corner when we need her, wouldn't you?' Marshall's sarcasm raised a few smiles, as it often did.

'May we ask where in Australia?' Sniggers from the corner of the room.

'Don't know. She's only been there a week, maybe two. Admin at KP will have her previous address in the UK. Get it, go round there, knock on a few neighbour's doors. See if anyone knows anything. You never know, we may get lucky. She may have left a forwarding address with a neighbour or something. Janet, when you've got all the details about Mrs Braithwaite, get an LOR[23] out to Australia. We'll see if they can help. And get the contact details of the other salesmen and women who were in the

---

[23] Abbreviation of ILOR. International Letter of Request, for foreign help with an investigation.

308

waiting room at the same time as our killer. I want all of them interviewed. The receptionist will help with that, but tread carefully, as she discovered the body and is still in shock.'

Marshall pauses to get a marker pen and proceeds to draw a slapdash diagram of the killer's route of escape on to a whiteboard. 'CCTV inside the building tells us that he must have turned right along this corridor after leaving the reception and waiting area here and taken the stairs down. Taking him past this room used for storage of cleaning materials, and adjacent to this, a sort of canteen used by the company's maintenance staff. Now, domestic and maintenance staff are the only people who would normally be in this area, and here we have a visiting salesman, running, presumably, through it, to get to the car park. Somebody must have seen or heard something, or he may have dropped something that a member of staff may have picked up. Uniform will be searching the building. Anything of any significance, I want to know. OK? Off you go.'

Marshall and his sergeant retraced the killer's steps out of the building, while officers scoured the premises in vain for the murder weapon or any possible clues. Fingerprints found in Porter's office matched those on handrails and doors along the escape route, but didn't match those of any other known criminals: the only source of comparison at their disposal.

Baffling it most certainly was. Not a professional killing, Marshall surmised. A lone person with a grudge? Not of the criminal fraternity? None of the maintenance men present in their hut, that the killer must surely have passed en route to the car park, had noticed a suspicious, fast-moving salesman exit the building. The receptionist on the fateful morning spoke of hearing no raised voices during the appointment, and, as there was no sign of a struggle, it suggested that Porter either didn't know his killer, or immediately recognise him as an enemy, and that all was quite normal until the visitor produced a knife. She recalled a moderately well-spoken man with no obvious regional accent, pony-tailed hair, a briefcase and an engaging smile as he left. She squirmed as she recalled the smile, now with the painful awareness that its owner had just slashed the throat of her beloved boss, causing her to then be confronted with the gruesome aftermath. Other salespeople present in the waiting room at the time were interviewed, revealing nothing more than descriptions of a man looking 'oddly out of place', and 'rather too intense', as he sat on the edge of his seat.

The team had already spoken to Porter's secretary who rang Jonathan, aka Ryan Walker, offering him the Tuesday morning appointment. But it was just another call, telling the person the time and date at which to attend, much like the numerous others of the same she had made that day. Of which, there was no recording of either the conversation or the phone number that had been rung. So nothing of any significance had been obtained from her.

Jonathan had had a more lengthy and revealing conversation with Mrs Braithwaite, who the police could only hope had a good memory when she was found. Maybe nothing would be achieved with her either, but Marshall had to move in that direction. There was not a lot else and he had to be seen to be doing something, and could only relax when he was. But the Australian authorities were dragging their feet trying to locate her. As they had only a witness to a serious crime committed elsewhere, not a serious criminal in their country, there was no great urgency. On her job application form, the former telephonist had given her husband's name as next of kin. He couldn't be traced and was presumably with her, somewhere in Australia. The surname was sufficiently common for it to hinder the search for any relatives the couple may have left behind in the local area. Her previous Sheffield address was empty, and ex-neighbours mostly shook their heads vacantly, saying the family at No. 7 had kept themselves to themselves.

More shakes of the head were obtained at the school the Braithwaite's children had attended. And, in the requested scouring of Porter's business activities, various minor breaches of contract with other companies came to light. But that was the worst of the man's known misdemeanours, and not the sort of thing to which people usually bear grudges inspiring them to commit murder.

Unbeknown to Jonathan (as he didn't have a telly), he had earned himself a spot on a national TV show that appealed for the public's help in solving major crimes. In it, CCTV images were shown of him walking, and later running, through corridors at KP Construction. And also an appeal for help to trace a 'possibly blue' Ford Sierra, the assailant was suspected of driving. As old age had now made them a rare sight on the nation's roads, it was considered worth mentioning. But that, for the moment, was all South Yorkshire Police had. The images were not exactly close up and nobody else knew enough about Jonathan's schooldays to make the connection, with the possible exception of ex-classmates: Marsden and Reynolds in particular. But they, like ninety nine per cent of the population, were probably of the opinion that school bullying was a trivial matter and not a motive for murder. And, as the murder of a high-profile, successful businessman had been committed, others who had done business with him seemed like a good place to start looking. And so, contrary to Jonathan's fears, his arrest was far from imminent.

With the whole business of the missing Roger Llewellyn, ex-colleague of Porter's, gnawing away at him, Marshall made visits to the man's nearest and dearest. Looking for anyone showing signs of a long-standing grudge against Porter, who didn't have an alibi for the fateful Tuesday morning. And, who shared the same opinion as his: that the businessman was either solely responsible or complicit in Mr Llewellyn's disappearance. Ever since his schooldays, Porter was somebody with a talent for accumulating male friends and getting them to collaborate in whatever cause he wished. The well incident being a prime example. So, complicit was far more likely.

As far as Marshall was concerned, it was more than a coincidence that Llewellyn and the evidence of embezzlement he had so strongly insisted that he had, had gone missing at the same time, so soon after the man's accusations. But, his ex-wife, now remarried, didn't exactly describe her marriage to Roger as a happy one. No sign of a grudge there, or with any other friends and relatives the helpful ex-wife had pointed Marshall in the direction of. And, they had alibis for the morning of the murder. Some not exactly made of cast iron, but he could sense that the people he spoke to had moved on with their lives and were not harbouring serious grudges. Another dead end, but another stone not left unturned, as he tried to think of them as.

Throughout these particular questionings, Marshall had endured an uncomfortable feeling: that if he got lucky and stumbled upon a still-grieving loved one of Mr Llewelyn who turned out to be the guilty party, he may have to give them a pat on the back before locking them up. Those occasions when the job was forcing him to do what was the opposite of his own personal feelings. Piling on the misery of those with understandable grudges. But luckily, or unluckily (he wasn't quite sure which), it hadn't been necessary.

On the inspector's return to the station, a constable knocked on his door having discovered some 'interesting information'. Marshall was getting desperate for some good news but didn't dare raise his hopes that this was it.

'Well sir, apparently Kevin Porter was under investigation for embezzlement in 2005, and a man named Roger Llewellyn—'

Marshall groaned and put his head in his hands.

'Go round all the graveyards in Sheffield. Look for a stone with Roger Llewelyn on it. When you find it, we'll gather round it, get one of those people who contacts the dead, and have a seance!'

'Sir?'

'Never mind.'

Marshall's sarcasm was legendary in his department, and after the latest outburst of it, he congratulates the constable on his excellent work and escorts the bewildered young man to the door. It had been another hard day of achieving nothing, and being told what he already knew right at the end of it just about finished it off, and him. Despite him almost planning the event.

This was a high-profile case, and the more that nothing was being achieved with it, the more likely it would then be that the name of its senior officer would be known for all the wrong reasons. A fact that the strained and promotion-chasing DI Marshall was all too aware.

An Unlikely Mourner

At the cottage, in between the usual pain and discomfort, there were sporadic moments of joy as it slowly began to sink in what he had achieved. The person that had had such a negative influence on his life, now dead, and of his creation! It was glorious, unreal, the stuff of dreams. And no sympathy whatsoever for the man's bereaved loved ones. Misguided fools to waste their affection on such a person.

But with the achievement came increased isolation, with it being such an enormous and deeply personal thing that couldn't be spoken about to anybody. As though a contagious disease, that whoever was told about would then be cursed with the decision whether or not to shop him to the police. The phone never rang and he never had visitors. A smile and a 'good morning' to the postman was the full extent of his social life. Sad, but inevitable

To survive financially he stopped paying the mortgage, figuring that he would surely be long gone by the time his home was repossessed. And a far easier option than attempting to claim benefits for the terminally ill. The prospect of filling out the endless forms for such, and then dragging himself down to the doctor's surgery for the required signature to complete it, was just too much to bear. And may lead to his anonymity being compromised, somehow.

Another drain on his finances were the regular taxi fares, now his car was at the bottom of a lake. Prompting a scouring of the classified ads in a local newspaper for the cheapest car money could buy. Many sensible healthcare professionals would surely be united in the opinion that he was no longer fit to drive, with the sudden spasms of pain while at the wheel and subsequent painkiller-induced drowsiness. But driving, and feeling terrible for whatever reason, were two things he had a lot of experience of doing simultaneously, long before any diagnosis of cancer. He was in no fit state to starve either, as that seemed like a possible consequence for no longer driving, due to the severe lack of public transport locally. Just as his crime had isolated him, so too did it dictate the life of independence that must be maintained. And as such, transport to the shops for food and medicinal supplies was essential. His next, and hopefully last taxi ride took him to a large luxurious house where such a vehicle was being sold, at which, he told the driver to wait in case he wasn't buying. But the attractive, smiling lady of about his own age who answered the door, was a vision of loveliness to a man so starved of company, causing his mind to wander off in various non-car related directions. Almost immediately, she gave him the keys, inviting him to check the car over in her absence as it sat in the driveway. It was trust, which fortunately on this occasion he didn't have to abuse, such was the increasing desperation of his life. She didn't seem the type to knowingly sell a car that wouldn't make it to the local shops and back, and with no further plans for long-distance crime, that was all that was required. A seemingly good, if aged, Japanese car and generously priced, and judging by the surroundings, perhaps because its owner could afford to be generous.

After paying his taxi fare and letting its driver go, cash and keys changed hands over tea and cake in the ladies' sumptuous and traditionally furnished lounge. Despite the charming distractions, he just managed to remain sufficiently focused on the task in hand to have the good sense to fill in her section of the vehicle's logbook with a false name and address. Considering his good fortune at still being a free man, despite having fled KP Construction in a car that could so easily be traced to his front door, it felt like greater caution in such matters was needed. It would surely take time for the falsity to be discovered, and almost certainly, he wouldn't be around when it was. A factor that was now increasingly influencing his decision making.

With transaction completed, seller and buyer sat in opposing armchairs and he took a slice of Battenberg off the cake stand to accompany his tea, as if having suddenly entered another world. He complimented her on her flowing locks of curly brown hair, to which she turned away with the most gorgeous of embarrassed smiles as she ran her fingers through it.

'Ah, do you like it?'

'It's lovely, and so rare these days to see a woman with curly hair. Is it naturally curly?'

'Oh no, I wish it was. It costs a lot of money to keep it like this,' she remarked, still with a beaming smile as though not quite recovered from the compliment.

314

'Well, it's certainly worth it,' Jonathan assured.

There followed a 'things aren't what they used to be' type of discussion, about all that was wrong with the world today including the all too common straightness of women's hair. To his astonishment, the conversation flowed so easily and she genuinely seemed to enjoy his company. But as the bliss continued, he became overwhelmed with something like the old, familiar, eleven o'clock-in-the-pub feeling from his drinking days, when fully anaesthetised by the booze and unable to muster the required movement for the dreaded return to the outside world. He was in danger of either falling in love or falling asleep if he sat there much longer. And almost wished the car he had just bought would not survive the journey to the end of her driveway. Her presence, although wonderful, filled him with regret at what he had never had and was surely never going to have. That if life had been a little more normal and less disturbed, he may have ended up with a house like this and a wife like that, to look after him in his final days. Something he craved so much, he was in danger of blurting out the most pitiful and resistible of chat-up lines. Thus, that he was dying of cancer, and would she care to look after him while he did? But, as if able to read his mind, she commented that her husband would be home from work soon: an intrusion of the type he had endured many times before, but right now was particularly damaging, although inevitable, with photos of her and what was obviously a male loved one in various photos dotted about the place.

And so, with extreme reluctance he rose to his feet, and as he did so, caught a glimpse of himself in a mirror on the wall. The chaos of now greying pony-tailed hair and face that seemed to be returning to that of a skeleton were a shock to behold, and he felt foolish to have entertained any such romantic ambitions. It brought him abruptly back to his senses and grim reality, and just like Quasimodo[24], felt the need to conceal his ugliness while in the presence of such beauty. Waving to her as he drove down the driveway, he gave a farewell toot of the horn which didn't work. An MOT failure of course, for those with time to worry about such things.

His next stop was a barber in the town just before closing time, with a sudden awareness of his appearance after the unpleasant brush with a

---

[24] The hunchback of Notre-Dame.

mirror. Partly for reasons of vanity but mostly for disguise, he had all his hair shaved off. Deciding that to become a bald-headed, heavily bearded man was probably a good idea under the circumstances. After which, he returned home with his supplies; as always, partly expecting the police to be there also, with new car, new bald head and new cap to put on it. It had been a successful afternoon and he sat in the lounge, contented. Although a far cry from the luxurious one he had enjoyed tea and cake in earlier that day, it was better than prison, he reflected. And he was lucky not to be there.

He spent hours on the internet, surveying the general consequence of his actions in that part of the country. Amongst the information was an appeal for help in tracing the man now dubbed 'the pony-tailed killer', shown in a still image in a corridor at KP Construction. To which, he congratulated himself on the wisdom of his recent, drastic change of appearance. Also, there was endless nonsense about the victim, written adoringly by people lucky enough not to have met him. A mother, whose teenage daughter had recently made a miraculous recovery while at the formerly beleaguered hospital, chose to publicly thank Kevin Porter for 'keeping the hospital and my daughter alive' rather than the surgeons who successfully operated on her. It was barmy. The funeral was next Wednesday apparently and expected to be very well attended.

'But not just by family and friends. He has touched the hearts of ordinary people with his generosity, and many are expected to be there to show their respects.'

He continued reading similar nauseating stuff honouring the great man. As if those doing the honouring were not really sure why, other than it was socially acceptable right now and they didn't want to be left out. Give it a few months and the media circus surrounding what was Kevin Porter will have moved on in its forever desperate search for something else to shock and outrage the public with; and the name will be forgotten.

As Jonathan read, ideas were just starting to organise themselves in his brain. This seemed like the sort of funeral where there would be a crowd that one could blend in with, and no invitations needed. And one person who would be sure to be there was Alan 'I always said he belonged in a sewer' Marsden. He predicted long ago that these two would be as inseparable in their adult lives as they were as schoolboys. So, if the man

316

was still alive, that is where he would be next Wednesday. Although enjoying his freedom and the rarity of having got away with something devious, there was a need to continue the slaughter if an opportunity presented itself. And for that luxury, freedom would have to be sacrificed. He knew it was a miracle he still had it. But in a strange, almost paranormal way, it felt like who or whatever had bestowed him with such a miracle was urging him to do something positive with it. And *what* could possibly be more positive than the destruction of the boy Porter's second in command? If he had the strength. Which was a big if.

The next day he made a note of the time and location of the funeral as displayed on the KP Construction website, inviting all to attend. He had distant memories of reluctantly attending the funeral of a family friend at the same Sheffield Catholic church as a teenager, so at least had some idea where it was. He decided to just go up there and hope for the best. Crazy perhaps, but a welcome distraction from his forthcoming death and self-pity that preceded it, and would surely be an experience to wander among the bereaved at a funeral of his creation.

Sadly, he had disposed of the knife and sheath that had been so successful in the murder of Porter. Then, with his appointment, he had had some idea where the murder was likely to be committed and had that in mind when buying a suitable weapon. This time he had no such idea, but nevertheless, went back to the same camping shop and bought the same hunting knife and sheath just in case it was needed. And in more visual preparation, with no hair on his head and a reasonable amount of beard, he put on a pair of reading glasses, looked in a mirror, and satisfied himself that he looked nothing like the 'Ryan Walker' that had wreaked havoc at KP Construction.

After finding a cheap hotel advertised on the internet with close proximity to the church, he withheld his number and rang. Booking wasn't necessary and he could pay in cash on arrival. Sounds like his sort of place. And, they would definitely have rooms if he just turned up on Tuesday, so he was told. He bought a cheap black blazer for the occasion as the loose-fitting sleeves were again ideal for the concealment of, and quick access to, the upside-down knife on his forearm, and placed a hammer under the driver's seat for extra venom before setting off.

On the long drive, there were doubts as to the success of a second murderous mission, with so many obstacles in the way. His appointment with Porter had more or less assured him of a face-to-face meeting with the intended victim. That now felt like one hell of a luxury, as the speculation gathered pace in his mind. Marsden had to be there, and recognizable, somehow. His anger and hatred of the human race didn't stretch to being content with killing someone who *might* be his co-abuser from school, forty years on. It had to be him. And preferably alone. As neither was he keen on the idea of killing the man in front of his family, and at a funeral. Once again, in danger of paralysing himself with conjecture, he gave himself some stern words: *just go and stand in the crowd and wait for opportunities, and if none arise just come home;* willing himself to the idea of nonchalance. But once there, and the enemy in sight, there was sure to be bucket loads of adrenalin.

After a comfortable night at the hotel without the intense pressure that had preceded Porter's demise, he arrived at the church on time. Or so he thought. But to his increasing unease, the proceedings hadn't kicked off yet. Thus giving plenty of opportunity for the few that had so far arrived to check each other out and chat, perhaps about how they knew the deceased and their fond memories of him. This was scary stuff, not what was expected, and with no hymn or prayer book to conveniently hide his face in, soon found himself in the thick of it, dreading having to try and explain who he was and his reasons for being there. And as such, looked around nervously for anyone who could possibly be a middle-aged Alan Marsden, while at the same time trying to avoid meeting the gaze of anyone who looked like they may be about to approach.

When suddenly, while looking intensely in the opposite direction, he felt a hand on his shoulder. Feeling much like a newly arrived missionary on an island of cannibals, he leapt out of his skin and turned to meet his fate.

'Oh, I'm sorry to startle you.'

'Ah, that's OK, Father.'

To his relief, it was neither police nor security guard, or well-meaning ex-classmate that recognized him and wanted to chat about old times. But the priest, in full battledress ready for the service.

'Forgive me. I saw you from a distance and you looked a bit lost, so I thought I'd just come over and have a quick word.'

'That's very kind of you, Father.'

Jonathan struggled to maintain the necessary normalities to conceal the malicious intent going on in his head. The extent of which felt like must surely be visible to others, and as such, almost assuming he was being watched as a possible security threat, wondered if that could be the man's reasons for wanting a 'quick word'. But the more the conversation went on, the more he realised that wasn't the case, and this seemed like the kind of priest who had a soothing effect on just about everyone he spoke to.

'It's a terribly sad occasion of course. Did you know the deceased well?'

How should he begin to answer a question like that, without mention of having killed him? *Well, I did, very well, then I didn't for a long time, until recently when I suddenly did again, briefly.* That would be an honest one. Once again, it was the normal, simple, expected questions that he had the most trouble with. What with him being forever abnormal, complicated and unexpected. And he could sense that another "what are you doing here?" would have to be grappled with; like the one that had caused so much unrest in a mental hospital of his past, if his answer to the cleric's first question wasn't good enough.

This was a kindly priest of the sort that people liked to confide in, with the gentlest of Irish accents. Definitely not the sort that tells unexpected visitors to piss off, like the last one he'd spoken to in Horsham. And one to whom Jonathan himself was in grave danger of telling the truth: an almost conditional response from the confessional boxes of his Roman Catholic youth. And as such, if he wasn't careful, too much of it would be given before he was even aware he had given it. But he attempted something of a reply.

'Ah, well, yes. Well, yes and no really, Father. It's a strange thing, but you know, the last time I saw Kevin, I was stuck in a hole in the ground about ten foot down. Like a disused well it was. Kevin had thrown me in there, and he then urinated in the well on top of my head and just left me there.'

Jonathan's words were very matter of fact, void of emotion, which somehow increased their powers of disturbance. Far too tense for any displays of emotion, he was just answering the question with a little too much truth than was appropriate. And the priest *was* disturbed. This wasn't the kind of thing he was used to hearing while mingling with the bereaved before a funeral, offering his condolences. Jonathan then came to his senses, realizing that his honesty had to be curtailed before it did any more damage, and the conversation suddenly changed direction.

Strange, that such priests were not brought into police interrogation rooms as a last resort, after hours of no confession being obtained from a Catholic suspect.

'But you know, Father, I was angry for a long time. But then I heard about his donation to the hospital appeal, and I thought, what a great man he must have turned out to be.'

Jonathan's lies were equally convincing as his truth. As though, if he must deceive the most holy of men, it must be done with sincerity. All of a sudden they were back on track with what was more like normal pre-funeral conversation. The priest nodded his understanding and approval continuously from mid-sentence and 'hospital appeal'.

'So, I thought I'd just turn up and briefly, quietly, pay my respects and then leave, Father.' Again, the priest touched his shoulder. Jonathan felt close to tears, partly with relief at his surely Oscar-winning performance that he knew instinctively would successfully smooth things over, and even the priest, hardened as he was to tragedy in all its forms, now seemed in a similar emotional state.

'That's very commendable, my son. The lord has given you the power to forgive!'

At 'the lord', he raised his voice, his hands, and his eyes in the direction of the sky, as though addressing his creator personally, with pure emotion, almost in a trance of gratitude to the almighty.

'It's good to talk to you. Be strong now.'

He came down to earth again, finishing with a touch of Jonathan's upper arm as though it were a blessing.

'Thank you, Father.'

Jonathan felt blessed. There was a big part of him that wished his words were the truth, and therefore acceptable to priests everywhere. He didn't like to deceive the one person who felt more like a friend than any other, among those present. It felt like they were somehow comrades: both outsiders. The only non-members at this meeting of the Kevin Porter fan club. The priest, just doing his job of officiating at the event, and Jonathan, its creator, only there to do more damage. Deception felt like a lonely business as the cleric walked away.

The outside of the church with its large graveyard was starting to fill up rapidly. The expected crowd that he could blend in with had at last arrived. He saw a pile of order of service leaflets and picked one up. Now perusing it with reading glasses on he felt sufficiently disguised as a regular mourner but kept up the observation with the odd glance over the top of them for any sign of the enemy. And a quick feel for the knife on his inner forearm, just in case the priest was a master pickpocket with all the touching. It was still there.

The service began inside the church. Jonathan was outside. One of around a hundred or so ordinary mourners: members of the public who were 'touched by his generosity'. Loud speakers had been erected all around the outside of the church, amplifying the service for the benefit of the crowd. All seemed hopeless in terms of locating and identifying Marsden. If he was here, he would surely be inside the church with close family and friends. Security guards stood at its door to keep journalists, weirdos, would-be serial killers and other undesirables out, and he hadn't been able to get a good look at who went in. Whose idea was this?

But then, flicking through the order of service, on page four, came a glimmer of hope: "Return, oh Happy Wanderer to Thee", 'A poem, read by Alan Marsden'.

Jonathan temporarily stopped breathing. There it was, in all its glory, unmistakable evidence that his predictions about the two boy's future friendship was absolutely spot on. His heart pounded throughout the singing of 'Abide with Me', a hymn that had stirred passion in many, and now did the same for him. He followed the order of service, eagerly awaiting the inevitable, and quietly manoeuvred himself to somewhere he could get a glimpse of the action inside, hopefully, without drawing attention to himself. Close to a secluded outside wall, he gathered several empty plastic baskets used to carry the mass of leaflets and stacked them on top of each other. He then stood on his construction trying to peer through a stained-glass window, desperately trying to ignore the pain in his stomach that had just emerged. It was impossible.

But, to his relief, there was one clear bit of window for such emergencies, and he transferred himself to it, keeping just out of view of the crowd and security guards. Standing on tip toes, stretching his feeble body to its limits, he just managed to get a brief, clear sight of the action.

'And now, one of Kevin's oldest friends, best man at his wedding and lifelong best mate, Alan Marsden, will read a specially selected poem: "Return, oh Happy Wanderer to Thee".'

A slightly built, shaven-headed, impeccably dressed man steps up to the microphone and starts to read. Jonathan focuses intensely on the image for means of identification, before his tower of plastic collapses under him, attracting the attention of the two security guards round the other side. One of them attends, so as not to leave the main entrance unguarded. Essential security for the funeral of 'a kind, warm-hearted, loving, generous man', in order to keep his enemies out.

'Oy! No photos. Get out of there!'

Despite the order, Jonathan was temporarily incapacitated, and going nowhere immediately. But had to do whatever it took to defuse the situation when confronted by a thick-set young man seemingly ready for violence. The progress made at getting a glimpse of Marsden wouldn't be much use if he was now slung out and didn't get to see the man leave.

'Sorry. I'm not a reporter. I haven't got a camera or nothing. I was just... erm...'

He struggled to speak as he struggled to breath, desperately trying to get himself upright and composed without resorting to having to beg for assistance. Not easy, while lying on a downward slope of grass, head nethermost, and a broken plastic basket somehow entangled around one's shin. The pitiful scene fortunately prompted no more than a menacing stare from the bouncer, as an exhausted Jonathan, unable to speak, finally rose to his feet with surrendering, apologetic hand gestures. Bouncer retreated to his post, shaking his head in disbelief, as Jonathan returned to the safety of the crowd where he got a few puzzled looks from the curious. But he was too busy to notice, nervously feeling for the knife at his forearm and relieved at finding it, still secured by its elastic band. Still struggling for breath and wincing with pain from the aggravated tumours, while concentrating hard on the brief image of Marsden for future reference.

The service inside gradually moved outside, and the coffin was being carried to its burial plot, by amongst others, Alan Marsden. A few umbrellas were raised in the crowd at the first few spots of rain.

'Oh, merciful father, we ask you humbly to receive our dear departed brother, Kevin Porter. Loved and treasured in life, and now in death. That he may rise...'

The cries and sniffles of loved ones eventually drown out the priest's Irish accented words coming through the speakers.

Jonathan recognized the distinguished figure of the 'officer leading the investigation', from film he'd seen on the internet.

Marshall stood shoulder to shoulder with Hennessy, who held an umbrella over both of them. The inspector's hands clasped together in front of him. The two coppers were unmistakable as such; looking deadly serious, but with more unease with their surroundings than actual grief. Forced to witness the emotion of Porter's close family and the large attendance of the public, as a reminder of just how high-pressured this case was becoming. And if the truth were told (which it never was) were here largely because there wasn't a lot else to do, thus unable to avoid it with protests to their superiors of being too busy. Marsden's straight face was more of a grimace, suppressing anger and a need for retribution. Jonathan had endured a lifetime of such feeling. But the tables had turned, and those that had given him that feeling were now getting it.

As the funeral neared its end, much of the large crowd started to leave, eager to avoid the crush of departing traffic. Jonathan, aware that very soon the watching would be over and the doing of whatever would begin, felt increasingly incapable of doing it. Having been standing for the last two hours, he was now weak and in pain. Despite the urgent need to keep sight of his target, he risked a walk back to the car, parked an inconspicuous distance away. And luckily, managed to barge his way through the mass of pedestrians to bring it back again, where the post-funeral mingling was now taking place; and stayed in it, with Marsden still visible through a pair of binoculars. He ate a bar of chocolate, washed down with large swigs of energy drink, and took just two paracetamol so as not to knock himself out completely. An inadequate defence against the tumours. Morphine now a more adequate one. But he was determined to ignore his physical condition as far as possible, stay alert, and take advantage of any opportunity that may present itself, while predicting that some intense driving would play a big part in any such opportunity. Marsden's grimace and menacing stare never left his face, even when consoled by fellow mourners and the priest. Such was the bond between best mates, united in their abuse of the long-forgotten Jonathan Piper and in just about everything else since. Until now.

As Marshall and Hennessy walked hastily past the front of his car to get to theirs, Jonathan felt a rush of excitement and power, as if somehow controlling the fates of those he was watching. The two coppers didn't yet know it but were looking for him, and Marsden was equally ignorant of being the next intended victim.

The outdoor chat and condolences were brief, as the rain started chucking down hard and people dispersed to the shelter of their cars. Marsden walked briskly to his, several cars in front of Jonathan's. To whose relief, the man was alone and got into an empty car. All was looking good and under control right now, and he dare not think any further ahead than that. Jonathan followed him as he drove off, and soon became aware that a lot of other cars were following both of them.

Eventually, Marsden turns into the car park of a working men's club. Jonathan, on his tail and not realizing at first how small an area it was, followed, and to his annoyance, the convoy behind did the same. Obviously, this was the location of the post-funeral reception to which he wasn't invited, and the prospect of being surrounded by those grieving the loss of someone he had killed was suddenly very real, and terrifying, and definitely not part of the plan. Acting purely on instinct with no time for thought, he frantically tries to turn the car round and free himself before the avalanche of new arrivals block him in completely, creating an audience of onlookers waiting to see if he was going to hit other cars in the confined space as he did so; and annoyance to the pedestrians he was obstructing, as they tried to get inside and out of the now torrential rain.

Now safely out of there and parked anonymously on the main road outside, it took a while for him to calm down. He had been close to acting on impulse with the knife, when in a split second, Marsden had got out of his car so close to his. But, with the subsequent invasion of funeral traffic, it would surely have been a bloodbath (his included!), with any escape having to be attempted on foot. Things had gone from being under control to out of it in a matter of seconds.

He sat in the car, wondering if he was ever to have the luxury of being that close to the enemy again. And considered that if he wasn't, he could so easily end up being locked up for just the murder of Porter and would then curse himself for failing to send Marsden to the same place. Hell, no doubt, if there actually was such a place, and they still had room for a few more despite the overcrowding. Once again, what had seemed so simple in theory when you're three hundred miles away imagining it, was definitely not in practice.

While still trying to keep watch for any sudden Marsden departure, he risked the short walk to a petrol station for a sandwich and coffee: not wanting to lose his perfectly situated parking space for optimum vision. And as quickly as possible, brought his refreshments back to the car and rearranged himself in the driver's seat ready for action. But the sandwich stirred one of the now frequent attacks of nausea the lady doctor who diagnosed his cancer had said he should expect. And as the coffee activated his bladder into an unstoppable force, he soon found himself having to pee in its empty cardboard cup while still seated, and, being sick in the empty carrier bag next to him, almost simultaneously. Occasionally missing his target with both streams of bodily fluid, he then makes a futile attempt to clear up the mess with tissues. This was followed by about half an hour of uninterrupted self-pity, while overlooking his good fortune of there having been no sudden appearance of Marsden's car while he was otherwise engaged. Thus forcing him to give chase, mid-flow!

The waiting continued, and as the hours slowly ticked by his mind wandered in and out of memories of school: of his clothes being nicked while in the shower after P.E. to everyone's amusement except his; of being alone, freezing and terrified in the pitch darkness of the well; of Porter and Marsden as boys, and their now undying friendship as men. All now serving the purpose of gradually adrenalizing him into an unstoppable rage. Relishing the prospect of declaring himself as the killer of the man's beloved best mate, and excitement at having this opportunity to put things right, and well and truly obliterate the past.

Eventually, cars emerge from the working men's club. One of them was Marsden's, and from what he could see, the man was still alone. Now, a real intensity and determination to accomplish his mission took hold of Jonathan. The rain having eased off had now started again, hard, and it was close to dusk as he followed, trying to keep an inconspicuous distance but doubting his ability to keep up with the high-powered, four exhaust-piped machine should its driver decide to put his foot down.

A few nicely timed red traffic lights slowed the thing down when it seemed he was about to do just that, before another possible advantage swung Jonathan's way. Marsden, having left the funeral of his lifelong best buddy, who possibly exceeded Mrs Marsden in terms of importance, was in no mood for the kind of compromise that usually restricts one's intake of alcohol before driving. Jonathan watched from behind as the

BMW gradually veered towards the pavement on one side of the road, and then suddenly to the other before being rectified to a straighter path and slower speed. Only to then cruise straight through the next red traffic light, as if oblivious to it and a van swerving to avoid him.

Jonathan's pleasure at the man's vulnerability was short lived as he had no choice but to attempt the same reckless manoeuvre through red light, barging his way through the now slow-moving traffic crossing his path by any means possible while being blasted with horns, as the BMW roars off in the distance. Jonathan's heart pounds and his hand thumps the steering wheel in frustration at having now lost sight of his target completely. But as he roars over the brow of a hill, to his joy, there it is again in the distance, and as both cars approach a dimly lit dual carriageway, there's no stopping Jonathan. It was now or never. Possessed with rage, his foot hits the floor, forcing the comparatively inadequate 1200cc engine of his second-hand car to way beyond its limits as he thumps the BMW from behind. The collision has the desired effect and the car pulls over on to the hard shoulder. Jonathan follows suit.

Marsden leaps from his car with rage, but as he runs towards Jonathan's there are signs of the same alcohol-induced imbalance that had affected his driving: straying into the carriageway, oblivious to the traffic while being showered with spray. Jonathan grabs the hammer from under his seat and gets out of the car just before his opponent reaches it.

'Jonathan Piper, remember me?' he shouts, relishing every second, despite the incessant rain and his obvious physical inferiority.

But with one almighty swing of the hammer aimed at his opponent's head, he loses it; it leaves his hand and propels into the rear window of Marsden's car, shattering it. And this time, there's no time to reach for the knife on his forearm, and a full-scale brawl ensues with traffic whizzing past a few feet away, half drowning them in spray. Inside Jonathan, there was complete acceptance that this *was* the end, but with it, an insane amount of determination to make his body do things that cancer sufferers can no longer do, to ensure that this bastard was going with him. With all the internal rage saved up from years of suppression being finally released; energised by pure anger and hatred, and very little else.

Among the chaos of gouges, punches and kicks, a semi-drunken Marsden throws a punch that misses its target and throws him further off balance, allowing Jonathan to land a more accurate, if feeble one to the man's face. But it's enough to cause Marsden to stumble, and a renewed burst of confidence in Jonathan.

'I've already killed your mate Porter!' he shouts, determined to get his words in despite gasping for breath as the two repeatedly bounce off the crash barrier. 'Best man at his wedding, eh. Very nice!'

'You're gonna die, you fucking piece of shit!' Marsden responds.

'Yeah, like what belongs in a sewer!' Jonathan shouts back, repeating the insult he heard as a boy looking up at his gloating abusers from inside the well.

But his words have the effect of energising his opponent, and Jonathan finds himself taking repeated punches to the face and head before sinking nearer to the ground, gasping for breath, with arms tightly wrapped around Marsden's legs with no particular plan, other than trying to stop himself collapsing to the ground, and possibly being kicked to death when he does. But then, still with the tightest grip as if clinging on to life itself, and with every bit of strength he has left, he hauls the man up by his legs as if tossing a caper in very slow motion, letting out a deafening roar as he does so. And despite the continued battering of Jonathan's head, up and over the crash barrier Marsden goes. And, to his joy and relief, there's nothing but fresh air on the other side of it as they're on an elevated section of carriageway. With the same satisfaction of watching the blood draining from Kevin Porter's throat, he now watches Marsden plummet about fifty feet to the ground. Arms aloft, laughing and shrieking joyfully with complete abandon, as his helpless victim hits the deserted concrete below.

His legs give way and he collapses to his knees in an almighty puddle, wheezing uncontrollably with head bowed, one hand on the crash barrier and the other clutching his stomach. Now with plenty of time to feel the agony coming from it. Such was the noise of traffic and almost zero visibility, being showered with surface water as each vehicle passes, he has no idea who or what is around him. But, as he slowly regains consciousness of his surroundings, to his amazement, he is completely alone. No police with handcuffs; no wailing of sirens. Nothing.

He staggers back to the car, its key still in the ignition, and fumbles frantically for painkillers. And as he does, is reminded of the knife as he feels its handle pressing against his forearm. Somehow, still there, and completely forgotten about in the chaos. He manages a smile as he

327

unbuckles its sheath, and places it next to him on the passenger's seat. Miraculously, it had passed its security test with flying colours, but in the end, proved inaccessible for other unforeseen reasons. And strangely enough, hadn't been necessary. Weird and wonderful, it most certainly was.

Indicating right, he clumsily pulls out onto the carriageway, forcing the traffic to brake and swerve into the outer lane, bibbing and flashing at him as they go. But he was immune to their protests, and despite being exhausted, saturated, bruised and battered, let out another shriek of joy. So close to death but getting more out of life than he had ever done, he was just going to drive and drive and keep driving, until either the police stopped him, or he made it home.

Such was his elation, he didn't care which.

He made his way to the motorway, not far from where his elderly parents still lived in the home of his troubled Sheffield youth. As he drove, his mind wandered off into a fantasy of paying them a visit, and the customary dry pyjamas and hot water bottle before bedtime that would almost certainly be enjoyed if he did. And soon, his mind was further adrift with happy memories of *past* home comforts. How he'd love to return to the innocence of his Horsham childhood: drinking Cream Soda through a straw in sunny pub gardens with swings after mass on Sunday, wearing his elasticated bow tie. Thursday night swimming lessons followed by *Top of the Pops* and its glam-rock superstars and psychedelic camera trickery, with Mum drying his hair while he gazed at the telly in wonderment. All this grappling with the adult world was just too much – something he'd never been cut out for.

But suddenly, he's forced back to the present day with a blue flashing light in his rear-view mirror, gaining on him fast. Calmly surrendering to his fate, he pulls over to the left, ready to get out, only for the ambulance to then roar past him at speed. The top half of his body collapses on the steering wheel, in a much needed interval of stillness and silence.

He drives on through the half-deserted roads of late evening, trying to resist the urge to take more painkillers, as was usual, with so much driving and staying awake to be done. Despite the serious illness, there was no regret at the lack of medical assistance. The constant repeat prescriptions of painkillers until he dropped dead, seemed the only form of treatment necessary. Thus, avoiding the empty promises of this and that, while clinging on to the faintest of hope.

Having got as far as Northampton, with increased exhaustion, came greater urgency to get home to comfort, dry clothes and rest. And as such, had to remind himself of what he'd done, which made it unthinkable. It was like climbing Mount Everest and expecting there to be a jacuzzi at the top of it. To expect too much was to make oneself vulnerable. To expect the worst had been his only defence in many a situation. Even if he made it home, the chances are the police would already be there, without dry pyjamas and hot water bottles before bedtime. In psychological preparation for such an event, with its inevitability of being treated like a monster, he told himself rigidly that there would be no regrets. He wasn't one. His reasons for it all were sound and clear. Even if the sudden mass of people he would be surrounded by from then on, would neither know nor care what they were. Just as his abusing classmates, headmaster and teachers, neither knew nor cared what the effect of his 'education' had been.

Eventually, that what had seemed so nice it shouldn't dared be thought about, happened. He made it to the summit; there *was* a jacuzzi, and no sign of police. The end of another successful murderous excursion.

It was the most tranquil and remote place to come home to, that made you feel safe even if you weren't. The local wildlife that regularly squawked, hooted and whistled were like pets that he adored. At his first viewing of it, there wasn't much other than the 'For Sale' sign that gave any clues to there being anything there. Now there was even less, with no sign, and its grounds overgrown to that of a jungle. He had got into the habit of giving specific instructions to taxi offices: to look out for the birdhouse attached to the pine tree on your left and turn right immediately after it. But they invariably, in typical transport-office style, didn't bother to tell the driver. Even the police would have trouble finding it. No street lighting, barely visible from the road and a driveway that couldn't really be described as such. More of a dirt track, with no hint of there being anything worth seeing at the end of it. The perfect hideout.

For as long as he could remember, revenge had been something that couldn't be indulged in. Time after time, the need for it had to be suppressed for life and liberty to continue. To avoid incarceration in the sort of places where his habitual quick getaways were not an option. Doubtless, with people who would seek to abuse him further, thus multiplying the need for it. A no win situation. But now, he had taken full advantage of what was surely the only benefit of terminal illness. No future.

Under Pressure

Marshall arrived for work at six a.m. to be given the news that a prominent mourner at yesterday's funeral had fallen off a dual carriageway and was now dead. And that a Mrs Marsden had reported her husband missing, as it was 'most unlike him to stay out all night'. Never an early riser out of choice so nothing made much sense at that hour of the morning. But just as he was beginning to try and make sense of it, he received a rude awakening when informed that the media also knew, as it had just been given out on local radio news.

'Who the hell...!'

The inspector didn't bother to finish his sentence, realizing the futility of it. The source of the leak among his *trusted colleagues* as always unknown. Anything even loosely connected to the late Kevin Porter being a valuable commodity to the forever prying media, determined to prolong the sensation.

Marshall sits, deep in thought, quietly absorbing the latest events, oblivious to everything around him, including his sergeant. But during the silence, there's a tension in the air for Hennessy as he wonders if he dare break it by expressing an opinion. But goes for it nonetheless, clearing his throat before proceeding.

'It sounds a bit like road rage, I thought,' he says awkwardly, prepared for the worst: his words being mocked and a possible outbreak of the all too familiar brand of Marshall sarcasm.

Marshall raises his eyes to the sergeant as if being woken from a trance.

'Well, you know,' Hennessy continues, 'a car accidentally goes into the back of Marsden's, in wet weather, he gets out, there's a scuffle, he ends up going over the top. Those crash barriers aren't always that high. Other guy panics and scarpers.'

Marshall remains silent with no expression, with only his half-open eyes as a clue that he's actually awake. A pensive Hennessy awaits the verdict. And finally gets it.

'Bit more than a scuffle wouldn't you say, with flying hammers about?'

'Yes, of course.'

'But I know what you mean.'

A relieved Hennessy exhales, having been aware that this was perhaps not what the inspector wanted to hear, and of how scathing the man can be when caught at the wrong moment.

Marshall continues, 'In other words, not necessarily connected to Porter and the funeral at all. And where does that leave us? But it still smells a bit like our killer with an almighty grudge against Porter, goes to the funeral for his own amusement, is made aware of the best mate and his poem, sees him leave, follows, and thinks, *why not?* Another way of getting back at Porter? Or, already knew about Marsden, for some reason had a similar grudge against him, and went to the funeral to seek him out? Anyway, we shall see.'

A troubled Marshall was aware that this latest fatality, with the question marks hanging over it, had made things rather untidy. And in this business, tidiness was the only thing that pleased those that had to be pleased. But with it came a flicker of relief that at last they had something to investigate rather than trying to look busy while sitting around waiting for the Aussies to locate their only potentially useful source of information.

A more thorough forensic examination of the scene on the dual carriageway commenced as an overcast daylight began to emerge. The car's registration number quickly traced to Alan Marsden. The hammer retrieved and bagged. The damage done to the rear of the car as it was rammed from behind, examined, with samples of the offending vehicle's paint collected as the body lay in a morgue awaiting identification and post-mortem. The inspector, still grappling uneasily with the current obscurity surrounding the mourner's death, stresses the urgency of being informed of any results.

The phone rings in Marshall's office. Hennessy answers it. 'For you. Father O'Brien.'

Marshall looks puzzled as he takes the phone. There was only one

'Father' about and that was the one that did the honours at the funeral. What on earth could he want?

'Father, how are you?'

'Fine, thank you, inspector. Deeply distressed though to hear about this. It surely wasn't one of the family. Lord knows they've been through enough.'

'No, it wasn't, Father, but at the moment I can't say any more that, you understand.'

'No, no, of course not.'

Marshall was comforted that at least some sanity had prevailed, and the victim's identity didn't seem to be out there yet before the body had been formally identified.

'How can I help?'

'Well, I don't know if this is any help, but I had a rather strange conversation with a gentleman just before the service yesterday. Unsettling in a way, I thought.'

'Oh yes.'

'He appeared to be alone and looked nervous, as though looking for someone. And he didn't look at all well. Pale and thin in the face. I asked him if he'd known the deceased well, and he told me that the last time he had seen him, he was stuck in a disused well of some kind and was being urinated on by Kevin, who had thrown him in there.'

'Really. Did he say when this was?'

'No, I'm afraid not. He just said that he was very angry about it, but when he heard about his donation to the hospital appeal, he realised what a great man Mr Porter must have become. As if that had somehow made him able to forgive.'

'Did he have a ponytail in his hair, by any chance?'

'No, not that I recall. Hardly any hair, in fact. Look, I don't want to waste your precious time, inspector, but I've been in turmoil since I heard about this. Thinking, should I tell you, or shouldn't I.'

As Marshall listened, various colleagues entered his office and he engaged in sign language with them: taps of wrist watches, nods, and thumbs up, that kind of thing. But still listening attentively.

'Well, thank you, Father. I'm very glad you did. We need all the help we can get right now. Will you stay on the line a minute and I'll pass you over to someone who'll take down a quick description of the man from

333

you, for our records? Thanks again, Father. Take care now.'

Marshall was being pestered about the arranged briefing of his team, after the latest events. Not sure what they were doing or supposed to be doing until their great leader tells them. And also, about the arranged accompanying of Mrs Marsden to identify her husband's body. As the inspector gets to his feet, deep in thought, with unusual doubt as to what to say to his team, a smiling Hennessy puts his head round the door.

'Sir, just had a call. Fingerprints on the hammer match those taken from Porter's office and the escape route at KP Construction. It's the same man.'

With barely time to respond before the sergeant's head disappears, Marshall stands motionless in a semi-trance of contentment. Clarity of something, and a cure perhaps for the chronic stagnancy of the investigation. It now seemed like he had two choices: assume that the killing of Marsden was preplanned, that there was something else linking the two men that linked them with someone else who wanted them dead, or assume that their killer, with just a grudge against Porter, now sought to obliterate the man's loved ones as a further insult. And just wait for him to strike again?

With the details of Father O'Brien's phone call and this latest news of the matching fingerprints buzzing around his head, Marshall felt like he needed time to prepare before addressing his team. But there wasn't any. Even with the knowledge they were now dealing with a double murderer, there was further uncertainty ahead. Such was the attendance at the funeral, it hardly seemed worth mentioning that the killer may have been there. Or the fact that the seventeenth century church wasn't equipped with CCTV to assist them. And as such, would be like trying to jog memories of one particular person who may have been at Waterloo station in the rush hour. And he hadn't yet had a chance to consider if the conversation the priest had before the funeral was actually relevant. He enters the room with his mind still a fog of indecision, but with a suitably officious exterior to conceal it.

As usual, with a clap of his hands, it falls silent.

'Right, ladies and gentlemen, as I'm sure you all know, we have another fatality. Strictly *off* the record, as he hasn't yet been formally identified; and if there's any blabbering outside of this room I'll find whoever's responsible, Alan Marsden, whose body was found having fallen from an elevated section of road. And whose car was found on that section of road, with rear window smashed in and an order of service from Kevin Porter's funeral in it, at which he had read a poem. I can now confirm that Kevin Porter's killer, our mysterious Ryan Walker, was at the scene. And so, we're treating it as double murder committed by the same man. I want to know what connects these two men, apart from the obvious. Yes, they were best mates, from childhood possibly. But were they ever in business together? Would they have the same enemies from doing business together?'

'Excuse me, sir. We *have* already checked Porter's business and work history, thoroughly.'

'Look again!' Marshall's response was fierce, to the point, and accompanied by a prolonged stare.

'Now, there's a strong possibility that the killer was at the funeral and followed Marsden as he left. But so were a lot of other people, too many to find and question individually, and most of them unknown to the deceased. But, as I've just discovered, the reception after the funeral took place at the Langley working men's club, where only close friends and family would have attended. Was Marsden there? Get down there and ask around. Were Porter and Marsden regulars there, or have contacts there? From what we already know of the murder of Porter, it's fair to assume our killer is either a stranger, or not immediately recognizable to his two victims. So, was there anyone inside the club or lurking about outside that those attending the wake didn't recognize? If so, I want descriptions of them. Get as many names and addresses of those who were there as you can. I want them all found and spoken to. Even if Marsden wasn't there. If they attended the wake, it stands to reason they were close to one or both victims.'

Marshall chose to go all out with the details of Father O'Brien's call. At least on this rare occasion he had the most honest and sincere of informers, despite the content being somewhat bewildering.

'Now, I've just received some information about a conversation that took place just before the funeral, between the priest and a man, a mourner, shall we say. This man spoke of violent, humiliating abuse he had suffered at the hands of Kevin Porter. Of being stuck in a disused well that Porter had thrown him in, who then urinated in the well, onto the man.'

There commenced a pause in which Marshall exhaled deeply, as though needing time to recover from the strain of interpreting the obscure information as clearly as possible. And to try and think of his next sentence, which should contain some instructions as to what the team were meant to do with this new information. As Marshall looked up from the floor, he noticed signs of amusement on a few faces in the audience. And suddenly, with a sickening feeling of being on display, like a puppet whose sole purpose was for their entertainment, the spectacle of Marshall at his fiercest is ignited. He grabs a thick folder full of paperwork and slams it down hard on the table in front of him, looking directly at the chief smirker on this occasion, and before, at the mention of Australia being the current location of a 'vital witness'.

'Anyone who feels they would rather not be part of this investigation can leave, now! There's the door! It's that big rectangular thing over there!' Arm raised, pointing to it, eyes still focused on the cause of his unease. But this time, there are no smiles at the sarcasm, just the defiant smirk on the face of the young man remaining, which took a while to disintegrate. Marshall waited patiently until it did, during which you could hear a pin drop in the room until Hennessy entered it.

'Sir.'

The sergeant got no response and quickly realised this was a moment when it was best to join in the silence. Marshall then continued grappling with Father O'Brien's words, with a renewed sense of determination to treat them with respect. And an abandonment of his ego, refusing to care what he looked or sounded like as he picked his brain out loud on the matter, with eyes to the floor. As there had been no time to do so earlier, now, he considered, was as good as any.

'What this man described to the priest may well have been a reference to bullying. Childhood bullying. School bullying, perhaps. The man also said, that having heard about Porter's hospital appeal donation, now admired him for it, umm... realised what a great *man* Porter must have become. As if perhaps he were not a *man* when the incident occurred. That could be cods wallop about admiring him, but also a clue as to when the incident occurred. Childhood...' His last few sentences trailed off into more of a private mumble, but ironically, the more unprofessional the inspector appeared to be as he paced the floor, seemingly in conversation with himself, the nearer to the truth he was getting. Something that had been buzzing around his subconscious since his conversation with Father O'Brien, had miraculously found a way out. And the cleric's bewildering phone call had, somehow, pushed the investigation in something like the right direction.

'We have to consider that the person who held a grudge against Porter enough to kill him, and possibly Marsden, was at that funeral. And this could be the man. If it is, and he followed Marsden as he left the funeral, and Marsden then went to the reception, so *too* did our man who the priest spoke to before the funeral. And Father... er...'

'O'Brien,' Hennessy assists from the doorway.

'Father O'Brien described this man as looking ill and being pale and thin in the face. So, more questions to be asked at the working men's club. Was Marsden there? Was a pale faced, ill looking stranger also there, possibly lurking about outside? Or a car that left the place immediately after Marsden left? OK?'

There were nods in the audience, signifying that the inspector was back on track and his words were now getting serious attention. Something of an achievement for a man desperately trying to organise the flimsiest of evidence into something he can point his team in the right direction with. Knowing that if he paused for a moment's thought on that direction, would cause an avalanche of doubt.

He continues, 'And school. Where did the two victims go to school? Did they go to the same school? How far back does Porter and Marsden's friendship go? Anything significant about their childhood or schooldays that connects them, I want to know. Any questions?'

'Sir, are we allowed to visit close relatives of the victims to get that information?'

A good question, and one that prompted some hesitation before answering. Marshall had been feeling the strain of another problem, and this was a prime example of it. Too large a team. A knee-jerk reaction from above to a case sure to have the media sniffing around it. With the supposed wisdom that the more people you throw at it the more likely you are to get a result. Not in this case. There just wasn't enough leads for them to pursue. And he now felt compelled to slow them down in pursuit of this one.

'No. Do it without for the moment. See what you can get from the working men's club. Porter and Marsden may have had close contacts there. And look on the KP Construction website. There's a lot on there about Porter and may be stuff about where he grew up. Check out schools in that area. Myself and DS Hennessy will get what we can from the families. OK, ladies and gentlemen, let's get on with it.'

There were disgruntled murmurs from the team as they dispersed, wondering how they were expected to get such information about the victim's childhoods without talking to the families. But the last thing Marshall needed now was complaints from fragile, bereaved relatives about insensitive treatment from the police in their quest for information. And knew, that some of his more competitive members would be determined to be the first to get it.

The room empties with the exception of Hennessy, still eager to give his message. Marshall sinks into a swivel chair and sighs, as though having just performed a musical version of King Lear at the National Theatre to an audience of sceptics.

'Yes, sergeant, what is it?'

'Sir, you were due at the mortuary for Mrs Marsden's identification ten minutes ago.'

'Why the hell didn't you…! OK, thank you. Ring them, apologise, and tell them I'm on my way.'

The body was not a pretty sight when first discovered, but as usual, the make-up artists had done a miraculous job of transforming the fifty-three-year-old builder. But it wasn't enough to stem the flow of Mrs Marsden's uncontrollable tears. Her world had caved in. She was very much the traditional, devoted, unquestionably loyal wife, who didn't argue with her husband, even when the loyalty wasn't reciprocated. There were questions the inspector desperately wanted to ask about her late husband's friendship with Kevin Porter. He offered her a lift home with the intention of doing just that. Over tea and biscuits in her front room he tried but it just prompted lengthy pauses for more tears between sentences, and he wished he had brought a WPC with him for back up, to provide emergency comfort. So he gave up for the moment, hoping his team had had more success. He expressed concern at leaving her alone in her distraught condition, but was assured 'the family' would be round shortly. It didn't seem appropriate to ask if she would mind if he just remained in his comfy armchair and had a quiet doze until they arrived. As that's exactly what he would have wished if given the choice, thinking that 'the family' may be a tad less emotional, and therefore, more capable of answering his questions. But alas, he finished his tea and left, graciously as always, without a trace of the frustration he was feeling at the lack of information obtained.

He returned to the station to devastating news: a press conference had been arranged for this afternoon and there had been 'orders from above' that he must attend. This was the bit of police work that he hated the most. The job that he would most like to pass on to a junior colleague to deal with if he could. But it was inevitable there would be one sooner or later, as rumours of a serial killer on the loose were beginning to flourish, helped as always by the scaremongering press. The trick was to say something without actually saying anything, but which somehow created a feeling of everything being under control. Hennessy, he felt, was far more talented in that direction and would doubtless relish the opportunity. But alas, only senior officers could be thrown into the arena, and the superintendent was still off with a 'bad cold'. Marshall had enjoyed the man's absence, until now. Not that he wouldn't enjoy talking to civilians who were genuinely interested in police work, as he was. But these civilians were only interested in one thing: a sensational headline, ideally about police incompetence. The slightest detection of which, would be exaggerated to the point where Inspector Marshall could find himself being compared with Inspector Clouseau[25]. No, he was not a buyer of his sergeant's argument that the press played a vital role in alerting the public to things, who in turn could help the police, or some such positive-sounding gibberish he had never managed to make sense of! More evidence that Hennessy should be dealing with them, and not him!

On one such occasion in a previous pantomime of publicity, he made the big mistake of giving too much away, which included a statement that turned out not to be the case. Only to then be keenly reminded of this at the next press conference, by a young, gloating reporter, desperate to be the first to weed out any police blunders. Marshall was essentially a humble, down to earth public servant, who would have gladly given the truth if it were allowed: that he was mistaken, as all human beings were

---

[25] The bungling French detective of the 'Pink Panther' films.

from time to time. But that would have led to such headlines as, *Police Lose Control,* and there would have been hell to pay with his superiors, that 'the lid wasn't on tight enough'. A valuable lesson that it was all a game in which there was no room whatsoever for the truth.

Marshall kicks off, 'In the early hours of this morning a body was discovered which has now been identified as being that of Alan Marsden. We are investigating the possible cause of his death.'

Always a good idea to try and make everything sound as dull and uninteresting as possible, to stem the hysteria the media so desperately craved.

'Is it true there's a serial killer out there who's targeting loved ones of Kevin Porter?'

'We can't confirm that at this stage.'

'But you don't deny it, that it could be a possibility?'

'I don't deny it or confirm it.'

Definitely 1–0 to the police at this early stage of the game. And Marshall privately congratulated himself on such a dull response with an expressionless face to match. But the question left him with an unsettling feeling that if such rumours were not quelled, he could find himself with the added problem of said loved ones demanding police protection. Such was the power of the media.

'Do you believe both murders were committed by the same man?'

The truthful answer was a resounding yes, but again, no need to reveal the truth if it's a little too exciting.

'If it's established that Mr Marsden was actually murdered, then that's something we'll be looking into, but at the moment we can't rule anything out. We're trying to establish a link between the two deaths. When we've done that, we'll have a better idea.'

That was three sentences. Two more than the suggested amount! Had he got away with it? Had he said too much? He would doubtless be told later if he had.

'But they were good friends, weren't they? Isn't that a link?'

'Possibly, but it's the only one at present. Our deepest sympathies are with all concerned, and we're doing everything we can to find those responsible.'

The final well-worn cliché was a verbal panic button, and a cue for an understanding colleague to come on stage and rescue him, due to a prior arrangement. Thus, not giving him enough time to put his foot in it.

'I'm sorry, ladies and gentlemen, there's no more time.'

It was done with impeccable timing. The secret of all great comedy. The press left frustrated. What possible sensational headline could be prised out of such blandness? Marshall was reasonably pleased, almost daring to predict that there wouldn't be too much of a scandal about his performance. Never before had the words, *I haven't got a clue*, been put so eloquently. Not by him, anyway.

He was ushered out of the venue through a rear door, straight into a car which sped away, passing the hullabaloo of expectant media with cameras and microphones poised at its front entrance. Relieved to be back in the privacy of the station, he accepted a few "Nice one, sir"'s with a knowing smile and a roll of the eyes. It felt like outside the vultures were still squawking, only now he couldn't hear them. The pressure was immense. Who knows where he was at now with his promotion prospects, that had looked so promising before this investigation?

A bit of good news to end a frustrating day: Mrs Braithwaite had been found, and she had a phone number.

'Hello, is that Julia Braithwaite? Good morning. Inspector Marshall from South Yorkshire Police here. I'm sorry to trouble you so early but it's rather important.'

After all the arduous thinking of the day, he still managed to correctly deduce that if it was nearly going home time over here, it must be early morning over there.

'I'm guessing you must have rather a lot going on at the moment, having just arrived, but I'll try and be brief. Well, as you may know we've had a bit of a murder over here at KP Construction. Probably soon after you left, in fact.'

He laughs at the lady's response as she pleads her innocence of the crime with self-mockery.

He was definitely in the mood for some light-hearted banter with an ordinary member of the public after the previous theatrics with the media, despite this one being inadvertently responsible for a large chunk of the complications he had endured so far.

'Oh, don't worry about that, Mrs Braithwaite. You're quite safe. Even if you had, I think you'd be let off with a caution, as I don't think South

Yorkshire Police would want to fork out for my plane fare to come and get you!'

Much laughter. Gifted he was at putting female members of the public at ease. But got back to the serious matter in hand.

'Well, if you can cast your mind back to when you first spoke to a man who we feel must have given the name Ryan Walker. Because at the time of the murder, the receptionist had a list of names of those that you yourself would have spoken to when they rang up to request an appointment with Mr Porter. Yes, that's right. And what she had written down for that particular appointment slot was a Ryan Walker from Plasterboard Direct. Does that ring any bells at all?'

'Yes, it does. I vaguely remember the guy saying the company was based in Liskeard, Cornwall. He sounded a bit nervous and confused. But he gave me a telephone number where he could be reached with an area code I didn't recognize. I'm really sorry, I don't have that phone number now. But definitely Liskeard, that's what he said, and that they were now able to do business elsewhere, not just Cornwall. Something like that.'

'Did the man speak with any particular accent at all, or give any other information about himself?'

'No, not that I remember. I'm sorry I can't be any more help than that. But Mr Porter's secretary will have rung that number if he had got an appointment, so maybe she might have it.'

She tried desperately to be helpful, but suddenly recalled trying to delete her own personal calls made on the company's phones and deleting a few too many in the process. All had happened in a flash at the touch of a wrong button before she knew what was happening. And so now, with much embarrassment, assumed that said call to Ryan Walker, as well as the one from him, were probably among the casualties, hence the long-distance phone call from the police. She had always been an honest, conscientious worker, and her clumsy attempts to cover her tracks so soon before leaving for the other side of the world, were somehow testimony to that. Others wouldn't care. Now, with a flicker of realization of the problems she must have caused the inspector, she became anxious to end the call to avoid the embarrassment. Keen to get on with her new life with any past misdemeanours now far away. Marshall, satisfied that he may have moved the investigation forward an inch or two, thanked her, wished her well in Australia, and went home.

As he drove, he struggled to get his mind off the case and the lack of real progress after the much anticipated conversation with his only witness. What had he got? Liskeard. But that too could be bogus, like Ryan Walker and Plasterboard Direct! What was he supposed to do, contact Devon and Cornwall and tell them to keep an eye out for a man who may have a Ford Sierra, a ponytail, and could be in Liskeard?

As he came in through the front door, his wife, having just seen him on telly, voiced her disappointment.

'That was short and sweet wasn't it.'

'What?'

'Well, you didn't say much, did you?'

'No, I didn't!' he agreed, triumphantly. 'That's the whole point. What were you expecting? A few jokes, a tap dance, and a stirring rendition of 'Climb Every Mountain'?'

This was followed by a gentle chuckle of amusement at his own wit.

Armed and Dangerous

Jonathan's second successful mission of revenge had left him physically weakened but spiritually uplifted. And with his good fortune at being free to return home once again, felt almost like he was being assisted by unseen forces for good, and that this is what he should be doing with what little time and energy he had left.

His thoughts turned to his third abuser present at the scene, Phillip Reynolds. He googled the name on his computer, more out of curiosity than serious planning. The mind was willing, but the body was getting ready to pack up at any moment.

Sadly, there was a lot of them about: interior designers, plumbers, convicted criminals. He spent hours wading through the possibilities, and while in pursuit of another one, found himself directed to a website for so-called 'high flyers'. For successful companies to scour its profiles and 'head hunt' others for their important positions, seemed to be the purpose of it. And one such profile was that of a Phillip Reynolds, managing director of a hydraulics company. But, to his annoyance, in order to see it, Jonathan had to create a profile for himself, followed by username and password, just to get information on another possible red herring. But, despite preferring to spend the evening trying to nail his own eyelids to his computer table than think of acceptable bullshit to put on his profile, he got on with it, only to find that his creation was unacceptable without a photo. And so, much fumbling about with a camera resulted in a photo of himself, looking about as unlike a 'high flyer' or in any way legitimate user of such a website as it was possible to get, being added to his fictitious profile. Which, having been submitted, was now being 'considered for suitability'. But more importantly, had somehow given him access to further details of this particular 'Phillip Reynolds'.

The same age as himself, as ex-classmates often were. This was getting more interesting, and he sat upright in his chair with renewed intensity. The photo wasn't much help: a rather smug, lop-sided grin in a shirt and tie, looking younger than his years. He read on eagerly, looking for more clues.

"Educated in Sheffield and the London School of Economics."

From his distant memory, the boy had seemed like an academic, but determined to fit in with the yobbos at his new school, as if for his own protection. And if that meant participating in the regular pastime of bullying Jonathan Piper, so be it. But only ever did so when fully armed with the presence of the other two, as did all of them.

It had to be him. Jonathan's enthusiasm escalated until he read:

"Recently relocated to south-west France, having been promoted to Managing Director of the company's French headquarters."

Deep sigh! He switches the machine off. The disappointment affected him mentally and physically. Now in agony again: his enthusiasm having been like an out of body experience making him sit forward for too long, oblivious to his physical state, cramping his stomach as he stared intensely at the screen. He moves to a more comfy chair with glass of water and strong painkillers, and a feeling of surrender to his condition. If there was to be a third victim, they needed to be living down the road for any serious plans for their destruction to be considered.

After the rare miracle of a good night's sleep and with a clearer head, the subject of Phillip Reynolds is returned to, with more positive information as to the man's identity being gathered. Now, a more difficult and serious decision to make, he pondered on his future. Was he up to it? He wouldn't know until he tried. If he set off for France and then found he wasn't, what would be the consequences? Dying in France? As good a place as any. And if he didn't survive the journey, what better place to die than at sea, on the ferry from Plymouth. And as such, would be providing the authorities with the perfect place to dispose of him, if they had the good sense to take advantage of it. But there were more serious arguments in favour of going, and it was definitely a more attractive plan for the future than sitting around here waiting for the police to arrive, flinching with every unexpected noise. His chances of killing Reynolds were of course slim, but, as his mum had advised many times, often misguidedly, he needed a holiday. And on this occasion, she would be right.

There would be no option about keeping his name a secret. It was on his soon-to-expire passport, with a photo of a much younger and healthier looking Jonathan Piper. So, if he was going it had to be now, while the passport was still valid, and the name Jonathan Piper hadn't yet become a household one. As when it did, and its connection with Liskeard had been established, border officials at Plymouth would be on red alert, and any departure impossible. His enthusiasm for the trip was growing rapidly.

On the outskirts of the French city of Bordeaux stood the headquarters of 'Euro Hydraulic Solutions' about a six-hour drive from the ferry port of Roscoff. Although warming to the idea of his escape, he conceded that a more thorough attempt at identifying the suspect needed to be made. Looking at the website, he scribbles down a phone number and a few notes to assist him. He rings the number and hears a voice at the other end.

'Hello! Bonjour!' he shouts to it, eagerly, but it continues oblivious.

It was a French recorded message, probably saying something like, 'all calls are recorded for quality and training purposes'. Only less excruciating when you didn't understand a word of it. Silence.

'Bonjour. Is anybody there?'

'Bonjour, monsieur,' a female voice now speaks. And to his delight, the 'monsieur' was something with which it seemed could be distinguished that there was now a human being at the other end of the phone and not some kind of virtual one.

'Parler vous Anglais[26]?'

'Yes, I do, sir. How can I help?'

That was at least one obstacle overcome. No doubt, the first of many. 'Can I speak to Mr Phillip Reynolds, please?'

'Yes, I will see if he is in his office. Can I ask who is calling, please?' He should have prepared something for this.

'Umm, it's Mr Walker. An associate from England.'

With such a feeble introduction, he wasn't now expecting to actually speak to the man.

'Thank you. One moment, please.'

The next voice Jonathan hears is a distinctly English male one. 'Hello.'

'Good morning, is that Phillip Reynolds?'

'Yes, speaking. Who is this?'

---

[26] Do you speak English?

After a deep breath to compose himself, Jonathan gets into his stride, determined to capitalize on his good fortune.

'My name is James Walker from PD Hydraulics in England. I've been asked to give you a ring. It's regarding your profile on toppeople.com.'

'Oh yes. What about it?' Reynolds asks, with a hint of irritation, signifying that the grovelling needed to commence before he hangs up.

'Well, we at PD were most impressed with your profile and are looking for new recruits'

'PD Hydraulics, did you say? I've never heard of it.'

'Well, we're a fairly new company, based in Sheffield. Very up and coming you might say. And very eager to get the right people.'

So far so good. Managing to sound just like the sort of person that made him feel sick. Hopefully, he wouldn't be asked anything too technical, like what type of hydraulics his company deals in. Doubtless, prompting an answer like, 'the type with liquid in that makes things go up and down', thus, managing to fit in his entire knowledge of the subject, thus, killing the facade stone dead. But without realizing it, his misdemeanours so far and the dialogue involved in creating opportunities for them, had honed his skills of deception. Determined to worm his way in on the unsuspecting, getting the information he needed. And his words needed to sound normal, so as not to cause a tightening of security at Euro Hydraulics. Just in case he found himself outside the place, trying to bullshit his way in.

Keen to check out the legitimacy of the phone call, Reynolds did his best to google PD Hydraulics while Jonathan spoke. But his broadband speed wasn't quite up to it and so was forced to give the phone call the respect it didn't deserve.

'I appreciate your interest in me, but I'm now settled here in France and would not consider a move back to the UK.'

'Yes, of course, I understand completely. I'll pass that on to my superiors. Can I just ask you something, Mr Reynolds? I'm dying to know. Might you be the Phillip Reynolds who attended the Langley Park Comprehensive in Sheffield, around the late seventies perhaps?'

There was a pause, in which Reynolds, blissfully ignorant of the murders in Sheffield or any other British news, but still cautious, hesitated before answering. But his curiosity got the better of him.

'Yes, that's right. How did you know?' Again, a hint of irritation, and

347

now suspicion in his voice.

As much as Jonathan yearned to hang up immediately now the information he wanted was obtained, it really was best not to arouse suspicion. And so, continued with the charade.

'Good heavens! Small world, isn't it? I think I was in the year below you. I thought it rung a few bells. Anyway, I've taken up far too much of your time, Mr Reynolds. So, I'll leave you in peace and have a good day.'

Jonathan hangs up. First part of mission accomplished. Now, more eager than ever to get to France, and give Mr Reynolds a very bad day, very soon.

Reynolds spent a few subdued minutes with phone still in hand making a continuous tone, reflecting on what had just occurred. It was intriguing, unsettling almost. He was left feeling much the same as the priest at Porter's funeral, after Jonathan's words to him. But it wasn't long before more of the usual calls came in, requesting his attention to this, that, or the other. And being fairly new in his current position, was anxious to please. PD Hydraulics and the phone call were forgotten.

He pondered the task ahead. Memories of grappling with Marsden on a flooded hard shoulder had left him in no doubt, that no way could his body cope with any more such physical exertion. Any fisticuffs, with even the most feeble of centenarians, would be over very quickly, resulting in him being the victim. A gun would make things far easier. But what did he know about guns and how to get them? About as much as he knew about hydraulics. But suspected, that a license was needed to buy one from a shop, and to buy one without would mean dealing with some right dodgy people, and probably paying three times as much. But there was no guarantee he would ever come face to face with the enemy. One of the many obstacles like ill-health, or death, could easily get in the way. And therefore, would be a waste of a large chunk of his already dwindling savings if he didn't.

After further indecision, it was eventually decided that a gun would make him more determined to come face to face with the enemy, and possibly increase the chances of it, with it perhaps being pointed at someone who would then kindly direct him to the enemy. And so, a visit would be paid to the only place he knew where there was an abundance of dodgy people, possibly the same ones that had destroyed his council flat a few years previous. But not because he wanted to improve his social life. It was the last place he wanted to return to after saying his goodbyes with cooking oil. But if a gun was needed, then so too was a mercenary attitude in acquiring one. He would call in there on his way back from the booking office at Plymouth ferry port tomorrow.

The next day, he bought a single ticket to Roscoff to sail in a few days' time, with the certainty that any return would either be in a coffin or the company of British police who would presumably pay the fare. A gun to accompany him was important but mustn't delay his departure.

Early evening just before dusk was considered a suitable time, when the campaign for the removal of puffs, ponces and weirdos had always been at their headquarters. And luckily, still were. Or unluckily, he wasn't too sure, as he contemplates a larger-than-previously-seen crowd gathered at the bus shelter. And, as it was their second home, the only one in the area whose glass was still intact and flimsy plastic seating hadn't been ripped out. He walks towards it wearing sunglasses, a feeble attempt at disguise, just to avoid the past complicating the already complicated present. But luckily, there are no familiar faces in this most undesirable of social clubs.

'Have you lost your guide dog?' was a quip from its most senior member, prompting laughter from his juniors.

Those that were too busy fiddling with mobile phones were satisfied that others were laughing or scowling at the visitor. Now, with increased immunity to the triviality of the opinion of others, Jonathan explained the purpose of his visit.

'Do you know anyone round here that can sell me a small gun? Like a pistol, with bullets.'

'Yeah, there's a toy shop down the road.' Collective laughter.

Jonathan waits for it to die down. 'Well, do you?'

'I might. What's in it for me?' was the predictable response.

'If I get a gun and bullets for it, there'll be £500 for whoever brings it round to my place and shows me how to use it, plus 200 for them to give to you.'

With about as much idea of the usual cost of handguns on the black market as he had of shooting people with them, he sensed the need for a substantial figure to at least arouse sufficient interest in the young man to get anything moving. If anything was going to move, which seemed

349

increasingly doubtful.

'Ooh, shows you how to use it, eh.' More laughter.

Well used to being the butt of jokes, but now far less sensitive and fully focused on the mission ahead. And as he looked around at this most depressing of quintessentially British surrounding, felt a flicker of gratitude that he was leaving.

Jonathan hands him a piece of paper.

'There's my phone number. Give it to someone you know who can do it or forget it. You've got two days.'

Jonathan's stern words caused a silence and the straightening of faces in the shelter with none of its occupants able to think of a suitably witty insult for his departure.

Was this a crazy idea? He had asked himself that question a lot recently, and one crazy idea after another had proved successful. He fantasized about running amok with the loaded gun if he were to get it. Starting with the slaughter of whoever brings it to him expecting money in return, followed by this second-rate comedian and his low-life audience. But such gratification would probably end up being instead of going to France, rather than as well as. His life was descending into a real life farce of scary proportions. But far better than just fading away quietly at the convenience of others, as so much of his life had been. Forced into saying and doing nothing for it to continue.

He busied himself on the day before departure with packing essentials. Once again, difficult for such an uncertain trip. Clean underwear for wherever he drops down dead? Another 'final' letter of warning arrived about his non-payment of mortgage, causing him some sadness, sealing his fate that there would be no more blissful returns to the peace and tranquillity of the cottage after the mayhem. It was inevitable but unsettling: his home having been a great source of comfort and security since his diagnosis. Despite its still dilapidated, unrestored state, from which he had once been so obsessed with transforming, in what now felt like a previous life.

The usual pain, frequent visits to the loo and much indecision kept him awake most of the night. He got up early and started packing the car, ready to sail at lunchtime.

The phone rings. 'Is that Jonny?'

'Yeah.'

'It's the bloke about the gun.'

He sighed, not quite sure whether to be happy or sad. 'What, the bloke I saw in the bus shelter?'

'Doesn't matter. I've got a gun and bullets like you wanted.'

Jonathan, having almost given up on it, struggled to get his brain to keep up with his words. 'Where are you?' he asks.

'Plymouth.'

'Have you got a car?'

'Yeah.'

'I'm near Liskeard. I need you to come here with it, and alone. But you'll have to be quick. I've only got a few hours.'

'Have you got the money?'

'Yeah.'

'Well, you come here then.'

Deep sigh! Jonathan was close to hanging up, doubting the wisdom in his choice of gun supplier.

'No, I can't do that. I need to fire it to make absolutely sure, and we can do that at my place.' After a few predictable "forget it" and a "what is this!" an agreement was finally reached to meet at a petrol station on the A38 near the turning of the narrow country lane on which the cottage stood. In normal circumstances this was the riskiest of operations, but now, with so little of life remaining, the whole concept of risk had been re-evaluated.

Jonathan arrived early and used its cash machine, so as to have the agreed money just in case it was needed. Quite prepared to part with it if he got what he wanted, but that was a big if, and getting bigger with every minute that passed after the agreed time to meet. But just as Jonathan gives up and gets back in his car to go home, the man finally appears. And looks disturbingly familiar.

'Don't I know you from somewhere?' the gun dealer asks, with the same menacing glare as the one Jonathan had endured the day after the trashing of his flat.

'I don't think so,' Jonathan replies, as calmly as possible, despite strong suspicions that this was one half of the perilous duo whose flat he had soaked with as much cooking oil as possible without gaining entry to it. And that man was now a few years older, and presumably armed, judging by the small box that sat on the passenger seat next to him. Jonathan's death was imminent of course, but this was definitely *not* how he intended to go.

The two men stare into each other's eyes, silently, as if a decision was being made as to whether a near collision on a council estate a few years previous, was going to obstruct the intended transaction. After which, Jonathan gathered enough composure to proceed with his mission.

'Can I see the gun?'

He endured the delay in getting an answer as the man continued the stare, concealing his unease at the identity crisis with a sickly, mocking smile. But eventually opens the box.

'Bullets?'

The man showed the magazine and smiled again, already enjoying the ignorance of the customer he had come to do business with. He was shaven-headed and heavily tattooed, with a talent for smiling and snarling simultaneously. Jonathan looked completely harmless in comparison: skin faintly tinged with yellow, and frail, like a strong enough gust of wind would finish him off. Nothing like a double-murderer, aspiring to his treble.

As predicted after the edgy phone call, this was someone he wouldn't wish to do business with over the sale of a packet of chewing gum, let alone a gun. But the expected ordeal that would have to be endured for the purchase of the illegal item. He had hoped for someone older, who had outgrown the whole concept of bravado attached to what they were selling. A quick, straightforward transaction with someone he'd never clapped eyes on before, with a bit of mutual cooperation and trust thrown in. But alas, for that kind of service, one surely needed a gun license and a gun shop to visit nearby. Or, to go to a foreign country where guns were legal and buy one there, without all the cloak and dagger that surrounded it here. It was obvious that trust, or the lack of it, was going to play a major part in whatever was to follow. Jonathan was unsure whether he wanted to continue. The destruction of Reynolds was still craved of course, but if his attempts to get a gun to do it with endangered himself or the trip itself, he was ready to pull out. If he had sufficient warning. Not a luxury one always enjoyed when guns were involved. And, they were about to leave the relative safety of a public place, for the potential dangers of a private one. But he persevered, for better or worse, determined not to be intimidated.

'Where's the money then? £700.'

'At my cottage. We can go there now. You follow me.'

'You'd better not be messing me about.'

'I told you, I've got to fire it myself and watch you doing it, loading it, so I know it's all right and I know what I'm doing. We can do it at my place outside. There's no one about there.'

It felt like his words had just tripped over themselves several times, which prompted another smile from the gun dealer, looking straight into his eyes, sensing his fear and unease.

'All right, let's go,' the man said, satisfied that he was dealing with someone who wouldn't dare mess him about.

On arrival, the man marches towards the open cottage door to establish if they were alone. Jonathan's word that they were, being nowhere near good enough. He waits outside while the man searches inside. The outdoor experiments with the gun still foremost in his mind.

'You hear a fair bit of gun fire round here. Farmers I suppose, shooting rabbits or birds,' Jonathan explains, trying to ease the tension.

'Let's get on with it,' the man says, impatiently.

Jonathan's loathing of his guest had increased rapidly in the time so far spent in his company. This was slime of the worst kind that he'd had the misfortune to stumble upon so often in life: a big part of the inspiration for his post-diagnosis vengeance. The man smiled at him in much the same way as Porter and Marsden and other abusers had done. But Porter and Marsden's smiling days were over, thanks to his good work. This was similar vermin who deserved to go the same way, who he would relish the chance to shoot in the back with the test shot he was so eager to try. But, as the gun was in the hands of someone whose shoulder needed to be looked over, to get as much information as possible as to how the thing works, it was surely impossible.

'Money!'

'When I've fired it,' Jonathan replied, determined to stay in control of the situation.

The two men glare at each other, Jonathan more nervously. But, with previous concerns about how, where, or if they'd met before, now seemingly put aside, the demonstration commenced. He watches closely, as the man takes the pistol and magazine out of its box, as close as you

353

want to get to an enemy with a soon to be loaded gun.

'There's bullets in there, is there?' Jonathan points at the magazine.

'Yeah.'

'How many?'

Another pause before the dealer's answer, with indecision as to whether he was willing to give such information without money.

'Ten.'

Jonathan felt like a *Blue Peter* presenter, after the usual words from the studio, 'And I went along to find out', followed by the outdoor observation of what an expert on something was doing. Only, *his* observation was done with much less cooperation from the expert. Trying to put his revulsion of the man to one side, he was learning, on the principle that to be properly educated one needed to be immune to the unpleasantness of the teacher.

'Could you take those bullets out and then put them back in again? Please.'

The 'please' prompted eye to eye contact and another smile/snarl from the dealer who then obliged, so quickly Jonathan could hardly make out what was going on. But just managed to establish that the cartridges loaded one on top of another in some kind of spring mechanism, holding them in the magazine securely. Forever inquisitive and eager to learn, and, in this case, determined to only pay for something that works. Thus, not being a victim of that council estate or any of its slippery associates a second time. The man then pushes the magazine up into the rest of the gun, now enjoying being watched, convinced he was dealing with a harmless imbecile in awe of his expertise, as Jonathan watches closely. The slide shutter is pulled back, then released into its firing position. All done in a second, like a magician concealing his methods. With the gun now ready for firing, Jonathan, fully absorbed with the practicalities of the moment, suggests a few bags of fertilizer propped up against his shed, as a target for the test shot. But the dealer had very different plans for the loaded gun.

Now, with complete control over everything, he points it straight at Jonathan's head from a few metres away, and once again, smiles. Jonathan is suddenly paralysed with shock. His determination to understand the workings of the weapon was supposed to give him greater control, and yet somehow, in a split second, he had none. And it was a blatant reminder of the scum he was dealing with, who, having provided the demonstration on loading the thing, as requested, now had a loaded gun with which to start giving the orders.

'I know where I've seen you before. When your flat got done over. And that little trick with the bottles of oil. That was you, wasn't it?' Another smile, relishing the fear in his victim.

Jonathan does the most convincing display of bewilderment he was capable of, while at the same time preparing himself for death as the gun is still pointed firmly at him.

'Money. 700, as agreed, now!' No smile.

Jonathan suddenly realises what a fool he's been. The man could easily shoot him dead after he hands over the money and take his gun with him. And would almost certainly never be caught, with it being such an isolated spot that he himself had so keenly advertised as the perfect place for the firing of guns. While behaving like an apprentice wood turner about to get his first experience on the lathe, it had slipped his mind that this was a gun, a killing machine, he was in pursuit of getting his first experience of. And its owner had been found via a contact at the dreaded bus shelter.

'I'll just go and get it.'

'Yes, you will,' the man gloats.

Jonathan turns and walks to the cottage, deflated and humiliated, doing his best to hide the turmoil going on inside him. Although having the full amount in the wallet in his pocket, he made the pretence of having to return to the cottage to get it, just to give himself time. For what, he had no idea. But as he walked, to his relief, the young man didn't follow, distracted, like so many others of his age, by his mobile phone and the noises coming from it. Just standing there casually, gun in one hand, phone in the other, pressing buttons, grinning at some source of amusement from it.

However potentially lethal the young dealer appeared to be with his loaded gun, underneath the layers of bravado, this was a man with no expectations of shooting anyone with it. Just playing games, enjoying the power the weapon gave him and the terror it inflicted on others. At worst, he would just drive off with his gun and his £700: a satisfactory transaction with another mug, where money was taken and no goods

355

delivered. Another source of amusement with his mates when he got home. But that was more than this customer could stand. Parting with a large chunk of the meagre savings supposed to keep him in his final days, while relying solely on a gesture of goodwill to actually get the thing he had paid for. Sickening, and definitely not part of the plan of going out in style, causing as much havoc as possible to those that deserved it.

And this man deserved it.

As he entered the cottage, Jonathan mulled over ideas for the destruction of his guest, that would surely end up being his demise and no one else's. The man had a loaded gun. Not an easy thing to argue with. But kitchens were perilous places, and he heads straight for it, its weaponry being his only means of defence. Still with no real plan having properly formed in his brain, he fills up an electric kettle with water and switches it on, hoping it had time to boil before the inevitable: gun dealer coming in to find out the reason for the delay in getting his money. The sound of the young man's voice from outside, still distracted, as if without a care in the world as he chatted and laughed into his mobile phone, was a comforting one, giving him time. After rummaging through a few drawers, he finds the hunting knife previously bought for the killing of Marsden, still in its sheath, never used. But, with no time to start trying to attach it to his forearm, places it down his trousers, tightening his belt to keep it secure. The kettle boils. Silence from outside. He grabs it, removes its lid, and positions himself behind the lounge door, just as he hears footsteps approaching.

'Oi! Money, now!'

This was surely suicide, but what the hell. Life had to end somehow. But preferably quickly, without any more pain.

The young man enters and takes careful steps through the narrow hallway.

'Don't be silly. I've got a loaded gun here, you dickhead.' Now with a hint of nervousness at the possibility of having to use the thing as a weapon, rather than a fashion accessory.

He fires it outside the front door to prove his point, and then continues up the hallway further into the house. Jonathan watches through a gap between the door frame and door as the man slowly comes into view, who then kicks the opposing door to the dining room open. The man's mobile phone then bleeps, and Jonathan takes advantage of the break of silence to move himself nearer to the lounge doorway, kettle poised. But the slightest noise of a foot touching the floor is enough for the dealer to turn, suddenly, and with a sudden jerk of Jonathan's arm gets the full capacity of the boiled kettle in the face.

'Argghh!'

As he screeches, his body tilts backwards slightly with the shock, and his finger squeezes the trigger in instinctive defence, but with no proper aim due to the temporary blindness. As the bullet hits the door frame just above its intended victim's head, Jonathan manages to follow up with an almighty lunge of the knife into the man's chest. The gun falls to the ground, the dealer's body follows it, and Jonathan losing his balance follows them both. The dealer moans as Jonathan grabs the gun, and kneeling over him, finally gets the chance to do his practice shot about a foot from the man's face.

Despite the shock of firing a gun for the first time, the noise it made, and the unrecognizable mess of the face of its owner, there was now only one thing on his mind: having to get on that ferry. And with relief, learns that he's still got an hour to do so. Dithering as to what should be done with the body, he fights his way to the sack truck in his shed, surrounded by all kinds of cobweb-covered junk. Perfect for shifting filing cabinets full of records, but not so easy with lifeless human beings. He lays it down flat, drags the body by its feet onto it, and wheels it down to the river at the bottom of the garden, with one hand holding it upright. With the relief and exhaustion of a marathon runner crossing the finish line, he tips the thing over and watches the body transported away with the current.

Scampering back to the cottage, he gets the gun and chucks it on the passenger seat of the car. He then swallows two strong painkillers with a swig of energy drink, to hopefully counteract the usual agonizing consequence of such exertion when it arrives. After one last check in his hold-all bag for passport and ticket, he sets off, leaving the front door wide open. He roars down the country lane, then slows down to squeeze past an oncoming car driven by a bewildered looking lady who stares straight at him as they pass. He had the vaguest suspicion it was 'Cathy' the nurse, making another attempted visit to 'monitor' him. But he roared on, determined to put her and all other English concerns behind him forever. Over the Tamar Bridge, and the usual stop to fumble about for change for the toll. He hands over the coinage and the man sitting in his booth takes it, before noticing the gun on the passenger seat.

'What you doing with that thing?'

Jonathan hasn't the faintest idea what he's talking about, until the man points to it. The full horror of the situation sinks into his already overloaded brain, as he realises he is at the man's mercy. There was now a serious risk of him missing that ferry, the consequences of which didn't bear thinking about.

'Oh, it's just a toy. A replica. It doesn't fire.'

The man just stares vacantly at him as if unconvinced. Jonathan stares intensely back.

'I make them. It's what I do for a living. For museums that kind of thing. I'm just on my way to show it to a client now. But I'm really in a hurry, so if you wouldn't mind.'

The man looks around as if searching for a colleague to seek further advice, hence, trying to put a bit of excitement into his otherwise monotonous day, until the prolonged bibbing of horns signifies the impatience of the now assembled queue behind, and the barrier opens.

He roars on, with worried looks at both the clock and the obviously far-too visible gun sitting next to him, before braking suddenly at the sight of a layby ahead. In search of a suitable hiding place, he opens the boot, and after emptying much of its contents on the ground outside, raises the mat, exposing the spare wheel sitting neatly in its well. He lifts the thing out, straining every bit of his knackered body in the process, and then removes the magazine from the gun for safety: his brief education of its workings not covering that of the safety catch. Luckily, there's just enough room for both bits of gun to sit in the well, with wheel then replaced on top of them, and sitting flush as it had done before. After replacing the mat and his belongings, he roars off once more, exhausted and in pain, but his mind now at rest on the matter. Surely, only the most suspicious and dedicated of border control official would think to look there.

Never had he been so relieved to see a queue and join the back of it, with its glimmer of hope that the ship was still there and could be boarded. With ticket and passport in hand he moves slowly forward. But his now gaunt features and much less hair are in direct contrast to the photo in it, and it causes a puzzled look from the official who asks Jonathan to remove his cap. More suspense when he hadn't fully recovered from the last lot. It would be typical irony if he couldn't board the ship because of failing to look like his passport photo, when there was such far worse things he was guilty of, which of course would then be discovered if he didn't.

He wondered whether to offer a brief explanation, or if that might make things worse.

'I know. It was taken a while ago, and I've lost rather a lot of weight recently,' he says, with a strained smile, and as much fake nonchalance as can be achieved in such desperate circumstances.

But after a few more glances in his direction, it seemed to do the trick, and he is allowed to move on to the next potential obstacle. The vehicle checkers, who give a look of tired dismay at the passport check office for letting more cars through so close to sailing time. They give it an unenthusiastic going over. An increasingly weary Jonathan, standing outside the car as the boot is raised, looks to the sky in a – *what will be will be* – gesture. Luckily, no dogs, trained to sniff out a recently fired pistol. Maybe next week when his name is splashed all over the papers, there would be. The relief at finally being allowed to proceed onto the ship was almost a metamorphosis, as he moves slowly forward while in a trance, eyes glazed, foot on pedal but no hands on steering wheel, as though ready to collapse on to it at any moment.

With car safely stowed, he wandered about slowly using an umbrella as a walking stick. Up on deck he sampled the fresh air, enjoying being a carefree pedestrian after all the frantic driving. As the ship sounded its deafening horn and started to move, he let out a prolonged cheer of joy with arms raised, as Great Britain and its troubles slowly began to fade into the distance, attracting the odd glance from fellow passengers as the wind tore into him. It was an exhilarating feeling that was very familiar: the joy of escape, of being nowhere, of slowly drifting between one source of anxiety and another. Only this time, multiplied by the fact of leaving a country that it felt had kept him prisoner for almost his entire existence, and one where he had left a trail of destruction as a final farewell. The joy seemed to spread to his withering body with the sudden re-emergence of a lost appetite, enjoying the best meal he'd had in ages, followed by a sea sickness pill and painkillers. After which, the traumatic morning and sudden relaxation and fresh air began to overwhelm him. He asked if they had any spare private cabins as he was 'feeling a bit weary', and his

359

general appearance was more than enough evidence to substantiate it. A lady on the desk said she would see what she could do after he agreed to pay the necessary in cash, which he had rather a lot of, since his good fortune of parting with none of it for the gun. The lady returns with a key and a smile and resisting the urge to climb over the desk and give her a kiss in celebration, he thanks her calmly, hands over the cash, and slowly makes his way to the cabin without a care in the world.

Throwing his bag on the floor and himself on the bed, it was peace at last. His thoughts turn to the gun, how precious it was, what he'd had to go through to get it, and how lucky he was not to have been shot with it. And how forging a firearms license and buying a gun from a proper gun shop, would surely have been a far easier option.

Once again, the crown jewels were safely back in the tower. But those metaphorical gems used to be referred to when successfully getting his giro, or his belongings out of one crummy bedsit and into another. Complicated enough, if he remembered rightly. How life had changed.

But now the chaos was his creation, inflicting it on others for his own pleasure. And about time too.

Too tired to take in the full extent of the day's good fortunes so far, he drifts away into contented sleep.

An Educated Guess

Marshall survived his ordeal by television without further comment, having said nothing that could be open to misinterpretation. Or, that nobody had successfully found a way to misinterpret. But he hoped his superiors weren't so impressed with his performance, that he would be ordered to repeat it anytime soon.

Never usually one to take the psychological strains of his work home with him, but recent events had made it difficult not to. Much to the dismay of Mrs Marshall, who now found herself reporting her activities of the day to a husband who made the right noises of response in the right places but was actually somewhere far away. She would occasionally make mention of such gibberish as returning home with the shopping on the back of a passing elephant due to the lack of buses, just to catch him out, to which he would respond with the usual 'mmm's, 'ah's and 'oh yes's. Fortunately, their sense of humour was a large part of the cement that had sustained the marriage for so long, and such dialogue was usually followed by laughter. But he desperately needed a breakthrough with this case before he was removed from it, and that was a serious matter. Not just because of it being considered a blemish by a future promotion board, but because of himself, who he was. And underneath the layers of sarcasm and cynicism, he was a man who took great pride in what he did.

With the lack of progress came a mixed blessing: a drastic reduction of his team. Their services now considered far more worthwhile, assisting with a sudden spate of burglaries being reported in an affluent area of Sheffield on an almost weekly basis. Good news for Marshall, just as long as he wasn't about to be ordered to follow them. He'd endured several unavoidable progress reports to his now recovered superintendent, who had shown a similar facial reaction to some of his team when told of Father O'Brien's pre-funeral conversation. Only this time, Marshall had to suppress the desire to thump something heavy on the nearest available item of furniture and glare at his assumed critic menacingly. His superior's look of amused doubt had said to him loud and clear that he was clutching at straws, with no words required. But Marshall's instinct told him, that although there wasn't even a straw to be clutched in all this, the said conversation would somehow prove to be relevant. But there was no point in trying to explain that to a fellow policeman of lesser intuition; and there were lots of them about.

Another doubter of the investigation's direction was Sergeant Hennessy, who hadn't spent a minute reflecting on his good fortune of not being the one who had to push it in the right direction; whatever that was. But, with high aspirations for his career, would surely feel that pressure in the not too distant future. As ordered, he paid a visit to the sumptuous residence of Kevin Porter's widow to get whatever he could about the history of Porter and Marsden's association. Now less distraught than Marsden's, but still a lady with a black cloud hanging over her. Her only smiles where when she reminisced about her and 'Kev''s early days, while almost in a trance, as if alone. But the sergeant listened attentively to her words, resisting the urge to take notes for fear of appearing insensitive. She spoke of them attending neighbouring schools and waiting at the same bus stop to go home, eventually getting the courage to talk to each other.

After establishing that both boys had attended Langley Park Comprehensive and were in the same class, the sergeant was now feeling a bit more positive about things. Without quoting the disturbing words of a 'mourner' to the priest before her husband's funeral, he gently went round the outside edges of the possibility that her husband may have bullied other boys.

Maybe one in particular, perhaps?

'Oh no, I don't think so. Not Kev. I'm sure he would have told me. We had no secrets from each other,' she told him sternly.

Never a cynical man, but he had enough experience of the job to know that that last sentence was dubious to say the least, and that books the thickness of any encyclopaedia could be written on the secrets of people who apparently didn't have any. But he certainly wasn't going to push it any further. To do so, would be to cast aspersions on the marriage of a recently widowed wife of a murder victim. And they didn't pay him enough for that.

With this new information, Hennessy wasted no time in getting down to the school. But it was a long time ago and felt like the most he could hope for was confirmation of what Mrs Porter had already told him. A school clerk browsed through archive records, now computerized.

'Around the mid to late seventies if you could, please.'

'Ah, Mr Delaney, headmaster. No longer with us. Porter, Marsden, bingo! Yes, in the same class throughout, for five years.'

The clerk looked pleased with himself as he gave the information asked for, but the copper needed more, a lot more, and after the initial optimism that had brought him here, began to wonder why he had bothered.

With the assumption that a child stuck in a disused well (if one actually was!) may have warranted the attention of the police or emergency services at the time, the sergeant probed further.

'Is there any information about anything significant to do with Porter and Marsden and other pupils at the school, or in the same class perhaps?'

'No, it wouldn't have that information. Just names. Who was there, who arrived, who left.'

'Umm…' Hennessy racked his brain, with a feeling that he may be on the cusp of something interesting but wasn't quite sure how to proceed.

'Well, could I have a printout of all the names of other pupils that were in the same class as Porter and Marsden?'

'Of what year?'

'Ahhh, better do it for every year that they were at the school. If possible.'

Hennessy's words were accompanied by a feeling of inner clumsiness and lack of preparation. And a faint smile of embarrassment, as though his request were on behalf of a domineering superior officer who he could only hope would be satisfied. A deadly serious murder investigation this was, but he had the lacklustre of someone being pushed in a futile direction and a feeling that his time could be better spent pursuing other more promising lines of enquiry. If he only knew what they were.

'Yes, that shouldn't be a problem.'

As the young man set to work and his printer made the usual noises of being awakened, Hennessy sat back in his chair for the welcome interval of not being required to speak.

The sergeant left with his printouts, feeling like he had achieved a lot in terms of following orders, but still doubtful as to where those orders were getting them. All this, because someone had implied they had been the victim of abuse, which sounded like it might be school bullying! It was all too vague. Although he hadn't said it, for fear of another clash of opinions with Marshall, the man the priest spoke to sounded a bit like he wasn't playing with a full deck. And the priest was perhaps too kindly a man to spot it. But the pursuit of business acquaintances/enemies that both men might have had; in which he himself had had much to do with the painstaking research, was a dead end. No evidence had been found that Porter and Marsden were anything other than best mates who played golf and had barbecues in each other's gardens. So what else was there?

Jonathan's car number plate had been picked up on cameras in various places, including the working men's club. The team examined footage of a man described as 'suspicious', doing something like a six-point turn in its car park as a convoy of funeral goers arrived. But Jonathan's flash of wisdom with the logbook had paid off and it couldn't be traced to him, but it could and was traced to the car's previous owner, a Mrs Geraldine Smyth of Liskeard, who described to Devon and Cornwall Police the frail looking, pony-tailed man she had sold it to, who had said he lived locally. This sudden burst of progress was deemed important enough to warrant a knock on Marshall's door, who got to his feet on hearing confirmation that Liskeard *was* a key factor – not just another fabrication, like 'Ryan Walker' and 'Plasterboard Direct'. And a ponytail! As he himself had seen on the suspect on CCTV footage, as he fled the scene at KP Construction shortly after KP's murder. Whoever Mrs Geraldine Smyth of Liskeard had sold her car to, had to be the man they were after, and all they had to do was find him. After his initial excitement, the inspector conceded that there was still much to be done for that to happen. He sat down again and continued wading his way through written reports of burglaries. But at least he now had something resembling progress on their most crucial case to throw at the superintendent at his next summons.

Names on the printouts from the school were examined, a few of which were noted as being present in one year but then absent for the next. Anything even slightly unusual among the monotonous wall of names being seized upon, to try and prise out one particular one. A few addresses were then coupled with names, by any means at their disposal. One, from her criminal record for prostitution and shoplifting, which she was keen to point out to her visitor was 'ancient history'. She took some convincing that the WDC on her doorstep was not interested in her past, or even present.

'I just need to talk to you about your schooldays at Langley Park Comprehensive if that's all right, Carol.'

'You mean Porter and Marsden, don't you?'

'Well, anything significant. Were they the bullies?'

'Not half.'

'Was there anyone in particular they would bully?'

The constable already had the name 'Jonathan Piper' written down in front of her, among a few others who had left the school prematurely for reasons unknown.

'Yeah, there was a boy. They were always on at him. But he left. There were rumours he'd gone to the luni-bin. Mental hospital. That's what we used to call it then, you know, being kids.'

'Can you remember his name?'

'Oh, it's so long ago. The only reason I remember the other two is 'cos they've been in the news recently. Er... Jonathan, something beginning with P. Sorry, it's been a long time.'

'That's OK... Jonathan Piper?'

'That's it, Piper. Very quiet. Shy sort.'

'Was there any particular incident that you can remember involving Kevin Porter and Alan Marsden and Jonathan, or other boys perhaps?'

'Well, there was lots of them really, but nothing stands out. They'd nick his bag and chuck his sandwiches in the bin. Throw stuff at him. His sandwiches once, I remember. But otherwise, just general name-calling, the odd scrap in the playground, that kind of thing.'

'Anyone specifically who was doing all this?'

'Porter. He really hated Jonathan. Don't know why. But Marsden and a few others always joined in. It was like Porter had some sort of power over them or something. You don't think it was him do you, Piper? I mean, that was years ago!'

'Thank you, Carol. You've been very helpful.'

'Is that it?'

'That's it. I'll see myself out.'

The constable, being fairly new to the investigation, wasn't fully aware of its blunders and stagnancy so far, and therefore, unaware of the staggering amount of progress she had just made. She returned to the station where her reports of the visit to an ex-pupil prompted the leaping out of chairs of colleagues, from one computer screen to another.

The name Jonathan Piper was immediately typed into the police computer system, hoping for a recent entry that would show up an address. Nothing. However, a further search, revealing a council tax payer of the same name and similar age to the victims to have been an ex-classmate, and, living in Liskeard, triggered far more excitement. This latest addition to their growing number of Liskeard associations, told them they must surely now have their man – as they already had Mrs Braithwaite's statement that the 'Ryan Walker' she spoke to mentioned Liskeard as his company's base, and a Mrs Smyth's statement that she sold her car in Liskeard to a man saying he was local, the same car that was picked up on cameras at the working men's club; and now, a Jonathan Piper in Liskeard who was previously well acquainted with and had good reason to hate the two victims, it felt like they were home and dry. There were cheers and high fives going on at the station the next day in the most unusual of high-spirited briefing.

As he watched the celebrations, Marshall couldn't quite make sense of how they had got to where they had got to, or if they were actually there, such was his mental fatigue. But he appealed for calm, reminding them that they hadn't actually got him yet. And, as he knew only too well, only when they had and a guilty verdict was announced, would it satisfy the press, the public, and his superiors.

Devon and Cornwall Police were notified immediately, and their armed officers would have invaded the suspect's address immediately; if they could find it. After much exasperation and a few awkward 3-point turns of their mini-bus in the narrow country lane, one officer volunteered for the steady jog up the long driveway of a neighbouring farmhouse to ask for the whereabouts of the elusive 'No. 2'. The Piper residence being only one of three numbered houses in the half-mile long lane, vastly outnumbered by named cottages and farms, just to add to the confusion. His semi-automatic assault rifle and mini-bus full of colleagues, safely out of view to avoid unnecessary alarm.

After much fake nonchalance on the doorstep, trying to look as least like a policeman as possible, he returned with the information that a car had often been seen going in and coming out of the gap in the bushes about a hundred yards up the road: as much knowledge as Jonathan's closest neighbours had of him. They eventually find it and storm in, cautiously. With a car parked outside, people are expected inside, and those people, as always, are expected to be armed. They spread out and surround the building, sophisticated weaponry pointing at windows and doors blocking any means of escape. There was no need for doors to be kicked in. This one had been left open for them. They proceed inside, forever alert, the noise of a scurrying mouse prompting a sudden turn and a point of a gun. Satisfied they were alone, they examine the chaos of the dining room doorway.

Although there was no body to confirm it, this looked very much like a murder scene: one bullet lodged in a door frame, another in the floorboards, a blood-stained knife and a kettle left on the ground, and a vast pool of blood and water close by. This was about to become their second home, as when senior officers were alerted, they immediately ordered a twenty-four-hour armed police presence.

A blood-stained sack truck left on the riverbank was a clear indication of where the body had gone, and so police divers were called in. The river was on a slight downhill slope with always a fierce current, so a body could have easily travelled a fair distance along its route. That was deemed to be the likelihood, as the diver's only success was the recovery of a waterlogged mobile phone which, in itself, was a minor miracle, as some reported of losing their own hand after it was last seen at the end of their arm. Such was the visibility in the fusion of water, mud, silt and general grime in the nether regions of the river which, on its beautiful, clear, flowing surface, could have adorned many a postcard showing a typical, picturesque Cornish scene.

Nobody had been reported missing. The car left at the scene had false number plates, and fingerprints found in it hadn't matched those of any other known criminals so far. There was nothing else in it to identify who'd been driving it. The deceased mobile phone was pushed and prodded in vain for any sign of life, before being bagged for further examination. But, with its vital, unique numbering so obscured, proved impossible to trace to anything or anybody.

The cottage, although apparently somebody's home, looked ready for demolition, and now the scene of a horrific crime, it seemed unlikely anyone would return to it. And nobody did. With such consistency, that after the initial invasion of forensic examiners, the officers stationed there were going half-mad with boredom: well and truly sick of playing cards, telling rude jokes, and the occasional pointing of guns at the postman at the sound of approaching footsteps.

The annoying absence of a body, thus making it impossible to determine if suspected double-murderer and homeowner Jonathan Piper had killed again or been killed, continued. Until one morning, further along the river, from the balcony of another riverside property, a foot is spotted sticking out of the water by a traumatized lady hanging out her washing. Police rush down there before it frees itself and continues its journey downstream. To their joy, it was attached to a body, something they had been craving since the discovery of the murder scene, stopped in its tracks by a large rock, surrounded by fast moving water in one of the river's shallower areas.

The immediate deductions were that it had been shot at close range in the face, stabbed in the chest, and hadn't been in the water very long; and, more importantly, seemed a little too youthful to be the Jonathan Piper as described by their northern colleagues. So, not the infamous owner of the cottage a few miles upriver where it had almost certainly come from. Eventually, its fingerprints were taken and matched to ones found at the cottage, in the car left at the scene, and intriguingly, on an empty small box left on the ground. With two holes in it: one, the shape of a magazine, the other, a pistol. All evidence that suggested the now deceased visitor to the cottage had brought a brand new gun with him, somehow ended up being shot with it before being dumped in the river. The fact that nobody had reported him missing suggested he was a man immersed in skulduggery, whose nearest and dearest were perhaps more used to avoiding the police than seeking their assistance. As if to do so, would be to risk exposing a wider network of crime, possibly illegal gun distribution.

That, at least, was the conclusion arrived at by the experts at Devon and Cornwall Police. The latest events were passed on to their colleagues up north, eager for any news on the case, who were now left with the uncomfortable feeling that it was expanding, rather than drawing to a close, as had previously been thought.

But evidence so far gained about Jonathan Piper suggested he was no such gun-carrying, career criminal. And hadn't used one in his two murders so far. But, as this latest murder was surely his work, with it having been committed on his premises, he was now suspected of being very much alive and in possession of a firearm. And Devon and Cornwall Police now had good reason to brace themselves for more casualties, and more involvement in this case than they had originally bargained for – with a killer possibly still on their patch, who it seemed wasn't restricting himself to the slaughter of those he went to school with.

Parler Vous Anglais?

Jonathan leaves the ferry, as refreshed as anyone in his condition can be, after the long rest in the cabin. After some wobbly driving, while wondering why a sensible Anglo-French agreement couldn't be reached to drive on the same side of the road, he finds a lay-by and checks on his most precious possession. Still there, under the spare wheel, and had better stay there for the time being out of harm's way, he decides. The sight of a passing police car reminds him of the legal requirements for driving in France that he had forgotten to bring with him, having been otherwise distracted in his last few hours on British soil. So, GB sticker, first aid kit, breathalyser and other such mundane items, would have to be found soon. Preferably, before he was stopped by police and fined, and more importantly, the lack of said essentials for the law-abiding British tourist arousing suspicion and prompting a more thorough search of the vehicle. Fully aware as he was, that even the most trivial of unplanned occurrence could bring about an abrupt halt to his mission before it had even started. Another essential he didn't have was a place to sleep tonight. But for the moment, felt strong enough to fit in some serious mileage before bedtime, thinking he would stumble upon somewhere to rest his head at a suitable hour. There were doubts as to how the enemy would be found, assuming he had managed to conquer the first challenge of finding the French HQ of Euro Hydraulic Solutions. But all mere trivia, he reminded himself, compared to what he had so successfully avoided in England. He was still alive and still a free man, currently enjoying the comparative anonymity of being in a foreign country, and with a worthwhile mission to accomplish while he still had the strength. Blessings he had to remember to count.

After a few hours of driving he stops at a deserted lay-by on a dual carriageway for a painkiller and a snooze. And as he awakens, wonders whether the woodland next to it was sufficiently secluded for him to familiarize himself with the gun; with traffic whizzing by, surely too fast to notice anything. He retrieves it from its hiding place, attaches the magazine and enters the woodland. Despite having already fired the thing, the circumstances were now very different, and he felt clumsy and apprehensive. In the pandemonium at the cottage with the not-quite-dead gun dealer, there was no time for any such feelings. The trigger had to be squeezed and the best hoped for, that it would finish him off. And that, it most certainly did.

But now, with more time to think, he was aware that the weapon had to be properly mastered if he was to do the required damage with it. As he waded through the mass of trees looking for a suitable spot for a practice shot, he worried that a bullet might ricochet off one and hit him. Do bullets ricochet off trees? If a woodpecker's beak was sufficient to put a hole in one, so surely was a bullet, he figured, with what seemed like sound logic. So maybe not. Not something he'd ever had to think about before, but did now, knowing that to accidentally shoot himself would be a real spanner in the works. And he didn't even know the French equivalent of 999 if he was still alive afterwards to ring it! But, as was also often the case near a British lay-by, there were various man-made abandoned things littering the place, including a mattress. Never the most desirable of items after being left outside in all weathers, but on this occasion, just what was needed. After a quick look back to check that the lay-by was still empty, he pulls the shutter back, anxiously checking to see that a cartridge was where it looked like it should be for the next shot. He releases the shutter, flinching nervously as it springs forward, all the time trying to memorize his now deceased tutor's actions. Gripping it with both hands, he points the gun at the mattress with it rested vertically against a tree, and squeezes the trigger, trying to remain still and composed. To his relief, it fires, he is still alive and unharmed, and there's now a hole in the mattress. He repeats the process, only this time without pulling the shutter back first. It fires again, thus teaching him that no preparation was needed for the next shot. A crucial lesson, having had visions of clumsily missing his human target with the first shot, only to then have to fumble about with the thing to get it to fire its second! And there not being much time for the fumbling! His only certainty in all this was that the super-slick demonstrations of using a gun, as provided by the makers of endless Hollywood westerns and action thrillers, shouldn't be relied upon. With any such fumbling quickly erased by editing.

His experiment stirred memories of buying a realistic-looking pistol cigarette lighter for Dennis, thinking it would amuse his piano-playing friend whose birthday was approaching. After leaving the shop – where he had already checked to see if it was working – he then decides on one last check of the unusually expensive charity shop item. And so, 'gun' in hand, he goes down what he thinks is a deserted alleyway, squeezes the trigger, and a flame appears once more. Satisfied it was fit for purpose, he puts it back in his carrier bag and enters the chemist next door in search of indigestion tablets and cigarette lighter gas.

After about ten minutes of browsing the medicinals, looking about as menacing as a boy scout helping an old lady cross the road, he hears a quiet voice behind him. Trying very hard not to alarm other shoppers, the voice tells him to stand against the wall and raise his hands. On realizing it is a bullet-proof vested copper accompanied by a few armed colleagues doing the telling, Jonathan obliges, to gasps of sudden shock from shop assistants close by. Once established that it was a cigarette lighter incident they had been called out to deal with, the officer gave Jonathan a stern lecture and didn't seem to want to leave until he got what he considered an appropriate response to it: agreement from the 'armed man' that he had done something 'very stupid indeed'. But Jonathan, who had just wanted to make doubly sure that a flame would appear when the trigger was squeezed before leaving the area for his bus ride home, didn't think he had. But sensed that the uniformed invaders were themselves feeling a tad stupid, and would feel a bit less so, if he were to admit his wrongdoing and apologise humbly for the nuisance he had caused. Despite giving them no such satisfaction, thankfully, he wasn't arrested for stupidity or being in possession of a gun-shaped cigarette lighter or anything else, and Dennis *was* amused by his birthday present and his friend's bizarre story of acquiring it. But now, tears form in his eyes as he reflects on the real gun in his hand, how it may come in handy for his suicide, how serious and solitary life had become, and how much he would love to see his old friend from those long-lost frivolous days once more.

***

Now recovered from his melancholy, confidence with the weapon gained, and satisfied that he could at least hit a mattress at close range, he replaces the gun in its hiding place and resumes the journey.

At nearly midnight, tired and in great pain, it was surely too late to get a comfortable place to rest his head for the night. He looks around a large motorway services/shopping centre, with many things now closed. Except a petrol station. After filling up and purchasing a few overpriced legal essentials for his journey, he now had to attempt the asking of the lady behind the counter if there was a hotel nearby, and if so, where. He starts the conversation with what felt like the pitiful cry of the Brits.

'Parler vous Anglais?'

But it's a 'non', and a shake of the head.

From past education, he remembers the word 'hotel' being conveniently the same in both languages, and it's enough to trigger a smile, a 'Oui, Oui!' and sign language, in the tired looking night-shift worker. He thanks her with a warm 'merci beaucoup, madamoiselle' while fellow customers cringe in the queue behind him. Was there anything as nauseating as the British holding up queues while trying to tackle the very basic of French? But his mission was difficult enough without the learning of a foreign language. His intended victim would be sure to understand English and the reminder of the past he was so yearning to give. That was all that had seemed to matter.

Sure enough, at the end of the road that goes behind the petrol station, by the roundabout, as indicated by circular movements of the lady's hand, stood what at first appeared to be a palace, but was actually a hotel. All lit up in its magnificence with Roman-style pillars outside its front door, and a fountain in its front garden. And they had a room for the night. A godsend for such a weary traveller. But an expensive one. To his unease, the only room they had left wasn't a room, but a 'suite', preceded by an unpronounceable French name beginning with P. And when given the price for it, he embarrassingly mistook it for being that of a week's stay in it. In his pre-cancer days, this would have prompted a quick exit and seeing if he could get away with leaving the car in a remote corner of their car park overnight, while he slept in it and paid nothing. Alas, those days were gone, and, as it was now the early hours of tomorrow and way past his bedtime, he made himself comfortable in the four-poster bed with depressing concern at his financial state. Surely a hot water bottle could be thrown in at this price! And they were stingy with the essentials for proper tea-making! His good fortune at getting a free gun (without having taken advantage of a special offer) had led to some carefree spending. But now, after the cabin on the ferry, the petrol, and the 'Presidential' Suite he had yet to pay for, his savings were dwindling fast, and he guessed there would be no special benefits that visiting terminally ill serial killers could claim whilst in the country. Death, when it comes, would solve a major financial problem. It would have to be soon. But hopefully, not before he had the chance to put an end to what was surely the well-heeled existence of Euro Hydraulic Solutions managing director.

In his pre-cancer days, the fabulous looking buffet breakfast on display on a large table would have been relished. And at these prices, something needed relishing. Especially as the only redeeming feature of the bed he had just had a restless night on, was the fact that it had four posts! One would have been enough! But, having awoken with the severest of nausea rivalling that of the morning sickness of pregnant women, he wondered what on earth was going on in his stomach to cause it; before a moment of gratitude that he hadn't been shown X-ray images of it, accompanied by a grisly, accurate explanation. And knowing he needed to eat something to give him strength for what was sure to be an eventful day, it was a case of forcing down what he thought he may get away with without it suddenly re-appearing in the lavish dining room in full view of the prestigious clientele. And so, some muesli with a fruit cocktail and yoghurt was attempted, followed by a croissant, the usual strong coffee, painkillers and anti-sickness pills that he doubted were doing their job.

Even without being sick, he noticed the occasional curious look in his direction from smartly dressed fellow diners obviously on "business", which caused him a degree of self-consciousness. Since his rapid weight loss, he hadn't bothered to invest in a new wardrobe, and his clothes were now at least a few sizes too big. Fearing that he may be confronted by what looked like the type of impoverished character created by Charles Dickens, he avoided the many full-length mirrors in the place.

Having at least made it to the privacy of the en-suite bathroom for the re-appearance of his breakfast, he reluctantly paid the extortionate hotel bill before leaving, without daring to think of its possible consequences. The temptation to leave without paying being only just resisted, having noticed the cameras in the car park and considered the potential disaster of being apprehended *before* carrying out his mission. With a full tank of petrol in the car and an adequate supply of energy drink and chocolate on the passenger seat, for when or if his nausea passes, he sets off. Like twice before, there was apprehension and pointless speculation.

Would this be a big place? He presumed so. Would that make things easier, or not? Easier to blend in with a crowd perhaps, or, impossible to find its chief organ-grinder? But one thing was sure, there would be tight security. He must expect it. Gates or turnstiles only able to be opened by the press of a button by a security guard, who needed good reason to do so. Doors only able to be opened with a fob or plastic card. This was definitely the British way, and more than likely, the French also. It was certainly the way of KP Construction, but then, he had a legitimate reason for being there (despite it being illegitimate) with his appointment with the boss. The fact that he intended to kill the boss at that appointment was neither here nor there. It meant that he could simply press the intercom button at the entrance, declare himself 'Ryan Walker' with an appointment with Kevin Porter, and proceed without suspicion. And that appointment was more or less a guarantee of being alone in a room with the intended victim. What luxury! Couldn't he have performed the same miracle with this mission? He was beginning to wish he had tried. But his energy levels, mental and physical, were sagging, and was getting new pain in different areas of his body where he hadn't previously, suggesting the tumours were spreading rapidly. Doubtless, he would be getting regular updates on their progress of ravaging his body if he hadn't absconded from the care system and was being 'monitored' by Cathy and other professionals.

At the next motorway services, he debated whether to invest in an expensive English-French dictionary, which would surely come in useful. There wasn't going to be a big sign with an arrow on it saying '*Phillip Reynolds. This way please*', especially for the man's English enemies. Bullshit may have to be given, and possibly in French. Despite his financial insecurities, he buys the book, opens it in the car and wonders what it is he would be likely to have to say. He gets as far as 'rendezvous' for appointment, before conceding it was premature as he hadn't found the place yet, and that may prove a big enough obstacle.

So he closes the book and studies the European road atlas instead before resuming the journey, eventually finding himself on a ring road around Bordeaux. With not much more than instinct to guide him, he takes a gamble on an exit, and looking right and left at everything as he drives, suddenly brakes sharply on seeing a sign that looks vaguely similar to the French he's got scribbled on a piece of paper next to him. He turns in and tucked away behind the premises of various smaller companies, he finds Euro Hydraulic Solutions. He exhales, with a mixture of relief and apprehension.

It was a big place surrounded by high fencing, and as expected, he finds himself on the wrong side of a large gate with a camera pointing at him and an intercom next to it. After reversing back to the relative safety of a wall with other parked cars against it, he gets the gun; heart thumping, adrenalin largely overriding the pain as he again grapples with the spare wheel, still with no idea of his next move. Prepared for the worst: having to try and converse with a non-English speaking person in control of the gate, he flicks through the dictionary for suitable words to accompany his 'rendezvous'. Better, he decides, to just pretend that he has one with a made-up French name and hope for the best. To pretend he has one with Phillip Reynolds would surely lead to some serious checking, that could then lead to the tightening of security, thus ruining his chances of ever getting near the bloke. He pulls up close to the gate once more and spots another CCTV camera that suddenly rotates on top of its pole. Figuring that he could well be being watched by someone who correctly perceives his behaviour as suspicious, it felt like it was time for action. He gets out of the car with some prepared French bullshit at the ready and presses the intercom button. It bleeps. He hears crackles followed by a French voice saying something unintelligible.

Assuming it's a person, not a machine, he responds to it.

'Bonjour! Um… Je m'appelle John Martin. Je avez rendezvous avec Pierre…'

Whether his slow, robotic attempt at speaking French had actually done the trick, or it was a beautifully-timed technical fault, he would never know, but nonetheless, the gates open, and he rushes back to the car before they close again. Having got through the gates successfully, he drives on. Relieved, but not quite daring to class it as good fortune, and on seeing them close again in his rear-view mirror had the uneasy feeling of being a prisoner, who could only hope they would open as easily when he needed to escape.

He parks in a large car park outside the main building and manages to conceal the pistol down his trousers. Not an easy task while still sat in the driver's seat for added privacy, feeling sure his every move was being watched. How he could do with one of those holsters that goes across the chest with gun sitting just below the armpit, nicely concealed by a jacket, as seen in many an American TV cop show. But sadly, not widely available in duty-free shops on ferries, or motorway services.

He gets out of the car and walks across the car park, visibly carrying only reading glasses and translation book. Passing two impeccably dressed male executive types made him feel much like the only partygoer to arrive in fancy dress having been confused about the dress code. In his thick jumper with circular patterns, baggy beige trousers and baseball cap with a kangaroo on the front, he wasn't going to be mistaken for an employee of the place. Or, one of its shareholders. His unkempt and slightly eccentric appearance often raised a few eyebrows in certain places, such as this one, but not much in the way of suspicion. Conspicuous he may have felt, largely due to his murderous intentions, but his general demeanour of harmlessness was a definite advantage to getting what he wanted, without attracting unwanted attention by demanding it.

The car park was densely populated with top of the range, high-powered saloon cars. All neatly parked with hardly anyone about getting in or out of them. All belonging to employees perhaps, of what seemed a purely office environment with no trace of manufacturing. And no noise, apart from Jonathan's footsteps and rummaging in pockets, checking he had all that he thought may be necessary. His thoughts turn to the gun concealed in his trousers: doubting its usefulness right now as it seemed unlikely he was about to come face to face with the enemy without an appointment, and worrying that it may ruin his chances of getting one, depending on what security they had in there. With a mind in the chaos of indecision, he debated whether to return to the car with the weapon that could well be a liability. But after considering the increased attention to himself that that may cause, chose to continue with caution, looking out for any security guards and the possibility of being searched.

As he walks towards large glass double doors at the main entrance, he is prepared for the worst, wondering what kind of technology was about to stop him. But, to his pleasant surprise, the technology does the opposite and the doors open automatically on his approach. But once inside, to his horror, is confronted by his most feared: security guards and an airport-style detector that would have to be walked through. And in light of recent terrorist activity in France, it wasn't just airports that were operating them, so it seemed. Begging the question, *why didn't he leave the gun in the car?* Deep sigh! And worse still, when he turns round to exit the place to do just that, the glass double doors refuse to open, manually or automatically. But, to his slight advantage, there's a small queue of visitors waiting to walk through the detector, the security guards are busy guiding them through it, and there's a small forest of indoor plants in pots immediately to his right. With eyes darting around at everyone and everything in close proximity, and with lightning speed, the gun comes out of his trousers and is deposited amongst the sturdy leaves of a cactus. After which, he is beckoned forward by a seemingly unsuspecting security guard who instructs him to remove the other harmless metal items from his person and walk through.

Having made it safely through another obstacle – but with anxious, intermittent glances back at the plants by the door, wondering how the hell he was going to recover the weapon (if a security guard hadn't already done so) – he finds himself in another queue. This one, to speak to one of a long line of receptionists seated the other side of a long counter, all female and wearing the same uniform. And behind them, is a long line of clocks on the wall showing the time in various major cities of the globe. A spectacle of efficiency. The floor so clean you could almost see your own reflection in it. Two transparent glass lifts go up and down, fully loaded with their all-important human cargo.

When smiled at, he proceeds forward to a white-toothed, glowing, gorgeous example of receptionism, without daring to risk another glance back at the plants or let his mind wander from the immediate task in hand. Which was another difficult one.

'Good morning, sir.'

How did she know he was English? He was suspicious of it, and everything else, including his own shadow. She was probably highly trained to detect these things, and not to laugh when confronted with strange looking men in ill-fitting clothes, just in case they were eccentric multi-millionaires making a peculiar fashion statement.

'I'm looking for a Mr Phillip Reynolds. I believe he works here.'

The inevitable question then followed. 'Do you have an appointment, sir?'

'Ah, no I don't, but I have a gun,' before placing it at the woman's temple. If only life were that simple! 'Ah, no I don't.'

'Well, you will need one in order to see him. But if you give me your name, sir, I might be able to get his secretary who can give you an appointment for another day, perhaps. He's actually working from home at the moment nearby while his office is being re-decorated, so maybe he could see you there.'

To his good fortune, the standard of receptionism was high. Both informative and helpful, the lady was clearly doing her absolute best to ensure, albeit unwittingly, that her managing director's days were numbered. But he couldn't give a name, his, or any other. Reynolds' secretary was surely not in the habit of giving appointments to strangers as easily as at KP Construction. That was a fluke that couldn't be expected to be repeated. He had to think of an alternative route around the problem, and quick!

'Oh, good heavens! Is that the time? Sorry, I must go. I wonder if I could possibly take down his home address and then I could—'

'I'm sorry, sir. I wouldn't be able to give you that information.'

'Yes, of course, I understand. Well, if I could just take his telephone number perhaps, and then I'll ring later and try and make an appointment if that's all right.'

'Yes, of course, sir.'

She hands him a card with the man's name, telephone number and email address on it.

'He has a secretary at home, so if you ring that number you will speak to her and she can give you an appointment.'

'Thank you very much. That's wonderful.'

'No problem, sir. Have a nice day,' She smiles.

It was the speech equivalent of ballroom dancing when performed at its finest. Smooth and graceful. Almost making him forget the next arduous problem to be tackled before leaving. Maybe British doctor's surgery receptionists should come here for some intensive training, he mused.

Jonathan turns to leave, with the lack of uproar suggesting that his gun was still laying there undiscovered amongst the plant life. Good news, of sorts. But the damn thing had to be retrieved, somehow! And as he gets nearer to the exit, receives another smile and a courteous bow of the head, this time from the well-built security guard that had previously guided him through the detector, who now stands idly due to the lack of new arrivals, legs apart, wearing a suit, with hands clasped around a walkie-talkie in front of him. Jonathan attempts a return of the smile despite it being the last thing he felt like doing, with the man so inconveniently positioned just a few feet away from his most precious possession that he couldn't bear the thought of leaving without. And despite the apparent goodwill, there was a real hint of menace about the security guard, as though it was being reserved for visitors with more devious intentions. Like Jonathan. Never before had courtesy been so unsettling. It was like something out of a gangster flick, where the recipient of the smile is immediately garrotted as soon as he leaves the place.

Temporarily unable to find sufficient acceptance to just say a quiet, solemn goodbye to the gun and leave without it, he asks the security guard if he can use a toilet if only to delay the inevitable. Hoping that sign language for the presumably Frenchman to understand, wouldn't be necessary. Having successfully found his way to the loo, he takes a much needed moment of solitary contemplation. Spotting a smoke alarm above him, he wishes he had the essentials for starting a fire, as the sudden panic and evacuation of the building thereafter, seemed like the only type of distraction that would enable the retrieval of the weapon to be possible.

Again, he walks towards the exit with the security guard still unknowingly standing guard over the gun. But was now psychologically prepared for the trauma of having to leave the thing behind and the seeking of alternative weaponry to accomplish his mission. If he ever did have the good fortune of making the acquaintance of Phillip Reynolds. But, as he gets closer to the double doors, after returning another of the security guard's unsettling smiles, the man then suddenly changes position, moving in the direction of a button situated on the opposite side of the doors, presumably, in order to press it and open them. And in less than a second as button is pressed and doors open, with the guard's attention momentarily diverted, the cactus is spotted, gun is retrieved and shoved under jumper, and Jonathan walks out, leaving the bewildered guard with no more than a flicker of awareness that something had just occurred, but with no idea what it actually was. And was too embarrassed to ask. Safely back at the car and hiding the troublesome gun under the driver's seat temporarily, his only concern now was getting out of the place. And there was only one thing stopping him. The gates. Which, unnervingly, on this side, didn't appear to have any buttons to press or intercoms with which to request help. They will either open, or they won't. And if they won't, the most awkward return to the reception area would have to be endured. But they do, and off he goes, allowing himself to breathe normally again.

Once outside the place, cured of his claustrophobia and capable of rational thought, he reflects that now having the man's phone number and being told he works from home, was a lot more progress than he could have expected. All he needed now was a whole lot more of it to actually find the man's home.

He finds a cafe close by for a welcome sit down, while sampling some exquisite patisserie with a strong coffee to help keep him awake and alert. Not a caffeine addict out of choice, but having to have something in his blood stream fighting against the constant drowsing effect of painkillers.

He racked his brain further. He had a phone number but needed an address to go with it. To get an address, he would need an appointment, and to get an appointment, all kinds of bullshit would have to be conjured from somewhere, and possibly in French. The cafe was just about empty, except for a group of French teenagers talking loudly and excitedly: an annoying distraction to his intense thought. But despite it, a plan was beginning to develop as to how he could get over the next obstacle in front of him. With memories of his commercial driving days, he recalled that when unable to find a place where he had to deliver, if he had the phone number, he would often ring the company for directions.

He had his mobile phone with him. Forever a technophobe, it was something that in a few years' time could possibly be sold as an antique. But he had done the necessary nonsense required to use it abroad, and it worked. Ringing the number and pretending to be a parcel delivery driver seemed like a good plan until it occurred to him that such pretence would need to be done in French, as such a person asking for directions would be expected to speak French fluently, and not English. This being France, and them being ordinary workers in their own country and not bi-lingual receptionists. And whatever was expected, must happen, consistently, right up until the moment the extreme unexpected took over. This was a definite snag for which he had no answer. But noticing a sign that says 'Wi-Fi' on the wall, the girl behind the counter gives him a password and he gets his laptop from the car, with hopes of translating the charade into French at the touch of a button. Determination was once again overriding common sense, as it had done many times before, with the inevitable stumbling block of him having to understand the directions when given to him, being overlooked. Along with a few others. And there's more problems with the precarious plan. He enters the password. It doesn't work. And after several attempts, he gives up, orders another coffee, puts his laptop back in the car and sits down again, frustrated, fumbling with a new packet of strong painkillers. A stupid idea, perhaps. But the only one.

From across the room, the gathering of noisy teenagers appears to be disbanding. Lots of waving and hugging and people going in different directions. But one bespectacled young man remains seated with his head in a book, and all is quiet. After a few minutes, it occurs to Jonathan that the solution to his dilemma could be sitting right there. He wanders over, nonchalantly, with glasses and English-French dictionary, trying to look hopeless rather than threatening. And didn't have to try too hard.

'Pardon, monsieur. Je suis Anglais. Parler vous Anglais?

'Yes, a little,' the young man replied with a smile.

He was around sixteen or seventeen and had books and writing pads with him, suggesting he was involved in some kind of education, and by all appearance, didn't seem to mind the interruption to his studying. Jonathan was anxious to get to the point, to prove that there was a point to the interruption. And that it wasn't sexual. As himself at that age, when approached by a man several decades his senior, would have immediately assumed that it was. And chose to remain standing while trying to explain it, until invited to sit.

After Jonathan's first sentence in English is received with a confused expression, he attempts the French.

'Je avez, une…'

There commences much flicking through the book as he searches frantically for the word *problem*, and once found, points to its French equivalent. Following it with what he hoped was sign language for *small*, with thumb and finger, and a pained expression on his face. Doing his best to understate the *big* problem that he had, for the sake of appearing normal and concealing his desperation.

'Petite?' The teenager offers.

'Petite! Yes, Oui, Oui!' Jonathan responds, in a sudden moment of irrational joy with arms outstretched as if having found something far more valuable than a correct word.

The conversation staggers on in similar fashion, but crucially, a rapport begins to develop as both men smile and laugh simultaneously at the verbal fumbling. Jonathan is invited to sit, and after 'Je m'appelles's are exchanged, learns that he's in the company of 'Marcel' who is studying English. Thus, the communication challenge could almost be considered a useful inclusion into the man's education. Hence, Jonathan hadn't so far been told to 'bugger off', in French. But, of course, he has to proceed with the more serious side of the matter in hand, and as he does, treads carefully, looking closely at Marcel's face for signs of suspicion and confusion. But thankfully, there wasn't too much of that, and after much arduous alternating between English, pidgin French, sign language and flicking through his translation book, the young Frenchman appeared to understand his unusual task of pretending to be a parcel delivery driver when handed a mobile phone. And to Jonathan, determined to persevere with what was his only hope of a meeting with Phillip Reynolds, it seemed an appropriate moment to get his wallet out and place fifty Euros on the table, albeit with reluctance, as he was well aware that his plan may fail miserably, thus becoming an expensive waste of time as well as an ordinary waste of time. And, that he hadn't yet paid for tonight's accommodation, wherever that may be (assuming of course, that he wouldn't be partaking of the free accommodation that usually followed being arrested for murder!). But at the same time, in a passing flicker of positivity, considered that the presence of money may in some way help his plan to work, and the man needed rewarding for his efforts and patience thus far.

Marcel's face lit up at the sight of the money. Not just with the quantity, but the fact that it somehow added a bit of excitement to the proceedings. He was being paid for his services as an interpreter which made him feel important. And to Jonathan, he most certainly was. He was just at the right age to be sufficiently competent, and, to consider it exciting enough to want to participate, but also naïve enough to not question the likely dubious motive for such a bizarre request. So, while Jonathan had his assistant, there was hope.

Jonathan, full of anticipation, rings the number, and when he hears a female voice passes the phone to his friend who almost immediately passes it back again. Once established that it's a voicemail message, Jonathan hangs up, exhales, and sits silently with head in hands, feeling the strain, with thoughts like: *why the hell didn't he kill the bastards at school, years ago, when they were there, and he was forced to endure their company on a daily basis! Maybe life would have turned out easier if he had.*

'It's OK. We will repeat. Err... do it again.' Marcel offers words of comfort, sensing the despair.

To which Jonathan raises his head with a weary smile and thanks his friend who sits the other side of the table suitably prepared with pen in hand and notepad close by.

They try again, and this time with more luck, as Marcel takes the phone. Jonathan was relieved but still apprehensive. He could only hope there would be no confusion regarding the parcel itself, what it looked like, whether or not they were expecting it, and so forth. If Marcel were to look at him with a worried expression while in mid-conversation, he would guess that there was, and it would be perhaps time to give up, and hang up, for good.

A fast French conversation commenced, with Marcel scribbling away on his notepad. And despite Jonathan not understanding a word of it, his assistant's relaxed demeanour told him that all was well, causing him to sit back in his chair and enjoy the welcome interval of not being required to speak, listen, to be understood or understand. Just sitting there with a finger poised in readiness to point to the name Phillip Reynolds that he had written previously, in case his interpreter needed it. The conversation seemed polite and amicable and ended with a 'merci' and an 'au revoir'. Marcel smiled as he handed the phone back to Jonathan. Having already written down the elusive address (after shrewdly explaining to the lady that the address on the parcel was unclear), he then set to work drawing a detailed map, now almost as determined as Jonathan for it to be found.

'Joie de vivre! Vive le France! Toulouse-Lautrec!'

To Marcel's amusement, Jonathan shouts what bit of French he *does* know in deranged jubilation, before moving the fifty Euros across the table to his new-found friend.

With half the day gone, it was time to move on with the precious information he had. The two men shake hands and Jonathan leaves with the necessary bits of paper, resisting the temptation to ask the super-efficient Frenchman to come with him to assist further. And, for the much needed company. Sad it was, to part with the rarity of a friend while alone in a foreign country, on something very different from the average holiday.

After the latest communication challenge Jonathan was more in the mood for a lie down than merciless revenge, but reminded himself of the horrors of school and of Sheffield in those early days, and of the devious, arrogant, manipulative teenager that Phillip Reynolds had been. And he was certain, that just like the other two, would need a reminder of their distant past. Thus, school bullying being a far too trivial matter to give any thought to. Until somebody turns up with a long memory, and a gun.

Metamorphosis

Jonathan set off for the challenge of trying to find the residence of his next intended victim. It was his intention to remind the man of his crimes if circumstances allowed it. But niggling doubts were going on somewhere in the back of his mind, that if, during the course of such a reminder; and crucially, *before* the gun was shown, genuine looking remorse was visible, he may not be able to go through with it. Thus, making his possession of a gun, that so much of his recent life had been centred around, pointless. But that was unlikely, he predicted. The likelihood being, that it wasn't regarded as a serious matter then, and with the time that had elapsed, was now so trivial, it may not even be a distant memory. Hence, his cue to start shooting. With the deaths of Porter and Marsden, there had been no such opportunity for discussion and certainly no regrets, figuring that they probably didn't know what remorse was anyway, in order to feel it. And as such, were now, justifiably, dead. But would someone who attended the *London School of Economics* be different? He would have to wait and see.

Marcel's map was excellent. But in amongst a maze of country lanes things got a bit nerve-racking, with some awkward turning round in people's driveways, causing dogs to be woken from slumber to check out the intruder. And also, with a mystifying French word written in big letters on the map as if important, he wished he had asked the writer what it was. Could be anything. But, as he drove along what he thought must surely be the right road, he noticed a wooden block on the ground with the same word carved into it. It was the name of the house. He had arrived. A momentous occasion perhaps, that warranted at least a sigh of relief after all the effort in getting here. But one that was ignored, as he turned into its driveway with a heart pounding with excitement and anticipation.

Slowly he made his way towards what looked like a barn conversion surrounded by fields. This was far more the sort of place where what he had in mind seemed possible. No cameras or intercoms, no gates that opened and closed when they felt like it. As he approached the house, no one came out, despite two parked cars outside and a glass sliding door half open to the right of it with curtains blowing in the wind. Maybe, he considered, that as they were now expecting an imminent parcel delivery, assumed that the noise they could hear was it. Thus, giving him a possible advantage in catching them off guard. All was going smoothly, but he had yet to come face to face with a human. And his apprehension of such was similar to that of a newly arrived specimen to planet earth, who had heard all about humans but so far not encountered one.

As he turned the engine off, the silence all around felt convenient, like something that shouldn't be disturbed. With that in mind, he reached for a pen and a piece of paper in case it was needed for some silent communication. He got out of the car and felt for the gun under the seat, which now, he definitely *would* take with him, allowing himself a rare feeling of confidence and power as he conceals it down his trousers and tightens his belt. There was still enough bullets for the task ahead, and a few more, in case of missing his target. Always a possibility for the inexperienced. And hopefully, for the removal of others who may get in the way. This was a much feared possibility that he'd been lucky enough to avoid in his previous killings so far. But as he tip-toed in through the open sliding door to see a busy lady secretary talking on the phone, he wondered if his luck with that was about to run out. Still engrossed in fast French conversation while facing the wall, she didn't immediately notice him standing there. And even when she sensed a presence in the room, didn't flinch, assuming it was the parcel man wanting a signature. When she eventually turned her head and her swivel chair in his direction to see a gun pointing at her, he was prepared for her scream. As her mouth opened as if about to do so, he gave a prolonged 'Ssshhh!' with forefinger on his lips, as she stared at the gun and him in shock.

The lady was young and French, he assumed, from her chat on the phone, which now continues without her participation, as the phone dangles from her limp hand and she sits in silence gazing up at him. She presses the button to hang up without turning her eyes away. He approaches her desk slowly, pen and paper in one hand, gun in the other, and quickly scribbles *parler vous Anglais?* followed by another 'Ssshhh', trying to prompt either a silent nod or a shake of the head. Luckily, it's a nod, and he scribbles further, with gun now close to her face to compensate for the distraction, while trying to keep a safe distance between finger and trigger. *I am trying to save your life.* Which, although not immediately obvious, in a peculiar, round-about way, he was. *But if you make a noise I'll kill you.*

Again, as was so often the case, he didn't really know what he was doing, but what he was doing was correct. Somewhere in his brain there was an idea of how he wanted this to go, and he was moving quietly towards it. He wanted to be alone and undisturbed with Reynolds, *not* the man suddenly coming out of one of the internal doors, his attention then being diverted from the lady who may then run. And the situation quickly descending into chaos, with the wrong person possibly being shot. But for the moment, there was complete silence from the rest of the house, and all he could do was hope that that silence didn't mean Reynolds wasn't there.

With just the movement of the gun, he orders her to get up and go out through the sliding door. As she starts to move, her hand touches a mobile phone on the desk that he pushes away with the end of the gun, with relief at having noticed it. Perilous things, with the potential of getting the police here quick and ruining everything.

'Where is Phillip Reynolds?' he whispers in her ear when they're safely outside, but with menace in his voice and gun touching her head. Doing his best to ignore the regret he was feeling at causing the innocent girl such distress as tears begin to leave her eyes. A necessary evil that had to be maintained.

With a hand trembling with fear, she points to a door inside her office, and soon after, he hears a male English voice engaged in jovial chat, as though starting a telephone conversation with a friend, with no sound of anyone else responding to his words. Jonathan exhales at the good news. The man was here, distracted, and hopefully alone. With the only possible place he could think of to incarcerate the woman out of harm's way, he orders her towards his car and opens the boot, only to be reminded that just about everything he owned was in it. Ho-Hum! Just what was needed when you're about to order someone to get in it at gunpoint! Ordering her to stand the other side of the car away from the building, he starts flinging the stuff out of the boot and onto the ground, one-handed, completely oblivious to what it is, and without taking the gun and his eyes off her for more than a second.

'Get in, or I'll have to shoot!'

It wasn't just an idle threat. With his belongings (including laptop) scattered all over the place, he'd passed the point of no return and was ready to kill her, Reynolds, and himself in the next few seconds if necessary. And his face showed it.

After some hesitation, the whimpering girl obliges and begins to climb in, but already, an exasperated Jonathan feels the impending doom of being confronted with his next obstacle. The now empty, but not exactly spacious boot, was not quite big enough to contain the generously proportioned captive. In between anxious glances back towards the sliding doors of her office and repeated warnings to the lady to remain silent, he frantically pushes and prods her downwards at whatever part of her anatomy appeared to be causing the problem. How was it that in every film he'd ever seen where such a scenario had occurred, the human luggage was more petite and fitted neatly into whatever car boot they were being forced to enter? With one final lunge at her shoulders and chest, she's in, but looking up at him with venom and terror and a seething determination to prosecute for sexual assault if she survived her ordeal, with no thought whatsoever that that was exactly what her attacker was trying to achieve. He considers the lack of tape to silence her, knowing he's got a roll of it somewhere among the pile of discarded essentials on the ground. But not daring to attempt the search, he makes do with one final warning.

'If you make any noise, I'll kill you! If you shut up, you'll be all right, I promise.'

Doubting whether his promise was much comfort to the prisoner, he closes the boot, locks the car, replaces the gun down his trousers, and tries to compose himself as he makes his way back to her office. Which, to his relief, is just as he had left it: empty, with the sound of her boss still in conversation from an adjoining room. And by the sound of it, not with the police, as feared. But suddenly, a sharp spasm of pain shoots around his stomach and back, almost causing him to collapse to the ground. With all the exertion, something like it was inevitable. But he manages to conceal himself outside in a recess in the wall next to the sliding door for the paralysing few minutes of being unable to do anything except wince. But eventually, as expected, Reynolds comes out of it, oblivious to Jonathan's presence just a few yards behind him and disgruntled at his missing secretary.

'Anna. Anna! Where are you?'

Luckily, there's no sound of her responding to his call from the boot of the car, as feared, and Jonathan remains leaning against the brick wall for support and concealment. The pain now eased slightly having removed the gun from his trousers to relieve the pressure on his stomach. Despite the anguish and uncertainty of it all, everything appeared to have fallen into place. And at last, Jonathan has his reward: the enemy in sight, and him in a good position and holding a gun that's ready to fire. With his target still standing motionless with his back to him, he prepares to do just that, taking aim, fearing that it may be his only opportunity. But the phone rings and Reynolds turns and goes back inside to answer it, shaking his head in irritation, assuming that, with the presence of a now third car in the driveway, Anna had had a visitor who was far more important than her work, and had uncharacteristically abandoned her duties.

Jonathan, now sufficiently recovered, quietly follows him inside with gun now back in his trousers and concealed. Now standing at his secretary's desk with hand reaching for the phone as it rings, Reynolds turns sharply to face whatever is following him. Startled, then puzzled, as if trying to work out if there's a connection between the unusual disappearance of Anna, and the equally unusual appearance of an uninvited, frail looking stranger on his premises. Who somehow didn't look like he was delivering a parcel.

The phone stops ringing. Now, with the pain bearable and secretary safely out the way, Jonathan feels far more relaxed and in control, knowing the gun is close by, concealed, and ready to fire.

He smiles at the enemy before speaking, trying to appear as gentle, confused, and non-threatening as possible. 'Hello, I'm looking for Mr Phillip Reynolds.'

'Yes! That's me.'

The annoyance was obvious in the man's reply but showing no sign of feeling threatened. Jonathan's efforts had paid off. Looking sufficiently harmless to get the answer he was hoping for, just in case of any mistaken identity. Fearing that even the slightest hint of menace from himself (the uninvited guest) may have prompted a far less helpful response.

'Who are you? Where's my secretary? She was here a minute ago.'
'Oh, was that the young girl, quite large?'

'Yes! Yes!'

'Well, she just told me that she had to pop out but will be back in ten minutes. Can I help at all?'

'Who are you? Are you delivering a parcel or something?' Reynolds asks, with increasing impatience.

Jonathan was at last enjoying himself. He shakes his head and allows himself a smile, unsettling the managing director even further. Visitors were not in the habit of just turning up without appointments, and this one didn't look like the sort of person he had ever had an appointment with, or ever wished to, and his secretary was certainly not in the habit of just 'popping out'. This was weird.

'Well, my name's Jonathan Piper.'

The two men now have direct, unwavering eye contact, although Reynolds had wandered off somewhere in his mind. Jonathan waits patiently for his name to sink in, like a hypnotherapist with a patient about to come out of a trance. Reynolds' lips are pursed as if he's about to say the word *what*, but nothing comes out. Eventually, it sinks in, and a smile appears on his face.

'My god, that's a long time ago. What are you doing here?' Bewildered, and failing to grasp the seriousness of the visit.

'I just wanted to talk to you about you and the others at school, Kevin Porter and Alan Marsden in particular. What you did to me. Throwing me down that well and urinating on me.' Jonathan's manner remained non-threatening and unemotional throughout his explanation. Exhibiting all the menace of a priest just calling round to check that his parishioners were all right, as he hadn't seen them in church recently. The calmness in his voice was purely down to the presence of the gun, invisible to his ex-classmate. There was a deathly silence apart from the two men's words.

'You can't be serious!' Reynolds laughed, throwing his head back as he did, exactly the same as he did when the regular victim of the bullying was trapped helpless beneath him. And seemingly now, to be getting the same pleasure out of being reminded of his boyhood actions as he did of actually doing them all those years ago. Once again, Jonathan was providing the entertainment. But now, the audience's amusement was just the inspiration he needed.

'You mean, you've come all the way from England to talk to me about that?'

The man's words were accompanied by a smile of disbelief, somehow reminiscent of the boy: filled with arrogance, as if everything outside of himself was clumsy, stupid, and in urgent need of ridicule. But his thoughts then return to his missing secretary and he moves towards the window. Such was his apparent concern for the lady and lack of suspicion of his intruder, he seemed far more likely to request Jonathan's help in the search than accuse him of trespassing and ordering him to leave before the police are called.

'Strange. Her car's still there. Is that yours next to it?'

Jonathan didn't answer. He could tell by the man's tone of voice that he was used to getting quick answers. Not this time. But expected that at any moment the pile of his discarded belongings would be spotted next to one of the cars, prompting a whole new line of questioning.

'How did you find this place, anyway?' Reynolds continued with the questions, still staring out the window with net curtains pulled aside, unconcerned at having his back to his harmless visitor and seemingly oblivious to the lack of answers. But in a sudden surge of impatience and irritation, he turns his full attention back to Jonathan, moving back towards his secretary's desk as he speaks.

'So, what exactly are you hoping to achieve by coming here?'

Oh, you'll find out soon enough. Jonathan remains silent, answering the question in his head. Conversation was pointless, with what he knew and what Reynolds didn't.

'You can speak, you know. You've had a bit of a wasted journey if you don't.'

Reynolds' words were spoken with another amused grin, as if in no doubt as to the inferiority of who he was speaking to. But was experiencing the annoyance of not being able to focus fully on one problem or another: the missing secretary or the unexpected guest, and was still miles away from making the connection between the two. And as such, the expressions on his face alternated between amusement: at the sight of his visitor, who looked like he had just walked from Sheffield to Bordeaux to talk to him about their schooldays, and disturbed bewilderment: at not being able to quite make sense of what was going on. Or decide if he was in control of it.

Jonathan's task of wiping out his two boyhood abusers so far had been an easy one, morally speaking. His hatred of Porter the businessman was equal to that he had felt as a boy, without having to try, in order to justify the slaughter. He'd not had much of a chance to survey Marsden the man, but his choice of 'lifelong best mates' said all that was needed about his personality. From what he'd seen of the third one, Phillip Reynolds seemed equally incapable of remorse, and as such, would be no exception.

'Look, when you said you'd seen Anna, my secretary, which way was she going?'

Reynolds returns to the straight-faced, disturbed bewilderment once more as he further investigates his missing employee and starts to move towards the sliding door as if about to leave and conduct his own search. But Jonathan changes the subject, and his words stop Reynolds in his tracks.

'They're dead, you know.'

'Who?'

'Porter and Marsden.'

'Oh!' Reynolds responds, with exasperated indifference, assuming his visitor had recently attended some kind of class reunion to have got that information and wondering what it all had to do with him, completely unprepared for the explanation that was to follow.

'I killed them.'

Jonathan's words were made more disturbing by the blandness with which they were delivered. Without a hint of aggression. Just casually stating a fact, as though trying to make conversation. But it's enough to make Reynolds' mouth open in surrender to the bizarreness surrounding him; vague memories of the unsettling phone call, in which the English caller asked if he had attended Langley Park Comprehensive, flickered around the subconscious of the managing director. Was this the caller? Was he in the presence of a killer? Had he killed his secretary? And just as all was beginning to make horrible, disturbing sense, the man's thoughts are abruptly halted.

Suddenly, the gun appears, and Jonathan shoots the man twice in quick succession, aiming for both kneecaps. The first shot misses, hitting the lower thigh, the second is on target, judging by its effect on its victim. Reynolds collapses to the floor, screaming in agony.

Jonathan, like somebody possessed by the devil, screams his uncontrollable rage.

'Laugh now! Laugh now! Laugh now!' In between kicking the man as he writhes on the floor. He stands over him, unzips his trousers and urinates over the man's head, just to return the favour.

'That's what it feels like to be pissed on when you think you're gonna die!' he shouts at the now pitiful, defenceless figure beneath him, loud enough to be heard above the screams. The victim's torture comes to an abrupt end as Jonathan fires another bullet into his head. He stops writhing. He stops screaming. Silence.

Jonathan turns and walks calmly back to the car, gun in hand. The metamorphosis that had occurred at the release of his internal rage, leaving him in a trance. Without a flicker of awareness of his belongings still on the ground, he walks over them and gets in the car, throwing the gun on the passenger seat next to him, lacking the usual common sense to conceal it. He drives, still in a trance, anywhere, away, it doesn't matter. But soon realises that he's got to return to his senses to negotiate getting back to the main road.

After U-turns, three-point turns and sitting in traffic queues going in the wrong direction with a brain unable to focus, he finally makes it to the Bordeaux ring road, and from there to the motorway, exhausted, but still adrenalized by the afternoon's activities. On closing his window against the harsh wind as he hits eighty mph, is then startled by noises from somewhere in the car.

Suddenly remembering the secretary in the boot, he veers across quickly to the hard shoulder and opens it, to find the lady staring up at him with terror in her eyes. With the sudden image of her lying there in his boot, he finds himself forced to consider how attractive she now looks, and how, in very different circumstances, their association could have been a far happier one. That if he were perhaps a film star and she were his make-up artist, or their profiles had accidentally collided among the mass of internet daters, they may have actually fallen in love and had several children. But alas, in this particular circus of misunderstanding, like so many other previous ones in a life littered with them, the lady in question, having heard the gunshots while in the boot, assumes her boss is dead, and that she, being the only witness, is about to be shot herself. But a now unarmed Jonathan, relieved at being able to keep his promise to her, takes her hands as he helps her out of her prison as if it's the obvious thing to do. After which, she immediately runs away from him along the hard shoulder, minus one shoe, screaming, as if trying to escape the grip of a monster. He calls out to her waving the shoe, but she seems intent on doing a four-minute mile without it and eventually disappears into the distance. Now it was his turn to be bewildered.

He drives on in the late afternoon, with a brain miles away from the task of finding shelter for the night and a need to just keep on driving without thinking about stopping. But after a while, begins to feel physically worse than ever, in agony, and has no idea where his painkillers are or if he still has any. Now desperate to stop, to his relief there are services up ahead and he turns off. Realizing that the recently opened pack of strong painkillers were gone, along with just about all other useful possessions, he buys the French equivalent of paracetamol. After a handful of them swigged down with coffee, a short nap and a sandwich, he feels just about able to continue the journey. But still being in something of a trance-like state of shock at his own actions, was living purely in the moment, and as such, hadn't got round to asking himself the most fundamental of questions for any journey: to where? And why? As far from the afternoon's mayhem as possible seemed a good enough plan for the moment. Albeit an unconscious one.

Turning out of the services to re-join the motorway, he sees two cold and demoralized looking hitchhikers, male and female, holding a sign saying, *St Malo. North. Please! Si vu plate!* Brits, possibly, with either a good sense of humour or very poor spelling. He pulls over, keen to do a good deed and ease his conscience after witnessing the terror he had induced in Reynolds' secretary. Not that there was any regret at what he had done to induce such terror, but she had incorrectly assumed he was a monster. Which made him feel like one. Another incentive was the vague notion that he was falling apart, and as such, becoming increasingly desperate for help of some kind, without really knowing what. By helping others, he stood a better chance of himself being helped. But in no part of his still dazed brain, was there any sign of a connection between what he had done and the likelihood of him now being pursued by French fuzz! And therefore, perhaps not such a good time for the picking up of hitchhikers.

'Get in!' he shouts.

They didn't need encouraging. 'Thanks ever so much, mate.'

'No problem.'

He felt a bit less of a monster. But only just managed to get the gun off the passenger seat and shove it underneath it before male hitchhiker put his bum on it.

'Merci beaucoup!' lady hitchhiker chirps, getting in the back seat with two suitcases.

'He's English, you silly sod,' male hitchhiker corrects.

'How ya doing?' Jonathan asks.

'Oh, don't ask. I'm Dave, this is Julie.'

'Hiya folks, I'm Jonny.'

In normal circumstances, never one to seek British company on his few previous expeditions to a foreign country, but on this occasion, the social interaction was helping him to feel something like human again.

'So, St Malo. You're getting the ferry back to ah…?'

'Portsmouth, yeah.'

Dave was obviously a talker. Julie preferred the view out the window. 'We've had a terrible time, haven't we, love? First, we lose the key to our chalet and get locked out–'

'Excuse me! *You* lose the key to the chalet!' Julie corrects.

'All right! All right! He don't wanna know the finer details, thank you! Anyway, where was I? Oh yeah. Then the car packs up back there near Bordeaux. We waited so long for them to come out to us, we decided to get a lift off a bloke and just leave the car, as we're gonna miss our ferry and she's gotta get back for…'

Jonathan stopped listening and went into a world of his own. A world that was becoming increasingly blurred, where he was unable to focus on anything for too long.

'So where are you heading, Jonny?' Julie asked.

A normal question to which he hadn't as yet given any thought and so had to think before answering. A truthful answer of *'I don't know'* may seem a bit odd, and not the sort that passengers want to hear from their driver as he moves them speedily to their destination. Such had been the challenge of locating and killing Reynolds, that he had given no thought whatsoever to life after it. If there was any. But now there was, it seemed, and he was just wandering aimlessly through what felt like a thick fog.

'Oh, umm… Roscoff, but I'm not in a hurry, so I'll take you as near as I can.'

A normal answer that thankfully prompted no more discussion. But the fact that he sort of believed that Roscoff (and therefore Plymouth?) was his final destination, was evidence of a psychologically damaged mind. But gradually, the reality of his situation began to sink in, and memory restored of buying only a single ticket for his trip, and for good reason. The UK was a no-go area, probably now crawling with police looking for him. Only to be returned to by force. No longer home. So, with where he definitely *wasn't* going now firmly established, the question of where he *was* going still remained. The more he tried to answer that, the deeper into confusion he seemed to go before eventually arriving at the inescapable conclusion that there was nowhere to go, and even if there was, pretty soon there would be no money left for petrol to get there. And as such, the time had come to take advantage of the few bullets remaining in the gun and their ability to provide an instant, painless death, now his mission and everything was over. And vowed to do just that, as soon as he had offloaded his passengers at St Malo – the only purpose in life that remained.

As he continued driving, with Julie dozing in the back and Dave fiddling with mobile phone in the front, his condition began to feel less like a kind of post-traumatic stress disorder, and more like his brain was rapidly trying to catch up with the rest of his body in terms of deterioration. He was gradually losing consciousness and struggling to get it back again, but without being tired. Everything was becoming blurred, without it affecting his vision. It was weird. Like an LSD trip, but without the pleasure. Really, he should be tense and alert after what he'd done and overly conscious of the feared blue flashing light in the rear-view mirror. But he wasn't. Just getting more and more relaxed, with seemingly little choice in the matter. As though drifting away, somewhere. And what rational thoughts he had, couldn't be maintained, and subsequently fizzled out into a confused, muddled mess, like somebody fluctuating in and out of dementia.

'We've gotta get back to Pompey. She's gotta have a scan tomorrow, haven't you, love?'

'Yeah, I'm pregnant, aren't I, Dave?'

'Well, you should know, love,' Dave jokes.

'Yeah, it's great. Six months now,' Julie says, smiling at Dave and touching his shoulder. Jonathan felt a little uncomfortable for being there at such a private moment, not wanting to intrude on the lover's conversation or sure whether he was actually included in it.

But just manages the usual response: 'Oh, congratulations!'

The conversation had brought him out of a coma. Briefly. But it was followed by more silence, and soon, the only awareness he had was that he was moving, straight. He couldn't recall anything else, as to who or where he was. The motorway bended to the left. The driver didn't, and was heading straight for the hard shoulder and a crash barrier on the edge of it.

'Wo. Wo. Wo!' Dave shouts, grabbing the wheel and steering it left.

Suddenly, Jonathan is back to full consciousness and all too aware of the seriousness of the situation.

'Pull over. Pull over!' Dave shouts, and they slowly come to a stop in the hard shoulder. 'What ya doing, mate? She's pregnant, you know!'

'Sorry folks.'

'Are you all right, Jonny?' Julie asks.

'Umm…' Another obvious question for which he didn't know where to begin with an answer. It was always these simple, basic questions, that he seemed to have the most trouble with: *what are you doing'? 'where are you heading'? 'are you all right'?* And now, in his current degenerative state, was incapable of treating them with the usual dishonesty to make things sound acceptable.

'Not really,' he answers, in hopeless surrender to his predicament.

The couple are silent, as neither can think what to say. Just waiting for their driver to elaborate, with hopefully, something moderately sensible.

Suddenly, he has a flicker of inspiration as to what should be their next move. 'Listen folks, could we get to a hospital? Now.'

'What!' Dave expresses his disbelief with extreme agitation.

'Shut up, Dave!' Julie restores order.

Jonathan continues: 'And you two just leave me there and take the car to St Malo. Maybe you could just leave it somewhere and get on your ferry without it or take it with you.'

He was well aware of the lunacy of his words, and not what hitchhikers were used to hearing. But he'd had a lifetime of lunacy, and on occasions managed to solve a few problems with it. Against all odds.

'I've got cancer and I'm on the way out. I'm not gonna make it home.'

Dave was speechless and for once turns to Julie for assistance, as though not equipped to deal with anything so bizarre, despite Jonathan concealing the far more bizarre aspects of the situation with the mention of 'home'. As if he had one to return to.

'Shouldn't we just ring for an ambulance?' Julie comes out with the obvious suggestion.

'No, please, I'd rather you didn't.'

Jonathan didn't really know why he was refusing the most logical solution; such was the general confusion. But instinct told him, that if forced to alert the authorities to himself for reasons of ill-health, would rather do it in a quieter, less obvious fashion, and preferably, without the need of blue flashing lights as used by police and ambulance. As the two French emergency services would no doubt collaborate, especially in this case, with an unwelcome British maniac in their country. Despite his faculties diminishing rapidly, he still clung to the faintest thread of survivalist wisdom.

Julie exhales deeply, trying to take it all in, and starts fiddling with her mobile phone, sensing that it was herself who was expected to perform the necessary miracles to get them out of the current mess. 'Where are we now?' she asks.

Dave can just make out a sign in the distance. 'Saintes. 10 miles.'

'Please don't ring for an ambulance though, Julie. I know it's crazy, but if I just turn off at the next junction, I'm sure I can find a hospital,' Jonathan pleads his case, with an increasingly uncomfortable feeling of dependency on the couple.

Dave sighs, wondering at what point he should insist that he and his beloved just get out of the car and resume the hitchhiking. Julie scours the internet.

'Yeah, there is a hospital at this Saintes place. Look, I'll drive. We'll swap over, Jonny. OK?'

Jonathan nods his agreement, as if just about the only physical movement he's now capable of. She gets out and helps him out of the driver's seat and into the back: a humiliating end for a lorry driver who had always taken great pride in his driving. The couple have an almost silent argument in the front, with much shrugging of shoulders, stern looks and dismissive hand gestures. But soon they're off and exiting the motorway, eagerly following signs with a red cross on them.

After much chaotic driving and raised voices from the front seats, they arrive at the main entrance to a large hospital. Again, Julie helps him out, as a feeling of giddiness and imminent physical collapse takes over him.

'I'll stay here and make sure we don't get clamped or towed away,' Dave remarks, with a roll of the eyes, wondering if their already calamitous holiday could get any worse.

399

'Have you got everything you need, Jonny? Like, in the boot, or whatever,' Julie asks, expecting at least a bit of rummaging around for a few essentials to be about to commence.

'Oh no, don't worry. If you can just help me in there.'

To the slightly bewildered couple, it felt like the subject of Jonathan's possessions, some of which they assumed were in the car, perhaps warranted a bit more discussion than what had just taken place. Jonathan's complete lack of interest in the matter, coupled with his refusal to accept an ambulance being called, had aroused a flicker of curiosity in them as to who he actually was; certainly no ordinary terminally ill holidaymaker, they now quietly suspected, and having been previously uninterested in their driver, now were, slightly.

Without himself being aware of it, this had become very much Jonathan's style: on the surface, completely unremarkable, arousing more pity and often ridicule than actual interest, but also leaving people with a slightly unsettling feeling of not knowing quite enough about him than they perhaps should. But *these* people, as well as getting the same slightly unsettling feeling, were getting a car to replace their abandoned one, transport to where they needed to go, and were no longer dependent on the strangest of strangers to get them there. So, possibly a godsend in disguise.

Jonathan takes Julie's arm, and slowly they enter a busy hospital reception area where nobody notices their presence. With only the clothes he was just about standing up in, he could only hope the hospital would be merciful to a wayward Englishman. She sits him on one of the few vacant hard plastic seats. He looks up at her.

'Thank you, darling. You get off now. I'll be fine. Good luck with the baby.'

'If it's a boy I'll call it Jonny, all right?' She smiles, with a twinkle in her eyes.

Jonathan nods and smiles, with a tinge of sadness. She kisses his cheek and leaves him.

The couple speed away into the night. Jonathan falls off his seat, prompting shouts from people around him, prompting staff to come to his aid. It was mostly accidental, but with a whiff of intent. How he needed staff to come to his aid. How he needed looking after.

A Trail of Destruction

Julie and Dave continued their journey north in Jonathan's car, and the further away they got from him the more relaxed they became. They muddled over the decision of what to do with the car, which although a bit old and clapped out for their tastes was serving a useful purpose right now. And so, in their determination for Julie to attend her next appointment (preferably without the prospect of further uncertainty caused by public transport), excited and desperate for confirmation that all was well with the baby, they decided to take it all the way home. Now tired and hungry, they figured on just having enough time for a 'drive-thru' at a fast food place near the port, and take it with them to eat in the queue to board. The radio played some upbeat music as they ate, happily moving a few yards forward every five minutes. The car was then routinely searched, and one of the places where officials had a quick feel was under the passenger seat, which revealed the 9mm semi-automatic pistol, causing the bewildered couple to be bustled away to a nearby interrogation room. Dave was beside himself with rage, Julie slightly less so, as she tries to calm her spouse who she could see was about to get himself locked up.

'She's pregnant. Can't you see that you fucking—'

As if that fact alone should guarantee them onward passage with no more said.

Julie interjects to stop him finishing his sentence before it reaches its anti-French conclusion. 'We don't know anything about it, honest. It's nothing to do with us.'

Just how much more incident on what was supposed to be a holiday could the couple stand. They waited in a portakabin for a more senior border official to arrive, and when he did, began to pour out a far-fetched story about hitchhiking, taking the sick driver to a hospital, and 'NOT!' stealing his car. But with the couple unable to show any proof of ownership of the car, and a gun being found in it, it directed suspicion more towards carjacking than hitchhiking.

'He said his name was Jonny and he was going to Roscoff,' Julie added.

'British?'

'Yes! We've already told the other bloke!'

Dave did the shouting. Julie did the talking, feeling the need to provide an antidote to the volume. The French official shook his head and rolled his eyes as he turned to a smiling colleague. Problems with the British, who'd lost their tickets, their passports or their marbles, was a major part of the job.

'What is the name of the hospital where you took this man?' the official asked casually, knowing this would catch them out if they were guilty.

'Oh, I dunno. Santos or something, wasn't it, love? Just off the motorway,' Dave offers, unaware of the importance of his words, still clinging to the naïve assumption that their innocence was enough.

'Saintes?'

At last, somebody pronounced it correctly. 'Yeah, I think so.'

Julie gave a more detailed description of the man, from her previous 'he didn't look well'.

'We will have to check this. Wait here.'

'Look, we're gonna miss our ferry in a minute! She's pregnant. She can't stay here all night. She's got an appointment at the hospital tomorrow!'

'Nobody is going anywhere until we check this out. Attempting to export a firearm without the legal documentation is a very serious offence.'

'Don't give me all that cods wallop!'

The couple wait anxiously, not quite surrendered to missing their ferry. Dave looks at his watch frequently in between pacing up and down in the cabin and looking out the window. For the moment, he can see the rapidly decreasing queue of traffic waiting to be searched.

'I knew there was something not right about that bloke. I could sense it,' Dave offers his belated observations, with more of a surrendering tone of despair than the previous rage. To which Julie can only manage a sigh of response, as she quietly wishes she had actually gone to the reception with Jonny instead of just leaving him there, so someone would have actually seen them arrive. Thus, surely making the verifying of their story a lot easier and quicker.

The official returns, smiling.

'Yes, an Englishman of that description was admitted to Saintes hospital earlier today.' The couple look at each other with relief, now expecting to be set free to board the ferry. 'Right, let's go.'

'I'm sorry, but we cannot let you go until your story has been verified.'

'But you just said—'

'Yes, a man of that description was admitted, but has a different name, and we have not been able to actually speak to him for him to confirm your story.'

Dave watches out the window as the ferry departs. Julie is still seated, now crying.

'Look what you've done now!' Dave shouts at the official, pointing at the mum-to-be. 'If she has a miscarriage, we'll sue you!'

'The police are on their way.'

The official's assurance of haste being made was meant to be comforting, but sadly, wasn't.

'Police!'

The police arrive and insist the couple and the gun be taken to the nearest police station for fingerprints to be taken and the weapon examined. As they are armed and look generally more menacing than border control officials, Dave's protests become a little more restrained but no less felt. As they are taken away to a waiting police car, the official, with twinges of guilt at the stress caused to the expectant mother, tries to offer more comfort.

'It will not take long at the police station, and I will keep trying the hospital to verify your story.' Although carefully avoiding making any promises of freedom, he was in little doubt as to the couple's innocence. Actual gun smugglers would choose a far better hiding place for the weapon and wouldn't show that much exasperation. Unless they were very good actors.

Jonathan, having enjoyed a restful first evening on a ward at the hospital, is woken from a morphine-induced coma at one thirty a.m., unsure where he is. But after being informed that he is wanted urgently on the telephone, does his best to regain consciousness. He is then wheeled along a corridor to an office with too much florescent light. But it helps to waken him, and on recovering some awareness of what was currently going on in his life, reluctantly takes the phone with a sense of impending doom.

'Hello, who is it I am speaking to, please?' a French accent asks him.

'Ah, Jo—' Jonathan, suddenly remembering the need to remain anonymous and the false name he had given soon after arrival, composes himself accordingly. 'Martin Smith speaking.'

Martin, being his confirmation name[27] in the Catholic church of his youth, and Smith, being all he could think of at that precise moment. 'Good morning, Mr Smith, this is border control at St Malo, and we have two people here who say they transported a man named Jonny to the hospital yesterday. Their description of this Jonny is similar to the hospital's description of you. They are driving this man's car which we have here. Can you tell us more, please?'

The official, having already heard the couple's version of events, wisely chose to give little of it away to see if the mysterious hospital patient's version matched it. Jonathan, realizing the unfortunate couple had somehow found themselves up to their ears in bureaucracy, felt the need to cooperate fully. He confirmed that they were hitchhikers who brought him to the hospital in his car when he was too ill to drive, and had willingly given them the car.

'So who is Jonny?

'Oh, that's me. It's just a nickname that people know me as in England. But my real name is Martin Smith.'

'Ah, I see.'

So far, so good, but completely unprepared for the next question he was about to be clobbered with. The official had a rather unsettling, if unconscious habit, of putting people at ease before he clobbered them.

'But what about the gun, Mr Smith?'

Suddenly, everything was starting to make sense, but didn't make life any easier. He began to wonder whether this conversation was purely to ensure the couple's freedom to continue their journey to Portsmouth, or to see if he was going to drop himself in it. And he was getting dangerously close to doing just that.

---

[27] The custom of adopting the name of a saint, at one's confirmation into the Christian church.

'Gun! What gun?' Jonathan's charades had become more convincing with practice, but it now felt as though he was talking himself off a cliff, with no idea what line of questioning would follow if he continued with this line of answering. The verbal tightrope walking continued, despite a growing feeling that it was all too much like hard work and the time had come to confess to everything and surrender to wherever he was about to be sent.

'I'm sorry, I don't know about any gun. I've not had the car very long. I bought it a while ago in England. It must have been left there.'

His explanation wobbled precariously as he spoke, very nearly collapsing completely with a badly timed 'under the seat'. But just about managed to bring his sentence to an abrupt halt before it did any more damage, and compose himself once more.

'Where did you find it in the car, may I ask?'

'Under one of the seats, Mr Smith.'

Realizing his words could determine not only his future, but also whether Julie's baby would be born in a prison hospital, with its volatile father possibly in a straightjacket in another French institution, Jonathan felt the pressure of responsibility and sweated, but tried to stay calm to get both himself and the couple in the clear.

'Well, I'm sorry, officer, I know nothing about it. To think, that all this time it's been under the seat without me knowing! Ah! But please, let these people go. They wouldn't know anything about it either. I gave them the car as they were kind enough to bring me here, and they desperately needed to get home.'

The official was satisfied that at least the two versions of events actually corroborated, and therefore, it seemed, the couple were not attempting to smuggle a stolen car and a firearm into the UK which, as a border control official, was his primary concern. But he was still waiting for the all-important gun and fingerprint report from the police, and as he did, began to wonder how his job had suddenly become so much like theirs.

After the call ended courteously, but with Jonathan doubting whether his performance had successfully put an end to the matter, he slumped back in his wheelchair, mopping his forehead with a hanky. That was one stressful phone call, eclipsing that of his contact with KP Construction and the one made from a phone box to his mum that eventually secured a roof over his head at Auntie Pauline's. Still alone, he had time to recover before being wheeled back to bed where he had no more sleep. The phone call being equivalent to about fifty of his usual night-time disturbance: his visits to the lav.

Eventually, the police return with the suspects and the official is given the information that fingerprints *were* found on the 'recently fired' gun, but none belonging to the couple which, together with the assurance of the 'Jonny', or 'Martin Smith', or whatever his name was, satisfied him of their innocence and he let them go. Also, on witnessing the increasingly traumatized looking but now strangely silent innocent couple before him, didn't have the heart to confiscate their car for further examination and let that go with them on the four a.m. ferry to Portsmouth. It was a decision made out of fatigue, exasperation, and an urgent need to see the back of the British couple and the car. Somehow, in a momentary loss of rational thought, it seemed like a good way of removing the problem altogether, which had been just about the biggest he had known in his time in the job. But his police colleagues were not consulted in that decision, and the all-important 'recently fired' bit of the information they had supplied was completely overlooked in the making of it.

The sleep-starved couple turn up for Julie's appointment the next day, vowing never to return to France. And unbeknown to Jonathan, his passport, driving license, and just about any other means of identifying him, had safely left the country in the glovebox of his car.

A rainswept, disorientated, young French lady with only one shoe had made her way to a police station in two cars: the first, belonging to a lone male with inappropriate intentions, from whom she managed to escape while he stopped to have a pee against a wall; the second, to a couple with three children, who all squeezed up to make room for their distraught passenger. She told of her confinement in the boot of a car, and that she heard three shots while in there and feared for the life of her English boss. She could offer no description of the car other than it had a British number plate, as was its driver. Bordeaux police, some 50 km away, were alerted and immediately attended the scene where her car was still parked in the driveway. She was driven to it by a young female officer. It was all so shocking and unbelievable. Why would anyone want to hurt such a 'charming, kind man'? The young copper nods her agreement but had seen other similarly described men in similar conditions, and not of their own doing. Even the most charming and kind had enemies, it seemed.

Bordeaux police survey the scene. The three bullet wounds were no surprise, as reported, but the smell of urine around the head and traces of it on the ground, was, and somewhat macabre, it was felt, by officers first at the scene. Like an animal marking its territory, or the bizarre calling card of a serial killer, were the initial vague thoughts that sprung to mind. The bullet wound to the knee suggested the work of a sadistic maniac, but they were completely baffled by the abandoned belongings on the ground. The killer's, perhaps? An English victim and an English killer, in the most genteel of Bordeaux suburbs. Intriguing.

The secretary arrives with her escort, and to her distress, identifies her boss's body which is then shifted. She explains about the contents of the boot of the killer's car now on the ground, which she was then forced into. She told how the killer had asked where the victim was by name, so there was nothing random about it. Mr Reynolds had enemies. But when it was further looked into, he didn't. At least, no obvious ones. But this enemy was far from obvious.

The Anonymous Patient

The French hospital staff had so far been merciful to their English patient, with generous supplies of oxygen, morphine, proper meals, toothpaste and soap amongst other delights: all helping to create a slight rejuvenation, especially in his mental agility. Which, he quickly began to realise, desperately needed preserving; as along with the hospitality came a barrage of awkward questions, all of which must be evaded if he was to be left in peace to end his days here in a comfortable bed. Not wanting to even think about the possibility of an enforced return to his homeland, to satisfy any misguided belief that he must be seen to be facing justice.

The false name he had given was a small step in the right direction but knew it wouldn't be enough to silence the more inquisitive of interrogator. And so, began to experiment with various other methods of evasion: the feigning of amnesia, unconsciousness and pain, his inability to understand French and most of the staff's inability to understand English, all came in useful. But one bit of truth he was happy to assist them with, was his diagnosis of tumours in the pancreas and liver while in England, which, to his annoyance, was then followed by more questions as to why he and his tumours had made the strange decision to come to France.

'I just wanted to visit a dear French friend, one last time,' he explained, with levels of fake sincerity only ever usually achieved by politicians.

To which the member of staff respectfully nodded their understanding while he congratulated himself on his quick-wittedness in deflecting another awkward question, only for it to be swiftly followed by another one asking for the name and address of the 'dear friend' so as to be considered a next of kin. Which in turn, was swiftly followed by a well-timed spasm of pain causing him to spill a cup of specially requested English tea. When the staff kindly returned with another one, he made an equally convincing display of sleep. Thus, postponing the questioning until further notice. If he could just keep the postponing going a little longer, it would surely mean that the inevitable hullabaloo would occur posthumously.

After a scan and his body found to be riddled with the tumours as described, to his distress, he then suddenly found himself being moved out of the ward, while wondering if his new home was to be judicial or medical. His escort wasn't giving any clues, and as he was wheeled past a fellow patient with whom he had previously exchanged a few comforting smiles, to another building with a sign outside saying 'Soins de Palliatif', the lack of English translation didn't help to settle his nerves. But once inside, it soon became clear that this was a hospice where patients would come to end their days. He was given a guided tour of the bright and beautifully decorated residence with the most tranquil of gardens out the back, during which several "bonjour, monsieurs"'s were directed at him from smiling ladies as he was whisked around the place. By the time he was safely installed in his new room with birds twittering from outside the open window, felt utterly content with what he hoped would be his final resting place; as well as a tinge of unworthiness of such surroundings, having expected far worse from the aftermath of his killings. But, with his sixth sense for detecting the too good to be true, reminded himself that even if the French had an NHS, unidentifiable foreigners wouldn't be included in it. And therefore, such comfort would have to be paid for, and wondered if there was anything left in his bank account to do so.

At his new home, the pressure from the more administrative-natured of the staff continued, with forms being regularly put in front of him which sadly, they had English versions of. As had so often been the case in the past, his unusual circumstances were never going to fit neatly into the confines of a form, however much they were prodded. In the business of terminal illness it seemed, even more important than the patient's name being supplied was that of a next of kin: someone to take charge of his dead body and the shifting of it to wherever it was going. And, last but not least, the paying of any outstanding bills. But not everyone had one of those, as he was keen to point out to a fluent English-speaking lady specially selected to interrogate him.

'I've never been married, was an only child and my parents died years ago. I have nobody.'

It wasn't just a frivolous attempt to make life difficult for his French saviours, to whom he was truly grateful for the care and shelter. But for that to continue, so must the deception; as his parents were the only people he had who could remotely fit the description of next of kin, and there was more than enough reasons why they shouldn't be contacted. Despite the enormous inconvenience, they would make every effort to visit if they knew his condition and where he was. And he couldn't face them if they did. They surely knew by now of at least his Sheffield crimes, for which an explanation would be required. And there would be no point in even attempting one. The prevailing and immovable theory being that school bullying was a trivial matter compared to loss of life, life being God-given, and sacred. He could almost hear his well-meaning mother saying the words and see his despairing father looking to the sky with a where-did- it-all-go-wrong expression on his face. But most importantly, they needed protecting from knowing his whereabouts, and the trauma of then having to decide whether or not to tell the police. He neither wanted to be disturbed nor force his parents into the role of major contributors to that disturbance. If he gave their contact details with the strict instructions that they are not to be contacted until he is dead, they would be, immediately. He was sure of it. Just to check out the validity of the foreign patient's supposed 'next of kin'. The biggest favour he could do them right now, was to remain a missing person.

One morning, he was handed a piece of paper by a man whose bi-linguals were equally inadequate to his own. Among the few things on it he could make sense of, were his name, 'Martin Smith', some numbers, and the Euro symbol. It was inevitable, and he dreaded the complications that would follow if he couldn't pay it. But, with no time to speculate on the matter, asked for his trousers in which was his wallet, and after pointing to his bank card was promptly wheeled to the main hospital. At least he enjoyed the spectacle of the hustle and bustle of French medics going about their work, and patients emerging from lifts and being wheeled here, there and everywhere. But, as he is wheeled straight past a cash machine after his request to stop is ignored, is overcome with an unsettling feeling of being about to enter the unknown. He does, and it's an office, manned by a stern looking lady with glasses on the end of her nose, and she looks over the top of them at the wheel-chaired man and his escort. Jonathan was immediately tense. He had a phobia of offices and a long-held belief that nothing good ever came from them. And a strong feeling that this one posed a threat to his anonymity. Giving the lady his bill, she points to a card reader on the table in front of him. But he worried that as his real name was on the card, it would also be recorded somewhere on something they would retain for their own devious pleasure if he made the transaction with it. So, evasion tactics were called upon once more, as he deliberately enters the wrong pin number, followed by a look of surprise as if the card reader was faulty. After another fake failed attempt without the card being fully inserted, his efforts in being a nuisance are finally rewarded and he is turned around and wheeled out again. Thankfully, to the ATM they had passed on the way, where his request to stop is now granted, and he can hopefully withdraw cash and settle his bill with it in a more anonymous transaction.

To his relief, he could and he did, and the settled bill seemed to have a tranquillizing effect on his interrogators. But with now barely 150 Euros with which to avoid the more intense questioning that non-payers of rent could expect to receive, could only hope it was the last.

St Malo police informed their colleagues at Saintes that they have a recently fired pistol with fingerprints on it and are most anxious to trace the fingers that left them. Found under the seat of a car previously owned by a Martin Smith, now a patient at their local hospital, who claims to know nothing about it. Saintes police sent their most proficient English-speaking officer down there.

There was alarm at the sight of a uniformed policeman entering the hospice, the first one that had ever done so in its entire history. What could he possibly want with anyone here? But when he was later seen knocking on the door of the mysterious Englishman, it was confirmation of what many of the staff had already suspected: he was hiding something.

Jonathan repeated much of his previous statement to the St Malo border control man. Yes, it was his car, and yes, he gave it to the couple who brought him here, and he made another convincing display of horror at the mention of the gun found in it. He had bought the car in England and just never noticed it. To the visiting French copper, it seemed implausible that such a frail man residing in such a place could have done anything in his recent past that might warrant their attention. But the overwhelming evidence he had, suggested the man was lying. And when he put to the suspect the most damning of evidence, that the gun he claims must have just been left there without him knowing had recently been fired, Jonathan's heart temporarily stopped beating. It was all over, surely. But, with the officer's seeming ignorance of exactly where, when, and at whom, the thing was fired, chose to cling to the final thread from which he was hanging, and continue with the bluff.

'Well, I'm sorry officer, I know nothing about it. It sounds as if someone is trying to frame me for something, but I can't think who or why!'

The face of the policeman showed definite signs of suspicion, but only of something peculiar going on of which perhaps this unfortunate man was a victim. Stranger things had been known. 'Has anyone else been in your car recently apart from the British couple?'

The ice under Jonathan's feet was beginning to melt.

'No, not that I know of. That's what is so baffling. Maybe I forgot to lock it and someone needed to get rid of the gun in a hurry!'

Jonathan's words were accompanied by a shrug of the shoulders and a widening of the eyes. He was giving the charade all he had left, with the increasing fear of being removed from his tranquil surroundings to face justice, and whatever all that may involve for someone in his condition. And such was his display of bewilderment, it was almost shared by his uniformed visitor who didn't feel the need to say any more. However, following orders from above, he had brought his fingerprint pad with him, and Jonathan's heart sank a bit further at the sight of it. It really was over. They had the gun, and his prints would be all over it. Jonathan surrenders a finger, wondering whether to resort to some undignified screaming in agony to prove he was unfit to be moved. But the officer, with no such intention, leaves with a smile and a courteous raising of his hand, and a naïve assumption that when checked, the fingerprints he had taken would prove the innocence of the innocent looking hospice patient. Jonathan does his best to return the courtesy, but one thing was certain: the copper, or his superiors, would be back.

And next time, not so courteous.

First Love, And Last

The focal point of the hospice was the large day room where patients could chat, have meals, get their medicine, watch TV or play board games. Jonathan had so far managed to avoid it. But such avoidance had made him unpopular with the nursing and domestic staff who disapproved of his unsociableness and, it seemed, had had enough of bringing meals and medicine to the room of a reclusive patient who was quite capable of leaving it with the Zimmer frame they had provided. But it wasn't apathy that prevented Jonathan making the slow crawl to the day room. It was fear: of conversation, of not speaking French, of questions, of being misunderstood, or understood and revealing too much, or, as a foreigner, being rejected and ignored. And a general feeling that human contact was a threat to the anonymity that must be maintained. But, not wishing to offend the non-administrative workers who kindly never asked him awkward questions concerning his identity, and had been so welcoming on his arrival at the hospice, the withering eight-stone Englishman at last ventured out to the day room for lunch with similar apprehension of a child's first day at school. After joining what seemed to be the right queue, he contemplated the precarious task of getting himself, his lunch, and his frame to a table without major catastrophe. But as he stared intensely at the contents of the room with further anticipation, felt a pair of hands touching his arm. Startled, he turned round suddenly, half expecting to see handcuffs. But the hands belonged to a lady with the most wonderful smile, but whose eyes looked sad and tired as though she had been waiting a long time for something to smile about and had now found it. It was clear from her equally emaciated appearance that she was a patient suffering from something much the same as himself. As he returned the smile, the grip on his arm became more of a caress as their eyes locked together, and for a man who had become so accustomed to avoiding human contact, it was sheer bliss. She obviously wasn't the least bit interested in either the name and address of his next of kin or his previous doctor's surgery.

413

She carried his lunch to a table and sat with him as he ate, saying nothing. She seemed like someone who was content with silence, and her eyes and face communicated so much, almost making speech obsolete. But during the silence, only broken by the sound of him eating, he desperately tried to think of something funny, interesting, and amazing to say before she got up and left. And preferably in French. But suspected that another 'Toulouse-Lautrec!' with a mouthful of 'quiche aux asperges' wasn't going to cut it. The most honest and heartfelt thing he could say to her right at this moment, would be one almighty thank you for touching his arm. Which, on the surface, could be perceived as an unremarkable gesture of affection, but in this case, had somehow transformed everything. But not having a clue as to the French words required for such a sentence, and not wanting to appear ignorant by saying it in English, he made do with a solitary 'merci'. And for what, would have to remain unknown. One thing was becoming painfully obvious: that if he still had it, his English-French dictionary would be his most precious possession. Without it, he felt like a ventriloquist who'd lost his dummy.

'You are English, yes?' she asked, after patiently waiting for him to finish his lunch.

After the awkward silence, her words were like Chopin's 'Raindrop' Prelude to his ears: his all-time favourite of Dennis's classical renditions. And the fact that she was still sitting with him to speak them, felt like a miracle for which mere words could not express.

'Yes, eh. Oui.'

Her smile at his 'oui' stirred him into more challenging attempts at speaking French. So wanting to see her smile again, even if he wasn't understood.

'Je suis Anglais. Je m'appelle Martin.' Education hadn't been a total disaster. At least not the French bit of it.

'Wooh! Tres bien!' she responds, smiling, with a pretend look of being impressed. 'Parler vous Francais?' she asks, with continued amusement, as if already knowing the answer.

'No,' he replies, smiling and shaking his head in self-deprecation.

It felt like he had been mocked in the most charming way possible, and for some reason, yearned for more. Her big brown eyes constantly looking straight at his, as if no force whatsoever could turn them away.

'Eh.. appelle?' Pointing at her and smiling.

'Francoise.'

'Francoise!' Genuinely affected by the beauty of the name, his eyes lit up as he repeated it.

'Tres bien pour moi…' Pointing to himself.

She watches him with a contented smile as he twiddles his fingers in the air with eyes raised to the ceiling and a pained expression on his face, as though trying to contact the dead. Deep in thought, determined to finish his sentence.

'… parler Francais avec Francoise[28].' That was as funny, interesting and amazing as anything he could say in French was ever going to get. But even that got the most enchanting of reactions.

'Tres bien! Magnifique!' she exclaims, applauding with mock admiration.

To which, he raises his hands in a feigned appeal for calm, as though having just mastered every language of the planet. Her smile was irresistible and he was somehow lost in it as he watched her. Never before had he had so much pleasure in making someone laugh. This moment made all the ridicule and abuse at the hands of people who thought that a clown was something you stuck pins in or threw into holes in the ground, worthwhile. Someone, much like himself, without much reason to laugh, was laughing.

For some reason that he couldn't quite comprehend, trying to communicate with this lady was a joy, and the more she was amused at his French, the more determined he was to continue. But also, wanted to express some more serious things to her. How much he appreciated her sitting with him, which was quite overwhelming. How awkward he had felt about coming into the day room; being English and different, and how great he now felt because she was there. But, feeling unable to do so in either language for different reasons, made do with what he thought was an apology for his lack of language skills.

'Je suis desole, je ne pas parler Francais.' His words were slow with the usual intense thought and lengthy pauses in between, looking down at the table with a feeling of inadequacy as he spoke. But they were understood, and she reaches across the table and places her hands around his, with a now serious look on her face. They look into each other's eyes.

---

[28] Trying to say, 'very nice for me to speak French with Francoise'.

415

Something special was happening. Something perhaps too strong to be held back by any language barrier.

The conversation was being overheard by a lady member of staff, who, upon hearing of his struggle, taps him on the shoulder and smiles. 'Pardon, monsieur.'

He turns round, a little embarrassed that his attempts at speaking French had attracted an audience. She hands him a book, and on seeing that it is a replacement for the English-French dictionary he had lost, lets out a 'Wah'! of joy. The lady points to the large bookshelf in the corner of the room where it had come from, and he thanks her enthusiastically. In a brief moment of bliss, it felt as if he had everything he could ever want: a beautiful female companion, and a book with which to try and communicate with her.

On returning to his room with the book, he reflected on the wonderful afternoon of clumsy French speaking and smiles. After so much solitude and intense private thought since his diagnosis and during the subsequent killing, it seemed almost unreal at conversing with anyone in such a light-hearted, frivolous manner. And his thoughts turn to Francoise, and that only by her touching the arm of a stranger had his wonderful afternoon happened. She must be thanked, properly, in the most fluent French he was capable of.

That evening, after discovering that her room was just a little way down the corridor, he studied the book intensely. Not one to ever wish to invade another's privacy (unless he was trying to kill them), he anticipated the brief saying of what he had to say before leaving the lady in peace. But in the back of his mind, knew how much he wanted to see her again, almost for confirmation that she was actually real and not a hallucinogenic side effect of morphine or any of the other medicines he was being given. He had experienced similar such delusion with large quantities of booze, being helped by its mixture with the anti-psychotics and depressants he was then taking. Which, on one memorable occasion, had so enhanced the personality and beauty of a girl in a pub he fell madly, briefly, in love with. Only to then fall out of it, suddenly, at their second meeting the next day, wondering what had happened. Could such feelings be trusted?

But nonetheless, feeling like he needed a legitimate reason for disturbing her, brought along his glasses and book as though a clergyman about to read a passage from the bible. He knocked on her door and heard her call out something he didn't recognize. When she called it again, he thought it might be *come in*, so took a chance and opened it slowly.

'Martin!' she says loudly, as if delighted to see him.

She was definitely real. And someone he wouldn't chose to deceive with his false name or anything else, given the choice. Having indulged in so much petty but necessary deceit, to stop it now would surely be problematic. But it was just a name. Nothing of great importance. And to erase Jonathan Piper was surely the best way of staying where he was, in the company of his beautiful new friend.

She was standing, looking for something in a draw, but then turns to him smiling, which was so nice that momentarily he struggled to remember the purpose of his visit. But then looks down at his book at stuff he had scribbled in it.

'Bonsoir, Francoise. Merci d'avoir touche mon bras cet apres-midi[29].'

His pronunciation was predictably bad, but pointed to the limb in question in case of any confusion. It was something of an anti-climax, coming across with all the emotion of a first-aid demonstration rather than the sincere expression of gratitude as intended. But she graciously nods her understanding, smiles again, and looks straight into his eyes as they move themselves closer. Unable to resist each other any longer, they hugged and kissed passionately as if taken over by an uncontrollable force, gripping each other tightly as if in danger of losing each other if they didn't. They fall onto the bed, but their passion is interrupted by a knock at the door. Stuff was called out in French he didn't understand but he enjoyed listening to Francoise's equally unintelligible response to it. It was time for her medication, and she gets to her feet as the lady nurse enters the room to Jonathan's embarrassment. Luckily, no clothes were removed, but lying on the bed of a female patient may be frowned upon, he considered. And was there anything worse for a British citizen in a foreign country than being frowned upon? But it wasn't, and the nurse kindly asked him if he was all right. Francoise translated, answering the nurse's question for him.

'Oui, il va bien[30],' she says, as the two women look down at him smiling as though he were a new-born baby.

---

[29] Good evening, Francoise. Thank you for touching my arm this afternoon.
[30] Yes, he is all right.

It was a strangely surreal moment of comfort. The appreciation was weird but wonderful. Something he would normally assume was the result of a misunderstanding or a case of mistaken identity.

The nurse left them alone again, and unable to recover the energy to resume their passion, they lay in each other's arms. Alternating between the two languages and flicking through his dictionary pointing to words he didn't understand, she explained her rapid decline in the last five years as she approached fifty. How her marriage to an unfaithful husband had started to collapse before being diagnosed with ovarian cancer. Children? Three, grown up, and when she pointed to their photos that adorned the room, tears began to form in her eyes. There was obviously a sad story here, and when she explained further, Jonathan, not quite understanding, squeezed her tightly to his chest as if to compensate for his lack of comforting words. Later, when she asked him how long he had lived in France, it seemed an appropriate moment to tell her how tired she looked, which prompted a yawn. After which, they had a final kiss and a hug before he departed to his room, anxious to avoid further questions and outstaying his welcome. But the final image of her of the day, smiling and blowing kisses to him as he pushed his frame along the corridor, was one that stayed with him all night, causing the most blissful of sleeps. Ending the most heavenly day.

To see her smile and wink at him from across the day room the next morning as he entered for breakfast, was something that made the enormous effort of washing, dressing, and getting there, so worthwhile. He was in love. And almost to his disbelief, the feeling appeared to be mutual. Had he spent his whole life in the wrong country? Would this have happened sooner if he had moved to France or somewhere else years ago? If it had, would he have been so determined to avenge the abuse of his past? Who knows...

Since their first meeting, anything that happened before that had become a distant memory. So it came as a rude awakening when during a lively game of cards with Francoise and her lady patient friend in the day room, he was told he had visitors. The women smiled as though pleased for him and Jonathan did his best to do the same, despite the fear that it could be the last smile of his beloved that he would ever see.

'Visitors', in his own personal language, could mean only one thing: Police. And this time, three of them. One, armed and uniformed, the other

418

a lieutenant, plus an interpreter. All of whom are swiftly ushered, with Jonathan, into the privacy of his room, where extra seating is provided. Now remembering the previous visit from the fingerprint pad-carrying officer, he feared the worst. But braced himself, that whatever was to follow was the inevitable consequence of a successful mission, which he must NOT allow himself to regret, despite his current romance making the expected punishment of removal from the premises a far more severe one.

Not only had his fingerprints been matched to those on the gun found under the seat, as expected, but a description of the killer of a Phillip Reynolds in Bordeaux, provided by his secretary, bore a striking resemblance to him. Him being English and this being France, narrowed it down somewhat. On top of that, just in case he wished to discuss the unreliability of the lady's eyesight, bullets removed from the body of the victim matched those that remained in the gun, found under the seat, of his car, that he had claimed he knew nothing about. Game, set, and match, to the police.

Confronted with this new evidence, Jonathan signed a written confession to the killing of Reynolds, clumsily starting his signature with the usual J before quickly replacing it with an M. Such was the strain of the constant deceit on the increasingly feeble minded as well as feeble bodied. The lieutenant looked at him with a half-smile of more admiration than he would care to admit. This was the first killer he had interviewed in a hospice, and just how this frail patient hobbling along with his frame had so recently managed to achieve it, was something of a miracle. Or rather, the opposite of one.

Jonathan's thoughts were firmly fixed on the only thing he now cared about: separation from Francoise. He had bounced off many people in his life with comparative ease, some very dear to him who he had treasured memories of who were here one minute and gone the next. But this was something totally different. Something it felt like he had waited his whole life for. He pleaded in his defence, that he had been similarly victimised by Mr Reynolds who had a history of being a toerag and deserved all he got, keen to get across the fact that he was not a cold-blooded killer. More of a public servant, who had rid France of the most despicable of English vermin, for which he did not require any thanks. And therefore, completely harmless to anyone else. Anything to try and influence a favourable decision as to where he was now going.

With himself and his colleagues having done their jobs impeccably so far, the lieutenant was left with the unenviable task of deciding what to do next, with there being no standard procedure for such circumstance that he was aware of. The prisoner was obviously harmless, and to move him seemed pointless and potentially damaging. He may not survive the journey to wherever they chose to send him, and deaths in police custody, even among the terminally ill, were the stuff of serious investigation. He was being well cared for here, and would have to be cared for somewhere else, so what was the point? But then again, to let a self-confessed killer come and go as he pleased as if nothing had happened, was not only contrary to criminal law, but frankly, weird, and did nothing to satisfy grieving relatives and the general public that justice was being done.

After leaving the room to consult with the manager of the hospice, the lieutenant returned with a decision that the prisoner was to be detained in his room with an armed officer standing outside the door, 'guarding' him twenty-four-hours a day, who would be under strict orders to let only staff in, who must be searched before entering, and the prisoner could only leave the room if accompanied by them, to the toilet or shower. Satisfying himself that he had dealt with the troubling situation in a suitably officious manner, the lieutenant then insisted on seeing the man's passport. To which Jonathan explained that he no longer had it, or any other form of ID, having left it all in the glove box of the car the couple had taken over. That was the truth, except for the bank card in his wallet which fortunately they didn't ask to see.

So, for the moment, Jonathan Piper could remain Martin Smith, with only his Bordeaux crime in the French awareness, and the lieutenant leaves with his interpreter and his signed confession, leaving his armed colleague to start his first monotonous shift outside the door.

The lady card players, still unaware of the judicial goings-on, gave up all hope of him returning to the game after his visitors. Francoise was quietly upset that he had obviously found something more important to do than play cards and gaze at her adoringly from across the table.

All highly officious in its triviality, but punishment it most certainly was, purely for the fact of it causing him to lose contact with his reason for living. He wondered what she was doing, and thinking, especially about the unavoidable sight of a uniformed copper standing outside his door. He thought about her smiles, her laugh, and her tears at the mention of her children. How she needed comforting. And, as time went on, if she was still alive.

As Jonathan's solitary confinement continued, the presence of its enforcers caused growing unrest in the hospice. The staff were overworked already without bringing all manner of essentials to the room of a harmless patient, who was quite capable of leaving it unaccompanied. Not to mention the intrusion of being searched before they did. They hadn't been told anything as to why the police were there in the first place. The hospice manager had been told but decided it would be better if they were not. The whole fiasco led to the occasional heated exchange between staff and whichever unfortunate officer happened to be outside his door on their twenty-four-hour rota system. Unsettling for Jonathan, who couldn't understand a word of it. The place had suffered a communication breakdown, and it was nothing to do with his clumsy attempts to speak the language.

Francoise *was* still alive and grieving the loss of her new-found friend in equal measure to his grief from the solitude of his room. But hers was tinged with a sprinkling of hostility, as she grappled with the decision as to whether or not the keeping of an almighty secret qualified as deceit. Their painful separation was the kind of thing she had had an overdose of with her family in recent years, and just wasn't in the mood for any more of it. Time was running out for both of them, as they wondered if they were ever going to be lucky enough to catch a glimpse of each other in the corridor one day, before it did.

But with his isolation came plenty of time for thought, and even a few positive ones managed to make their way to the surface. Among them, was the triumph of having thrown every ounce of ingenuity he possessed into making sure some much-deserving people perished. The joy of silencing Reynolds' laughter when the man was reminded of what were surely to him, the good old days. And the slime that was Porter and Marsden, who, having achieved their ambition of bringing their comparatively well-to-do classmate down to a level far beneath theirs, had themselves been so suitably plunged. All beyond the wildest dreams of the recently condemned man when he first stumbled upon the disturbing newspaper headline, and with it, the first flicker of a grisly idea. In spite of it all, here he was in the most comfortable of surroundings with a copper on his door, which at least had served the purpose of silencing his interrogators with their questions and their forms. Who, he imagined, had now realised that there were far more serious concerns regarding the mysterious English patient than his unclaimed dead body and unpaid bills.

After a month, with no visits from their superiors and a gradual thawing of relations between police and staff, there was more of a surrender to the lunacy of such a harmless man being so closely guarded. The restrictions rigidly put in place to control the prisoner's movements and the searching of anyone who went near him, were unofficially relaxed, in exchange for tea, coffee, the occasional glass of wine and whatever food was going. The partaking of such delights in the day room meant that the door of the patient/criminal was more frequently left unguarded. This led to a breakthrough moment similar to that of the destruction of the Berlin Wall, where east and west were at last free to wander in each other's territory, as a now more feeble Jonathan emerged from his room, accompanied only by his frame, reading glasses and dictionary.

He entered the day room apprehensively with eyes all over the room, just like how he used to enter the Tea Bar when he owed someone money or vice-versa or been out with someone the previous evening and couldn't remember how it ended. Only now, all he wanted was a glimpse of that most treasured woman, who had perhaps forgotten about him and found a new male companion or was dead. His recent futile enquiries about her well-being to the less linguistically gifted visitor to his room, having consisted of only two words: a 'Francoise?' from him, prompting a reply of 'oui'; whatever that meant. It was all going on in his head as he skulked around among the chatters, the book readers and monopoly players. But there was no sign of her. The sun shone in through the open doors that led to the garden. He followed it, and to his relief, excitement and joy, there she was, in conversation with her lady patient friend. He stood still at the doorway, admiring the view he had been starved of for so long, as she sat among the gladioli, looking much like a silent film star. Her cloche hat, like those worn by ladies of the period, somehow enhanced the curls of dark hair that hung beneath it. A round face, with big eyes and high cheekbones, that seemed to sparkle, even without a smile. Her petite, frail, cancer-ravaged skeletal figure (the envy of perhaps all current female celebrities of the western world), was covered by a colourful crocheted blanket. And the rhapsody of her voice as she spoke French, unspoilt in its unintelligibility.

Suddenly, his time of still, silent pleasure was over, as her friend noticed his presence, causing Francoise to turn in his direction. Their eyes met briefly with no smiles before she turned away. It was macabre, purely for the fact of being unusual. He moved himself awkwardly towards her and her friend left them alone. He looked into her eyes for any clues as to whether he was a friend or foe. The latter, it seemed.

'I've missed you so much, darling.' His words could not have been more sincere. But there was no response. Not even a flicker of movement in the eyes. As was often the choice: either say it in English and risk not being understood or say it in French like a robot while looking down at a book. And now, more than ever, he needed not only his words to be understood, but also the feeling behind them.

Francoise's descent started with her husband's infidelity and continued with his persuasion of their beloved children that he was the more innocent parent, as the marriage staggered in the direction of divorce. This was the main reason Jonathan, to his surprise, had not seen anyone visit her. Visitors were, after all, a common sight in the place. And often crying. The fact that *his* only visitors were the police, who didn't cry, was to be expected, and something he suffered no self-pity about. He had all he needed in Francoise. But men were not high on her list of heroes right now and were closely linked with deceit. Him, in his harmless, humorous way, had been a most welcome antidote to her husband. Until now.

'How are you, darling? Comment, eh... vous.'

He starts an attempt at translation but shakes his head in exasperation when he can't finish it. Desperately wanting to be understood. Suspecting that she did but needing to be sure. Her eyes, so often a means of communication, now unavailable, as she looks as far away from him as possible. But suddenly, turns to meet his gaze. Her deadly serious face was strangely unfamiliar, and he cursed himself for being the cause of it.

'Why the police on your room?'

The joy of hearing her speak flooded his whole body, causing a slight imbalance and a firmer grip on his frame. The relief of knowing he was still important enough for her to ask, was overwhelming. But once again, in his crazy, private world that made sense to him only, it was the most obvious questions that he had the most trouble with. Where could he possibly begin with an answer? And should he, sensing that an overdue library book or unpaid parking ticket wasn't going to cut it?

Putting his frame aside, he kneels down in front of her on the hard stone of paving slabs so he's at eye level with hers as she sits, causing alarm among onlooking staff, wondering if he had collapsed. The joy of now being closer to her and her eyes meeting his, causing complete immunity to the pain of putting his decrepit body in such a position. He places his hand on top of hers. She pulls it away.

He continues undeterred: 'I love you so much. Je t'aime, Francoise. Je t'aime.'

He knew exactly what that meant from the erotic 1960s hit record in which it was repeated over and over. At least he could translate that most important of words, without the usual putting on of glasses and turning of pages.

'Why?' She starts to repeat her unanswered question.

'Ssshhh. It doesn't matter now,' he whispers, with unwavering sincerity.

And how right he was. There was no more reason for the armed guard than the officer's superiors turning up unannounced to check it was being maintained. And right now, it wasn't. As the 'guard' sits at a table with a hot beverage, flicking through a magazine while waiting for his pudding, happily oblivious to the whereabouts of the 'prisoner'.

Jonathan opens his book in case his words were not understood. Frantically turning pages, still kneeling, while she sits, staring vacantly at flowers in the garden. The bewildering scene attracted some curious looks from slow-moving passers-by, being ever so quiet, wondering if some sort of religious ceremony was taking place.

His behaviour was that of a man on the verge of losing the woman he had planned to spend the rest of his life with, which he was, even though that was half an hour, a day, a week? The shortness of it didn't make it any less painful. But just didn't have what it took to answer her question. The truth would surely take a lot of flicking through his book, and even if spoken in perfect French was likely to do more harm than good. Like many things he had done in his life, its potential for misunderstanding was vast. Since he had met her, the world outside the hospice had ceased to exist and wasn't worth talking about. But to her, it was, and for that reason he wished he could. And for them to fall into each other's arms after it.

'Ca n'a pas d'importance maintenant[31],' he incorrectly pronounces while reading from his book. It didn't get a laugh, and by the time he had looked it up and given it its usual deciphering-of- a-code-like treatment, was futile. He sensed defeat, but in a rare moment of selfless acceptance smiles at her, expecting nothing in return. And gets nothing, as she looks away. Which, with anyone else, would be enough to flood his brain with all manner of antagonistic thought. But in this rare exception while in *her* presence, felt strangely incapable of such, and the love for her just continued.

As he struggled to get to his feet, he didn't notice but she made the first inch of movement as if to help him, only to be beaten to it by a nurse who helped him back to his room. He didn't look back at her, trying to regain some resilience to sudden separation and rejection that was all too familiar. But after this particular instance of it, was left desolate, with a feeling that to return to his room was to return to nothing. And that maybe, underneath it all, he was just a lowlife who didn't deserve the love of someone like Francoise. Or anyone else.

---

[31] It doesn't matter now.

'Mr Piper, I Presume'

To Jonathan's blissful ignorance, he had achieved the notoriety of being currently the UK's most famous wanted criminal. His name having been mentioned numerous times on local, and now national news, with air and ferry ports having also been alerted to the possibility of the escaping fugitive. But the initial furore of a name suddenly being attached to the shocking murder of the well-known Sheffield businessman and his chief mourner, had begun to fizzle out with the lack of an actual person being attached to that name. There was an air of despondency at Devon and Cornwall Police among those waiting for him to return to his cottage near Liskeard. Which was a bit like waiting for the second coming of Christ. Weeks had gone by since their officers had set up camp there, and it was beginning to feel like a waste of manpower. But it was the home of a suspected double-murderer that South Yorkshire Police wanted to question. And now, after the discovery of another body close by, the home of a suspected single-murderer they wanted to question. And as such, had little choice but to sit there in case anything significant happened. Further bulletins had been given out on the crime-solving TV show requesting information from viewers as to the whereabouts of the missing Liskeard-based suspect, who, 'we believe to be armed and should not be approached'. To which, the only significant response came from a Liskeard camping and outdoor living shop assistant, determined to report the unhinged customer that had so keenly fiddled with the knives and sheaths. But alas, bringing them no closer to their man.

Jonathan's parents were now in their seventies, and still residing in the Sheffield area to their increasing unease. Now increased further by the visit from the police they had been dreading. Having avoided newspapers and television news as much as possible, with the fear of the half-expected image of their son handcuffed to a policeman, they were unaware of recent developments in the case. The last they heard was that the police were looking for a Jonathan Piper, and had been clinging to the faint hope that it was a different one. Those hopes were now well and truly dashed, as they reluctantly nodded their agreement to the suggestion their son knew his two victims from school; and with it, the distant, forgotten past came flooding back. It was a motive the troubled parents had quietly suspected but had tried to obliterate from their minds. After sitting down to steady themselves, they reluctantly and emotionally gave the police Jonathan's address in Liskeard, only to learn that their visitors already had it, but there was no sign whatsoever of him in it. The police didn't add to their trauma with a mention of what *had* been found in it, and in the river nearby. With at least a flicker of relief that they hadn't just put an end to their son's freedom, the couple pleaded their ignorance of his whereabouts now, and were believed. But reluctantly promised to contact the police immediately if they were unlucky enough to find out. Such were the perils of being law-abiding citizens when you had children that weren't, was a passing thought of the increasingly tired and bewildered Mr Piper, who wondered what kind of evil force had possessed the mind of his son who had just made the positive step towards homeownership when they had last spoken. All the visit had achieved was to confirm their worst fears and cause the twitching of a few curtains in the quiet cul-de-sac. All they were left with was the knowledge that their son was a missing person, and a strange, obscure feeling that under the circumstances that might be a blessing. Thus, maybe they would be spared the torture of seeing him paraded in front of the nation.

Once again, the investigation had returned to its state of play after the murder of Kevin Porter: long periods of nothing until the killer decides to kill again. And him either doing that, or returning to his cottage voluntarily after a serious bout of homesickness, was beginning to feel like the only solution. Unlikely, yes, but they needed to be there and prepared for it in case he did. At least, that was the idea handed down from the Chief Constable. Although it was never actually spoken, the twenty-four-hour police presence needed to be prepared for something else. A full-scale media invasion of the place, once it was leaked that this was the hub of activity in the Jonathan Piper case. Or in reality, wasn't. There was only one positive aspect of such an invasion: it would provide welcome relief from the boredom for the officers stationed there.

The postman, now getting more used to having the occasional gun pointed at him by the ever cautious police, continued to deliver letters and assorted junk addressed to Mr J. Piper on a daily basis: all of which were being scoured in vain for clues as to his whereabouts, just in case one of them was confirmation of a recently made reservation at a local hotel, with an address conveniently included. But one highly interesting letter from the oncology department of the South-East Cornwall health authority, had led detectives to Jonathan's former doctor's surgery, where what was inferred in the letter was confirmed. He had terminal cancer. But, with the relevant lady doctor also confirming that the Jonathan Piper she had diagnosed had revealed nothing of any plans to travel, that line of inquiry soon came to a disappointing halt. It did however shed some light on the possibly medically-based whereabouts of the killer, if they knew where to start looking, and that perhaps the armed man they were looking for was not quite so dangerous as was feared, and whose killing days were obviously numbered. But, in an administrative blunder of the type that occasionally occurred when two separate police forces were engaged in the same investigation, this most intriguing and possibly useful information never made it to the headquarters of South Yorkshire Police, and as such, the home of Mr and Mrs Piper. Which perhaps was a blessing for the already traumatized couple who certainly wouldn't relish adding terminal illness to the current woes of their son.

One company that was no longer contributing to the usual mass of paper arriving at the cottage, was the mortgage provider, who had finally run out of patience. In their last letter, that Jonathan himself had thrown in the bin, they had warned that they would repossess on a certain date if they didn't hear from him. They didn't, and today was that certain date, resulting in an unnecessarily large convoy of vehicles down the narrow country lane for what little there was to be shifted. The bailiffs that accompanied it were always prepared for resistance on such occasions, but definitely not in the form of armed police, who suddenly leapt into action ordering them off the site immediately. But after officially stamped bits of paper were banded about giving the visitors permission to carry out their task, the police, keen as they were to keep a tight lid on what was going on there, were forced into revealing that it was a crime scene; which perhaps didn't need explaining due to the assault rifles on display.

The sudden storm quickly reverted to its normal calm after phone calls were made and negotiations went on elsewhere between the authorities of both parties. The assembled re-possessors got out of their vehicles to stretch their legs and enjoy the rural tranquillity. After an hour, tea and coffee was served to one and all with a choice of biscuits. But just before the guests got too comfortable with the refreshments and inactivity, they were ordered off the site by their mortgage-providing bosses. Hierarchy of Devon and Cornwall Police having been disturbed for such a serious matter, explained that a murder investigation was being carried out there, while divulging as little detail as possible. This resulted in much awkward manoeuvring of vans and 7.5 tonne lorries being reversed back along the dirt track to the narrow country lane, and the gritting of building society teeth, having painstakingly got the necessary documentation to recover their losses.

In Sheffield, during the pause in the Piper case, its leaders, Inspector Marshall and Sergeant Hennessy found themselves up to their ears in more pressing matters. Largely, their attempts to quash a spate of burglaries that had caused near rioting on one of their less salubrious council estates, deemed to be the residence of the culprits. But the lack of firm proof of it stirred the locals into accusations of police harassment. On top of that, the glorious invention of DNA meant that an unsolved, thirty-year-old murder case had now reopened, and they were busy getting new DNA samples whilst being snowed under with ones they already had. But although they were now submerged in new investigations, the old one hadn't quite gone away. After the news from Liskeard that Piper's home was now a murder scene, and more recent updates that their Cornish colleagues had neither found him or identified what was thought to be his third victim, it felt like that investigation had done a U-turn and was now going backwards. Marshall was summoned to the office of his superior where much sighing and shaking of heads was done.

'What can we do?' Superintendent Foster asked with unease, more accustomed to telling what will be done rather than asking what can be done, still preoccupied with the stagnancy of what remained their most high-profile case, despite the burglaries and subsequent social unrest threatening to eclipse it. He could sense the imminence of another press conference, with such delightful questions being asked like: was it true they had a suspect but have now lost him? Fully aware of the media's power to stir the public into a near frenzy of demanding justice for the killing of their charity-donating hero, he had successfully avoided the last one with a beautifully-timed bout of flu, forcing his inspector to step in.

But such good fortune couldn't be relied upon to be repeated.

'There's not a lot we can do at the moment, sir. It's just a question of finding him, and we're doing all we can with that.'

'What about family, relatives?'

'No. We've tried, sir. They don't know anything. Good people.'

'And you believe them? They're not protecting him?'

The inspector shook his head despairingly. It seemed a good moment to change the subject completely with progress being made elsewhere.

Just as they were getting somewhere with the burglaries, Marshall's attention was diverted from it by a complaint made about one of his officers. And by a woman, making it all the more sensitive. Something like this was almost inevitable, as officers made house to house enquiries in an area with a 'strong sense of community', and all the proceeds of the burglaries in it, somewhere! Probably in one of the many locked garages they currently didn't quite have enough evidence to get a warrant to gain access to. If the police did not appear to be putting enough pressure on said area ('ideal for first-time buyers' with machine guns), they would then incur further complaints from the more affluent area where the burglaries had taken place: the sort of area where the complaining was usually done via the local Conservative MP. It was the most precarious of balancing acts.

Marshall wasn't sleeping well and had a nightmare the previous night. He was the star turn at a press conference where the journalists suddenly turned into giant gorillas that were slowly making their way to the table at the front where he was sitting. He had suddenly woken up at three a.m., shouting 'It wasn't me!' 'It wasn't me!', according to his wife. He had started to tell Hennessy about it earlier in the day thinking they could both do with a laugh but changed his mind after the first sentence. His sergeant seemed gifted at many things outside of police work and he feared that amateur psychology might be one of them, thus causing an outbreak of psychoanalysis instead of the planned laughter. Which would be typical of the direction his attempts at humorous conversation with the sergeant often went. What started as wit, soon turned into a particularly repugnant form of the plague.

Word of the Reynolds murder had gradually made its way from France to the National Crime Agency in London, and from there to the office of

Superintendent Foster. Marshall was again summoned to it, much to his frustration, having been deep in conversation on the phone wading through the 'tittle-tattle' of what his officer was supposed to have done to warrant the complaint. Something he had been ordered to attend to, without delay. As he climbed the stairs to the superintendent's office, he could sense there was something else he was about to be ordered to attend to, without delay.

'There's been a murder.'

'Oh.'

'In France.'

'Ah, pleased to hear it, sir. French police are dealing with it are they, or did you want me to sort it out?' Marshall retorted with the legendary sarcasm, failing to recognize the significance.

'If you'll let me finish, inspector.'

'Sorry, sir.'

'A man named Phillip Reynolds, English, shot dead in Bordeaux. Similar age to our other two. Might be worth a look. Oh, and another Englishman has confessed and is in custody.' Suddenly, Marshall is all ears.

'Name?'

'Doesn't say.'

Marshall sighs. There was often a touch of Chinese whispers about this type of information on far away crimes. It being passed through many departments with slight changes here and there and important bits left out along the way.

'But check it out anyway and let me know.'

'Yes, sir.'

Forced to continue with the publicity side of things, Marshall makes another phone call about the complaint as so little was gained from the last one due to its interruption. To give it to a more junior officer to deal with would smell of not taking the matter seriously. Which he didn't, but had to be seen to be. It was all part of the fun of twenty-first century coppering. Hennessy enters the room and is immediately given the job of checking out the French murder, as Marshall waves the relevant piece of paper at him.

'A man's in custody with no name, apparently. Get one, will you.

Hello, am I speaking to a Mrs ah…?

Hennessy left the room puzzled, not having had the chance to respond as the boss resumed his telephone conversation. As it couldn't possibly have anything to do with anything else they were currently working on, he was left to assume it was to do with the Jonathan Piper case. But in France?

Marshall came off the phone exasperated at what he considered to be non-police work that he simply wasn't cut out for. He sat back in his chair throwing his pen on the desk and began to try and make sense of the never-ending struggle since the downfall of Kevin Porter. And with it, his own, it seemed. Before that, he was floating along, as his nostalgia remembered it, waiting for what he was led to believe was inevitable: promotion. More money, and a little bit closer to he and Mrs Marshall's dream of a modest second home in Bridlington. Then, after almighty setbacks with the Porter case, he gets the name and address of a Liskeard dweller, which fitted in nicely with Mrs what-ever-her-name-was's version of events. The man fitted all kinds of descriptions and just happened to be bullied by the two victims while at school. Which was a motive, an extreme one, yes, but so was the bullying by the sound of it. A result, by anybody's standards. Then, after that, for a brief moment, he relaxed, with the feeling that the case was as good as closed and he was surely back on track with his promotion prospects. But since then, the suspect had not only disappeared, but notched up a third victim before doing so. And not much more had been established about that victim, other than the fact that he had not gone to school with his killer and had somehow supplied him with a firearm before being shot with it. So, with a now 'armed' Jonathan Piper still out there somewhere, this whole burglary lark turning into more of a battle against bad publicity, and the DNA samples they had now taken from almost every ex-employee of a factory close to the thirty-year-old murder scene proving only the innocence of all of them, he seemed to have lost interest in promotion altogether. The only thing he craved about the job now, was retirement. And perhaps a beach hut in Bridlington, if he was lucky.

At the hospice, Jonathan, now with more freedom to leave his room, had reverted back to doing all he could to stay in it, with exaggerated displays of deterioration and pain. By doing so, he had successfully avoided

Françoise and the painful reminder of their last conversation. But as long as the birds continued to tweet outside his window when it was warm enough to open it, life without her smile was just about bearable.

One morning, there's a knock at the door and a quick entrance from a male nurse who doesn't wait for an 'entrez', but it was a matter of urgency on account of the bill he was holding.

Unsurprisingly, it was for a lot, and if he didn't have it, there would surely be more pressure on him to contact a suitably wealthy person who did: Mum and Dad. And a phone call to them begging for money to be put into his bank account without revealing his whereabouts and why he needed it, would surely be a problem. Another problem was the direct debits to various companies for services no longer received, that he had never got round to terminating, his brain having been fully occupied with other forms of termination. So the figure in his head for what he thought remained in his account, was surely by now an overestimated one.

'Office,' the man says sternly, as he starts the process of getting the patient into a wheelchair, increasing Jonathan's anxiety. He realises it's the same impetuous chauffeur who was so keen to get him to the office last time. So keen in fact, that it felt as if 'office' was the only English word he knew, having looked it up specially. With a mixture of sign language and pained facial expression, Jonathan expresses his reluctance at said destination, and the need to visit the ATM first. Obviously, *not* the usual procedure, judging by the look of derision on the face of his escort, as though a foreigner requesting the unusual procedure was his least favourite thing. But Jonathan's determination to preserve his anonymity was as rigid as ever. And that meant no inserting of cards in offices.

Despite the financial and identificational worries, he finds being wheeled along the corridor of the main building a welcome change of scenery, desperately needing some pleasure however small after his major heartache. But, as they proceed round a corner, the reason for that heartache comes round it in the opposite direction. Now walking with a frame for support, she spots him, his heart misses a few beats and his brain can't decide whether to look up, down, or out the window. And before any such crucial decision could be made, she puts herself and the frame directly in the path of his wheelchair forcing them to stop abruptly. 'Pardon, monsieur,' she says to the nurse, before bending down, cupping Jonathan's face with her hands and giving him a prolonged kiss on the lips. During which, she loses her footing and collapses on top of him, and Jonathan holding her arms is the only thing stopping her falling to the ground. But to him, in a state of ecstasy, all that mattered was that they were holding each other. They could be both falling down an endless flight of stairs for all he cared. There was barely enough time for him to look at her let alone return the affection before the disgruntled nurse helps her to her feet. The chaotic scene caused concerned looks in the bustle of the main building from fast moving passers-by, as though mistaking it for violence and somebody being restrained. The impatient nurse then steers the wheelchair around the obstacle, moving him swiftly onwards so the urgent matter of foreigners paying their medical bills could resume. All a stunned Jonathan could manage in the way of appreciation was a brush of his hand against hers as they passed each other speedily, and a continuous wave, now with his back to her. All he could do was feel, as he was whisked away: mesmerized, resurrected, overjoyed, his brain didn't know where to begin. Love was frightening at this level, where a gesture, a look, a smile, a touch, a kiss, or the lack of them, could have such a joyous or devastating effect.

By the time he arrived at the ATM he was in another world. And unfortunately, one where the remembering of previously important things like pin numbers was impossible. The nurse, having granted the patient's wish to be parked at the cash machine, looks at him sternly as if he had stretched his evasion techniques a little too far. Only this time, Jonathan's amnesia was genuine, a side effect of being embraced and forgiven by the only source of joy left in his world. He is wheeled out the way to let the impatient queue behind them proceed while he sits, eyes closed, fingers on temples, as though a mind-reader about to reveal the personal details of a member of the audience picked at random. But after a few more attempts, and just before he is locked out of his account completely, it worked, and the gods had embraced him once more as he just about had enough and the bill was settled, leaving him with nothing. Which seemed like a good time to dispose of the only thing he had left that could identify him. So, into a rubbish bin the card was thrown as he was whisked back to his room, completely submerged in euphoric thoughts of Francoise. He collapsed on the bed, wondering how being pushed around in a wheelchair could be so exhausting.

His so-called twenty-four-hour guard outside the room became more ludicrous as time went on. Different officers rotated the farce on its eight-hour shift pattern. Whether he could venture out on his own often depended on the level of conscientiousness of the officer outside his door, and, if he was actually outside the door, or in the day room, eating, drinking, and chatting to staff. Or smoking, in which case he may be in the garden, observing the 'No Smoking' regulations in the building. Thus, causing further abandonment of duty. In one such incident that typified the lunacy like no other, a guard was accidentally locked out of the building while smoking among the rose bushes after dark. Jonathan had emerged from the loo and entered the deserted day room to find a sudden rainstorm occurring outside and a desperate looking man bashing on the windows to get his attention. After a moment of concern that the hospital possibly had a psychiatric department close by, and this was an actual security threat to which the guard should be alerted, Jonathan realised it was the guard, and only after he had alerted the staff was the unfortunate man let back in and his 'guard' resumed.

During one of many such lapses in security, Jonathan opened his door and moved slowly along the corridor towards Francoise's, now unable to control the urge to see her any longer. It was ajar, and he could hear the most wonderful music coming from it. An old favourite that he hadn't heard for years and had forgotten how enchanting it was. 'People Make the World go Round', with its soft melody now sung in French by a female singer, with lovely, strange, atmospheric instrumentation. His eyes welled up with tears as he stood still, just listening, with a mixture of memories it stirred from the days of his wanderings around central London with what was then known as a 'Walkman' attached to his ears, and the joy of hearing it again in these most wonderful of circumstances.

The back of her came into view. Despite the invasion of cancer, there were still traces of a beautiful feminine figure as she gently swayed to the music, unaware she was being watched. For him standing there watching her, time had never been so still and nothing had ever been so perfect. But after an unsettling look from a passer-by that suddenly filled him with self-consciousness, he conformed to the more orthodox idea of knocking on a door rather than peering through a half-opened one. Now it was a magical moment as she turned in his direction. To see that smile again, with its warmth and seeming inability to not be flirtatious, after being certain he had seen the last of it, was overwhelming. His mouth opened and eyes lit up as he entered the room, pointing to the source of the music without needing words to comment on how much he was enjoying it. She opened her arms while remaining still and silent, and smiling, as though a goddess inviting the crippled to shuffle their way towards her for healing. They kissed and hugged, and she gently swayed him to the music as he unsteadily clung to her as a substitute for the frame he had discarded. It was bliss, the most wonderful moment of his life. The song ended, followed by another faster one causing them to try and keep up with it, clumsily jigging themselves about while laughing, still locked in embrace. Eventually, they collapse on her bed and fall asleep in each other's arms as the music played on, causing a slight security alert as to the prisoner's whereabouts until her door is gently pushed open and the couple are found, without disturbing their slumber. They became inseparable, with all previous concerns regarding the police presence forgotten forever.

Hennessy struggled in his task to get a name for the killer of a Phillip Reynolds in Bordeaux. And for good reason: the French, grappling with their egos. The police lieutenant of that city had travelled to Saintes to interview 'Martin Smith' and left with a signed confession. And also, the killer's assurance that his passport and any other means of identification was in the car the English couple had taken over (for what the assurance of a killer was worth). But with this particular killer being a terminally ill hospice patient, it had seemed somehow uncivilised to conduct a search of his room to check the validity of that assurance. Assuming, as he did, that the car 'the couple had taken over' in which the murder weapon had been found, was still around somewhere, in France, presumably St Malo. And that just a quick phone call to his colleagues there would trigger the searching of that car for positive means of identifying its former owner: the man who had just confessed to their Bordeaux murder. The fact that Dave and Julie were currently driving it around 'Pompey', had just bought a new baby seat for it in readiness for their new arrival, and had disposed of anything belonging to, and reminding them of, its previous owner and that terrible night in France, was something that just never occurred to him. So, to the collective embarrassment of French police involved in the case, the only name they could give their eager colleagues across the channel was 'Martin Smith', which was eventually given to the sergeant of South Yorkshire Police only because of his persistence to get something out of them in order to please his boss. And just what exactly was so embarrassing about the name 'Martin Smith'? It was given to them by the killer himself, and as such, something not to be relied upon, something not seen on an official document like a passport, and therefore, something he could have just made up off the top of his head. Which Jonathan Piper most certainly did. And so, it was with a certain amount of sheepishness that the French authorities gave the British detective the name 'Martin Smith' (without mention of the question mark somebody had put at the end of it), in the hope that he would now bugger off and stop asking awkward questions.

A scapegoat was sought and found in the shape of the senior border official at St Malo who, in the heat of the moment, could not bring himself to cause the innocent couple any further distress by confiscating their car. His plea of mitigating circumstances that the lady was expecting a baby fell on deaf ears. He had let a car leave the country that could have been loaded with evidence vital to police investigating what the gun found in it had been used for, and who used it. A crime, that when described by the usually conscientious official's superiors, sounded terrible, but in reality, given the circumstances, was understandable. But, as was so often the case, circumstances were something that superiors never came within a mile of. The Brits he had encountered on that fateful evening didn't exactly smell of gun smuggling and murder: an exasperated couple desperate to get home after a bad holiday, and a thoroughly innocent and bewildered sounding hospital patient. It was bizarre. Surrealistic almost. A senior border control official's worst nightmare. He was severely reprimanded. Never again would he be swayed from doing his solemn duty by hostile British holidaymakers. Pregnant or not.

After the most arduous of long-distance phone calls while failing to grasp the purpose of it, Hennessy finally returns with his inspector's wishes granted.

'Where have you been?' Marshall enquires. 'I thought you'd gone on holiday or something.'

Hennessy ignores the sarcasm and delivers his findings, 'Apparently, it's a Martin Smith they have in custody who has admitted killing a Phillip

Reynolds. Will that be all, sir?' with just a hint of Bertie Wooster's butler[32] and a counter-attack of sarcasm of his own.

'Mmmm, a likely story. You sure it wasn't John Smith, Granny Smith or Donald Duck?' Marshall refutes. As usual, spot on with his negativity.

Hennessy leaves the room with a clenched fist between his teeth, like a volcano trying not to erupt. But then, after a sudden brainwave, starts flicking through filing cabinets and makes a far more interesting discovery with the name Phillip Reynolds. It was among the list of names of pupils on the printout he got from the school, just a few down from Alan Marsden. The sergeant smiles, knowing he had properly identified the killer, and takes a moment to savour his solitary moment of joy: like a metal detectorist who'd just found a diamond ring after a tedious day of pacing up and down a beach. He cast his mind back to the day he acquired the now most treasured piece of paper, when all seemed hopeless, as he hesitantly asked for the names while not entirely sure what could be done with them or why he was asking for them. Doubting its usefulness as anything other than evidence of his blind obedience to a superior officer.

After drawing an asterisk next to the names of the now three dead pupils, he casually stands at Marshall's doorway as the man rummages through drawers. For once, completely immune to any put down the inspector may care to throw at him. He drops the printout on Marshall's desk and waits patiently for it to sink in.

'Have you seen my erm...? What's this?' Marshall puts on his reading glasses and examines it with increasing interest as though a newly discovered Roman artefact, before slowly turning to the sergeant with a sly grin and a loud clap of his hands. 'Well done, you old bugger! That deserves a pat on the back. Come 'ere!'

Hennessy walks towards him, joining in the fun, and has his back repeatedly thumped by the inspector with onlookers concerned that someone was choking. And despite the discomfort, relishes the rare moment of occupational joy. At last, something was really happening in at least one of their investigations, and miraculously, was due to his quick-wittedness.

'Don't complain that you haven't had a pat on the back! All right!' Marshall continues, pointing at Hennessy, still grinning. Aware that the

---

[32] Jeeves.

usual lack of appreciation was probably somewhere near the top of the often prickly, sensitive sergeant's long list of complaints.

With the strain that Marshall had been under for some time, the celebration was of the more manic, slightly deranged variety. But much-needed light relief nonetheless, and in a rare moment of togetherness, the two coppers laugh. Moments like this made it all worthwhile. A major breakthrough that solved several mysteries at once. Annoying, irritating ones, like the disappearance of chief suspects just as arduously obtained evidence was mounting up against them. 'Martin Smith' *was* in fact, Jonathan Piper, and was in France, and that would explain why he wasn't in Liskeard. All was starting to make sense once more after weeks in the wilderness.

After the celebrations had died down, there was concern for the safety of others on the list and the reliability of the report that stated a man had confessed and was 'in custody'. Marshall made a phone call, and with the usual stern, authoritarian voice, managed to get quick answers: being reassured that Martin Smith who had confessed to the murder of Phillip Reynolds was still in police custody in Saintes. It was the best assurance he could get for the moment before seeing it with his own eyes, and for a man not exactly noted for his confidence in others, was eager to do so. To the French, it was one murder; to the English, it was three (with the exclusion of the still unidentified gun dealer now known as 'the riverman'), and there was plenty more names on the list he may have a grudge against, and seemed to have an uncanny ability to find them.

'Right. Keep him there. We're on our way!' Marshall's words were impulsive without having consulted with any superiors as to who exactly was on their way, but never before had he been so keen to come face to face with the cause of all the trouble.

Superintendent Foster was reluctant to part with any of his coppers at such a crucial time, which was mainly all the time. But it was obvious that Marshall should go, and he ordered him to make contact once he'd questioned Piper and if more men were needed for any reason they would be sent. But when Hennessy revealed an O-level in French and spoke a few sentences with what appeared to be proficiency and confidence, the audience, not knowing what he was on about, were suitably impressed. Marshall expressed the need for a competent interpreter while thinking to himself that his sergeant's talents would be sure to come in useful in shops and restaurants, deciphering menus and the like. Vital code-breaking work for the successful avoidance of seafood and subsequent confinement to hotel bathrooms with food poisoning, he considered, recalling an incident of such in a previous visit to the country. And so, the sergeant's seat on the plane was secured.

'Well, chaps, we'll just have to leave this lovely complaint in your capable hands. I'm sure the good people on the Franklin Estate will be delighted to hear from you,' Marshall teased his unfortunate colleagues drafted in to take over their duties.

In all the furore, their Cornish colleagues were forgotten, and then remembered. After more detailed briefing of Marshall about exactly what was found at the murder scene at the cottage, it was mutually agreed that the two South Yorkshire detectives would fly out, and as well as question the suspect about the Sheffield murders would do their best to get answers on the Liskeard one. All that should be discussed was discussed, except for the *minor* issue of terminal illness, with the letter from the oncology department after a missed appointment, lost and forgotten amongst a load of other bits of paper at Devon and Cornwall Police HQ. The detectives that were previously in the know about it, now fully submerged in a particularly complex and challenging case of benefit fraud in and around Plymouth; now showing signs of spreading to Exeter it seemed, after having been transferred to it as a matter of urgency during the lull in the Piper case.

At the hospice, the harmony between the two lovers continued, as whatever Jonathan may have done to warrant the police presence faded into insignificance. Now with a constant supply of love and affection and medicine sufficient to deal with the pain, he had at last entered a period of peace and tranquillity. As he watched Francoise comforting other patients in the day room, he tried to emulate her behaviour and gradually became more sociable. And there was plenty of need for comfort: tears after visits from loved ones, tears because there were no visits from loved ones, tears from those who didn't seem to have any loved ones. But for Jonathan, the language barrier was a hindrance to giving such comfort and he was determined to improve. The shame he had felt when forced to respond with a 'Je suis desole, je ne comprend[33]', when spoken to by one such emotional fellow patient, supplying the incentive for progress.

He left her alone when she at last had a visit from her daughter, who he had seen in a photo being held by her beaming, curly-haired, youthful mother. After the visit, he stood quietly at her open doorway as she sat facing the wall in silence. Fearing that a knock on her door would be an intrusion at such a delicate moment, he returned to his room, shuffling past the guard with a cheery 'bonne apres-midi!' which was returned with a smile. But a sombre Francoise with eyes red from crying then made her way to *his* room, with a similar but less cheery greeting to its guard, who in his official capacity had the power to stop her and been ordered to do so, but just like his colleagues, had succumbed to the futility of it all, and on seeing the frail woman's obvious distress, courteously opens the door for her. To Jonathan, the vision of loveliness coming through his door was the kind of miracle that was now occurring on a daily basis. All of which, although wonderful, was slightly bewildering to a man previously far better acquainted with the pain of unrequited love. He guides her to a chair, enquiring if the visit from her daughter was 'OK'. She nods with a faint smile, which he interprets as mother and child settling any differences, and the tears being caused by their imminent parting. Wishing they could turn the clock back and relive their time of not speaking to each other. Her obvious, family-related grief made him almost grateful for the cold, occupational visits from the police, with whom he had no emotional ties.

A brief nap while lying together on his bed locked in embrace seemed to cure the melancholy, and they sit together while he attempts a compliment in French with book close by.

'Bonjour, madamoiselle, vous avez un beau souris.[34]'

'Souris?' she queries, correctly pronouncing the word without the 's' on the end and looking puzzled.

'Je n'ai pas de souris[35],' she says with a knowing smile.

'Ah! Right. Hang on a minute. Start again.'

He turns a few more pages as though a wizard whose first attempt at a trick had failed due to the wrong magic word being spoken.

---

[33] 'I'm sorry, I don't understand.'

[34] 'Hello, miss, you have a beautiful mouse', but meaning to say, 'smile' (sourire).

[35] 'I do not have a mouse.'

'Pardon, monsieur! Parler vous Francais?' she teases him at his lapse into English, aware of his determination not to.

After further consultation of his book, he looks up at her, smiling triumphantly.

'Attends une minute. Recommencer!'

Translating his previous lapse with the usual mispronunciation, followed by a 'yes!' and a point of a finger of defiance.

She laughs, gently kicking him under the table. Any physical contact with her however small seemed to do something to his entire body. Every moment in her company was glorious. He never wanted it to end.

Both detectives had no experience of international criminal law, extradition and the like, and when they turned to their superintendent for direction, despite the man's strong words about Piper facing justice in Sheffield, in reality, he too was none the wiser. It was something they had learned at college a long time ago and now forgotten due to lack of use. With their flight booked for this afternoon, there was barely enough time to pack their things let alone brush up on past education. More phone calls were made. The French assuring maximum assistance on their arrival, but the conversations amounted to no more than courteous bullshit from people who spoke fluent English, but whose entire knowledge of the case consisted of what little was displayed on the computer screen in front of them. And as such, there was no mention of hospitals, hospices or anything else associated with ill health. Merely, 'custody', with its variety of definitions. So, with not much more than their determination to ensure Jonathan Piper was incapable of doing any more harm, the two men set off.

On arrival at Saintes, they check into a five-star hotel. In a rare moment of harmonious thought, they agreed that South Yorkshire Police owed them a great deal and it was therefore appropriate that they were picking up the large bill which would now include the French lager and sandwiches brought up to their rooms, as it was too late for dinner. It was easy access to Saintes police station from there, so they opt to make their own way first thing the next morning. It had the potential for being a long and challenging day, but far more welcome challenges to the ones they had just about managed to escape from back home.

At the hospice, the besotted couple were determined to spend as much of what little time they had left with each other, and with the fear of being permanently parted during the hours of darkness, that included their nights. So, with this determination, they managed to spend most nights together in Jonathan's room, so the police could at least remain at their proper post with something to guard, in an atmosphere of mutual co-operation that now existed in the place. They would lay together in each other's arms, squeezed into a single bed. On occasions, their passion for each other was overwhelming and their love was successfully consummated without the need for medical intervention, supervision, or assistance; and quietly, so as not to disturb the sleep of the guard outside, if he was outside, or trigger a sudden entrance to check the prisoner was behaving himself. But Jonathan's good fortune at having such understanding captors and being able to spend his last nights in such blissful company, was usually enough enjoyment for his frail body. On one such evening of blissful togetherness, the couple settled down having finished kissing and hugging each other goodnight.

On arrival at the station, to their dismay, the two Brits are told that Martin Smith is not there. For a brief exasperating moment, it felt as though the elusive killer was forever going to be slipping through their hands. But after Hennessy translated the desk officer's words as best he could, it was established that the prisoner was under police guard in Saintes Hospital, and that they would be escorted there in due course.

Their chauffeur arrived in the form of a lieutenant from Saintes police, from whom Marshall immediately tried to ascertain the reasons for the hospitalization. But it became obvious that the lieutenant's knowledge of the case was not much greater than his, as was his language skills. So far, the assurances they had received of 'maximum assistance' were not forthcoming. But all had been hastily arranged on both sides of the channel, and Saintes police were only really on the case because it was where the killer of Phillip Reynolds had ended up, with their role in it being a more custodial one, guarding the prisoner for the relevant other forces, a point that the lieutenant tried to make to the English visitors. As they made their way to the hospital, he spoke of his colleagues in Bordeaux, as though alluding to the fact that it was they who were the experts on the case.

443

'Yes, of course, Bordeaux. The location of the murder,' Marshall agreed, with twinges of embarrassment at his lack of knowledge and preparation. As such, he felt an urge to explain that they had been up to their necks in it with burglaries and DNA samples, and therefore hadn't had time to fully grasp the new complexities of *this* case since it had suddenly relocated to France. But he didn't, thinking that not even his O-levelled sergeant could cope with the translation.

Marshall felt unusually out of his depth as they were whisked through unfamiliar surroundings in the early morning traffic. The case had taken a sharp turn into no man's land since the glorious day of obtaining Jonathan Piper's Liskeard address. The inspector couldn't help but speculate on what was to come. Even if the questioning of Piper went completely according to plan and a confession was obtained for all three murders in England, that would then leave a mountain of international protocol waiting to be climbed. And it was full of questions he had no answer to. He pondered them in turn. As it was a case of both a British killer and victim in a foreign country, would European law expect them to get their criminal out of that foreign country and prosecute him for the whole lot? Or would the law insist that the killer be tried for his one murder in a foreign country, in that foreign country? Or would the law, whatever it was, be put aside in favour of common sense? An idea to which he, although an enforcer of the law, was far more suited, and was all too aware that the two things didn't always run smoothly alongside each other. All matters for his superiors to grapple with perhaps, but Marshall was a perfectionist, a man who needed to know exactly what he was doing, and when he didn't, it bothered him. And relying on senior officers to tell him, was definitely not part of his ideology. His superintendent had stated confidently that Piper was 'our prisoner', who would stand trial for all of his four killings in Sheffield. But superintendents had to state everything confidently in case people thought they didn't know what they were doing. And very often, they didn't.

All this speculation of post-confession movement was on the assumption that the prisoner *could* actually be moved anywhere. And, as they were on their way to a hospital to interview him, for reasons as yet unknown, that was another cause for uncertainty in the already uncertain mind of the inspector. But one thing Marshall was supremely confident about, was questioning the suspect of the killings of Porter and Marsden.

444

A subject he knew inside out and back to front. Knowing exactly what he wanted to say and eager to do so while the finer details were still clear in his mind. And before this most complex of cases became a distant memory.

During the night, Francoise woke up, possibly disturbed by the unusual lack of movement and heartbeat of the man she had slept with her arms around. She gives Jonathan a shake. Nothing. He was gone. Although it had to be expected, the sudden severity of being alone and without him was too much. She cried and shouted as she pressed her face against his, with a relentless flow of tears running down her cheeks.

'Ne me laisse pas, Martin! Je t'aime, Martin! Je t'aime!' [36]

This attracts the attention of the guard outside who opens the door. She quickly gathers her senses before he has time to switch the light on, realizing that her deceased lover will be taken away immediately. And that, right now, was too much to bear. She calms the situation, explaining that she had just had a nightmare but was all right now. To which her door is then closed, and now, with some kind of acceptance of what is happening, she holds Jonathan close to her and eventually goes back to sleep. Forever. As if all that was keeping her heart beating and blood flowing through her veins, was him.

The three policemen arrive at the hospital reception. Hennessy does the talking, beautifully, except for asking to see a patient by the name of Jonathan Piper. As this was the first time the name had ever been mentioned in the hospital, it causes a slight delay while the lady scours her computer in vain.

'Non,' she says with a shake of the head.

'Try Martin Smith,' Marshall corrects, with a tired roll of the eyes and a touch of irritated disbelief at the importance the false name seemed to have acquired.

With the relevant patient now located, they are directed away from the main building to one of several within the grounds of the hospital. Marshall had the most precious of documents with him and was eager to show the list of names with asterisks against those that were now dead, that this 'Martin Smith' must surely have killed. Fully prepared as always

---

[36] 'Don't leave me, Martin! I love you, Martin! I love you.'

for a denial, and the subsequent barrage of evidence he would then throw at the suspect. With a determination to prove once and for all, that he was in fact the Jonathan Piper also on that list, with name circled.

They rang the bell and the lieutenant showed his badge at the door with a brief introduction. But the solemn lady who opened it looked only at the floor and said nothing as she gestured them to come in with a sweep of her hand. The now almost familiar sight of official-looking strangers in the building was largely ignored by patients having breakfast in the day room. The detectives pass a uniformed French officer holding a mug of coffee and a croissant, who suddenly turns his head away after seeing them. The trio were led through an open doorway, slightly baffled with the silence. They hadn't so far had the chance to ask for the man they wished to speak to, and so were not sure where they were being led.

It was all quite weird. But got weirder, as they entered the room to the sight of two lifeless bodies lying next to each other in a bed, with various staff in the room surrounding it. It could have been a scene from a horror film on the subject of devil worship after a ritualistic sacrifice, with the disciples standing in a circle around the bodies in expressionless silence. But the harmonious position of the lovers was testimony to the peace in which they died. She, with a protective arm around him, head tilted towards him; his head resting peacefully under her chin with an arm draped over her stomach. The deceased couple had only just been discovered by a nurse, having entered the room with Jonathan's early morning medication.

Marshall looked down at the bizarre spectacle, temporarily lost for words, with just a vague assumption that one of these people was Jonathan Piper. He checked the bodies for a pulse. The lack of it and their warmth suggested that death was very recent. Just trying to establish a few facts without the need for speech and translation. Nobody felt much like talking. Marshall then looked up at the assembled staff for any sign of an explanation. There was none, just a subdued awkwardness. One dead body in a bed in such a place was acceptable and normal. Two needed a bit more explanation, especially as one of them was a prisoner supposed to be under police guard, but nobody was brave enough to attempt it, and for the moment, Marshall didn't push them. It was slowly sinking in: Jonathan Piper had eluded him once more, and for the last time.

'Martin Smith?' Marshall breaks the silence, pointing to the male body, looking at the staff who nod their agreement. He exhales, with just a hint of relief. At least something had been established amongst all the obscurity.

The last thing the inspector felt like doing was launching a new enquiry into the death of a suspect 'in custody', and foreign custody, making it all the more complex. But to his eye, the scene was much like the aftermath of a suicide pact between two gravely ill people who would need access to medicine, and lots of it, in order to do so. Marshall expressed his concerns of such. But after some translation of his words by the lieutenant, the staff dismiss it with stern shakes of the head, adding that the bodies had only just been found and had not been disturbed by them, just in case of any further insinuation of their wrongdoing.

Marshall looks down again at the cause of all the trouble, who had so denied him the eagerly awaited opportunity to present with the facts, and then around the room at the few personal belongings in it.

'This is Martin Smith's room?' he asks. The staff again nod their agreement. 'Excuse me.'

The staff stand aside as Marshall reaches for a wallet sticking out of the pocket of a pair of trousers. He passes it to Hennessy without speaking or looking at anything except the floor. The sergeant knows what his boss is looking for but suffers slight anxiety when he can't find it. No bank or credit card, or it seems, any other form of ID. Just a five euro note, a receipt for petrol, some odd scraps of paper, and a few miscellaneous other cards. One of which, gets his attention. He removes it. It's very faded and difficult to read what's written on it, but when he holds it up to the light, it's just possible to make out the words, 'Liskeard Town Council Library Services', and, in the bottom right-hand corner: 'J. Piper'.

He hands it to Marshall who puts on his reading glasses and examines it. He removes his glasses, exhales deeply, and the two men look at each other with the weariest of smiles. 'That'll do.'